Voice of Freedom
Book 2
Against all Enemies Series

H.L. WEGLEY

Political Thriller with Romance

Cover Design: Samantha Fury
http://www.furycoverdesign.com/

Back Cover Design: Trinity Press International
http://trinitywebworks.com/

Interior Formatting: Trinity Press International
http://trinitywebworks.com/

DEDICATION

This book is dedicated to all the pilgrims who have been deeply wounded as they pursue God in this fallen world—especially to those who trust Him enough to change whenever He exposes flaws in their beliefs, allowing Him to mold them into the person they were meant to be. Such are the hero and heroine of this story, Steve and Julia.

ENDORSEMENTS

Endorsements and Praise for *Voice in the Wilderness*, Against All Enemies 1

What a powerful and compelling book! And to think it is "only" a fictitious portrait of modern America and things that may actually come to pass unless "We the people" do something to prevent them from happening. Multiple kudos to Mr. Wegley for having the courage to use his talents to "tell it like it is."
-- Author Roger Bruner

If you're looking for a rich and creative adventure through a dystopian future in the heart of America's powerbase, then *Voice in the Wilderness* will be a wild ride that you won't forget anytime soon.
-- Author John Staughton

H. L. Wegley has written an action-packed, politically terrifying, hair-raising thriller about the need to guard our freedoms--lest they be snatched away. An edge-of-your seat race to keep one man from taking over the United States--don't miss it!
-- Susan May Warren, RITA and Christy Award-winning, best-selling novelist

CONTENTS

ACKNOWLEDGMENTS

Thanks once again to my wife, Babe, for listening to me read to her several drafts of this story and for helping me fill the plot holes and fix the logic as the story iterated through the editing cycles. Thanks to my beta readers, Duke Gibson, Don and Carol Ruska, and to members of my critique group, Dawn Lily and Gayla Hiss, for their suggestions.

Thank you, Samantha Fury, for developing a cover that captures the feel of the story, and of the entire *Against All Enemies* series.

Thanks to the team at Trinity Web Works/Trinity Press International for their work in preparing this manuscript for publication, including editor, Dr. Caroline Savage, as well as Shawn Savage for web site work and book formatting. Thanks to their leader, Tony Marino, for planning the publishing and marketing of this novel and to Lynn Marino for managing book promotion.

Though I sometimes mourn for all that we have lost in America over the past fifty years, I still thank our Lord for allowing me to be born in the USA. May He bless and challenge us all through the lessons learned and the courage displayed by the hero and heroine featured in *Voice of Freedom*.

"If ever a time should come, when vain and aspiring men shall possess the highest seats in Government, our country will stand in need of its experienced patriots to prevent its ruin."
Founding Father, Samuel Adams

When the righteous rule, the people rejoice, but when an evil man rules, the people mourn.
Proverbs 29:2 (paraphrased)

Chapter 1

Week 4 on Israel's Coast, near Netanya Beach

Oh crud!

A tear tickled Julia Weiss's cheek. Crying at a wedding would only confirm everyone's opinion of her. Weiss the wimp, the weak link on this team.

What a wuss she'd become after her narrow win in her battle with Ebola, after being knocked out by a flashbang grenade, held captive by a demoniac who had some really bad plans for her, and after having guns held to her head more times than she could count.

But, putting things in perspective, shedding a few tears was preferable to full-blown PTSD. Besides, this wedding was special.

Maybe Julia *should* be crying. After all, she had been pursuing the groom only eight weeks ago. Julia grinned through watery eyes. On their mission trip to Guatemala, she had definitely been crushing on hunky Brock Daniels ... until she learned about Brock's childhood soulmate, KC.

No way would she wedge herself between those two. They belonged together. And now, on August 15, at 09:05 a.m. ...

"I now pronounce you man and wife." Pastor Michael, a fortysomething man with a small beard and a large Bible, stood at the end of the long living room, beaming a smile that spread the full width of his round face. He gestured to Brock. "You may kiss your bride."

Bride? Twenty-two-year-old KC Banning was more than that. With her green eyes and auburn hair highlighted in blazing red from a month in the blistering Israeli sun—sunshine which had also multiplied the sprinkling of freckles across the cheeks and nose of a perfectly sculpted face—KC might have been a Celtic Princess.

No. KC was a Celtic Princess, royalty in every sense of the word. While Julia, two years KC's senior, was a commoner, a weak, little—*enough self-deprecation. Just enjoy the wedding, Julia.*

Six-foot-five, two-hundred-thirty-five-pound athlete and writer, Brock Daniels, heart and soul of America—whatever President Hannan hadn't destroyed—kissed the Irish Princess.

Julia tried to shove tyrant, Abe Hannan, and the problems at home from her mind and simply delight in the union of these two people handcrafted for each other.

KC, dressed in a summer outfit that had some secret, special meaning for the two, returned Brock's kiss with all the passion of a heart-on-her-sleeve, stereotypical Irish girl.

As Brock and KC kissed, it seemed that a great wrong in the world had finally been set right. The rending of Brock's and KC's childhood relationship by KC's father seven years ago was almost as if it had never happened.

Please, God, let KC and Brock have their time together. Don't let Hannan finish what KC's father started ... especially not now.

Julia wiped her cheeks and looked up into the eyes of warrior, Steve Bancroft. The gaze of this handsome Army Ranger had been locked on her, intense and—there was no other interpretation—longing ... at the very time Brock and KC were kissing.

Steve hadn't a clue what he would be getting in Julia

Weiss and probably wouldn't want it once he found out. Regardless, his look of admiration continued, flattering but frustrating, because his warrior ways created a big problem, a problem she would soon have to deal with before it broke two hearts.

Uncomfortable with Steve's protracted study of her face, Julia looked away, focusing on Jeff and Allie Jacobs. They were the married couple who rounded out the band of six Americans protected by the Israelis in this spacious, fifth-floor suite near Netanya Beach on the Mediterranean Coast.

Beyond Jeff, at the far end of the living room, Benjamin Levy, their IDF Special Forces guard, stood by the main entry door. Loyal, devoted, vigilant, he had been with Major Katz in Oregon when the Israelis rescued the six from Hannan's thugs.

What was wrong with Benjamin? His eyes widened. He whirled toward the door and grabbed the knob. "Incoming—"

An invisible force cut off Benjamin's words.

It slammed Julia into Steve.

His arms circled her.

Their bodies smashed into the wall.

Julia collapsed on the floor beside Steve.

Her head throbbed. She rubbed it then tried to stand.

"No, Julia." Powerful arms pulled her down.

She shook her head to clear the fog, but now it clouded her vision, too.

When Julia drew a sharp breath, she gagged on acrid air, unfit to breathe.

She blinked her burning eyes. Not fog. Smoke!

With a whoosh, a tangle of flames leaped toward them, dancing, engulfing the far end of the living room, threatening their path of escape.

"Stay down, everybody!" Steve's voice. "There might be another incoming ..."

Incoming what? Regardless, they had been attacked.

That realization jolted Julia. It sent her pulse revving to somewhere near the red line.

Despite military guards and Israeli intelligence, the best intelligence in the world, they had been located and attacked.

KC and Brock didn't deserve this. And coming on their wedding day was beyond brutal. Somehow, President Hannan had found them.

At that thought, molten lava surged inside Julia. It erupted in a string of words describing Abe Hannan and the place she wanted to send him. Her tirade ended in a wheezing, coughing fit.

Brock sat up beside KC and coughed. "Julia's right. Hannan's doing. I'd bet on it."

Steve rose to his feet then quickly dropped to his knees. "Air's getting hot. Stay down near the floor." He scanned the group then looked across the smooth marble floor toward the door which had been blown off its hinges. "Come on. Let's—what the—the floor's gone!"

"So's Benjamin." Jeff's voice.

Julia crawled beside Steve. Barely visible through billows of smoke, a dark chasm had opened up in the marble floor. The hole extended all the way to the door. Now flames threatened to engulf their sanctuary in one end of the closed-off living room.

With the flames and the gaping hole, they couldn't reach the door, their only hope of escaping the inferno.

Julia looked at Brock, cradling a wide-eyed KC in his arms, then at Jeff and Allie. They would all die. Brock and KC would have one kiss as man and wife ... and nothing more.

Tears flowed again, tears from Julia's heart, not from the smoke.

Vacillating between tears and another tirade, she prayed that another explosion would come, sending them all quickly into God's presence, heaven. But the menacing orange and red blazes, licking at all things flammable, looked like heaven's antithesis. Julia's bare skin already stung from its radiant heat.

Benjamin had disappeared, his fate a mystery. With the living room rapidly becoming a smoke-filled oven, the fate of Julia and her friends was no mystery at all. For them, in a few more seconds, they would experience hell on earth. And burning to death was Julia's worst—

"Go, go, go!" Steve swept Brock and KC toward the hole in the floor with one stroke of his powerful right arm.

"To the suite below?" Brock pointed ahead to the smoke-shrouded hole.

"Yeah. Then out the door to the stairwell. Meet you there." Steve shot Pastor Michael a glance. "Go with them, pastor."

Brock tugged on KC's arm. "How fast can you crawl, Kace?"

"Faster than you."

Brock scurried after KC, both slowing as they approached the cavernous hole.

Crack!

Julia gasped.

A large section of floor broke, sending Brock and KC tumbling downward, out of sight.

Pastor Michael reached the edge of the enlarged hole, swung his legs down into it, and disappeared.

Steve's hand squeezed Julia's shoulder. "It's only ten feet. They'll be okay." He nudged Jeff. "You and Allie next."

Near the hole, flames lashed out at Jeff and Allie. Somehow the two dropped into the hole without the fire stopping them.

Julia shrank back against the wall, away from the flames that now danced like demons over the opening in the floor. The thought of burning to death sent a quivering nausea through her gut. As bile rose in her throat, she fought the urge to vomit.

"Our turn, Julia. Stay on the right side of—"

"Away from the flames?"

"Yeah. Let's go." Steve crawled ahead.

She didn't follow. Couldn't follow.

The fire leaped across the hole to the opposite wall. Now, blazes attacked from both sides of the opening.

Steve spun around on the floor and made eye contact. His eyes widened as he studied her face. He lunged toward her, hooking Julia under her arms with both hands.

She pulled away from him as images of flames licking the flesh off their bodies drove every sane thought from her mind. "Steve, I ... I'm not afraid to die, but please, not by burning."

"We're not going to die." He rose to his knees, gripped both of her wrists, and swung her body toward the opening in the floor.

Julia's body slid across the smooth floor toward the hole and the flames. She cried out as her legs dropped into the hole.

Steve's hands had clamped on her wrists so tightly her hands were going numb. "It's okay. I'll lower you down. Then it will be only a three- or four-foot drop. But roll out of the way. I'll be right behind you."

She hung suspended from Steve's hands in an opaque, gray cloud. Julia looked up at Steve.

Flames shot out from the nearest wall, hitting him.

He winced, and his grip loosened. One hand slipped loose, then the other.

Julia plunged downward, off balance and flailing to control her fall into the smoke-shrouded unknown.

Chapter 2

Julia tried to brace for the impact, but her right foot hit first—an object, not the floor.

The off-balance landing threw her forward to the left.

When she shoved out both hands to protect her face, her left hand hit the floor first, taking the full impact of her fall.

Julia's left arm screamed in complaint. The muscles in her forearm spasmed, turning her arm into a rigid bar of steel.

Steve. He would be right behind her.

She pulled her injured arm against her body and rolled away from her landing point. When she stopped rolling, Julia tried to flex her wrist. It resisted movement and, once again, screamed a loud complaint that echoed through her nervous system.

Steve's shoes slapped the floor behind her, followed by a loud crack.

Shards of flooring, mixed with flaming debris, pelted the marble floor. Somehow, the red-hot rain missed her.

Visibility was slightly better here. In front of Julia, a figure slumped over something large stretched out on the floor. She moved closer.

Auburn hair hung limp, dangling over a body. KC's hands moved furiously, exploring Brock's neck, trying to find a pulse.

Julia pinned her throbbing left arm to her body and moved behind KC, placing a hand on her shoulder.

"Why isn't there a pulse? There's got to be a pulse." The desperation in KC's voice hurt more than Julia's injured wrist.

Brock dead? That couldn't be. Steve said they would be okay.

At the thought of Brock's death, and with pain shooting through her arm, the quivering nausea returned. Julia swallowed hard, fighting the urge to vomit. Could God really be that cruel? Would He let Brock die on his wedding day?

What about Steve? She turned to see how he had fared.

Steve leaped by her toward KC.

Julia inhaled the cloud of smoke Steve brought with him. She coughed and choked until nausea won. Her breakfast splattered across the floor.

She needed to concentrate on something other than her quivering stomach, her throbbing wrist, and the smell of the smoke, or the vomiting wouldn't stop. Julia focused on Steve.

He slid beside KC, placing his fingers on Brock's neck. Steve took KC's hand and moved her fingers to the place his had been.

"He's alive!" KC gasped. It ended in a coughing fit.

Smoke had filled the apartment over the past few seconds, invading from the billows swirling down through the hole above them.

Steve nodded. "He's alive. But we've all got to get out of here, now."

More flaming debris rained down on them, sending glowing red embers and chunks of marble bouncing and sliding across the floor.

8

Steve bent over Brock, sheltering his body.

KC leaned across Brock's head.

Julia crouched beside them, left wrist pinned to her stomach, using it like a splint. She was useless. Just another burden.

When the clattering on the marble floor stopped, Steve knelt on one knee and grabbed Brock's arm. "Come on."

Julia and KC stood, stepping back as Steve swung Brock over his shoulders in a fireman's carry.

Steve turned toward the door. "Let's get out of here before the whole building comes down on us."

KC seemed oblivious, focused only on Brock. She stroked his head.

Julia took KC's hand and pulled her toward the front door.

The door stood partially open. Jeff, Allie, and Pastor Michael had probably gone through the doorway and should be waiting to meet them near the stairwell.

After Steve and KC moved into the corridor, Julia turned to close the door, but bumped her left elbow in the process. A lightning bolt of pain shot through her injured wrist. She tried to ignore the pain. After all, it was probably just a minor sprain.

Julia pulled the door closed.

No more heat. She had been too preoccupied to notice, but they were being slowly broiled by the flames dancing over the opening in the floor. Her cheeks were hot and the skin on her arms and bare legs stung like a bad sunburn. If that wasn't enough, her chest now felt like it was being squeezed in a vice. Each breath took more effort than the last.

A few feet ahead, KC reached for Brock's head, obviously wanting to stop and examine it.

Steve glanced her way. "Keep going! To the stairs at the end of the hall."

Through the smoky corridor, a man's figure moved toward them from the stairwell. Pastor Michael. "KC. Thank God you're okay. What happened to Brock?"

KC opened her mouth to reply, but only coughed.

Julia coughed, too. It didn't stop until smoky crud erupted from her burning chest. She spat it on the floor. The vice loosened and she could breathe freely again.

KC hurried toward Pastor Michael. "Please pray for Brock. He's unconscious."

Jeff and Allie moved away from the stairwell door as another figure burst through it. Someone in protective gear. The firemen were here. But what they needed most was an ambulance.

Steve glanced at KC as she stroked Brock's face. "He's alive, KC. But ..." Steve didn't finish.

How much alive and for how long? Somebody obviously wanted Brock dead. Anger surged inside Julia, replacing her feelings of helplessness.

Anger also flashed in KC's eyes. The signs of an imminent eruption. "Somebody needs to pay for this. Hannan. And I'll kill him, myself!"

Two more firemen appeared. One of them carried a radio. He stopped beside them. "An ambulance will be here in two minutes. Go to the front of the building." He looked at Steve. "Let me help you. I can carry him."

"No. I've got him," Steve said. "Come on. Let's get outside."

Outside? In front? Wasn't that where the attack had come from? Julia reached for Steve's arm to stop him.

Before she could voice her fears, KC spoke. "Steve, that shot probably came from somewhere near the beach."

Steve stopped at the head of the stairs.

Julia stopped beside him. "Isn't that the side of the building where we're meeting the ambulance?"

Steve shifted Brock's weight on his shoulders. "I'm guessing the Israelis are all over this by now. They don't take kindly to surprises ... like RPG attacks." He headed down the stairs.

An RPG? So that's what created the explosion and fire. The explosion had felt a lot like the flashbang grenade that knocked Julia out four weeks ago when Brock, Steve, and Jeff tried to rescue her.

Julia's shoes clattered down the metal steps of the stairwell. She trailed Steve now, barely able to keep up with him though he carried Brock. At least she could breathe. The smoke hadn't yet invaded the stairwell.

KC kept pace at Steve's side. "You'll check before we go outside, right?"

"I'll check, KC."

"Thanks."

KC said thanks, but there wasn't much thankfulness in the group at the moment. The man who had just become KC's husband had nearly been killed. He could still die.

Sometimes evil seemed to win on planet Earth. The Bible taught that true justice would only be realized at the end of time when God became judge and all wrongs were set right. If they had to wait until then, KC's heart would be broken. It looked like it was breaking now, like the dam holding back KC's emotions had cracked under the pressure. Tears streaked her cheeks.

Inside the stairwell, at floor three, Steve stopped to catch his breath.

When KC stopped, Julia placed her good hand on KC's shoulder. "I'm praying for him, KC. It's going to be okay."

As KC turned to face Julia, the dam burst. KC, who never cried, now sobbed in deep convulsions.

Julia held KC with her good arm and let her cry, hoping and praying that it really would be okay. To have the man she had loved since she was a girl taken from her only seconds after saying their wedding vows was too much for anyone to endure.

Tears now rolled down Julia's cheeks, too. She wanted to wipe them away. She wanted to wipe the whole incident away. But, holding KC with her only good arm, she couldn't.

"It's time to go." Steve resumed his descent of the stairs. "I hear another siren, probably the ambulance."

KC slid from Julia's embrace, studying her face for a moment. KC gave Julia a quick hug, then followed Steve down the stairwell.

For whatever reasons, KC had never developed a close relationship with Julia. At first, it had hurt her. But now a bond between her and KC had been forged. At least Julia believed it had. And she prayed KC would come to trust her, because who knew what KC might have to endure after they reached the hospital and heard Brock's diagnosis.

They exited the stairwell on the first floor and the front door of the building lay only a short distance ahead. Would there be more RPGs or bullets? Would there still be six of them left at the end of this day? What if someone had to die today?

A terrifying thought entered Julia's mind. Should she turn it into a prayer?

Please, God, if someone must die, let it be me ... not Brock.

Chapter 3

Fifteen minutes later, Julia, KC, and Steve sat side-by-side in the emergency-room waiting area at a large medical center in Netanya.

Benjamin, who'd been blown out into the corridor by the explosion, had survived with no apparent injuries and had remained at the burning apartment building with Jeff and Allie, waiting for Major Katz to arrive and bring them to the hospital.

Brock, still unconscious, had been wheeled away for an MRI, the only test the ER doctor thought would tell them the extent and nature of his head injuries.

For the past five minutes, KC's eyes had vacillated between glaring eyes filled with violence and haunted eyes that spilled her worries and fears onto her cheeks.

Julia's heart ached for her.

Only seconds after being pronounced man and wife, Brock's and KC's dreams had been shattered in a violent explosion. It seemed almost as cruel as that day in the Nigerian village, nine years ago, when the jihadists came and—Julia couldn't let her mind go there. Not now. And Julia's prayer to trade places with Brock seemed so futile. She was helpless, unable to do for Brock what he had done for her.

Brock had sacrificed himself for Julia. Less than five

weeks ago, he had walked into torture and almost certain death to ransom her with his life after Hannan's men captured her.

Once again, Julia Weiss was no help to anyone, especially KC, who desperately needed comfort. That thought only brought more tears.

Crying again. The name kids at school called her after she returned from Africa certainly fit. Weiss the wimp. Julia looked for a place to hide her face, a place to cry in private shame.

Steve's shoulder was the nearest thing to her. She buried her face in it.

When his huge arm wrapped around her shoulders, she relaxed against the strong warrior, gave in to her weakness, and let the tears flow.

A few moments later, a crash sounded from near the emergency room doors.

Julia pulled her head from Steve's shoulder.

A tall man in uniform had stiff-armed the emergency room door like a fullback shoving aside tacklers. It was Major Katz, commander of the Israeli team whose last-minute rescue had saved KC and Brock from Hannan's black ops team four weeks ago.

Allie and Jeff followed Katz into emergency then hurried toward KC.

Benjamin stood in the open doorway behind Jeff. The always vigilant Sayeret Matkal warrior scanned the room before entering.

Major Katz had promised to protect them in Israel. Had Katz's neglect permitted the attack? Julia chided herself for accusing the man who had taken huge risks and responsibilities to keep them alive.

KC stood, glaring at Major Katz. She'd probably made the same accusation as Julia—Katz, guilty as charged—and needed a target for her anger. Someone needed to defuse KC before she exploded.

Julia draped her good arm over KC's shoulders. "KC, I've been praying so hard. Brock is going to be okay. He has to be."

At Julia's words, KC deflated and collapsed on Julia's shoulder.

The emergency room went silent as KC's anger flowed away in tears and the sobbing of a broken heart.

When KC's sobbing subsided, Julia released her and looked up at Allie.

Lines of tension etched on Allie's permanently tan face deepened as she placed a hand on KC's shoulder. "Brock isn't ... I mean, he's still—"

KC raised her head, drew a breath, and blew it back out, slowly. "They're doing an MRI." She wiped her cheeks. "He's still unconscious. The doctor thinks the MRI will tell us why and..."

KC had stopped talking and the haunted look returned to her face. She still feared the worst. Then her face reddened and her eyes blazed as they bored into Katz.

He winced. He'd gotten the gist of the unspoken message. "Ms. Banning, Hamas sacrificed a valuable deep cover plant to execute the attack. They—"

"Hamas?" KC glared at the major again. "This is Hannan's doing. I'd swear it."

"You're probably right," Katz said, his eyes softening. "We caught two men trying to escape from their hiding place in a beach house. One was the Hamas spy. He's dead. But the other man seems willing to talk to save his own life. He indicated that someone paid Iran who paid Hamas to kill you and Brock."

"Hannan." Steve reached for Julia's hand. "And he probably used that old scoundrel, Eli Vance, to negotiate the whole thing."

Before she could react, Steve grasped her injured hand

and squeezed. She couldn't stifle a groan as pain shot from her wrist to her elbow.

"Sorry. I didn't mean to squeeze so hard." Steve looked down at Julia's right hand protecting her left. He studied her face.

Her eyes were welling from the piercing pain.

Steve released her hand and Julia quickly wiped her eyes.

"What's wrong with your left hand?"

She didn't reply.

"Julia, you're hurt aren't you?"

She nodded. "Just my wrist. Maybe I sprained it a little."

Steve cradled her injured hand gently in his enormous hands. "A sprain you say. Let me see you make a fist."

All eyes were on Julia now. They knew she was the weakling in the group, the one who had placed them in danger several times. She didn't want their pity, so she'd better make a fist.

Julia curled her fingers. Her jaw clenched at the ache that crippled her wrist.

"It hurt didn't it?" Steve drew her gaze.

"A little." Julia couldn't lie to him. Her wrist actually looked a little puffy, but maybe that was her imagination.

"Now move your hand up and down. The full range of motion."

"Come on, Steve. I—"

"Move it, or I'll do it for you." Steve set his jaw and stared her down.

He would win, eventually. She needed to just get it over with. Julia rotated her hand backward a couple of inches. Her hand stopped. Surprised at the limited range of motion, she paused before rotating her hand downward.

"Move it down. All the way." Steve reached for her hand.

She wasn't going to let him force it down. Julia pushed her palm down toward her wrist and nearly screamed from the agonizing jolt that shot up her arm. But her hand hardly moved.

All eyes were on her. On Julia Weiss, the great American wimp. Her face grew hot and, now, there was no place to hide her shame.

Allie gasped. "Julia, you're hurt."

"Yeah. She's hurt." Steve cradled her hand again, even more gently. "You've got a broken wrist. Probably one of the small bones at the base of your hand. We're getting you to X-ray, now." Steve stood, hooked an arm around her waist, and pulled her toward the emergency room desk. "Nurse, we've got another injury here. Maybe a broken wrist."

"Steve, you don't know that." More eyes focused on Julia. Maybe she could shake off the pain and persuade them it was nothing.

Too late. Now, a whole medical team converged on her.

The Israelis probably felt terrible about the RPG attack on their American guests. And the Israelis weren't stupid. If there were Americans here getting preferential treatment, it meant they were anti-Hannan, like Israel, and this tiny sliver of a nation, which fought daily for survival, had a vested interest in protecting them.

Julia stood to face the onslaught of attention.

Steve stood beside her. "You should have said something. Julia, if you're hurt and we don't know it, we might be depending on you to do something you can't do. It endangers everyone if you don't tell us."

She couldn't win. Either she was a whiny weakling or a stubborn stoic, jeopardizing the entire team. "What is it you want from me, Steve? I'm not KC Banning, I'm just Julia Weiss."

Julia regretted her words, words from a poison tongue. She had drawn everyone's focus from where it belonged, on Brock and KC, to Julia whose pain was insignificant.

Julia glanced at KC's face.

It held a puzzled frown.

What was KC thinking? What had Julia been thinking?

She fumbled for words. "Brock and KC needed us, Steve, I—they were the targets. Besides, you saved my life."

KC folded her arms and looked away from Julia.

Steve stood, hands on hips, while a young woman in scrubs pushed a wheelchair toward them.

Sixty seconds later, Julia sat in the wheelchair while the woman pushed her at a fast clip down a hallway toward a sign written in three languages. The bottom line read, Diagnostic Imaging.

Fifteen minutes later they wheeled Julia back toward emergency.

After her outburst about not being like KC, what kind of reception awaited her?

Steve stood waiting for her in the hallway to Diagnostic Imaging. His eyes went directly to the blue and white, fingerless Velcro glove on her hand, extending half way up her forearm.

She waved her injured hand at him. "It's called a scaphoid bone fracture. Actually, I just cracked it, so it's no big deal."

"No big deal?" Steve's frown and the piercing look in his eyes said he didn't believe that. He pointed at the Velcro cast. "How long?"

"Three weeks, then just whenever I'm stressing it for another three weeks."

Steve was still frowning as the wheelchair stopped in front of her previous seat in emergency.

KC put a hand on her shoulder, "How bad is it?"

KC, a young woman who, all alone, had carried the fate of the nation on her shoulders while riding a motorcycle from DC to Oregon, still cared about Julia, despite her bitter outburst. Maybe she should just move ahead and assume they'd forgiven her. "Just a little cracked bone. I'm fine. Any word about Brock?"

"No, but ..." KC turned toward a dark-haired man in scrubs, approaching them.

His intense eyes and pursed lips weren't what Julia hoped to see. She stopped breathing.

He walked straight to KC. "I'm Doctor Shemer. Ms. KC Banning?"

KC met the man's gaze, drew a sharp breath, and nodded. "Brock ... is he—"

The doctor pointed a thumb back over his shoulder and snorted. "He nearly destroyed a two-million-dollar imaging system housed in a half-million-dollar room."

Julia released the breath she'd been holding. Was this man telling them that Brock was alive and well?

"You mean he's okay?" KC's eyes widened, hopeful.

"He is in better shape than our MRI patient table." The doctor sighed and shook his head. "He regained consciousness while he was inside the bore, started thrashing and yelling your name. We barely got him out before he tore up the whole machine. He is one strong—what do you Americans say—dude?"

A smile spread across Jeff's face. "Just be glad he didn't start throwing things. He can stone you to death with one rock."

"Yeah." Steve said. "He—"

"Everyone, just stop!" KC crossed her hands then flung them wide, nearly hitting Steve in the chest with her incomplete pass signal. She looked at the doctor. "What did you find? Is he going to be alright?"

Dr. Shemer sighed again. "I guess I need to, as you Americans say, cut to the cheese."

"To the chase," Jeff said.

KC shot Jeff a glance that shut his mouth.

The doctor continued. "We think the explosion stunned or knocked him out, so he couldn't protect his head when he fell. He has a concussion."

"That's all? Just a concussion?" KC gave the doctor a puzzled frown.

"Yes. But, about his concussion ... he's not, as you say, out of the irons yet."

"You mean the woods," Jeff said.

The doctor nodded. "The woods. You'll have to excuse me. I'm not really into golfing."

Jeff rolled his eyes. "He's all yours, KC."

"Doctor Shemer, just give me your prognosis." KC glared at the doctor with clenched fists, looking like she might drive one of them into his large nose.

He studied her face for a moment, then seemed to be scanning her long red hair.

Please don't go there. Julia cringed.

"That explains it, Ms. Banning. You're Irish, aren't you?"

This doctor had no idea who he was dealing with in KC Banning. She erupted like a volcano, spewing hot lava and a few choice words Julia hadn't realized were in KC's vocabulary.

Julia moved beside her.

With fists clenched at her sides, KC stepped toward the doctor.

He took a quick step backward.

Julia moved to block KC's path.

Steve hooked KC's arm and pulled her back.

"You need to understand something." Jeff's voice. He pointed a thumb at KC. "She has two notches on her M4. There are two less special ops soldiers on the planet. Wanna go for three notches?"

Shemer's eyebrows raised. "I see."

"No, you *don't* see!" Steve shoved a finger in the man's face. "You tell her Brock's prognosis, now! And no more clumsy clichés, or I'll turn her loose."

The man had tried his best to make them feel at home.

But using clichés from another culture, when one was not completely familiar with it, wasn't wise.

"I... I see what you mean." The doctor turned toward KC. "Mr. Daniels's concussion doesn't seem to be severe, but it is a concern. We will keep him for a while longer. If all goes well, he will be discharged later today, or perhaps tomorrow morning."

"Finally," KC huffed. She paused and her face relaxed. "When can I see him?"

A woman in scrubs strode through a doorway behind Dr. Shemer and approached them. "You need to bring KC Banning now, doctor. If you don't hurry, we may have to shut down part of emergency. It's not safe in there."

The doctor motioned toward the door. "Then you should follow me, Ms. Banning."

"Will you all stop calling me Ms. Banning? I'm Mrs. Daniels."

Julia heaved a sigh of relief and, for the first time in an hour and a half, the tension drained from her. Though her arm ached, the dark cloud that had settled over her an hour ago was gone.

Thank God they had survived another attack from Abe Hannan. KC should be grateful, too. But that probably wouldn't happen until KC looked into Brock's eyes and read the message written there, the message saying that he really was okay.

Regardless, they had been found in Netanya and nearly killed. What would Major Katz do with them, now?

* * *

Steve Bancroft sighed long and loud, trying to drain the tension of the past hour from his heart, mind, and body. Brock was going to be okay.

Steve's gaze involuntarily locked on KC and tracked her

as she followed the doctor. With her anger painting her cheeks nearly as red as the long curls swinging behind a body that could easily compete with world-class models, how could he not watch?

In a few seconds, she disappeared through the double doors leading into the bowels of the hospital. Even her temper seemed to add to her stunning beauty. Brock was a lucky man.

Something bumped Steve's shoulder. He looked down into dark sparkling eyes and the delicate beauty of Julia's face, a face holding a quirky smile. She had nudged him.

"They're together again, Steve. The way it was meant to be."

"Well, I'm glad it's Brock with KC and not me. Courting a volcano doesn't seem like a safe thing to do. Marrying one could kill a guy."

Julia laughed softly. "She's certainly a woman of passion."

"Yeah. Passionate about everything she does, says, and probably thinks."

Julia's quirky smile morphed to an impish grin. "You mean you've never wondered what it would be like to have such a fiery, passionate woman in love with you?"

His face overheated like a Humvee engine with a blown water hose. "Julia ... I can't believe you would—"

"So, you *have*." She laughed again. "I'd have been worried if you hadn't."

What was going on with Julia, the woman who was always so calm, controlled, and almost prudish? He sensed something beneath the surface, smoldering inside her, waiting to catch fire. It piqued his curiosity. Whatever it was, Steve doubted Julia would ever erupt like KC.

He scanned the light brown waves of her hair, then focused on those dark brown eyes.

She looked up at him, her eyes hardly two feet away and

so deep that another universe might be hidden in them. They sucked him in like a black hole.

Steve looked away across the room while he could still escape their pull.

On the far side of the emergency room, Major Katz turned from the nurse at the desk and walked their way. "For security reasons, the hospital is moving Brock to a private room. We all need to have a meeting in his room, after we give KC and Brock a few moments alone. We've got some critical decisions to make and very little time to make them."

Julia slipped her arm inside Steve's and they followed the major down a hallway toward an elevator sign. Her arm, curled around Steve's, felt custom-made for his. But, beyond that arm, there were issues. They had begun discussing a big, mysterious one before the wedding. Now, that issue, whatever it was, would have to wait until Julia raised it again.

When they reached Brock's room a few minutes later, the door was only half closed.

The major knocked and pushed the door open.

Brock released KC from his arms and she sat up on his bedside, wiping away tears but smiling through them.

Behind Major Katz, Steve escorted Julia into the room, followed by Allie and Jeff. They circled Brock's bed.

Benjamin stood by the door, guarding them. The pained expression on his face said he hadn't come through the day unscathed either. After the attack, he probably thought he'd failed them.

Steve shared some of Benjamin's feelings. After all, Captain Craig had sent Steve to help watch out for the other five Americans. But, when the attack came, Steve was participating in a wedding ceremony.

Some protector of the group he was. Maybe he had become too personally involved in their lives. Regardless, this would not end like it had with his sister. No one Steve Bancroft protected would die on his watch. Never again.

Major Katz's voice drew Steve back to the hospital room. "Sorry for the intrusion," Katz said, looking down at Brock. "But we need a new plan to keep you safe and, after the events of the day, I'm afraid Israel won't do. Our country is too small and it's surrounded by enemies who know you're here."

KC sat on the edge of Brock's bed, holding his hand like she would never let go. "But we can't move Brock, not yet. So what do we do in the meantime?"

"We have a safe house ... actually a bit bigger than a house. It will accommodate the five of you and keep you safe until Brock is discharged. But it won't be anything like the suite overlooking Netanya Beach."

"Safe sounds good," Julia said. "That ocean view was nice, but it brought us an RPG."

This was a new and more vocal Julia than Steve had ever seen. Even after four weeks of as many one-on-one conversations as Steve could get, he still had a lot to learn about this young woman who was stealing his heart in huge chunks.

KC looked up at the major. "Will Brock be safe at the hospital overnight?"

"Let's hope it's not overnight. I would like to move you all today, but, yes. We'll have two men outside his room, others inside the facility, and observers hidden outside. And our intelligence organizations are on high alert. Brock is safe here."

"Then I'm staying with him." She met the major's gaze with an icy stare.

Steve had seen that look before. KC wasn't leaving Brock no matter who gave the orders.

"Kace." Brock raised his head, grimaced, and laid his head down on the pillow.

"I can sleep in the recliner by the door."

Katz shook his head. "I doubt that he will be staying overnight."

Brock grinned. "Haven't you learned, yet? Nobody changes KC Banning's mind, except her."

She pointed a finger at Brock's face, then softly traced his lips. "KC Daniels, sweetheart."

Brock kissed her finger then looked up at the major, "Sir, she could—"

"Overruled." Katz's commander's voice returned. "KC goes to the bunker until we leave."

"Bunker?" KC walked to the recliner and sat. "You're not splitting us up on our wedding night."

"It's not my intent to split you two up tonight."

KC sat up straight in the recliner.

Katz gave her the palm-out stop sign. "Just listen for a moment. Since Hannan pulled all the Americans out of Israel, both civilian workers and military, after he declared martial law, we've taken over Site 911. You'll be safe there from everything but a direct nuclear hit."

"Site 911?" Steve had heard of this secret project, but had never been given any important details about it. "Is that the underground complex about ten miles south of here?"

Major Katz nodded. "Bancroft ... changing the subject ..." Katz looked at Steve then Brock. "What is Craig's detachment up to?"

So the Israelis weren't giving out info about Site 911.

Brock's eyes narrowed. "I haven't heard anything from Craig in four days. It's not unusual to hear nothing for a day or two, when he's on the move. He has the secure satellite phone you gave him, but we've heard nothing. Right, Steve?"

"Yeah. Nothing since they started moving eastward four days ago. As he approaches DC, calling us gets riskier, even with the secure sat phones you gave us."

Major Katz stroked his short beard. "Regardless, we need

to move you all within the next twelve hours, preferably the next six. I've just got to decide where."

Steve ran a dozen countries through his mind, searching for a safe haven. Only one country seemed plausible, Canada. It was still friendly toward Israel, and both the Prime Minister and the Minister of National Defense hated Hannan. Would the major reveal his plan at this juncture? Steve turned toward Katz. "Where are you taking us, sir?"

"We're conducting negotiations with a country that I can't yet disclose. For now, Steve, you try to get a message to Craig to tell him we're moving you. It's a place we would like to hide you for two or three months."

So Katz wasn't going to tell them, yet. Canada was too close to the US to risk disclosure of their Canadian destination to the wrong person. "Will do, sir. He might have some valuable input."

Steve stepped closer to Brock.

A scowl formed on Brock's face. "Two or three months. I hope Hannan's history by then."

Steve nodded. "Yeah, history. And maybe painted a bright shade of hades." He shouldn't wish that on anyone, but mercy was in short supply in Steve Bancroft's heart today. Hannan had almost killed them. He'd injured Brock and Julia and, at this juncture, Hannan's demise in two or three months was far from certain.

If something had happened to Captain Craig and his Rangers, there might be no demise ... ever.

.

Chapter 4

Why was his private study so bright at eight o'clock in the morning? Hannan swiveled away from his desk until he faced the windows normally behind him while he worked. He squinted as sunlight stabbed his eyes, then he shielded them with a hand.

He should fire the horticulturist for cutting the shrubbery so low. A sniper with one of those precision-guided rifles could shoot Hannan in the back from the roof of the National Telecommunications and Information Administration building five or six hundred yards away. But this horticulturist had served six presidents. Firing him might cause a bigger rebellion than the one Hannan had been mired in for the past six weeks.

The state of the six-week-old rebellion was the reason for Hannan's sour mood and for holding this solo pity party in his private study. He needed some good news. Maybe something encouraging would come out of the meeting with his inner circle scheduled for eight thirty.

Since Hannan had declared martial law across United States, the nation had settled into a tense stalemate, a precarious balance of pro- and anti-Hannan factions. The population centers, heavily patrolled by military, were under Hannan's control. But in the rural areas, and in several states west of the Mississippi, dubbed the Red States, various militias, allied with state governments, were in control.

The National Guard was no longer *national*. Guards in the Red States had pledged allegiance to their state's governor. And despite the fact that Hannan had nationalized them, the true allegiance of other National Guard units remained questionable.

The last time the Union had fractured to this degree the division almost wiped out an entire generation of young men and, 150 years later, remnants of the bitterness from that war still plagued the nation.

Hannan knew the formula for seizing power. He knew it well. First create the demon, then the people will let the government subjugate them, using martial law and the Commander-in-Chief's power to control the demon. The CIC then assumes total control. It worked well enough for Hitler.

The problem was that, though Hannan had deflected the blame for the American catastrophes, some states and their intra-state militias viewed Hannan as the demon ... thanks to Brock Daniels. Consequently, many state's willingness to resist had far exceeded Hannan's worst-case predictions.

And if he couldn't stem the steady trickle of military defections, the defectors, especially from the Special Forces, would train more militia and the scales might be tipped against Hannan.

In the four weeks since he had been abandoned by the wealthy ideologues who brought him to power, the insurgents had become bolder, inspired by public enemy number one, blogger Brock Daniels. At times it seemed that Daniels was coordinating the chess moves made by the insurgency. But that wasn't possible. Was it?

The only victory Hannan could claim actually belonged to his Secretary of Health and Human Services, Dr. Patricia Weller, who had stopped the spread of a mutant, airborne version of Ebola, the strain his feckless former Secretary of Defense, Gerald Carter, had allowed to break out of control, threatening the entire nation.

Two firm knocks on Hannan's closed office door ended his pity party.

That would be Secretary of State, Eli Vance. Intelligent and perceptive, Eli seemed to have the pulse of every department and agency in the administration.

Since Hannan had launched his power play, nearly every other nation had closed their embassies in the US, pulled their ambassadors and staff, and were playing a waiting game.

Following the resultant isolation of the US by the rest of the world, the State Department had temporarily morphed into a department of internal affairs, with the various departments and agencies replacing foreign nations as Eli Vance's domain.

The knock sounded again.

Hannan had asked Vance to give him weekly state of the union reports, and Hannan needed to hear Eli's report before the meeting with his inner circle in less than a half hour. "Come in, Eli."

A long, narrow face wearing thick glasses that magnified already large eyes peered at Hannan from the doorway. That face and the gaunt body, bent at the waist from eighty years of living an unhealthy lifestyle, and with both hands reaching out to his cane, Eli resembled a praying mantis.

Hannan motioned toward the semi-circle of office chairs he'd arranged at the end of his desk.

"Has anyone taken any potshots at you this week?" Eli's quirky smile lifted one side of a gray mustache that spanned two-thirds of his face.

Hannan didn't reply. *Someone's going to shoot you.* That was Eli's continual, taunting remark.

Eli lowered his bent frame into the chair. "It's inevitable.

Someone's going to shoot you someday, Abe." He chuckled until it turned into a coughing spasm.

Hannan shook his head. "You won't be around to see it. Your cigarettes will kill you first."

The old ambassador folded his gnarled fingers, placing his hands in his lap. "Changing the subject."

"If the subject's your smoking, you always do."

He met Hannan's gaze, the man's large eyes intense, radiating intelligence. "The new stats say twenty-five percent of our population is for you and twenty-five percent against you, Abe."

"What happened to the other half of the people?"

"They're not taking sides." Eli shook his head. "They just want it to be over. But, do you want my opinion?"

"I'm going to get it anyway." Hannan waved a hand at Eli. "Go ahead."

"If you don't end the martial law soon, they will turn on you. When that happens ... let's just say you don't have enough troops to quell all of the violence. And they will be climbing the White House fences before you kill them all. Yes, somebody will shoot you."

Eli was right and Hannan still had received no report on his attempt to stop the one man who could incite a large-scale rebellion and keep the rebels stirred up, Brock Daniels. "What's Daniels's blog readership these days?"

Eli coughed, pulled out a handkerchief, and wiped his lips. "As near as we can tell from the network traffic bound for that Israeli server, about 100 million ... give or take twenty million."

"Blast it! Why in the blazes haven't we heard anything from Hamas?"

"You mean from Iran, don't you?" Eli raised his bushy eyebrows. "You need to watch your words, Abe. People will use them against you. We don't cut deals with terrorists. Not officially. Terrorist-supporting nations on the other hand ..."

"You didn't answer my question. Has Hamas made the attempt?"

"No word yet. You're forgetting that news doesn't travel as fast to the US these days. American reporters are viewed with suspicion, even among our former allies." Eli chuckled.

Control had been slipping away from Hannan for the past four weeks, both internationally and at home. He didn't have enough troops to control the entire nation. If he lost control of what remained of the Union, he could find himself swinging from a rope ... if someone didn't shoot him first.

Eli's grin suggested the old goat was reading Hannan's mind.

But, hopefully, Hamas would kill Daniels and the Banning girl that he ran off to Israel to marry. With a little luck, it would happen before the two obtained their marriage authorization. Daniels didn't deserve any kind of happiness after all the grief he'd brought Hannan.

With Daniels dead, Hannan could launch an offensive against the red states. A combination of threats and promises of rewards would bring them back into the fold. If that failed, he would be forced to take extreme measures to control the entire nation. A lot of people would die and history would brand him a ruthless tyrant, instead of the man who had ushered in a modern socialist utopia, ending capitalism in America.

"They're here." Eli's voice startled Hannan.

He needed to focus. The meeting with his newly formed inner circle would start in a few minutes and they had a full agenda, one that, for the first time in over a month, might not include Brock Daniels or KC Banning.

The first person through the door was his new Secretary of Defense, Harrison Brown, whose primary qualification was his loyalty to Hannan, not his expertise with military operations. At this point, loyalty trumped expertise.

Harry Brown sat beside Eli on Hannan's left.

31

Gregory Bell, Randall Washington's former subordinate, was an adequate Attorney General, though he didn't have Randy's efficiency or ruthlessness. But Randy had resigned and disappeared, while Greg had remained loyal.

Bell took the chair on Hannan's right.

Hannan had finally convinced Eli Vance to join the group. The old geezer had proven most useful in negotiating sensitive issues with unreliable allies like Iran. Eli had brokered the half-billion-dollar deal where Iran funded Hamas to kill Brock Daniels.

Hannan opened his mouth to speak, but stopped when a knock sounded on the study door. "Who is it?"

"Agent Belino with an urgent message for Secretary Vance."

"Very well. Come in, Belino."

The young Marine handed a folded sheet of paper to Eli, shot Hannan a curious glance, then excused himself.

Eli opened the page. As he read, his bushy eyebrows rose. Then his huge orbs focused on Hannan's face.

It couldn't be good news. "Well, Eli, would you mind sharing the news with the group?"

Eli grinned, but his large, luminous eyes staring at Hannan expressed anything but mirth. "Hamas launched an RPG 29 into the American's suite while Brock Daniels and KC Banning were inside." Eli stopped.

Maybe this would be good news after all. "You can continue. Anytime, Eli."

The old man sighed loud and long, a raspy hissing from worn out lungs.

An RPG 29 would fill most of the apartment with fire. The fire, with the explosion, would—

"Daniels survived." Eli coughed. It turned into a coughing fit.

"What the—how? How could anyone survive that?"

"All six Americans were inside, but they all survived," Eli

said. "Daniels went to a hospital for observation. Our spy thinks he's going to marry KC Banning—maybe he already did—and then leave Israel."

Hannan pounded his desk, stood, and cursed Brock Daniels, KC Banning, and their entire ancestry. "When does it ever end with these two? I want to know where they're going, and this time I'll kill them using my own men. No more unreliable—"

"You might want to rethink that, Abe." Eli cleared his throat. "We know that the Israelis negotiated something with the Canadian Department of National Defense, maybe with the deputy minister. And we know there was a Public Safety person present at the meeting, you know, the Mounties."

"And how do we know all this?"

"Abe, it's not like you don't have *any* supporters in the Canadian government. I know it's hard to believe, but their far left is further out on the west end of the political spectrum than you." Eli chuckled. "An underling in the Canadian DND has taken a personal interest in this matter. He's taken steps to ensure we will be able to track our target."

"So they're going to Canada. Where in Canada?"

"Don't worry, it's all under control."

Abe leaned back in his chair, propping his feet up on his desk. "But this involves Brock Daniels. He's the one who needs to be under control. He needs to be dead."

Eli studied Hannan's face for a moment. "All in good time. Our friend in Canada has other friends. We will soon know where Daniels and company will be staying."

Hannan ruminated for a moment on the information Eli had given him. "Okay ... we know they're in Canada, but we can't be caught violating Canada's sovereignty to kill them. So, what do you recommend, Eli?"

"By the time they arrive, the house will be bugged, so we'll know what they're planning. There's a US Army Ranger with them, a guy named Steve Bancroft. They also have a member of Israel's Sayeret Matkal, Benjamin Levy."

Where was Eli going with this? "And so ..."

Eli chuckled again. It ended with more coughing. Finally, looking exhausted, he looked up at Hannan. "So, here's how it will play out. The Israeli guy's no slouch. He will discover the bugs within a few hours, realize they've been compromised, and they'll move."

"Move? They don't have many options."

The old diplomat nodded. "They really only have one option. To come back to the US ... you know, to one of the areas where you don't have your thumb on the people."

"You mean the red areas?"

"Yes. Probably out west somewhere, where the dissidents and the insurgents are in control."

How did they get a Ranger assigned to them? It had to be someone who was with them the night they took out the Apache near Crooked River Ranch. That's when the Ranger detachment had first become involved.

If Hannan knew who the ranger was, perhaps he could identify the Ranger Captain C who said, in a Brock Daniels post, that he was coming to get Hannan. The bold threat had made him angry, but it had also given him nightmares. "I want to know everything about this Ranger Steve ... what's his name—"

"Bancroft." His new Secretary of Defense, Harry Brown, sat up in his chair. "I can have that information for you in about fifteen minutes."

Fifteen minutes later Harry returned with a paper in his hand. "Mr. President, the Ranger with Brock Daniels is Sergeant Steve Bancroft. He's assigned to a Ranger detachment commanded by a Captain David Craig, a man who seems to have gone AWOL.

So it *was* Captain C. Hannan recalled the threatening

words in Brock Daniels's blog post from the Ranger commander.

Some night you will awaken to fingers around your throat. They will be mine.

... Captain C. US Army Ranger

It had to be the same guy. If Hannan could capture Steve Bancroft when they went after Brock Daniels, maybe they could use Bancroft to flush out this Ranger Captain, or at least learn where Craig was. If Hannan could do this quickly, it could tear a huge hole in the insurgency. Maybe turn some red states back to true blue.

"I want all Israeli flights originating from Canada to be closely monitored for any Israeli aircraft that might be coming into the US. This group has to fly in. They can't use a border crossing or they'd be arrested. And when they do re-enter, we need to pounce on them before the vermin can scatter and hide." He paused. "Can you handle this, Harry?"

"I can handle it." Harrison Brown smiled. "If we find them in the air, we will have Air Defense interceptors waiting to shoot them down. If they manage to land—"

"Land? Doesn't NORAD track flights out to 200 miles?"

"Yes, Mr. President. If they approach from the Atlantic or Pacific Ocean, the Air Defense Identification Zone begins 200 miles out and sovereign airspace starts at twelve miles. But, like I was saying, if they land, I've got the best detachment of loyal Rangers ready to take them out."

If he wanted Bancroft alive, their landing wouldn't be a total loss. "And who's commanding these Rangers?"

"Captain Deke."

Hannan sat up in his chair. "Why Deke?"

Harry cocked his head. "Because, like I said, he's the best we've got."

Deke was also part of the contingent that would provide personal protection for Hannan should anyone make an assault on the White House. He hadn't made that public knowledge and didn't intend to.

Was it worth the risk of making POTUS a bit more vulnerable for the time it would take to rid himself of Daniels and KC Banning, the two thorns in Hannan's flesh? Yes, more than worth it.

"Then Deke it is. Let me know the minute you've located them, Harry."

"Yes, sir. Is that all, Mr. President?"

"No. Tell Deke that if those rebels manage to land and he captures any of them, make their death slow, make it hurt, and make sure they understand why no one should try to make Abe Hannan look like a fool. But I want Bancroft taken alive, if possible."

Hannan would call Deke, personally, with a special set of instructions for interrogating Sergeant Steve Bancroft, techniques pulled from Deke's considerable repertoire gleaned from the captain's study of the Islamic State. Sergeant Bancroft would tell them everything he knew in order to end the pain. Then Deke could end the traitor's pain, permanently.

Chapter 5

Julia scanned the long, dimly lit corridor ahead. How far underground were they? And where was all the security? Maybe it left with the Americans.

She had more questions about this gargantuan underground compound called Site 911, but she didn't want to voice them and let Steve and KC know how clueless Julia was about things related to national security.

They already viewed her as someone who couldn't pull her weight on the team and, now, a broken wrist only made matters worse.

Major Katz led them down the hallway and into a conference room. He flipped a switch on the wall and the ceiling glowed with some strange lighting system that lit the entire room.

The conference room could probably seat a hundred people. However, there were no seats in the middle of the room, only long padded benches, or very Spartan couches, lining the wall on the far side. The facility reflected Hannan's relationship with Israel, vacated, nothing of substance left.

The major motioned toward the couches and all five Americans crossed the room and sat.

Julia glanced at the large digital wall clock. 11:00 a.m. She looked at KC who was also staring at the clock. Probably wondering when they would release Brock, her husband of nearly two hours.

Steve stood and tugged on Jeff's arm. "Major, may Jeff and I check out that war room down the hall? Or is it classified?"

"Nothing in this part of the compound is classified. The US military made sure of that when they pulled all their people out of Israel. Yes, you may go exploring, but stay on this corridor and don't start flipping power switches." Katz gestured to the door where they entered and the two men were off like two boys on an exploring adventure.

KC shuffled her feet on the floor, wrung her hands, and stood to face the major. "How long are you going to wait before you check with the hospital?"

Katz blew out a sharp sigh. "KC, getting all six of you out of the country is my top priority. I told the hospital to contact me, immediately, when they had approval to discharge Brock."

Julia had seen that frown on KC's face before and, now her cheeks glowed red. She was either going to cry or explode. With her, one never knew.

Allie stood and hooked an arm around KC.

Julia did the same on KC's other side. She was trembling. Julia prepared for an explosion.

"Major ..." KC's gaze bored into Katz. "...what happens when they discharge Brock? This is our wedding day, you know. I—" A sob choked off her voice. Tears flowed again. Too many tears for a wedding day.

Now tears threatened to spill from Julia's eyes.

KC was like that. Whenever this striking young Irish woman walked into a room, her emotions seemed to go viral, infecting everyone in the place, sometimes inspiring them, other times driving them to anger ... or to tears.

"After Brock is discharged ..." Major Katz shook his head. "This is a very inconvenient thing to do to a newly married couple." He paused. "We take you all to Ben Gurion and put you on an eleven-hour flight."

Julia winced. Eleven hours on KC's wedding night? It seemed cruel and Julia grew angry just thinking about it. She glanced at KC.

She had calmed, as if she was taking it all in stride, until the twin frown lines returned. "Does that mean Brock and I have to spend our wedding night strapped into ursa chairs on a Gulfstream?"

"Technically, it will still be your wedding day when you land in ... uh ..." Katz cleared his throat. "At your destination."

"So we won't actually miss—I guess that works."

"But, KC, it will take favorable winds for you to get where you're staying by midnight." Katz pursed his lips.

Julia's heart ached for KC. This young woman had come through unsurmountable obstacles and almost certain death to reach this point and marry the love of her life. It wasn't fair. Julia stepped to the major's side and gripped his arm.

Katz looked her way with surprise in his eyes.

She had invaded the personal space of this dignified man. Julia had never seen anyone do that. But it was too late to back down now. "Major Katz, will you please tell the pilot it's pedal to the metal, all the way. Brock and KC deserve it; don't you think?"

Katz's cell rang and he stepped out into the hallway as he answered it.

Saved by the bell.

Had the major's frown been for her invasion of his space or the cell phone's interruption?

Major Katz usually looked confident, a man in control of himself and every situation. But, when he returned, his military bearing had disappeared and he wouldn't meet KC's probing gaze. "I just talked with Benjamin and something's happening at the hospital. One of the doctors doesn't want to discharge Brock."

39

"Is something else wrong with Brock?" KC moved toward the major, clenching her fists. "I should never have left him this morning, not until—"

"KC, we don't know that anything is wrong with Brock," Katz said. "But one of the doctors is delaying his discharge until he checks out something from one of the tests they ran earlier."

Katz's cell rang, again. "Excuse me while I take this. It's Benjamin."

What did this mean? Julia studied Katz's face, looking for answers. Could Brock have been injured more seriously than they first thought? He seemed to be okay except—

"Shots fired?" The major's body stiffened. "Get in there now, Benjamin!"

KC gasped. "What's happening?"

The major waved her off and headed for the doorway.

Alarm sent Julia's heart racing. She hooked KC's arm and reached for Allie with her other hand. "Allie, KC, we need to pray. Now."

KC turned toward Katz. "Not until I—"

He gave her the one-handed stop signal, then stepped out into the hallway with his cell planted in his ear.

The three women huddled and Julia prayed for Brock's safety. Before she was two sentences into her prayer, Katz's voice grew loud. "Sirens. It's the police responding."

Brock might be dead. At that thought, Julia's prayer intensified. But her fears turned to anger that burned like a shaft of white-hot steel had pierced her heart. The focus of her anger ... Abe Hannan.

I want to kill him myself.

The uncontrollable urge to commit a violent act against another human being shocked Julia. It went against her deeply held convictions, and it came while she was supposed to be talking to God.

KC's and Allie's gazes had locked on Julia's face. Were

her out-of-control emotions that evident?

"Julia?" KC looked frightened.

"What is it?"

"I... I... Just—"

The door flew open and Major Katz stepped in. He stopped when he saw the three women huddled together. The alarm on his face had been replaced by a squinting frown. "The shooter is down."

KC whirled toward him. "What about Brock?"

Katz closed his cell and huffed a blast of air. "Brock ..." He shook his head. "Brock has disappeared."

"What?" It was the second attack in less than twenty-four hours, both allowed by the man standing in front of Julia, the one supposedly in charge of their protection, Major Katz.

Julia opened her mouth, tempted to use words she never voluntarily allowed into her vocabulary, but KC beat her to the verbal attack.

In graphic language, KC called Hannan a monster from the pit, including a strong desire to send him back to that location. She glared at Katz and opened her mouth to continue, but words didn't come ... only tears.

The major's cell lit up and played a ringtone, some vaguely familiar Jewish folk song.

Julia circled KC's shoulders with her good arm and studied Katz as he talked on the phone.

Allie tilted her head toward the floor, lips moving as she prayed softly.

Katz left the room with his cell still in his ear. He strode back and forth past the open door to the hallway at a furious pace, then stopped and closed his cell.

When he came in, Allie ended her prayer.

"It appears that one of the technicians processing Brock's MRI scans said that he saw something disturbing in the images."

KC opened her mouth.

Katz raised an open hand. "Listen for a minute. The report was false. It was a ruse to hold Brock at the hospital longer than necessary to give Hamas time to get a shooter inside. But he didn't make it to Brock's room. The shooter was killed by one of my men as he emerged from the stairwell on Brock's floor. The technician, a deep cover operative working for Hamas, has been arrested."

"Where is Brock?" KC's voice broke.

The room went silent.

Katz shook his head. "KC, we still don't know."

"We've got to find him." KC ran out the door into the hallway.

Katz chased her with Julia and Allie behind him.

KC stopped and looked both ways down the empty hallway as if confused.

The major caught her and cut her off.

She turned away from him. Her eyes streamed tears for the fourth or fifth time this morning. The mascara she had brushed on for her wedding had run, creating two large, sad looking, black eyes.

Katz placed a hand on KC's shoulder. "Sorry, KC, but I can't let you go outside. It's not safe."

Behind Katz, near the end of the corridor, a door burst open.

Dressed in cargo shorts and a muscle shirt, a tall figure strode toward them ... Brock. His gaze had locked on KC.

Thank you. Julia brushed her tears away and smiled at KC.

Brock rushed to her. "Kace, what's wrong? You've been crying."

"Where were you, Brock?"

Hands on his hips, Katz studied Brock. "Yes, Mr. Daniels. I'd like to hear your explanation, too."

"I'm fine, but the stupid doctor wouldn't discharge me."

Brock wrapped KC up in his big arms.

KC looked up into his face. "We thought you'd been shot."

"Shot? Look ... some numbskull of a technician tried to keep them from discharging me, so I just went back to my room, jumped into my clothes, and left."

Major Katz pointed a finger at Brock. "Don't do that again. You were being guarded. You left my men defending an empty room and one of them was nearly shot."

"Come on, Katz. Don't tell me Hannan sent another terrorist after me in less than twenty-four hours."

"More likely Iran sent him. They want to get paid by Hannan and they were probably getting desperate." Katz paused and looked from KC to Brock. "How did you find this place?"

Brock loosened his hold on KC. "Ever heard of a taxi? Taxi drivers are better than a GPS. I said Site 911, he nodded, and here I am. But what happened to security here? I just walked in and nobody tried to stop me."

"For this part of the compound, it left with the Americans," Katz said.

Brock nodded, then turned all of his attention to KC. He lifted her chin. "You're so beautiful, Kace. Well, all but those two black eyes are beautiful. If somebody had given you two black eyes, I'd kill them with my bare hands. I'd strangle him."

KC took Brock's hands and placed his fingers on his neck. "Then start choking yourself, Mr. Daniels."

"Katz ... and now you, too? Kace, all I did was discharge myself to get here. It's our wedding day, and ... well, I was fine and I knew it."

Steve and Jeff entered the hallway and hurried toward them.

"Hey, bro," Jeff said. "It's about time. We thought you'd married KC and then left her standing at the altar."

"That'll be the day." Brock pulled KC into his arms and kissed her.

When Brock finally released her, KC smiled.

Julia's heart smiled, too. A woman's wedding day should be filled with smiles, not terror.

"Let's go, now," KC said. "We've got an eleven-hour flight before our honeymoon begins."

Brock looked at KC's eyes and frowned. "I'm not going on a honeymoon with a woman who's got two black eyes. Somebody might think I beat my wife ... on my wedding day, no less. Go wash."

KC grinned. "But I'm going on a honeymoon with a man who's got a concussion."

"Possible concussion, Kace."

"Whatever." KC turned toward Katz. "Where's the ladies' room in this place?"

Brock tugged on KC, pulling her into a warm embrace and kissed her, again.

"Sweetheart, I thought you wanted me to wash my face first."

Brock took her hands and broke out in a raspy rendition of Van Morrison's Brown Eyed Girl, substituting black for brown.

Julia giggled at Brock's cleverly improvised lyrics.

KC struggled to cover his mouth with her hand, but big, strong Brock refused to stop singing until the song approached "the stadium" stanza.

The room filled with a cacophony of laughter until Katz's booming voice called the room to attention. "It's 1300. Time to go to the airport." He snorted. "Americans ... immersed in their pop culture while the world around them burns."

"I resent that remark, sir." Brock's gaze bored into Katz.

Katz nodded. "I'll bet you do. You're one of the few Americans who has a legitimate right to. Now, on to Ben Gurion."

Chapter 6

The huge house in front of Julia glowed like a lantern with light beaming from its large windows. The waters of Alta Lake in Whistler Valley lapped the lakeshore in the darkness to her right.

Julia stepped down from the van they'd been riding in for the past hour and a half and stood on a paved circle driveway. She smiled as she looked back at KC in the van.

The winds had been favorable and at fifteen minutes before midnight, on what was technically still her wedding day, KC Daniels slid out of the van and waited for her husband, the man she'd sat beside for nearly eleven hours on the Gulfstream.

These two had run, hidden, fought, and even killed to reach this moment, and Julia prayed that nothing would rob them of the joy their shared love held in store for them.

Brock hooked an arm around KC as they both studied the rustic log house nestled in the woods.

After everyone got out, Steve stopped by Julia's side. "Listen to those two."

KC looked up at Brock. "We just flew over halfway around the world to spend our wedding night here and it's still our wedding night. Do you think anyone else has ever done that?"

Laughter broke out in the group of seven.

"Might be a world record, Kace." Brock scanned the house for the second or third time. "This looks bigger than Julia's house in Oregon. I think I could get attached to this place in a hurry."

"You're already attached, Mr. Daniels, to me."

A creaking sound came from the house and the large, wooden front door swung open.

A man in a suit stood in the doorway, motioning for them to come in. "Welcome to your new home away from home." His words came wrapped in a mild British accent.

Jeff stopped beside Brock and poked his shoulder. "Do your duty, bro. We'll wait here."

KC leaned close to Brock and whispered something in his ear.

"Uh... Kace... That's not the duty Jeff was referring to."

"Oh." She hid her face against Brock's big chest.

He scooped KC up in his arms and carried her through the doorway. "This is what Jeff was talking about."

Julia and Steve followed Brock and KC into a large room with polished wooden floors, a vaulted ceiling with huge logs for beams and stained logs for walls.

As KC and Brock passed the smiling man in the suit, he pointed down a long hallway to their left. "The master suite is ready for you. Last door on the left. Congratulations! And I hope you are satisfied with our Canadian hospitality."

"Thanks," KC croaked. Evidently, she still hadn't regained her composure.

Brock let her slide to the floor.

"See you two in the morning," Steve said.

"Or in the afternoon." Jeff's voice. "Ouch, that hurt, hon."

Allie waved a finger in Jeff's and Steve's faces. "That's enough, you two. Leave them alone."

When KC and Brock reached the door to the master

suite, Brock pushed it open and scooped up KC again. The door closed behind them.

What God had intended for these two was finally being fulfilled. Would Julia live long enough to find what KC had found in Brock? It was an unsettling question, like one equation with two unknowns, living and finding. For now, Julia needed to focus on the living part.

Five minutes later, she sat in a large easy chair in the living room.

Steve pulled up a small chair and sat beside her.

Jeff and Allie sat on the couch facing her. Allie's legs were crossed and her arms folded on her chest. Julia had seen this posture before, right before Allie exploded.

Benjamin had excused himself to check the perimeter of the house. After the RPG attack in Netanya, and the attempt to kill Brock at the hospital, Benjamin had gone from being cautious to clearly paranoid.

Jeff's and Steve's banter centered on the honeymooners.

Julia heard nothing crude, but their remarks soon bordered on things of an intimate nature.

Allie's laser eyes grew more intense with every word from Jeff. Her sometimes volatile temper appeared near its flashpoint.

Jeff smirked. "I'll bet Brock—"

"That's enough!" Allie leaped to her feet. "If I hear one more wisecrack about Brock and KC, I'm going to stick a cork in your mouth, Jeff Jacobs." She looked at Steve. "And in yours, too. Those two have loved each other since they were kids. This was meant to be and I'm not going to let anyone spoil their special time. And you'd better not embarrass them at breakfast tomorrow, or I'll use the biggest pan in the kitchen on your thick head." She turned to sit.

Jeff grinned. "Breakfast? They may not even show for lunch."

Allie whirled to face Jeff, hands on her hips. "That's it.

47

You're sleeping on the couch tonight."

"But, hon, that's where Benjamin's sleeping."

"Then you'd better pray he doesn't snore."

Allie stomped out of the room headed toward her bedroom.

Jeff caught her in the hallway outside the bedroom, a spot clearly visible from Julia's seat in the big chair.

Jeff pulled Allie's head against his chest and kissed her forehead. Julia couldn't hear the words they exchanged, but Allie's smile returned seconds before the two entered the bedroom. Their door closed.

Julia looked at Steve sitting beside her, eyes studying her. They were the odd couple out. A new kind of loneliness crept into Julia's heart, the kind that ached for fulfillment by someone to share life with, someone who was more than just a friend.

Steve took her uninjured hand. "Well, the old married couples have retired for the night." He squeezed it. "I think I'll wait up to see what Benjamin thinks of the security in our new digs."

If only she could be like those "old married couples" with someone to fill the empty spot in her heart. She had a prime candidate sitting beside her.

Julia looked at Steve and her cheeks grew hot. She was blushing, afraid that Steve might be reading her mind. But her embarrassment wasn't uncomfortable enough to send her off to bed where she'd be alone.

She looked across the room to the kitchen until she could again meet Steve's gaze. "I think I'll wait up with you, if you don't mind. Would you like some tea or coffee? Our hosts stocked the kitchen cupboards for us."

He smiled. "Coffee would be great."

Julia returned his smile with an even warmer one. For the moment, she would let Steve drive her loneliness away. Beyond this moment, however, there were issues lurking, issues they hadn't yet discussed, issues for which she saw only a faint hope of resolving. And those were only *her* issues. She was certain Steve had some of his own and he hadn't been willing to share them, yet.

Steve was handsome beyond belief, and he had so many wonderful qualities that things could get serious in a hurry, if it weren't for the biggest issue. It stood between them like a mountain—McKinley, maybe Everest—but Steve either didn't realize it, or he was avoiding the subject, completely.

On the plane, Julia had hinted at one of the lesser issues, Steve's name. Maybe that was a good place to start this discussion.

Steve gave her his grin, one that could disarm a battleship. "I've noticed that you seem to have an aversion to my name?"

Had he read her mind? "Not an aversion. Steve's a fine name, but it was my father's name, and it seems a little weird to ..." Julia's words had painted her into an awkward corner. "I mean it would be so ... uh ..."

"You mean, if we ever became more than friends who occasionally hold hands, it would weird you out to call me your dad's name one moment and then maybe ... kiss me the next?"

Steve's Ranger training was clearly on display. Detect the obstacle and remove it. But his direct approach had heated her cheeks somewhere near hot pink. "Uh ... something like that."

"You can call me anything you want ... well, almost anything." He reached for her uncasted hand.

She slipped her small hand into his large powerful one. "Steve's fine. I'll get used to it."

He grinned again. "I hope so."

Julia felt so safe with this powerful warrior beside her. But his being a warrior was the mountain between them, and she didn't know how to approach that subject. When she did, would Steve understand her beliefs about warfare? Would he understand her horror of it?

A cloud passed over his face, leaving a look Julia had only seen flash in his eyes once before. Steve's face had displayed that intense, wide-eyed expression when he gripped her hand in the tent before Abdul, the brute on Hannan's black ops team, had shot at Steve, forcing him to jump out of the tent, leaving Julia behind.

After the cloud passed, the warmth in his eyes returned. He peered into her eyes and studied her face for a moment. Soon, his gaze went through her, as if he were looking into another time or place ... or at another person.

Looking at, looking through—did he even see her? This was getting freaky. "Steve?"

"So I'm still Steve?" The man she was beginning to know returned, smiling, confident, and so easy on the eyes.

"Yes. Steve. You know, if I had changed your name, all five of us here may end up using whatever I chose."

"That'd be okay. After what we've been through together, you're all like family. All like ..." His eyes again looked away through some door to another world.

Would he open the door to this part of his life and let her in? She squeezed his hand. "You've been thinking about something ever since ..."

"Ever since I sat down beside you."

Did she have something to do with his mental excursions? "Would you mind sharing it?"

Steve sighed. "I've been thinking about my sister, Stephanie." He paused and looked down at the area rug in front of them. "Steph died ten years ago."

"Oh, Steve. I'm so sorry. You two were close, weren't you?"

"Twins usually are."

"Twins? I can't imagine how awful that must have been for you."

"But you remind me so much of her, Julia." The look he gave her was filled with torment and something else, something she couldn't interpret.

She looked like Steph? Was Steve trying to regain his sister through Julia? Was that why he liked her? Even without an answer, the question upset her. Maybe she wasn't as important to him as—

Julia Weiss, how can you be so selfish?

If it eased Steve's pain, she would be Steph for him. If they remained close friends and nothing more, then the mountain wouldn't matter. But one thing was certain, as Julia or Steph, with or without the mountain between, if she continued spending time with Steve, Julia Weiss could easily end up with a shattered heart. But if that's what it took to mend Steve's heart ...

The front door opened. Benjamin entered; his intense eyes flashed danger, just as they had after the RPG attack.

Benjamin motioned for Julia and Steve to follow him. He led them to the wide granite counter near the kitchen where a notepad lay beside the telephone.

Benjamin pulled out a pocket pen and began printing. "I think we're, as you Americans say, snug as a bug in a rug here." He finished the message on the notepad and moved his hand out of the way so they could read it.

Don't discuss anything about our plans or our mission. The house is bugged.

· Chapter 7

When Julia awoke at a quarter after six, the sun had already topped mountains to the east. It lit her room through the open curtains she had forgotten to close. With the house bugged and possibly under surveillance, how could she have been so careless?

Her bedroom window faced the east. When Julia pressed her face against the glass, she could see from Whistler Mountain and Blackcomb Peak northward to other mountains in the distance. Each peak had dazzling white glaciers clinging to its rocky crags, while large glaciers blanketed the saddles between peaks, inviting summertime skiers.

Brock said that some people skied the glaciers in their swimsuits and, at 6,000 feet above sea level, often suffered severe sunburn. Since danger had preceded them to this beautiful place, Julia doubted they would be able to enjoy the scenery any more intimately than she was currently doing from her bedroom window.

Benjamin told them that August in Whistler would be warm. The only clothing she had saved from their bombed out suite in Netanya was what Julia had worn that day. Major Katz had allowed them to pick up few items of clothing before their flight to Canada, but today was a day for something cool. She adjusted the cast on her wrist and slipped into her denim shorts and a sleeveless summer blouse while Benjamin's warning about the house being bugged played through her mind.

Wondering what Benjamin had decided they should do, Julia walked down the hallway to the large family-room window. Outside, near the lake, Steve and Benjamin sat at a picnic table in the back yard, overlooking the dark blue water of Alta Lake.

The two were locked in an intense discussion.

Julia exited through the kitchen's back door and headed across the lawn. The sun warmed her arms and legs, a sharp contrast to the icy chill growing inside her from the realization that the people monitoring them wanted to kill them.

Benjamin looked up as she approached. "Keep your voice down. I didn't see any mics outside, only a camera. But let's not take any chances."

She looked down into Benjamin's intense brown eyes. "If we have to whisper, even outside, we aren't safe here. What are we going to do about that?"

Steve moved over to make room for her and she slid in beside him.

"Do you suppose they're watching us right now?"

She got no reply. "What if they can read lips?"

Benjamin's eyes widened. "I think they just bugged the place with mics." He leaned across the table toward them, subtly shielding his mouth from view using his hand. "I've been on the satellite phone with Major Katz. He says we should finalize our plan today and be out of here before nightfall. But, until then, we shouldn't act like we know someone is listening."

Julia listened for the next thirty minutes as Steve and Benjamin strategized using military jargon that she only partly understood. Their conclusions seemed to be that the entire group needed to participate and buy in to the final decision. They all had a big stake in whatever decision they made, their lives.

Julia looked toward the house when a door opened.

Jeff and Allie stepped through the back door from the kitchen.

Steve waved them toward the table.

Jeff looked up as the two approached. "This place is beautiful. Why the grim faces this morning?"

"Keep your voice down." Steve said.

Benjamin shoved his note from last night in front of the two.

Allie gasped. "They're monitoring us. How awful for KC and Brock."

Jeff looked at her with raised eyebrows. "KC and Brock? Whoever did this doesn't give a rip about embarrassing us, they mean to kill us."

"Keep your voice down, Jeff," Benjamin said.

Allie's reaction had been completely unselfish, so unlike her own. Julia had only thought about her personal danger, not how violated KC and Brock might feel. Once again, Julia chided herself for her biggest failing. She was a weak, selfish woman.

Allie and Jeff slid onto the picnic table bench beside Benjamin.

Jeff looked at Steve, then Benjamin. "Well, what are we going to do about it?"

Benjamin's dark eyes flashed a menacing look as he met Jeff's gaze. "We're dealing with a traitor, a Hannan sympathizer, either among the Canadians or the Israelis. My guess is it's a Canadian."

Jeff nodded. "You're probably right, but you didn't answer my question."

"I called Katz." Benjamin scanned the faces around the table. "He says we need to leave today. We shouldn't spend another night here. Hannan won't violate Canada's sovereignty by sending US troops, but we saw the lengths he will go to when he sent Hamas after us. He might hire someone to kill us here."

"But didn't you say the group needs to reach consensus on this?" Steve said.

"We need to leave regardless. What we need consensus on is where we go. Any ideas?" Benjamin gave them a palms-up hand and waited.

It grew quiet. The only sounds were a few birds in the trees and the lake lapping the shore thirty steps away.

The raspy sound of a slider opening came from the deck off the dining room. KC and Brock.

Surprised to see them up already, Julia studied their faces for clues as to why the two newlyweds were up so early. Had their time not gone well?

No. Brock and KC exchanged warm looks, affectionate smiles, and KC held onto Brock's arm as if it were her most prized possession.

If it weren't for KC, Julia might be the person with Brock. She had gotten his attention in Guatemala after the incident with the Mayan girl. And she'd gotten a hug from him at the Redmond Airport.

Julia Weiss, what are you doing?

Was she actually envious of KC because of Brock? No. Julia was, for the first time, wanting a man to share her life with. Facing danger alone, without a person who loved you at your side, was a frightening proposition, even for someone who said they trusted God.

Julia was happy for Brock and KC. But the loneliness in Julia's heart and mind had crept in, creating an ache that, if she didn't squelch it, might soon turn to envy and then to fear—emotions that could drive a person into an ill-advised relationship.

Steve's gaze moved from Brock and KC to Julia's face,

where it remained.

For whatever reason, Steve was attracted to her, or thought he was, and his gaga eyes were clearly on display for all to see.

Her loneliness morphed to warm cheeks and embarrassment. Why did Steve—a thought blindsided her. Maybe Steve was lonely too, despite the dedication to his career as a Ranger. Maybe he needed more than a replacement for the twin sister he lost.

But Steve was a Ranger. A man of violence and killing. He was his detachment's weapons man, highly skilled in the art of blowing people up, shooting them, and instructing others in doing the same. As long as the six of them were stuck together, Steve would be their weapons man and that eliminated him as a candidate for her attention. Imagining them becoming a couple, seriously courting, was the stuff of fairy tales. Pure fantasy.

After he looked away, she stole a glance at Steve's handsome face. It was a very nice fairy tale, but one that had no chance of ending happily ever after.

KC and Brock stopped near the picnic table. She whispered something to Brock. He pulled KC's head near and kissed her forehead, then turned toward the table. "What's up? From the looks of you all, I'd say you're planning a funeral."

"That's what we're trying to avoid, bro." Jeff slid Benjamin's handwritten note in front of Brock and KC.

KC drew a sharp breath and looked back at the house.

Brock shook his head. "Hannan again. This isn't going to stop until that man's dead or locked in prison. Personally, I'd like to get my hands on—"

KC put her hand over his mouth. "Don't say it, sweetheart. Not today."

Benjamin's face saddened as he slumped in his seat on the bench. "I'm sorry for the bad news, KC. But this means we have to leave here today."

"But we—" KC stopped. Her gaze dropped to the ground. "I guess the honeymoon's over." She looked up into Brock's face and gave him a weak smile. "For now."

"Not over," Allie said. "To be continued. Same time, different place."

"The question we need to decide is..." Benjamin grabbed the note and shoved it into his pocket, "... where are we going?"

Brock sat down beside Benjamin and made room for KC. "Wherever we go, I assume Craig still wants me blogging on the Israeli server."

"Of course," KC said. "And it still works because the Israelis built-in a protected page to enter your posts and the messages for Craig. The submittal is handled with a CGI script that also does the encryption."

"Remind me why that's important, Kace." Brock brushed a stray curl from KC's face.

She kissed his hand. "Sweetheart, we were FTP'ing the posts. NSA knows about the Israeli server, so they could just search their network traffic database for an FTP to the Israeli server's IP address, get ours, and locate us."

"NSA may know about the server," Benjamin said. "But they can't take it down. Not even with a DOS attack."

"A what?" All this computer jargon frustrated Julia. She used technology as little as possible.

"A denial of service attack. We've got that covered," Benjamin said.

Brock sighed sharply. "Come on, guys. We need to move faster. Before the spies get suspicious. We need to ditch this place, this incredible place that I'd give almost anything to live in."

"Agreed," Steve said. "But we need transportation and a place to go. We don't have passports, or any ID, and we couldn't use them even if we did. That would only bring

Hannan's hounds down on us, immediately."

Jeff shook his head. "This isn't working out well. Technically, we're in Canada, illegally. If the police stop us, we're toast."

Benjamin stood. "Don't worry about ID or the police. In case things didn't work out here, Katz asked our pilot to stick around for a day or two. He can take us anywhere in the world with a runway that can handle our Gulfstream."

"Not quite anywhere," Steve said. "We don't want an Israeli plane flying into Hannan-controlled areas where its transponder might get it shot down. Hannan's not happy with Israel right now."

Brock gave a disgusted snort. "He's never been happy with Israel. Hannan was perfectly content to force the Israelis to sit there and take it while Hamas bombarded them daily with rockets fired from schools and hospitals. Hannan wouldn't stand for Mexican drug cartels shooting rockets at us every day across the border. I—sorry. Sometimes I get—"

"Carried away?" KC hooked an arm around him. "Brock is right. But there's probably no one with the birth name Abid who's ever going to be happy with Israel."

Benjamin shot KC a curious glance. "So his first name is really Abid, not Abe?"

"Yes. But he kept it secret, or he might not have been elected to his first term. Still, there were people who called him a closet Muslim."

"KC's right," Brock said. "But we need to stay on subject here. We're flying out of Vancouver, but anybody got a suggestion as to where?"

Allie stared at Jeff, as if waiting for him to say something. "Jeff ... are you going to tell them or should I?"

"Tell them what, hon?"

"*Mi amor*, about your house in Western Oregon. You know, where we first met."

Jeff rubbed his chin. "That could work. I was going to have it cleaned and painted before I rented it again. So, it's available."

Steve propped his elbows on the table. "How big is this house?"

"Three bedrooms and a den that could be a fourth bedroom. Two bathrooms and ..."

Allie shot Jeff a glaring glance. "Don't even mention that outhouse in the back."

Jeff grinned. "Now, I don't have to."

"That works," Steve said.

"Yeah." Jeff chuckled. "It always works. Never needs a plunger because you don't have to flush—"

"Enough, Jeff." Allie pointed a finger at his face.

Benjamin laid a hand on Jeff's shoulder. "You've got me interested. Now for the ... what do you Americans call it, the clincher?"

Jeff nodded. "Yep. The clincher."

"Where is the nearest landing strip at least 1,400 meters long?" Benjamin focused on Jeff.

"There's an old Forest Service runway near O'Brien. Smokejumpers used it years ago. I think they flew DC-3s out of there, but it's still used by the locals."

Benjamin rubbed his chin several times. "DC-3s you say. I'll call our pilot on my secure phone. He can check out the runway. If it's been maintained at all, we can probably use it. Though I'm a little worried about weight restrictions. With all of us onboard, our Gulfstream weighs almost twenty-three thousand kilograms."

"Southwestern Oregon is in red territory," Brock said. "We can probably get in and out of there, unless Hannan scrambles fighters from Portland or Kingsley Air Force Base in Klamath Falls?"

"Let's assume that won't happen," Benjamin said. "Our Gulfstream is identified as having diplomatic immunity. But, being Israeli, it could be risky to fly into a populated area."

Jeff shook his head. "O'Brien isn't a populated area."

"Are you okay with this?" Benjamin asked. "You know what could happen to your house, don't you?"

"It wouldn't be the first time." Allie sighed and propped her chin on her hand.

Benjamin gave her a strange look, but didn't pursue her strange comment. "Okay, here's our plan. We take off from Vancouver, reach cruising altitude, fly south. After we're out of ATC range, we descend to about 500 feet and shoot a radar gap to the Southern Oregon coast. We hug the mountains and drop into the valley by O'Brien."

Julia hadn't contributed to the discussion, but listening to it gave her an uneasy feeling. "But suppose they send a plane to intercept us. What happens then?"

Benjamin sighed, loud and long. "The Air Guards that Brock mentioned have all been federalized since Hannan declared martial law. We have electronic countermeasures on the Gulfstream, but it would be too late to use them. We would be at the pilot's mercy, and I can guarantee you what his orders from the Commander-in-Chief would be."

"Shoot them down."

Chapter 8

Fifty miles off the Oregon coast, the Gulfstream broke out of a low cloud bank and soared over the water nearly a thousand feet below. The sound of the engine changed. Or, was there a second engine's sound?

Steve looked out the window and recoiled from it when he saw a fighter off their wing.

He turned toward the front of the plane.

Benjamin stood by the door to the pilot's cabin.

"Benjamin, tell the captain we've got—"

"He knows." Benjamin glanced back at Steve, an intense expression frozen on his face.

"It's always something," KC said. "This is never going to be over until Hannan is dead."

"What's the pilot doing about it?" Jeff's voice came from across the cabin.

"He's broadcasting a message on several frequencies, hoping the pilot will hear."

"What's the message?" Brock's voice came from the rear of the cabin, laced with sarcasm. "Don't shoot, all we have on board is public enemy number one, Brock Daniels?"

"And enemy number two, KC Banning—I mean Daniels." KC's voice.

Benjamin heaved a sigh. "He's telling the fighter pilot we've got an aircraft emergency and will be making an emergency landing in fifteen minutes."

KC shook her head. "If Hannan's federalized the Air Guards, he could be giving direct orders to the pilot, right now, telling him to shoot us down while we're still over water."

"He didn't." Benjamin took his seat and buckled in. "We just made land and we're headed up a river valley."

Steve looked out, but couldn't see the fighter. "Where did he go, Benjamin?"

The copilot twisted in his seat and leaned toward the open door to the cabin. "He's following. Above and behind us now."

Steve pushed his face against the window and strained to look upward. Nothing. But ahead of them stood towering clouds that flattened and spread out on top surrounded by others that looked like giant kernels of popcorn. "What are we flying into? It looks downright ugly inland."

Turbulence jarred Steve, slamming him down in the seat then lifting him up until his seatbelt stopped him.

Julia gasped and grabbed his arm. "Are we going to crash?"

"Just stay buckled in. It's convective turbulence," Benjamin said. "At least it got rid of the fighter, temporarily."

"Speaking of convection," Jeff said, his face against the window. "Look at those CBs."

Getting safely onto the ground at O'Brien might take more than a softhearted fighter pilot.

"Thunderstorms? You've got to be kidding." Brock's voice.

"Not kidding, bro." Jeff pointed a thumb at the window. "In August and September, southwestern monsoon moisture works its way into the intermountain region and comes in the back door to Western Oregon, sucked in by our heat low.

Sometimes, like this afternoon, it sets off spectacular fireworks."

Brock pointed a finger at Jeff. "You've been holding out on me. You ... a meteorologist?"

"Only an amateur," Jeff said. "Took a few courses in college."

"Hang on, everybody!" Benjamin's voice.

Steve drew a sharp breath as darkness enveloped them. The buffeting grew violent, like repeated blows from a giant hammer, threatening to knock the plane from the sky.

Julia put her hand over her mouth.

Steve hooked her shoulder with an arm and pulled her as close as their fastened seat belts would allow.

A bright flash stole his vision. It disappeared leaving only blackness. He couldn't see Julia though he was holding her.

A deafening roar sounded, causing the plane to vibrate. Something pelted the body of the Gulfstream.

Julia's arms circled his neck and squeezed. Her cast dug into the side of his neck.

The roar continued as Steve sat weightless while the airplane fell downward in total darkness. With his stomach flip-flopping, he braced himself for a crash he would probably wouldn't even feel.

The roar intensified and his and Julia's bodies, locked tightly in each other's arms, seemed to be floating in the cabin of the falling airplane.

Was this how it would end? The group of six, who had survived so much together, becoming nothing but body parts scattered over the mountains of Western Oregon?

His last words. What did he want to say? Steve leaned toward Julia.

She pressed into him.

"I love you so much, Julia." He spoke the words into her ear.

She buried her head into his chest.

Tears splashed on Steve's arm.

Only a few seconds more, then ...

Steve lurched as light exploded into the cabin, transforming the darkness to bright daylight. His body dropped down onto his seat.

The quiet whine of the engine replaced the deafening roar.

Steve raised his head and looked out. Blue skies filled the openings between columns of white clouds. The mountaintops towered above them. They must be over the valley floor, otherwise ... His mind balked at describing that scenario.

Julia had raised her head, too. She wiped the tears from her cheek and gave Steve a long penetrating look that softened and then warmed.

The captain's voice came over the PA system. "Sorry about the hail shaft. But we needed to elude the fighter before he got trigger happy. I'll have you all on the ground in less than two minutes. You're safe now."

Steve's and Julia's gazes were still locked, searching, wondering, and questioning.

He needed to say something to break the awkwardness of the moment. "I thought we were going to crash, Julia."

"Nothing like a little shot of impending death." She gave him a weak smile. "Truth serum."

Just like every smile from Julia, cute morphed to beautiful.

"I..." He searched for words to explain his outburst, but found nothing except Julia's explanation. "Yeah. Truth serum."

As relief spread nervous chatter through the cabin, Julia buried her face in his shoulder and cried, softly.

Happy? Sad? Relieved? He didn't know and was afraid to ask. At least she hadn't pulled away. She'd pressed into him, held him while she cried. That had to be a good sign, didn't it?

"Hang on, again, but don't be alarmed." The pilot's voice. "I need to use the entire runway to set down. I'll break hard at the other end. Touching down in thirty seconds."

But where was the F-15? Would the fighter now strafe the runway while they sat on it, helpless?

More likely he would blow them away with a laser-guided bomb ... in about thirty seconds.

Chapter 9

How could Benjamin already be asking for an evacuation plan? They had just walked four long, hot miles from the landing strip to get to Jeff's house in O'Brien. Julia stared at Benjamin across the living room where the seven sat in a semicircle. "Why are you asking us that question? We just got here."

Benjamin leaned down from his chair and flipped open the case at his feet containing the tools of his trade. "We've got this automatic, a hand gun, and a couple of NODS." He lifted what appeared to be binoculars from the case.

"And we have my M4," Steve said.

They were ignoring her. Once again, treating her as if Julia Weiss wasn't a contributing member of this group. That was going to stop ... *now*. "Benjamin, you didn't answer my question. Why do we need an evacuation plan? Does someone know something I don't?"

Julia scanned each face in the room. Their blank expressions spoke for them. No one was going to answer. She looked at Benjamin, again. "Well?"

Steve took her hand. "Julia, we lost the fighter in the thunderstorm, but that was only about twenty miles northwest of here. When the pilot files his report, Hannan's going to know our approximate location."

At least Steve acknowledged that she existed.

"There's more." Jeff sat up on the couch. "The county put our tax records online a couple of years ago. If Hannan checks, one quick search and he has my address."

Heat rose on the back of her neck at the thought of being forced to run again so soon. "Then will someone please tell me why we decided to come here?"

Brock raised his eyebrows. "Do you prefer RPG's delivered by Hamas? Maybe you'd feel differently if they had Julia Weiss written on them instead of Brock Daniels."

Brock's words cut into her heart like a scalpel, exposing her selfishness. How could she be that way? "I'm sorry, Brock. Keeping you and KC alive is the most important thing. I just get so frustrated with Hannan..." Her eyes blurred with unshed tears.

Steve draped an arm over her shoulders. "Me too, Julia. Were all frustrated."

Allie sat, legs crossed, her top leg swinging like an old fashioned metronome set for presto. "And my parents live about ten miles from here. Put that together with Jeff owning a house here and..."

"I'm sorry, everybody." Julia slumped in her chair. "I guess we do need a plan."

Would there ever be an end to all the running and hiding? If Hannan's men found them tonight, it might end ... in one big, violent bloodbath. Julia shivered at the long buried, horrifying memories that thought resurrected.

A light flashed in the periphery of her vision. Benjamin's satellite phone.

He pulled it from its case and walked away from the group to the far side of Jeff's living room near the big picture window looking out to the mountains.

Benjamin spoke too softly to hear his words. But his body language spoke volumes—gaze boring into the carpeted floor, jaws clenching between his spoken words.

After Benjamin slipped his phone back into its case, he had the attention of everyone in the room.

"Well..." Brock cleared his throat. "What did Katz have to say?"

Benjamin's shrug was almost imperceptible, but that spoke volumes, too. If selfless Benjamin was trying to shrug off bad news, it probably meant danger for this young IDF Special Forces soldier.

"Just some instructions for me." Benjamin's smile looked forced, certainly not the warm, friendly smile he usually displayed.

What was he *not* telling them?

"Come on, Benjamin," Brock said. "If it's bad news, we can take it. Heaven knows, we've had enough of that to deal with over the past three days."

KC nudged Brock. "It hasn't all been bad, sweetheart." She gave him her coy smile.

Brock's head turned her way and he seemed to melt.

If two people were ever created for each other, it would be Brock and KC. Would Julia live long enough for someone to love her like Brock loved KC? Could anyone ever really love someone like her ... when they weren't in a plane about to crash?

Where had that come from? Regardless, the wake of the questions seemed to carry her heart away to the most distant place on the planet, leaving it isolated, alone in the freezing cold of an Arctic night. The thought of dying in such a state brought tears to her eyes.

Why were her emotions all over the place today? Was it the airplane incident where death seemed so certain?

Benjamin sighed and returned to his chair. "Major Katz said we need to decide where we're going and how we're going to get there. He suggested going deeper into red territory. He also said we need an emergency evacuation plan in case Hannan's men manage to surprise us here." He looked at Jeff. "This is your home turf. Got any ideas?"

Jeff nodded. "They'll try to approach from the trees across the road ... from the front of the house. The pastureland behind us doesn't provide any cover. We'd spot them 300 yards away."

Benjamin leaned over and put the NODs back in the case. "Any plan we come up with has to include two things."

Julia sat up in her chair waiting for more unpleasant news.

"For transportation, we need a vehicle that seats seven. And if they surprise us before we leave, we'll need to split up, a three-way split. When it's safe, we'll all rendezvous with the vehicle." Benjamin raised his eyebrows and scanned his audience.

"Split up?" Julia shook her head at the suggestion. "I don't understand. Aren't we stronger when we're together?"

Benjamin met her gaze. "If we split, they have to split. Our odds are better that way." He scanned the semicircle of people. "I suggest we decide right now who goes with whom, what our roles will be, and where we will rendezvous." He paused. "Jeff, you know this area. What do you suggest?"

Jeff sighed and glanced at Allie. "When Allie and I made our getaway from here—"

"What?" Benjamin turned toward Jeff. "You've done this before?"

"Yeah. Almost five years ago, Allie and I ran from drug cartel thugs. It's a long story. But one thing I learned is that the diciest part is getting away from the house. They nearly killed us while we drove away in my truck."

"Don't worry." Benjamin set his jaw and gave Jeff a look that bordered on scary. "I'll make sure you get away, safely."

Brock swiveled in his chair toward Benjamin. "Planning to be our dog soldier, Benjamin?"

KC gave Brock her you're-crazy look. It was the first time Julia had ever seen it directed toward him. "Talk sense, Brock. Dog soldier?"

Brock chuckled. "From an old movie, *Last of the Dog Men*. One of my favorites. The Comanches' rear guards were called Dog Men. They were the elite warriors, and theirs was often a suicide mission. Benjamin, we don't want you to die so we can live."

"Yeah," Jeff said. Without you, we're toast anyway."

"Wait a minute," Steve looked at the faces around him, then focused on Benjamin. "Craig sent me with this crew to protect you guys, too. I'll stay behind."

Steve's words knifed into Julia's heart. She drew a sharp breath, surprised that the thought of Steve being in danger had evoked such fierce emotions.

Benjamin relaxed, settling into his chair. "No, Steve. I will. And I'll be fine if we plan this well." He paused. "Brock and KC make a good team. They'll go together. Jeff and Allie need to get us a vehicle. They know people here. They'll go together. Steve will take care of Julia. Jeff, how would you recommend I escape from here during a firefight?"

Benjamin's words, *take care of Julia,* said it all. They viewed her as a little girl, a weak person who couldn't protect herself.

Couldn't or wouldn't?

She chose to ignore her unsettling question.

Making a vow never to kill another human being certainly complicated living in the dangerous world where she found herself. But this was an issue she wasn't wrong about. Anyone who'd seen what she saw would make that same vow.

Jeff stared across the room as if the answer to Benjamin's question about escaping was written on the wall. "There is a way out of here, but Allie and I had my truck parked in the garage. I had backed it in."

Benjamin nodded to Jeff. "Here's what I need. If I can disappear for a few seconds, while they're firing, then pop up in a place they don't expect me, I know a tactic that will get me out of here and will probably take out several of their men in the process."

Jeff stood. "Be right back." He walked to the hallway, opened the basement door, and clomped down the stairs.

"The cellar off the basement," Allie said. "That's where Jeff hid me."

A loud groaning sound came from the basement, then a crack and the sound of boards falling on the floor.

In a few seconds, Jeff emerged from the doorway in the hall. "I'd boarded up the old cellar, but it's unboarded now. If you go into the cellar, there's a trap door by the ladder at the far end. It opens outside, behind the garage."

"No one in front of the house can see me leave." Benjamin said. "That works. Now, Jeff, we need places where Brock and KC and Steve and Julia can hide for up to twenty-four hours after we split up. I can make sure you escape safely from the area near the house but, after that ... you need to be well hidden."

"Aren't you forgetting Allie and me?" Jeff said.

"I thought you'd probably know where to get a vehicle. I was planning to meet you there after I leave the house."

"Yeah. We can go to the church. I'll call Pastor McMillan. The church van probably isn't being used these days due to the martial law and curfews. If I explain what's happening, I'm sure he'll let us borrow it."

"Good. How far is it to the church?"

"Not quite two miles."

Benjamin nodded. "Give me the directions and I'll meet you there after the shooting stops. Now, what about the other two couples?"

"I've got an idea, Benjamin," Steve said. If you can send Brock and KC to a safe spot close by, a place where you can

71

pick them up quickly, I can make sure Hannan's bloodhounds follow me. That will keep the rest of you safe, especially if Benjamin takes out any that try to follow you three. So—"

"Hold that thought," Jeff said. Let's get Brock and KC to a safe place where I can pick them up." Jeff pointed out the living room window. A large hay field lay in the foreground, but the hay had been infiltrated with weeds, now scorched brown from the hot summer sun. "See that old irrigation ditch? It's been dry for two or three years, so Brock and KC can follow it across the fields. If it's dark and they stay low, attackers will never see them. Beyond the field, a short distance into the trees, there's a logging road. Go north on it, about a half mile, to the paved road. Wait there."

Jeff paused. "After Benjamin joins Allie and me at the church, we'll circle to the northeast of town and pick up Brock and KC. That keeps us away from whatever you're doing south of here, Steve."

Benjamin gave Steve a corner-of-the-eye look. Now, tell us how you are going to be our ... Dog Soldier, is it?"

"First, let me tell you where you'll be going, Steve." Jeff pointed out the living room window to the southeast. "See the nearest ridge?"

Steve studied the area for a moment. "How far is that ridge? About four miles?"

"I used to run the old logging roads up there for training," Jeff said. "It's four miles."

"Rugged terrain. I can lose them." Steve grinned. "Evasion is my specialty. And I'll be taking them farther from you, Allie, Brock and KC. I'll bait them as I leave, get several of them to follow me. It'll be easier for you to slip away toward town and get the van."

Benjamin shook his head. "Are you forgetting that Julia nearly died of Ebola six weeks ago? She—"

"I can elude Hannan's men and handle Julia."

"Handle me?" Julia's face grew hot. "What am I? A sack of potatoes that you throw over your shoulder?" Once again, they viewed her as nothing but dead weight to this group and she'd had enough.

Steve looked down at the floor.

Julia tried every other face in the room, but no one would make eye contact with her. She could do this without slowing Steve down. But the other six faces didn't look convinced. "I'm not helpless, you know. This cast won't slow me down, and I still hold the record for 100 meters at my high school."

Steve's head snapped up. He scanned her bare legs from her shorts down to her ankles, slowly ... very slowly.

Her anger evaporated and Julia stifled a giggle.

Steve's eyes held the same disbelief as those of her track coach when Julia first told him she was a sprinter.

But her coach hadn't smiled like Steve was doing. "Just the right amount of muscle in all the right places."

"No, Steve. The right *kind* of muscle. My coach said I have fast-twitch muscles, about the same percentage as the male sprinters, so I—would you all please stop staring at my legs."

"Yes, Mr. Daniels. Stop staring." KC slapped Brock's leg.

"But, Kace, I—"

KC's hand clamped on Brock's chin and turned his face toward her. "Whatever it is, Brock, don't say it."

Brock heaved a long sigh. "Yes, Mrs. Daniels."

Steve cleared his throat and slid his chair closer to Julia. "Back to the subject at hand." He hooked her arm with his. "Julia can sprint the irrigation ditch to the trees, while I become the bait. When I clear the house and reach the trees, we run hard toward that first ridge. What then?"

"Use your evasion tactics and try to lose them before they reach the first ridge," Jeff said. "On top of the ridge you'll cross Greyback Road. If you've lost them, follow it northward until you reach a four-way intersection with a sign marked Takilma. It's an easy, downhill jog. We'll pick you up there."

When Jeff paused, Steve looked at Julia and raised his eyebrows.

"I'll be fine, Steve."

Steve dipped his head then focused on Jeff. "And if we don't lose them at the first ridge?"

"Then you have to continue on to the next mountain, Bolan Peak. It's rugged, steep terrain with rock outcroppings and a lot of trees and brush in between the rocks."

That might tax Julia to her limits. Regardless of the bravado she had tried to project, she doubted that she was back to full strength after Ebola ravaged her body six weeks earlier. And she couldn't endanger Steve by slowing him down. But the dense vegetation Jeff described might hide them while she rested.

"How far to the peak and what kind of elevation rise are we talking?" Steve asked.

Jeff heaved a sigh. "Five more miles and a twenty-five-hundred-foot climb from the base of the peak to the top. Maybe you shouldn't—"

"Jeff?" Julia waited for him to look at her. "You said there were a lot of trees and bushes. Steve and I can find places to hide while we rest. I can do this, even if we have to climb the peak."

Jeff nodded, but his eyes didn't reflect the affirmation. "There's a lookout tower on top of the peak that provides shelter and visibility of this entire area. There's drinking water a short way down the back of the peak, and an outhouse near the lookout."

"An outhouse?" Steve's eyebrows pinched hard. "How long do Julia and I have to wait there? Where are we going to rendezvous?"

"I've got your sat phone number, so I can text you once we're in the clear. Then I can give you a better idea." Jeff paused. "But, if you two have to go all the way to the peak, it's going to be a while before we pick you up, because we'll have to circle around to Happy Camp and come in from the California side. You shouldn't leave the lookout until I give you the all clear. That means you and Julia might have to stay twenty-four hours at the lookout."

Benjamin reached for the bag at his feet. "I'll give you one of my NODs so you can follow their movements in the dark. If you don't lose them, at least they won't be able to sneak up on you."

"Thanks, Benjamin. With your nighttime optical device, I think Julia and I are good to go."

Brock's foot had been tapping out a snappy rhythm on the floor since the discussion about Steve's and Julia's role began. "Jeff ... can't we just cut to the chase here? You know, leave now, before Hannan's people can get here?"

Allie looked at Jeff. "Yes, *mi amor*. Let's leave now. Just sitting here doing nothing is—"

"We can't, Allie. We'll never make it to Eastern Oregon if anyone sees me leaving here driving that van," Jeff said.

Benjamin dropped the NOD into Steve's hands. "Jeff is right. As much as I hate waiting, we've got to leave under cover of darkness. When does it get dark here this time of year?" He looked at Jeff.

"About 9:45 p.m. The safest thing to do is leave then."

"Okay. As soon as gets dark, we split and leave," Benjamin said. "I'll stay behind until you're all clear, then meet Jeff and Allie at the church."

"After Benjamin meets Allie and me at the church, we'll circle to the northeast to pick up Brock and KC, then continue on to get Julia and Steve. If you're not there in an hour, we'll know you've been forced all the way to Bolan

Peak. In that case, it's goodbye O'Brien. We'll hit I-5 at Grants Pass and head for the California border."

Steve's arm tightened around Julia when Jeff mentioned California. "Jeff, California is a blue state. Will you be safe on I-5?"

Jeff grinned. "It doesn't turn blue until you drop down from the Siskiyous into the Central Valley, somewhere south of Redding. We'll be okay. We won't be going south of Weed, even when we head for Eastern Oregon. And we should be able to coordinate the timing by texting you before you and Julia leave the Bolan Peak lookout."

Jeff leaned over and placed a hand on Steve's shoulder. "That lookout on Bolan Peak was where Allie and I spent our honeymoon."

Julia's face grew warm. "What did you mean by that remark, Mr. Jacobs?"

"Just a statement of fact. It's also where we hid from the drug cartel. What I really meant to say is, if you hide there, it's all glass. You'll be visible from miles away, especially during daylight hours."

"Understood," Steve said.

"Next topic." Benjamin scanned their faces. "How quickly do you think Hannan's people can find us here?"

"The fighter pilot probably gave his report an hour ago," Steve said. "Hannan probably has it by now. I'd give Hannan about an hour to locate this place, and at least four hours to send some men to check it out. But it depends on who these men are and where they're coming from."

"It's 5:00 p.m. now." KC shook her head. "We could have Hannanis crawling all over this place by ten o'clock."

Chapter 10

The Israeli Gulfstream left Vancouver more than two hours ago. It was bad enough that Hannan's Canadian friend hadn't finished the job in Whistler. Now, the fighter pilot from Kingsley, sent to intercept the Gulfstream, wasn't reporting.

Hannan sat at his desk in his private study with his laptop plugged into the defense network. After he opened the worldwide comms program, he looked up Kingsley Air Force Base.

Since he had federalized the Air Guard, technically, the entire base in Klamath Falls was under his command. But Eastern Oregon had a favorite son, Brock Daniels. Who knew how deep and wide the loyalty to Daniels ran in Klamath Falls?

Another quick search yielded the number for the dispatcher's hotline at Kingsley. Hannan placed the call and waited.

"Kingsley dispatch, Sergeant Redwing here." A young woman's voice.

Redwing. Must be Native American. "I hope your name doesn't reflect your loyalties, Ms. Redwing."

"Sergeant Redwing, sir. And that remark was highly inappropriate. I took an oath when I enlisted. It specified my loyalties. And if you persist in casting slurs—"

"Look, Airman Redwing—"

"Sergeant Redwing, sir."

"I can turn sergeant to airman with one phone call. So I suggest you listen, closely. This is your Commander-In-Chief, President Hannan." He stopped and waited for his revelation to sink in.

Static from a sharp blast of air came through the phone. "Sir, assuming you are the CIC, what is the purpose of this call? We have a fighter on the runway and another approaching on final."

She hadn't cowered, wasn't intimidated. Hannan had to admire the spunky sergeant even if she was annoying. "The pilot of the F-15 who made the intercept near Pistol River on the Oregon Coast hasn't reported. Where is that blasted plane?"

"He's taxiing down the runway as we speak, Mr. President."

"Can you patch me through to him?"

"Can I? Yes. But it's a violation of —"

His patience gone, Hannan wrapped his demand to talk to the pilot in strong language crafted to demean and intimidate. "Now, put me through to the pilot."

No reply.

"If you cooperate, Ms. Redwing, you will not be disciplined. But if you don't, I'll rip those chevrons off your uniform and you'll never see them again. I promise you that."

"One moment, sir." Low mumbling came from the sergeant, then Hannan's line went silent. She had placed him on hold.

A few seconds later, a voice came through Hannan's phone amid the spitting and crackling of static. "Captain

Weber here, Mr. President. Dispatch says you need to talk to me, sir."

"It's about time. What in the blazes have you been up to? You should've reported in by now."

"Sir, we had weather problems. Severe thunderstorms over the coastal mountains."

"I didn't contact you to chat about the weather. Did you take down the Israeli aircraft that entered our airspace, illegally?"

"Mr. President, it wasn't an illegal entry. They had an aircraft emergency, tried for the nearest airfield, and flew through a hail shaft in the process. I thought for sure they had crashed."

"Did they?"

"No, sir. They made an emergency landing at—"

"You let them land?" Hannan swore at the captain until he ran out of crude synonyms for idiot.

Captain Weber didn't reply.

From somewhere in Hannan's distant past, an old adage about flies and honey came to mind. "Sorry, captain. But this is a serious matter of national security. Where did the plane land?"

"An old Forest Service landing strip near O'Brien, Oregon."

Southern Oregon. Did anyone in that group have ties to that area? Or, was this a real emergency?

"Did you copy, Mr. President?"

"Yes, I copied. Did they land safely?"

"CBs cut me off. But I caught a glimpse of the Gulfstream on the ground before I turned back to the base."

"An aircraft emergency. What next?" He spat the words out as he terminated the call.

Daniels and Banning—or was it Daniels and Daniels now—seemed to be living a charmed life, fortunate beyond mere coincidence. Supernatural protection? That was preposterous, but sometimes it seemed like it.

Hannan placed a call to his most trusted contact in the FBI and prepared to dangle a career-advancement carrot in front of her. She'd always taken it in the past. At Hannan's and Gregory Bell's request, the Bureau had accumulated a lot of information on the two terrorists and their friends. If Hannan was a gambling man, he would wager everything that someone in the group had ties to Southern Oregon, someplace near O'Brien.

Thirty minutes later, Hannan had the address of a house in O'Brien sitting on several acres of land—a house owned by Jeff Jacobs. He picked up his secure phone, keyed in Captain Deke's number, and placed the call.

Deke was the most trusted and capable Special Forces commander Hannan had. He'd deployed Deke's detachment nearby for defense in case of an unexpected attack on the White House, the West Wing, or any of its underground facilities. Supposedly, Harrison Brown had alerted Deke about a possible rapid deployment to hunt down Daniels.

"Captain Deke, here." He sounded sleepy.

Hannan's plan would certainly wake up the captain. But was it a wise plan? And was Deke the best person to offer advice on that issue?

"Hello?" Deke's deep voice raised half an octave.

"President Hannan. Deke, how quickly can you and your men be ready to deploy to the West Coast?"

"Sir, that depends on where you're sending us. Is it red territory?"

"More like pink. It's an area where insurgents seem to be in control, but they don't have a strong presence."

"We'll need more munitions. How long is this deployment, sir?"

"Maybe a week. Hopefully, less."

"We can be ready to fly out in four hours. But, Mr. President, are you sure you want to weaken your defensive posture in—"

"I'm sure, Captain Deke. We know where Daniels and company are hiding and, if we hurry, we can take them all out." And Hannan could rid himself of the pack of little, yapping dogs that had been nipping at his heels for the past six weeks. "I'll brief you when you get to Andrews." Hannan ended the call.

This would, as Deke mentioned, temporarily increase Hannan's vulnerability to an attack by the insurgency, but that was much less a concern than the vulnerability of having Daniels and Banning running loose, feeding treasonous fires, keeping false hopes alive, and prolonging resistance to the inevitable. And Deke had learned his lesson well from the deceased Captain Blanchard. Do not underestimate these rebels.

When he found them, Deke would hit them with everything he had and that would be that.

I believe your luck just ran out, Mr. Daniels.

Chapter 11

A tall black cloud with a wide anvil on top hung over a mountain west of Bolan Peak. The cloud flashed anger at its impending death. As it collapsed, the thunderstorm poured out its drenching fury on the mountain. In another hour, the sun would be gone, sunk below the western horizon, and the cloud would disappear. Hopefully, so would Steve and Julia.

Steve jumped as a hand slid down his bare arm. A small hand, soft and gentle. He smelled the citrus fragrance of her hair and took a calming breath before he looked down into a perfectly sculpted face adorned with deep brown eyes.

Thunder rumbled from the dying cloud nearly ten miles away, a cloud which seemed to darken Julia's face.

He took her hand. "Having second thoughts about this?"

She shook her head, sending waves of light brown hair dancing on her shoulders. "No. Just a few concerns."

"About running that ditch in a firefight?"

"I'll be fine. Just some concerns about Benjamin." She looked up into Steve's face. "And you."

Steve had revealed his feelings for Julia when the Gulfstream seemed about to crash. She hadn't reciprocated. But she was here now, holding his hand, concern for him in her eyes and in her words, maybe on the verge of—

An annoying tingle on his side and the flashing light

from the sat phone ended the moment. "Doggone phone."

Julia gave him her coy smile. "I thought Rangers couldn't survive without their comms."

What he couldn't survive without was Julia Weiss. He pulled his phone from its case. "It's Craig."

She pulled her hand from his. "Should ... should I leave?"

"No. You're in this all the way. For better or worse."

"You make it sound like a wedding."

Steve picked up the call. "Let's just hope it's not a funeral."

"A funeral? What's my weapons sergeant got himself into this time?"

Great. Craig had heard his remark.

"Captain Craig, we're secure, right?"

"Secure as we can be these days. So, where is my weapons sergeant and what's the status of his charges?"

"We're all present, accounted for and safe, sir, at least for another hour or so."

"You expecting company?"

"Yes, sir. They may have discovered our destination almost before we arrived. But where are you, captain?"

"We're holing up in a safe house in Virginia because ... Gano got hurt."

This was not a good development. Gano was Steve's replacement as weapons sergeant. "How badly hurt?"

"Broke his leg. Tibia and fibula, a compound fracture."

"Oh, man. That's eight weeks or more without him." Was Craig hinting that Steve—no, it wasn't possible, not right now.

"There's more." Craig paused. "Can you have someone get KC Banning?"

"You mean KC Daniels?"

"So, they got the papers and she married him. Good for KC. I'll bet Brock isn't complaining about it, either."

Steve pulled the phone away from his mouth. "Julia, would you bring KC. Craig needs to talk to her."

Julia brushed Steve's arm with her hand and walked out the door.

"While we wait for KC, would you like to tell me where in the heck you are and how you got there, sergeant?"

Steve sighed, then recounted the events from the RPG attack at the wedding until their arrival at Jeff's house. "So, we're in pink territory in Southwestern Oregon planning to head back to Central Oregon, east of the mountains. But we expect Hannan's men to show up anytime now. We have an evacuation plan, but things could get a bit dicey getting out of here."

"Bancroft ... you don't know the half of it."

"Come again, sir."

Julia returned with KC.

The other four followed behind them.

"The whole group just came into the room. I don't think we need to keep any secrets here so, with your permission, sir, I'll turn on my speakerphone."

"Permission granted. If your time is short there, I need to do a quick info dump and then speak to KC. Tell me when they're all gathered around."

"All here, sir. Go ahead."

Craig cleared his throat, then his voice rose. "As I told Sergeant Bancroft, we're holing up in a safe house in Virginia because our weapons sergeant, Gano, broke his leg. But we met someone here who's also hiding, and he had some interesting intel for us. He's Secret Service Agent Belino."

KC hopped a step closer and leaned toward the sat phone. "Belino? Is he okay? I thought Hannan might kill him."

Brock draped an arm over KC's shoulders. "Is this the guy who warned you, Kace?"

"Yes. Saved my life with two short text messages."

Craig chuckled. "Can I tell him you're okay, so he'll stop pestering me? I think he was falling hard for a young, freckle-faced, redheaded woman who worked under the West Wing."

KC's grin spread the width of her face. "Tell him that woman is married. He'll have to look for another woman. And everybody here is spoken for, or ..." She glanced at Steve and Julia.

"I noticed 'or' four weeks ago in my weapons sergeant's puppy dog eyes." Craig paused. "Back to the subject at hand. Belino did some spying before he had to bail. He's maintained one contact, an agent who's still in the White House. Maybe we can get some more intel. But what we've got now is enough to raise the hair on the back of my neck."

Steve leaned toward the phone. "Come again, sir."

"It's like this ... Hannan has released his most trusted Special Forces detachment, an elite team led by a brutal commander named Captain Deke. This team had been guarding the White House, serving as Hannan's private bodyguards in case of danger to the president. Deke is the only man Hannan trusts to keep him safe."

Steve cut in. "Released them to do what, sir?"

Silence.

"Sir?"

"To obliterate a target somewhere in Oregon."

Julia gasped.

Steve hooked his free arm around her. "Obliterate, sir?"

"Yes. Belino heard a couple of things mentioned. RPO-Ms and thermobaric rockets."

Steve blew out a big blast of air. "Russian flamethrower rockets on an RPG launcher."

Brock plopped his hand on Steve's shoulder. "Why Russian weapons?"

"Because ours are mostly for hard targets—tanks,

85

bunkers. Jeff's house is a soft target. This place will disintegrate in a big ball of fire. If the fire doesn't kill us, the concussion will literally rip us apart. They're not looking to take any prisoners, just take us out." Steve stared at Benjamin.

Benjamin returned Steve's gaze with equal intensity. "No, Steve. You're not staying behind. I'm still your dog soldier. This doesn't change anything."

"You won't be a dog soldier, just a roasted hotdog. We're all leaving at the first sign of trouble."

"Want my opinion." Craig's voice crackled from the speakerphone.

"Not sure I do, sir."

"Well, you're getting it anyway. Leave it to Benjamin's discretion, Steve. The Sayeret Matkal are the best trained in the world for these kinds of situations. He'll make the right decision."

"Is that an order, captain?"

"Yes. You know what you're up against now, so let Benjamin go with his gut on this."

Benjamin's hand plopped on Steve's shoulder. "I'll know when to leave, Steve. You and Julia carry out your roles and don't worry about me."

Craig's phone crackled with static then his voice returned. "Now that that's settled, the next message is for KC."

KC pushed her head between Steve and Julia. "I'm listening, Craig. But this had better be work-related."

"It is. Belino left the White House day before yesterday and, up until that time, Hannan was working from his private study most of the time, only retreating to the DUCC when security thought they detected threats."

KC picked up the sat phone. "Does that mean he still plugs it into the White House networks?"

"He does," Craig said. "But he spends a lot of time on the

defense networks using that network drop he had installed in his study."

KC grinned. "I've got the picture. Tell Belino thanks. But I'll need to stop running for a couple of days so I can use this hardened laptop the Israelis gave me."

"What do you intend to do with it?"

"I'm going to hack Hannan's laptop and leave a little Trojan Horse. When you make your assault on the White House, Hannan will run for the DUCC. You can thank me then for what I'm about to do."

Craig chuckled again. "That's nearly word-for-word what Belino said you would say ... Steve?"

"Yes, sir"

"I'd better let you go and get ready for Hannan. He dropped his guard when he sent his private bodyguards after you. It might give us the chance we've been looking for. The longer you can hold his men out there, and the more of them you can eliminate, the better our chances. But our chances would be even better if you could come back here and fill in for Gano."

"But, sir—"

"I know, Steve. It's risky. Think about it."

"Yes, sir."

"Call when you're settled in again."

"Will do, sir."

Steve looked down into Julia's eyes after he terminated the call.

Her welling eye spilled a tear onto her cheek.

* * *

Julia had faced death before ... alone. It had terrorized her, scarred her, emotionally. She had recently faced it with Steve by her side. Seeing the possibility of violent death still brought fear, but not terror, nothing like what she had experienced in Africa, because she wouldn't be alone. Or, would she?

She wiped her cheek and met Steve's tender gaze. "Are you going?"

"I... I don't know. Certainly not until I know you—that you are all safe without me."

What was she doing? Trying to make him stay? This wasn't just Julia's life and her selfish desires on the line, and it wasn't only the team's lives. America and all it stood for hung in the balance. "Benjamin can watch out for us. If Craig needs you, we'll be okay."

Steve touched her cheek, then turned toward the rest of the group. "You all heard what we're up against. Hannan wants to take us out in a blaze of glory. Exterminate us with thermobaric rockets. And, in this house, they won't need a SMAW II Serpent to do the job."

Benjamin's eyes widened. "You mean those cave-clearing rockets they used on the Taliban?"

Steve nodded.

"Regardless, it won't happen, Steve," Benjamin said. "You six will be gone, and I'll take out the first man who raises an RPG launcher. They will take cover, and I will disappear."

"Yeah," Jeff's voice grew loud and angry. "Then my house disappears in a big ball of fire."

Benjamin laid his hand on Jeff's shoulder. "That's going to happen to your house no matter what we do. They've already made that decision. We just need to get safely away."

All the talk of violent explosions and killing struck a raw nerve in Julia. And to think Benjamin had no qualms about ambushing and killing another man. She looked up and saw Benjamin studying her face. "Doesn't it bother you to just kill another human being with no warning, or is that what you do in Israel?"

The hurt and shock on Benjamin's face as he averted his

gaze stopped her breathing like someone had knocked the breath out of Julia.

Now all eyes were on her, and she had to defend the conviction she held, regardless. "Killing is wrong. I don't think—"

"That's right, Julia, *you don't think.*" Brock towered over her, glaring his disapproval.

"It's okay, Brock." Benjamin hooked Brock's arm and tried to pull him away from Julia.

The reaction of everyone, turning on her for her convictions, was a jumble of hurt, betrayal, and righteous indignation, so tangled inside her heart and mind that she couldn't think of anything coherent to say.

Brock blew out a sharp blast of air and turned away toward Benjamin. "It's never wrong to defend yourself. *Never.* How would pacifism fly in Israel? Tell us what life is like there."

Benjamin shook his head. "I don't think this is the right—"

"Oh, it's the right time. Tell her what you told me about kids waiting for the school bus ... come on, Benjamin."

Benjamin sighed. "In parts of the country, we build small bomb shelters beside the school bus stops. When the sirens go off, the kids have four to seven seconds to jump inside or they could be blown to ... as you say it, kingdom come."

Innocent kids? "How can the Palestinians be so—"

"Hamas." Benjamin cut her off. "It's Hamas controlling the politics, controlling the Palestinian people, infecting their children with jihadist ideas, aided by some radical Palestinians and funding from Iran."

This was evil, done by evil people. But was killing the solution?

Brock stuck out a thumb toward Julia. "Show her the picture of you and your girlfriend."

Benjamin smiled as he slid a picture from his wallet.

"Not my girlfriend. She's my fiancé." He handed the picture to Julia.

She studied the picture. A beautiful, young, olive-skinned woman in a skirt and blouse walked hand-in-hand with Benjamin on the sidewalk. Both smiling at each other ... with assault rifles slung over their shoulders.

"Date night." Benjamin shrugged. "As they say ... only in Israel. You see, we are attacked almost daily in some manner—stabbings, bombings, rockets. How would Americans like it if over 1,000 rockets a year were shot across your border into a city? I do not think Americans would stand for it."

Brock glared at Julia again. "But we force Israel to just sit there and take it. Especially, since Hannan's election. You see, Julia, it's always right to defend yourself and innocent people. It's no different than Nehemiah arming the people while rebuilding the walls of Jerusalem under threat of attack."

Julia knew better than to argue with Brock, the apologist, especially while his fierce gaze intimidated her. But she couldn't be wrong about this, could she? Her evidence was—no. She wouldn't go there now, not to Africa. Not in her mind and not in this discussion.

Julia looked out the window. The sun had set.

"Shouldn't we be watching for Hannan's men, or something?" Allie had cut off the discussion, rescuing Julia.

She looked up into Allie's warm brown eyes. Mothering them all, gluing them together into a cohesive whole—that seem to be the role Allie had taken since the six were thrown together in Oregon nearly six weeks ago.

Julia opened her mouth to thank Allie, but Julia's voice was gone.

"It's okay," Allie whispered to Julia. Allie smiled and stepped away.

Benjamin opened the slider in the family room and

walked onto the deck. He climbed onto the deck railing and pulled his tall slender body onto the roof. "It should be dark enough to leave in another thirty minutes, but I'm going to watch from the roof until then, just in case."

After Benjamin climbed onto the roof, Brock turned his attention to KC. Evidently, he wasn't going to resume their discussion.

Julia blew out a breath and tried to relax. She was right about killing, but why did being right make her feel so bad? Maybe because, if her friends acted on Julia's convictions, they would all die. She had never had to confront that situation since leaving Africa eight years ago, until today.

Please, God, don't let them die because of me.

Could Julia actually let someone die if she could stop the killer?

Her head snapped up as Benjamin dropped from the roof and thumped hard on the deck. He leaped toward the open slider. "Jeff ...," Benjamin stuck his head in the room. "How far are those mountains to the northwest?"

"Let's see. That's a little southwest of Cave Junction ... about five or six miles."

"Listen everyone." Benjamin's voice rose. "A chopper just dropped into the valley from a gap in those mountains and headed our way. I heard no engine or rotor sound."

Steve gripped Benjamin's shoulder. "No sound at all?"

Benjamin shook his head.

Steve blew out a blast of air. "They've got a Stealth Hawk. If I'm right, we'll have Hannan's men in our laps in five minutes."

Chapter 12

"Go, go, go, everybody. Get your packs and weapons."
Benjamin ran from the family room to the living room.

Julia followed Benjamin.

Steve pushed her along. "Julia, grab my pack, too. Wait for me by the family room slider."

She tripped when her foot kicked the leg of a chair but caught her balance as she stumbled into the living room. Julia snatched both her and Steve's packs with her good hand and turned to go back to the family room.

"Wait." Steve snagged her arm, unzipped a section of his pack, and pulled out two magazines. He stuffed them into a pocket on his cargo shorts.

What was he up to?

"Jeff, Allie, you need to go now before they can see you." Benjamin's voice rose above the chaos. "They could show in two or three minutes. Take the streambed into town, like we discussed."

Jeff and Allie ran through the family room and out the door, then veered left toward town and the tree-lined streambed that would cover them on their run to O'Brien.

Julia stopped by the slider and waited for Steve.

Brock and KC flew by her while KC's laptop case, slung over her shoulder, banged brutally against her side. They jumped off the low deck and sprinted toward the irrigation ditch.

It was supposed to be darker when they did this. "Benjamin ..."

He glanced Julia's way.

She stuck a thumb out toward the sky. "It's not dark, yet."

"I know, Julia. But Hannan's men aren't here yet, either. Brock, KC, Jeff and Allie will be fine."

Steve scurried into the family room holding his M4 like he meant to use it any second. "Julia, you need to run the ditch now and don't stop until you're fifty yards back into the trees. I'll be there in a few minutes."

"A few minutes? Steve, by then they'll see you. They'll shoot."

"That's the general idea. I'm the bait, remember?"

Benjamin jumped up on the deck rail. "I'll cover you from the roof until it gets too hot."

This wasn't how they had planned it. Steve would be a visible target, too visible. She had to do something, but what?

"Go, Julia!"

"I can't just leave—"

"You've got to. If you're here when they show, I'm dead."

She had to go, but she may never see Steve again this side of eternity. She needed to say something. "Steve, I—"

"Save it for later." He nudged her out the door and onto the deck then pointed across the field. "Sprint the ditch and don't climb out until you reach the bushes by the trees."

Save it for later? Would there be a later? Julia touched his cheek, turned, and ran. With her tiny pack on her back, she leaped off the deck like a long jumper and hopped at the end of her jump. Her shoes tore the sod in the backyard as she accelerated into an all-out sprint toward the dry irrigation ditch.

As she slid down the bank into the bottom of the ditch, Benjamin called out from his perch on the roof. "Hannani, 500 yards, across the road. One of their men just made a big blunder."

In the center of the ditch, Julia turned her head toward the house. What she saw sent an icy chill through her.

Steve lay in the prone firing position beside Benjamin at the peak of the roof.

This wasn't part of their plan either.

Now she knew their new plan, the one Steve and Benjamin had just improvised. There would be two dog soldiers instead of one.

Julia ran low, leaning forward and driving with her legs. As she flew down the ditch, with the warm evening air rushing by her ears, whistling like the wind, she sought some way to help Steve.

Please, give me a way to help him. America needs him ... I need him.

* * *

Steve glanced at Benjamin in the prone position beside him on the roof of Jeff's house. "We've got to time this right or that thermobaric rocket will—"

"Got it, Steve. Now, have you spotted the Hannani?"

"He's still about 500 yards out, in the trees in line with that big Madrone. He's going to regret exposing himself."

"He was probably trying to get line of sight in order to target us with their grenade launcher."

"So the plan is we hold them off with gunfire until—"

"Until I tell you that you need to head for the ditch and get to Julia."

Steve didn't like where this was heading. "What about you?"

"Like you said, it's all in the timing."

"So help me, Benjamin, if you're sacrificing yourself for us, I'll—"

"I'm—Steve, there he is."

Steve tagged the Ranger holding a bazooka-like weapon on his shoulder and squeezed off a shot.

The man fell, dropping his weapon.

"He's down."

"Good. But we've warned them, so the others will be harder to spot. Like you said, he was careless." Benjamin's body stiffened and he swung his weapon to the left. "They're flanking us on the left. Time for you to go, before the house no longer blocks their view of the irrigation ditch. You need to get to Julia ... now!"

"Dude, you've got to leave here before it gets too hot!" Steve rolled over and slid down the roof, out of view of Hannan's men, and dropped onto the deck. After several bounding strides, he jumped into the irrigation ditch.

A long, staccato burst of gunfire sounded from the roof. Benjamin was covering him.

Steve couldn't afford to look back. He needed to run hard, to reach Julia before any of the Hannanis flanking them saw his evacuation route.

A line of dust exploded along the top of the ditch. It ran by Steve's right side.

Too late. They had spotted him.

They had flanked Benjamin on the left and clearly knew what Steve was attempting. Their bullets had missed. Would they use a rocket on him?

He accelerated to top speed. If they hit near him with a thermal rocket, either the shock or the fire would kill him.

Another burst of fire from Benjamin.

Steve risked a glance back over his shoulder.

Benjamin jumped from the roof and scampered into the house.

Why, Benjamin?

If they shot a rocket at the house, he was dead.

Movement out of the corner of his eye. Hannanis on the road. The man had Steve in his line of sight and was swinging the launcher onto his shoulder.

When the rocket exploded, would Steve feel it? Or would he just—forget the speculation. He needed to run hard and pray.

With only a hundred yards to go, Steve looked ahead, down the ditch.

Movement caught his eye. Julia?

She stood at the edge of the trees, waving her arms, exposing herself to—

The whoosh of a rocket sounded. The sound of death.

Twilight brightened to midday.

An invisible hammer slammed Steve to the bottom of the ditch. He got up, stumbled forward. No severe pain, but that didn't mean some of his internal organs hadn't been ripped loose.

Another blast. A blinding light flashed from the house. Too late for Benjamin. It came only ten seconds after he ran inside. Maybe he ... no. He couldn't have survived.

Fifty yards ahead, a body lay in the ditch.

Please, God. Not Julia.

The blast must have knocked her into the ditch. Whatever they fired had to be bigger than an RPO-M. Maybe a SMAW with an even bigger thermobaric warhead.

Steve had seen death in battle many times before. He'd seen the death of a comrade, a fellow Ranger that he loved like a brother. But he'd never seen someone he could envision spending the rest of his life with lying dead. Seeing Julia face down in the ditch drove a spike into his chest. It drove another one into his gut and drained the life from his body.

Julia couldn't survive the effects of a thermobaric blast. The fiery explosion came wrapped in a warhead straight from hell, one that gave its victims a deadly preview of that place.

He stumbled toward Julia's body. His sense of balance, like his life, had been knocked askew. Somehow, he had to go on alone and fill his role, but he couldn't leave Julia's body lying there. Ranger's never did that. And, what made it worse, she'd been trying to warn him, drawing their fire even though it meant sacrificing herself for him.

Beyond Julia's body, flames attacked the dry pine forest.

How far back had the rocket hit? Thirty yards? That was roughly the weapon's kill radius.

If she lived, almost any injury would be fatal, given their circumstances ... needing to run up a mountain, no medical help for hours, maybe days.

Come on, Bancroft. Don't think that way.

Steve slid to a stop near Julia.

Surprise jolted him when she moved.

Julia rose to her knees and held her head.

Another explosion sounded from the house. It lit the valley as bright as midday and sealed Benjamin's fate.

Steve prayed that the blast killed Benjamin before the flames got him.

When Steve reached Julia, she fell into his arms. He lifted her and accelerated to a sprint as he ran up out of the ditch. He headed for the trees, praying there wouldn't be a fourth explosion.

Dust kicked up all around them. The roaring fire almost drowned the tat, tat, tat from automatic rifles.

No pain. They must have missed him.

"I'm sorry, Steve." Julia clung to him.

Her voice brought tears to his eyes. She didn't realize she was dying.

He ran harder, putting the flames between him and Hannan's men and hoping that would stop the shooting.

How had their plan gone so far awry?

"Steve," Julia choked out his name. "Please, don't be mad at me."

Mad? He just hoped her death wouldn't be painful. "It's okay, Julia. I've got you and I won't let them catch us."

She raised her head and looked over his shoulder as they ran into the darkness of the forest. "But they sure are trying to."

How could she be so alert, so cognizant? It wouldn't last. She would lapse into unconsciousness and then ... He forced his mind to focus on something else. "How many of them, Julia?"

"Four ran after us, but there were more near the house. Maybe six."

So, she was still clueless about her injuries. Soon the internal bleeding would kill her.

"Thanks. That helps." He gasped for air. Probably hyperventilating more than being winded. "You saved my life..." A sob choked off his words. Tears streamed from his eyes and blew away behind him.

He sprinted at top speed, holding the woman he loved, but knowing he would soon lose her. "Julia, I stayed behind ... tried to be the hero ... so stupid."

Julia's lips brushed his ear as she leaned her head near his. "Steve, I knew the risks when I stepped out of the trees. It's not your fault."

But it *was* his fault. Just like before. It was *always* his fault.

In the last of the twilight, an old, overgrown logging road came into view. It headed up the mountain in front of them, to the ridge, their first checkpoint.

Could he lose Hannan's men before reaching the ridge?

Did it even matter?

Yes, it mattered. Julia needed to know she was safe from Hannan's men and in the arms of someone who loved her when she died. No matter the cost, he would not let her die alone.

* * *

Julia's arms circled Steve's neck. She studied the darkness behind them as the powerful Ranger carried her at a furious pace up an old road toward the top of the ridge.

Steve's hoarse, raspy breathing told her he was struggling to maintain his pace. No one could run to the top of the mountain with a 110-pound load in his arms. But Steve didn't slow down. If anything, he accelerated.

This man had said he loved her when the Gulfstream appeared to be falling from the sky. Now he would kill himself for her. How could she convince him she wasn't worth it?

Julia turned her head toward his ear. "Steve, please don't do this. Slow down. Your heart will burst if you don't."

No reply.

"Put me down. I can run."

"No ... you can't ... don't understand." Deep breaths chopped apart his words.

Her words weren't going to stop him. She pounded on his shoulder. "Please. Put me down, now."

"No." He ignored her blows and ran even faster.

Julia gasped when a tat, tat, tat sounded in the distance. The smell of pitch burned her nostrils as bullets pruned a pine branch to the left of her head.

That was impossible. How could they get within shooting range? No one could match the pace Steve set.

Steve veered to the right and entered the darkness of a dense forest canopy. He also slowed as trees blocked the dim light from the crescent moon in the western sky.

"They've got ... night vision goggles ... got to avoid ... visual contact."

They emerged from the stand of timber and found another old timber access road. It ran along the contours of the mountain instead of up it.

Steve leaped onto the road and began an all-out sprint.

"Steve, please. You're killing yourself."

No reply. Only the sound of his feet pounding the ground on an old road, hardly more than a trail.

Steve pivoted hard and turned left, heading straight up the mountain at a pace that was insane.

His body jerked and his muscles spasmed with every breath.

Julia's cheeks were wet. Some of her tears had dropped onto Steve's neck.

His arms tightened around her. "Are you okay?"

Her voice was gone, so she nodded. How stupid. He couldn't see her nod.

Steve had said he loved her, but that was when their death was almost certain. Now he was proving his love, killing himself for her.

Julia tried to wipe her eyes and runny nose, but only managed to smear tears and mucous on Steve's neck.

After sprinting uphill for at least a full minute, Steve's pace slowed. He continued at a jog straight up the mountainside, following what looked like a dry stream bed.

"So, you are human after all."

Steve coughed out something that might have been a laugh.

Julia relaxed in the arms of this superhuman, determined to save her even if his heart burst in the process. Steve's power and sheer determination, all to save her, drove away her last vestiges of fear.

She stopped trying to persuade Steve to do anything. He would do whatever he intended. There was no stopping this man. And she felt safe though, two minutes earlier, enough bullets to fill an M4's magazine had zipped past her head.

Steve's ascent slowed, though she sensed he willed it not to. Even Steve, the nearest thing to superman she had ever seen, had his limits.

She turned her head and peered into the night sky in front of them. The ground had leveled. They had reached the top of the first ridge that Jeff described.

Steve had run the mountain carrying her, and she loved him for caring that much. But she wasn't supposed to love a man with a job description that included killing people. So much had happened so quickly that she would have to sort it all out later.

Steve slowed to a stop, gasping for breath. But he wouldn't put her down.

The vegetation ended. Was this a clearing, or a road?

She looked down at the moonlit ground. It was a road. They had reached the road Jeff said would take them to the rendezvous point.

"Steve, put me down. I can walk."

"Where do you hurt, Julia? The truth." His face against the night sky was a dark shadow, but she could feel his gaze bore into her.

Did he still believe she had some kind of injury? Why was he so persistent? "The only thing that hurts is my head. But it's okay."

Steve's breathing was controlled now, no longer gasping. "But it's *not* okay. Are you bleeding from your eyes, nose, ears or ... anywhere?"

"I don't think so."

"Then what's all over my neck?"

She was not going to tell him that she wiped her nose on his neck or even that she had cried there. "Well, it isn't blood."

"Do you feel like you're getting weaker?"

"No, but *you* obviously are. Why all these questions?"

"Julia, you were standing only a few yards from a thermobaric blast. A big one. That kind of blast can suck the air out of your lungs, destroying them, rip your internal organs loose, perforate your gut, and a lot of other things I'm not going to describe."

"Steve, I jumped into the ditch *before* the explosion. I hit my head on the ground because I lost my balance when something hit me in the back."

"That something hitting you in the back was the overpressure of the blast."

"But I was falling into the ditch when it happened. My arms stung a little, afterward, and I had a dull headache from toppling forward onto my head."

"So your back was turned to the flash?"

She nodded.

He slowly lowered her to the ground, setting her on her feet. "Can you stand?"

"Of course."

"Let me see your arms." Steve rubbed the backside of her upper arms. "Does that hurt?"

It did sting a little. "No more than a mild sunburn."

"And you can see okay?"

"Steve, I'm fine. I'm strong. I can run. Do you want to see me?" She gasped as a green light moved across Steve's shirt. "Steve, a green—"

Steve slapped a hand over her eyes and rolled her to the ground.

"What are you—"

Tat, tat, tat sounded somewhere in the distance.

Hannan's men had seen them. Forget the first rendezvous point.

He pulled her behind a stump at the edge of the road. "Are your eyes okay, Julia? Tell me."

"I already said they were."

102

"That laser sight is a 200 megawatt beam. It will fry your eyes, instantly."

Steve's paranoia had become really annoying. "Fried by thermal bears, fried by little green lights. I'm not fried, Steve. I'm fine. I'm not getting weaker, but you are. So, I'm not letting you carry me."

He pulled her to her feet but still held on to her, supporting most of her weight. "Is your broken wrist okay?"

"It's fine."

Steve heaved a blast of air. "We need to go. They know where we are, so we have to go to Bolan Peak, but we don't want them to know that. Let me carry you for about thirty yards, to cover our tracks. Then I'll put you down. I promise."

So he finally believed her. She leaned into Steve's outstretched arms.

He scooped her up and pulled her to his chest

Julia Weiss was safe here, pressed against the pounding heart of a powerful warrior, someone who loved her. For the moment, all her fear and horror of the past flowed away, leaving only peace.

Steve turned down the road toward the rendezvous point and walked that direction a few steps, then backtracked and stepped off the road onto some rocks. He picked his way carefully down the mountainside for another minute, then set Julia on her feet. "They'll be coming over the ridge in a couple of minutes. Lock hands around wrists with me ... your good hand. Try not to leave a trail for them. Take it easy and let me support you. Let's go."

Jeff had said they must lose these men before going up Bolan peak. If not ... they had made no plan for that contingency. But she trusted Steve.

Julia followed him as he pulled her silently down the mountainside toward a black valley below. Hopefully, a place where Hannan's soldiers wouldn't realize they had gone, a place where they could hide. It might be thirty-six hours before Jeff, Allie, and the others picked them up.

The overwhelming sense of peace she'd had in Steve's arms had come in like the ocean tide, but the tide was ebbing. Her old fears returned and with them came thoughts of the many ways she might die on this mountain.

At least the men chasing them wouldn't have thermal bears. Well, she didn't think they would. From her glimpse of the launchers and rockets, they looked too heavy for the men to carry while they chased Steve and her into the mountains. But they had little green lights that could burn your eyes out and who knew what other instruments of killing and maiming these monsters carried with them.

Julia shoved their pursuers out of her mind and focused on her steps as she clung to Steve's hand. She scampered down the mountain, trying to keep her balance, and praying they would both be alive in thirty-six hours.

Chapter 13

Running down the mountain with their hands locked on wrists, Steve struggled to maintain the right tension on Julia's arm to keep her on her feet. He feared yanking too hard. He might dislocate her shoulder.

She didn't seem overly protective of her injured wrist. The Velcro cast around her hand and forearm seemed to be doing its job, supporting the wrist with the cracked bone. It was an injury Steve had caused by dropping her off balance. He would not let her get hurt again.

A long shadowy object came into view. A rotting log. Steve adjusted his grip on Julia's wrist and hopped over it.

Julia's small hand tightened on his wrist as she followed him over the log.

He had heard nothing from the top of the ridge, had seen no lights and, thankfully, no more laser beams from guns. But their plans had been disrupted by the attack and the furious pursuit that had driven Steve and Julia up the mountain ... and by the loss of Benjamin. Without Benjamin, there was no way Steve would leave the five civilians to help Captain Craig in DC.

He needed time to think, but also needed to keep moving. Steve flipped the switch that placed his mind on autopilot, divorcing the physical from the mental. His reflexes and instincts took over the physical descent of the mountain while he analyzed the facts and plotted the next series of moves for this ragtag army of six.

At some point in the next few days, they had to eliminate this detachment of Rangers Hannan had sicced onto them. With Benjamin likely dead, the odds of winning such a confrontation were worse than betting on a long shot in the Kentucky Derby.

But could Benjamin have survived? Steve replayed those crucial seconds from the time Benjamin leaped off the roof and ran into the house until the first incendiary blast. Ten or eleven seconds max. Almost enough time, but not quite. It would've taken luck or divine intervention to save him. If only...

A yank on Steve's arm almost pulled him down onto his back.

Two hands clamped on his wrist pulling with surprising strength. "Steve, you were headed straight for that tree. Are you okay?"

Apparently not as okay as he thought. "Yeah. I'm fine." He turned toward Julia, her hands still locked onto his wrist.

"Did you hurt your broken wrist, pulling like that?"

The moonlight lit her hair through a hole in the forest canopy and silhouetted the contours of her face. "I'm fine. We have more important things than my wrist to worry about."

Steve's memory filled in the shadowed places of her face, the light brown hair, soft brown eyes, and full lips. Beyond all that, Julia was a woman who considered herself weak. But she was as tough as women came. She had no idea how strong she really was. What she had just come through would turn most women into blubbering quivering pools of Jell-O, but she—

"Steve, what's wrong? What do you see? Please don't tell me there are more green lights or thermal bears."

"Thermobaric. No, I don't see anything ..." *Nothing but you.*

Her hands relaxed their grip on his wrist. "Oh..." She drew the casted hand to her mouth and stared at him in the dim light.

She had read his mind. A fool's mind. He should be concentrating on keeping her alive, not depending on her to keep him from planting his face in the trunk of a fir tree while he entertained thoughts entirely inappropriate for someone running for his life. "Thanks. I didn't see the tree."

"And you were worried about my eyes being fried by little green lasers or thermal bears?"

"Thermobaric."

"I know."

"So what are thermal bears?"

"They're those little cloth bears filled with rice, I think. You heat them in the microwave then put them in your bed to keep your feet warm. Calling the rockets thermal bears makes them not so scary."

"Julia, they are scary, because—"

"You don't have to enumerate all the terrible things those bombs can do to a person's body. I get it, Steve. But, look. We're off the mountain and down in the valley."

"Yes. And we need this thick canopy for a while to lose the Hannanis."

"Hannanis? Why do you keep calling them that?"

"It's a pun Craig created from a term used in Afghanistan combined with Hannan's name. We needed a slang term to call our enemy. Soldiers always do that—redcoats, rebs, kraut's, Charlie—some I won't repeat in the presence of a lady."

"So now I'm a lady. What time is it?"

"Midnight. Zero hundred hours."

"Midnight? I think it's time to escort this lady home."

"Home?"

"You know, to that lookout tower on the peak."

Steve looked up at the black shape that blocked nearly half the stars in the sky. "Escort doesn't quite fit what we're about to do."

"Which is?"

"In the dark, with no trails to follow, as fast as we can, we're going to climb 2,500 feet in the next four miles."

She locked her good hand around his wrist. "Lead the way ... as long as you promise not to run into any more trees."

Was that a crooked smile on those full lips? It was too dark to tell. Besides, it was time to go.

Steve pulled Julia toward the edge of the stand of timber, but stopped when his sat phone buzzed, tickling his side. He dropped Julia's hand and pulled out the blinking phone. "Let's hope this is good news." After unlocking the phone, it lit up and he read the text message.

All clear here. U didn't show so moving to RV pt #2. See you in about 36h. Heard shots from mountain. Praying 4 U.

He replied with a K. "It says all clear, Julia."

"Does that mean Benjamin, too?"

"I don't know." There was no reason to worry Julia about Benjamin, yet. "Come on. We need to keep moving. We've got a rendezvous to make in about thirty-six hours."

A four-mile trek was, at best, a brisk one-hour walk on the level. But running up a forty-five-degree slope, would be two hours of torture.

Unsure how much time the climb had taken, Steve stopped below the rock cliff with the lookout on top. He looked at his G-Shock, bumped the light, and read 0135.

Impossible. He looked at Julia's dark silhouette, hands on her sides, breathing hard. She was incredible. "The last quarter mile, we just take the hidden path around the southwest side of the cliff and walk up the backside to the lookout. You ready, Julia?"

She turned away, scampered over the rocky ground to a cluster of scrubby bushes, and heaved. Once. Twice. She wasn't going to stop anytime soon.

Steve waited for her to return. He'd been where she was a time or two and didn't want to embarrass her.

A couple of minutes later, Julia walked his way, her casted hand gingerly rubbing her stomach, the other playing with strands of her hair. "I'm sorry, Steve. Guess I'm still out of shape after the Ebola. Any sign of the Hannanis?"

"No. But listen, Julia. I saw thirty women try to pass Ranger school. One did, with a whole lot of help. But none of them could have kept up with your climb up Bolan peak."

Her head lifted, gaze locked on him. "You're just trying to make me feel better after—"

"After you had the dry heaves? No. You should feel good about what you did. The dry heaves—that's from dehydration and lactic acid buildup. Only way to stop them is to make that run twice a week until they don't come back." Steve chuckled. "I heaved like that the first time I had to run two miles with a full pack on my back."

"Enough about puking. I'm okay, now. Let's get to the lookout. Jeff said, in normal times, people rent this place during the summer. They leave bottled water and other unused supplies for the next person."

Steve took her hand and headed to the left at a brisk walk to circle the mammoth promontory crowning Bolan peak, protecting it like a castle with high walls. He prayed it would protect them like Jeff said it had protected Allie and him.

* * *

Julia followed Steve as he held her hand and led her over the rocky, barren ground. After they circled a rock outcropping, the ground flattened.

Ahead of them, a dark silhouette filled part of the starry sky. The lookout.

"Oh, Steve. This is beautiful." She looked up at the stars, so bright it seemed that a person could reach out and hold them in their hand. And so many more than she could ever remember seeing, even in Eastern Oregon.

"No light pollution. At over 6,000 feet above sea level, the stars are a lot brighter. Unfortunately, enough brighter so night vision goggles can gather their light. They can see us from a mile away. Let's stay low while I figure out how to open the door underneath the tower."

Steve moved underneath the lookout. With his six-foot-four frame, he reached the lock on the door without climbing the short ladder. "That was nice of the last occupant. They left it unlocked." He pulled padlock from latch, pushed the door upward, and stepped up the ladder. Steve stuck his head inside the lookout. "It's still warm from the sunlight coming through all the glass. And nobody's home."

"No one but us." Julia climbed in behind Steve. The musty odor of old wood and the warm air left over from the day seemed familiar, almost like an African hut. With glass on all four sides, the inside was nearly as well-lit as the ground outside the lookout.

"Keep your head down, Julia. Their infrared sensors won't pick us up through the glass, but the light gathering component of their goggles might."

"You don't see them, do you?"

"No." Steve pulled out the NOD Benjamin had given him and scanned the mountains to the east. "But we've got to be cautious. We might be here for a while and we don't want any company."

Julia laughed. "People on their honeymoon generally don't want company."

Steve glanced her way.

What was he thinking? "I meant Jeff and Allie. I can see why they chose this place for ..." Her face grew hot.

Steve swiveled to face her, his eyes peering through the nighttime vision binoculars. "Do you have a temperature or something?"

Infrared sensors. Great. Steve could see her blushing through the NOD. She was probably glowing. "No. I'm fine. It's just that I've never spent the night with—" She stopped. "Changing the subject."

Steve set the binoculars down and held her by the shoulders. "Sometimes I wonder what's going through that pretty head of yours."

What was going through her head? To be sure there were repeated thoughts about being here alone with Steve Bancroft, a man Julia could not deny she had developed strong feelings for. A considerate, kind, handsome—she turned away from Steve.

Stop it Julia Weiss.

They could be killed before this night ended, and they needed to watch for anyone approaching. Besides all that, Steve still did not understand the strength or the source of her resolve to never kill a human being or have a relationship with someone who did.

"Can you believe this?" Steve touched her shoulder.

She whirled toward him, keenly aware of the conflicting emotions raised by him touching her. "Believe what?"

"Someone left a six pack of twenty-four-ounce water bottles."

He pushed one at her. "Not cold, but cool and wet."

She was thirsty. One look at the bottle of water and her mouth suddenly felt parched, dry as the Sahara. Julia grabbed the bottle, broke the seal, flipped the lid, and guzzled.

"Whoa, whoa. You keep that up and you'll be heaving again. But it won't be dry this time."

She pulled the bottle from her lips and let the water moisten her mouth, tongue, and throat. But it wasn't enough. A craving deep inside insisted she guzzle until she slaked her thirst. But this time she sucked on the bottle, let the cool water moisten her mouth and throat, then closed the lid.

"Atta girl." Steve's white teeth flashed in the starlight as he smiled at her.

"I'm not a girl, Steve."

"So I noticed."

"Shouldn't you be noticing the northeast slope, the way we came up?"

"Yeah. And you probably need some rest, if you can sleep on that wooden bed. I think visitors are supposed to bring their own air mattress to put on it."

"If I'm tired, I can sleep on anything. But ... I'm not tired."

He cocked his head. "Not tired?"

"I mean not sleepy tired. I can watch for a while if you want to sleep."

"Uh..." Steve shifted his feet. He was antsy.

"I get it. I'm not Special Forces trained. You wouldn't trust—"

Steve placed a finger over her lips. "That's not so. I would trust you with my life, any day. You've more than earned my trust. But I trust me more with your—but I don't mean I would—uh ... that didn't come out quite like—"

"Oh, it came out clear enough, Mr. Bancroft." How could she be here on a mountaintop, in the middle of the night, flirting with someone she swore she could have no serious relationship with?

Maybe it was time to tell Steve why. "Steve, you know that I'm a pacifist, don't you?"

The smile on Steve's face faded. "I thought you were a Christian."

"How could you doubt that after—"

"Because you don't subscribe to the Christian worldview ... not all of it."

The heat rose under the collar of her summer blouse. How dare he make that accusation? "What do you mean?"

"I just don't understand how a strong Christian like you can claim to be a pacifist. It doesn't fit in with the Christian worldview. Besides, pacifism is unlivable in a fallen world."

It took all her will to keep from yelling at him. She was letting Steve control the direction of this conversation. Julia needed to take control, to force Steve to face the real issue. Maybe he needed an example. "But people like the Amish live pacifism in this ... *fallen world.*"

"They can pretend to be pacifists only because other people risk their lives to protect the Amish. People even kill to protect them—police, military." He shook his head. "I'd be too ashamed to join any pacifist group."

She had totally lost control of the conversation, and the pressure building inside her, threatened to explode out of her mouth in words she would regret. "Are you saying I should be ashamed?"

"No, I'm suggesting that maybe you should tell me what changed you, what made you believe the way you do."

Steve had opened the door for the conversation she wanted them to have. But could she walk through the door to a place where so many horrific memories resided?

Haunting, terrorizing sounds came at her, full force. People screamed. Guns fired, hundreds of them. Then a gun pointed at her.

Julia's legs grew weak. The room seemed to rock back and forth.

Steve's arms wrapped around her. "You're shaking. It's okay, Julia. You're safe ... and I'm sorry. We don't have to talk about this if you don't want to."

"I don't *want* to, Steve. But I *need* to. You *need* to know." If he knew, maybe he would understand. She wasn't a coward, simply a person unwilling to commit atrocities against other people.

Steve eased her down to the wooden bed frame, sat beside Julia, and nodded to her.

"I'm an MK, missionaries' kid. From the time I was eight until I was fourteen, my parents ministered to the Yoruba Tribe in the northern part of Nigeria. Many members of the tribe had become Christians. I loved the Yoruba people, and it seemed we were a big, happy family. I can still hear their rhythmic music and see the colorful clothes they wore for tribal celebrations. They could dance, really dance.

"I had three close friends in our village, a girl, Bisi, my age. Her brother Jonathan, was two years older than me. He preferred to be called by his Yoruba name, Chibueze, because it means God is King. The third friend was their cousin, Ore, who was Jonathan's age.

"Bisi loved to sing and dance and, like Brock, she had a way with words. She was gentle, beautiful ... and so kind. Not long after we moved to the village, some older boys teased me, because even my dark brown tan was much lighter than their dark chocolate skin. In just two sentences, Bisi exposed the evil in their teasing. It shamed them and they stopped. From that day on, Bisi and I were best friends.

'She taught me their language and customs. Bisi, Jonathan, Ore, and I spent all of our spare time together. We played Ayo when it rained and hopscotch when it didn't. We—"

"Hopscotch. How did you get boys to—"

"We modified the rules. They had to jump two squares at a time. But it didn't matter, I was going to win because I could jump as far as the boys and run as fast as they could."

Julia drew a deep breath and let it back out, slowly, trying to savor the treasured moments before everything changed. "We sang and danced together. We attended church and school together. When I turned thirteen, and started looking at boys in a different way, I thought Jonathan and Ore were the most handsome guys I'd ever met. I seldom saw any white boys."

"Ore saved me from being bitten by Carpet Vipers at least three times while we played in the evenings. Once, Jonathan stood up for me when older boys from another village harassed me. He was outnumbered and beaten badly before some men stopped the fight. But he said he'd do it again, if he had to."

Steve grinned. "He sounds a bit like Benjamin."

She looked up into Steve's eyes. "Or you."

"Yeah, well ... what happened next?"

"The four of us couldn't have been closer if we were brothers and sisters ... until the Islamists showed up."

Steve draped an arm over her shoulders. "I think I know where this is going."

Julia leaned against Steve and tried to draw from his huge store of strength to continue her story. "After the men wearing mismatched pieces of military garb and carrying rifles came and started recruiting, it seemed like someone darkened the sun. It forgot to shine on our village. Those dark days began when I turned fourteen.

"From that time on, Jonathan stuck close to Bisi and me. It was like he thought he needed to protect us, though he would've been helpless against those men with automatic weapons. But Ore grew sullen and angry. He made cruel remarks to Bisi and me. We didn't understand it. It hurt us, deeply."

"I'll bet you noticed more than just a change in mood from him. I've learned a bit about radicalization." Steve's voice became hard-edged, full of cynicism. "It's a stupid word for people who become stupid when they believe lies straight from the pit."

"We noticed more than a mood change. We saw less and less of Ore. Sometimes he would walk to a place outside the village where the Islamists preached jihad and promised the young men—well, they promised them things so vile I won't even repeat them, things on earth and in their perverted version of heaven. The young men simply had to join in jihad and a sensual paradise was theirs."

Steve snorted in disgust. "People will believe anything they need to believe to justify fulfilling their selfish desires." He looked directly into her eyes.

Had Steve meant that for her, too? She shook off the thought and continued. "Well, one day, after Ore turned sixteen, he walked out of the village and didn't come back.

'Other young men left, too. Then we heard rumors of killings, kidnappings, and rapes occurring at other villages."

"Rapes." Steve's body stiffened against hers. "With radical Islam, or anywhere they practice Sharia law, it always comes back to that, men sexually abusing women and kids. You want to know why, Julia?"

"I'm not sure I do."

"They make such a big deal about sexual purity. But the men punish the women for the men's sexual incontinence. Wear a burqa. Paint the windows to your house so men can't see you. You might tempt them to sin. If a woman's sexually assaulted, it's her fault. All because their religion is impotent. There's no power in their false god, certainly no power over sin. The one true God puts His Spirit in us, empowering us to live a holy—sorry. I was preaching." He looked at Julia, studying her face as if he expected to see a negative reaction.

She gave him a big smile. "Keep on preachin', brother."
Steve chuckled.

Steve's words, and the conviction with which he spoke them, made her feel still more protected in his presence. Even alone on a mountaintop, in Jeff and Allie's "honeymoon suite," with emotions and attraction running high, this man would protect her ... in every way. With Steve Bancroft, she was safe.

"Where was I?" She paused. "We suspected that the perpetrators were affiliated with Al Qaeda. But soon they started calling themselves Boko Haram, meaning they were against all things Western, especially schools that provided a Western education.

"The elders armed the men in our village, as much as they could, and the men took turns standing guard twenty-four seven." She looked up at Steve.

Her mention of Al Qaeda and Boko Haram had brought the intense look of a warfighter to Steve's face. "I know the Nigerian government has been unstable at times, but didn't they help you?"

"No. The government was corrupt and seemed incapable of stopping the attacks ... or unwilling. Whenever the jihadists wanted more recruits, or more girls to use, they attacked another village."

Steve gently lifted her chin until he could peer into her eyes. "Don't you see, Julia, that's why I—"

"Let me finish, Steve. Please."

He moved his hand, cupping her cheek as disappointment filled his eyes. "Sure. Go ahead."

Julia looked away, out the window into the star-sprinkled darkness of the night sky. "One day, the American Embassy contacted my parents. The State Department wanted us to evacuate. Mom and Dad had been working with the Yoruban people for so long, they said they needed to pray about it first. The next day ... our village was attacked."

That day came storming back into Julia's consciousness, vivid and brutal.

Bisi gasped. Her eyes widened and she scanned the trees and huts around them.

Julia whirled toward the crashing noises and angry shouts of men.

An attack!

Jonathan grabbed the two girls' arms and pulled them behind a hut, out of sight of the attackers. He pointed toward the trees in front of them. Two hundred meters into the dense bushes and trees lay their secret hiding place, a place where Bisi, Julia, Jonathan, and Ore hid when they didn't want to be bothered by other kids. No one had ever found them there.

The three sprinted into the thick bushes and squirmed around trees, moving deep into the dense vegetation.

The staccato popping of automatic weapons sounded behind them. People yelling. People screaming.

Mom and Dad!

They were in their home at the far end of the village. Would these jihadists be brazen enough to kill American citizens?

Julia prayed they wouldn't. But the sheer volume of shots fired could've killed everyone in the village several times over.

The shrill screams of girls painted a picture of evil in Julia's mind that she couldn't erase. She recognized some of the crying voices. Pictured their faces.

The jihadists were demonic. What they did couldn't be explained in any other way. Beliefs and practices this evil must've come from Satan, himself, including their unholy book and their violent, power-crazed prophet.

Jonathan pulled the two girls into a tiny opening near the base of the tree.

This had been a place of sanctuary for them for five or six years.

Please, God, keep us safe.

"Bisi, Julia ..." Jonathan's hoarse whisper came between deep breaths. "... slow your breathing. Be still. Absolutely silent ... no matter what you hear. They won't find us."

Maybe they couldn't find the three of them, but all the others in the village would either be killed or taken as slaves. Where would Bisi and Jonathan go when this was over? What if Julia's mom and dad were killed or taken?

The swishing sound of bushes being pushed aside came from Julia's left. Someone moved through the tangle of vegetation, coming from the direction of the village.

Jonathan put a finger over his lips.

The sounds in the bushes grew louder. Now rapid footsteps came their way.

Jonathan pulled Julia and Bisi behind a large tree trunk.

A body leaped into the clearing on the other side of the tree.

Julia stiffened and slapped a hand over her mouth to stifle a scream.

A uniformed man holding an automatic rifle circled the tree. "Do not move!"

Ore. He pointed his weapon at Bisi. "If either of you move, she dies, kuffars."

"Come on, Ore," Jonathan pleaded. "We are your friends. You—"

"Shut up, dirty kuffars!" Ore raised his weapon.

Jonathan leaped toward Ore, but Ore pulled the trigger, firing point-blank into Bisi's face.

Julia covered her eyes. But she couldn't block the sounds of the two boys fighting, grunting, rolling on the ground in front of her.

Ore's rifle fired again.

Julia moved her hands from her face.

Jonathan yelped in pain, then roared in anger. "You are dead, Ore!"

Jonathan ripped Ore's rifle from his hands and emptied the magazine into Ore's body.

Blood pooled around Ore's still form on the ground.

Jonathan's knees bent and he fell on his side across Ore. Blood soaked the front of Jonathan's shirt. "You're safe, Julia. Stay here, until ..." He exhaled slowly and life left his body. Jonathan died at her feet.

Sounds of gunfire. Horrible cries of pain. Girls screaming. It went on for at least an hour, while Julia sat in the clearing holding Bisi's lifeless hand, unable to look at the disfigured face of her closest friend.

Julia shivered and pushed the memories from her mind ... for now. But they would return to hurt and haunt. They always returned. "Steve, that's why I could never—"

"That must've been horrible for you. But, Julia, don't you see? Your friend Jonathan saved you. He gave his life for yours. That's what Jesus did for us too, and you have a relationship with him. So ..."

She knew where Steve's logic was headed and it stopped her like she'd hit a mental brick wall. Steve's words were true, but there were big differences in what Jesus did. "Jesus didn't go around killing people."

"Not then. But one day He will. Because of God's justice, some people will be sentenced to eternal separation from God. Eternal death."

"I don't want to talk about it anymore." No logic could remove the horrible memories from Julia's mind. Right or wrong, words or thoughts of war would always reload the video of that day and force her to watch the vivid, gruesome images. How could she ever spend her life with someone whose job was to do such things to other human beings? She couldn't. Not even if they were handsome, chivalrous, caring—not even someone like Steve. At that thought tears began to flow. An incredible amount of tears for a dehydrated body.

How long had Julia been crying? Steve's shirt, where her head lay against it, was wet with her tears. And how had she ended up in Steve's arms? Sometimes the memories became so strong, they blocked out the present.

Steve stroked her hair. "I understand, Julia. I—"

"How can you say that?" She pulled free from Steve's arms.

He reached for her hand. "I know how you feel ... really, but—"

"There's always going to be a 'but', isn't there?" She pulled her hand away. "I'll never understand how—"

"How the horror of killing affects you, sickens you?" Steve paused. "Julia, the first time I saw someone shot to death in combat, a man in my detachment, one of my brothers, I puked my guts out. I..." Steve stopped as if he'd choked on his words.

She met Steve's intense gaze and saw the pain his eyes and face held. He knew about this horror and yet remained a warrior. "But you still kill people. I don't understand how anyone could do that, after..."

"Yeah. After..." Steve blew out a blast of air. "Look, God called me to be a warrior. How could I say no?"

"So you're using God as an excuse to justify—"

"I don't need to justify what I do. He called countless people in the Bible to do it. If we don't respond, who will protect people like the Amish ... or you?"

"Me? Maybe no one should."

"If no one fought oppression and evil, there would be no USA. Think about what that would mean. History would change. None of the thousands of missionaries that have gone out from America would've been sent. In fact, in the beginning, people like Cain would've killed all of the innocent people like Abel. No one in the world would think living here is a wonderful life. The world would be one big Pottersville. Is that what you want?"

"People like you kill to protect others, and it's still not a wonderful life."

"Some evil oppressors can only be stopped by killing them. Look ... everything we know about God's character says He hates oppression." Steve paused. "Julia, He doesn't call everyone to be a warrior. Brock and KC took that role for a while, but only when it became absolutely necessary. Not everyone can do that. Not everyone is asked to."

So Steve thought some people needed to be killed, but she was too weak to do it. Like the kids in elementary school, he had just called her Wimpy Weiss. Her body stiffened as a bolt of anger shot through her. "So, you're saying a weak person like me can't do what God wants?" She stared up into Steve's shadowy face.

"You're anything but weak." Steve's shoulders slumped. His voice softened. "I already told you that."

She opened her mouth to speak, then closed it, unsure about what to say and wondering where Steve was taking their discussion.

"The day you and Allie were taken ... we ambushed Blanchard's men and KC shot two of them. But, when I looked out the back door of Jeff's house to see if she was okay, KC was shaking while Brock held her."

"This discussion has gone on long enough." Julia wanted to end it, now. She would bring it to a head. "Why are you telling me all of this, Steve?"

"I would think it's obvious. Julia, I've waited a long time to find a strong, good woman like you, and—"

"But you don't think I'm very good. And people have to risk their lives to protect me, because I won't do it myself. So why do—"

"That's not what I think. You remind me of another person I swore to protect and..." Steve's voice caught, choking off his words.

Her fingers curled around Steve's hand and Julia waited.

Chapter 14

Steve studied Julia's wide, brown eyes, expectant eyes, no longer piecing. Her mood had changed. And her hand lay warm in his, as she waited for him to tell her the story he'd started to share in Whistler.

Telling the story would abrade away the protective shell around Steve's heart, leaving it raw and exposed to a woman who might very well reject it. If she did, what then? Was it worth the risk?

As the crescent moon began its rapid plunge below the western horizon, Steve studied Julia's face in the dim moonlight of a starry night.

More than worth it.

He pulled his hand gently from hers, rose, and crouched near the east-facing window. "I need to see if there's any sign of Hannan's men." He glanced back at Julia.

She sat, hands folded in her lap, staring at the floor.

"Just give me a couple of minutes."

He used the NOD Benjamin had given him to study the route he and Julia took from the ridge into the small valley and then up Bolan Mountain. Neither the infrared nor the light-gathering enhancements showed anything.

Maybe they really had taken the false trail he left them. It was dark and tracking would be difficult until morning.

Steve swung the device to the ridge line and followed it toward the first rendezvous point near Takilma. He stopped when five tiny bright objects appeared on the ridge. The five dots coalesced into one. "I can't believe it."

"What can't you believe?"

"According to Jeff, and our little jaunt up the mountain, that ridge we crossed is at least—if I remember my geometry—three miles away. And these guys are another half mile down the ridge."

"You mean you see them?"

"This is advanced infrared technology with a ten power scope. Yeah. I see them. They stopped moving toward that rendezvous point. Looks like they're having a confab ... now they're moving again, coming back along the ridge."

Shuffling sounds came from behind him, but Steve kept his eyes focused on the five images of human body heat captured and magnified by the incredible device Benjamin had given them.

A hand rested softly on his shoulder and Julia's breath tickled his ear. She pushed her head up beside his, peering into what her naked eyes would only see as darkness. "Are we going to be okay staying here in the lookout?"

"For a while. We didn't leave much of a trail near the ridge. I doubt they can pick it up before daylight, if even then. It should get light around 0600, and if they find our trail then, it's at least another three to four hours of tracking to get here."

"What time is it now, Steve?"

He pulled the glasses from his face and bumped the back light button on his G-Shock. "It's 0220."

"So we're safe for five or six hours?"

"Yeah, but I need to monitor them continuously starting about 0400, before first light."

She looked up at him, waiting.

125

"We have time. Besides, I need to tell you my story so you know who you're ..." Who she was what? Falling for? He suspected it but he didn't know that.

"Steve?" She pulled him to the wooden bed frame.

Steve sat beside her on the bench-like platform, drained his lungs with a long sigh, then drew a breath. "I told you in Whistler that Stephanie was my little sister. Six minutes younger than me, but at sixteen years of age, almost a foot shorter. She was about your height, light brown hair, brown eyes. So beautiful and gentle."

"I'm not actually beautiful, but it sounds as if I look a bit like her."

"So much that I gasped when I caught a glimpse of you and Abdul in the tent with his gun to your head. I froze. Nearly blew everything. I could have gotten us both killed."

Julia muted his lips with her fingers. "Hush. All that turned out right. God had a plan to save us all, and it was a lot better than anything we could have imagined. KC will tell you that, too ... tell me more about Stephanie."

After Julia moved her hand from his mouth, Steve held it. "Well, I was proud to call her my sister. And no guy ever got out of line with Steph. I let it be known what I would do to anyone who did."

She stuck out a thumb toward Steve's gun propped beside the bed. "But you didn't carry an M4 in those days."

"No. At sixteen, I worked out a lot and carried around a six-foot-three-inch frame with 215 pounds of muscle on it. I knew just enough martial arts to be dangerous."

As his mind jumped back to the night that changed everything, the old dark cloud returned, hanging over him, removing hope and joy, marking Steve Bancroft as a failure.

"Our parents were away at a church conference. Dad told me I was in charge of the house."

With clouds gathering, the Nebraska sky had grown dark before 10:00 p.m. on this warm, early June evening.

A scream stabbed Steve's ears, jolting him into action. It sounded like a woman in some horror movie. No, it sounded like Steph's scream.

He sprinted down the hallway toward his sister's room.

Steph stood, her back toward him, frozen stiff, one hand on her mouth, while the other hand pointed at the far wall.

Steve stopped beside her, circling her shoulders with his arm.

"Steve, a ... a spider. It's huge!"

Someday, his twin sister's arachnophobia would kill him—cardiac arrest. "Show me where it is, Steph."

"On the wall, just above my bed."

Great. The small house spider had at least a half dozen places to run and hide before he could reach it. But if Steve let it get away, he wouldn't get any sleep tonight.

"If you don't get him, I'm not sleeping in here tonight. No way."

"Well, you're not sleeping with me, Steph."

"Then you'd better kill him. Steve, he just moved. Hurry, before he gets away."

Steve grabbed a tissue on the nightstand and crept toward the spider.

The lively arachnid crawled downward, almost to bed level. It's preferred hiding place was obvious. If it got behind the bed, he'd have to fumigate the room before Steph would set foot in it again.

Desperation time. Steve slowly extended the hand with the tissue. He lunged at the spider, smashing his hand into the wall. Pain shot through his wrist. He cradled the throbbing wrist in his other hand and twisted his head to look at Stephanie.

"You let him get away." White completely encircled Steph's brown eyes.

Steve moaned. "No, I didn't. I got him, Steph." He rolled over on the bed onto his back and sat up facing her.

"Show me the proof. I have to—"

He opened the crumpled Kleenex and Steph squealed at the remains.

"Are you satisfied now?"

"Not until you flush him down the toilet."

"But you're not supposed to flush Kleenex down—"

"Just do it ... for me, Stevie. Please?"

When his sister's warm brown eyes looked at him like that, so innocent, completely reliant—he could never refuse Steph.

The spider and Kleenex disappeared down the toilet in a turbulent swirl of water followed by a gurgling sound.

When Steve emerged from the bathroom across the hall from Steph's bedroom, two slender, well-tanned arms circled his neck. She kissed his cheek. "My hero."

He gave her a warm hug. "Yeah. Big hero. I crushed a poor little terrified bug, running for its life. At least now, maybe I can get some sleep tonight."

"If the thunderstorms don't keep us awake. On tonight's news, the weatherman said a squall line will pass through our area."

"Thunder I can sleep through. But your screaming ..."

"I promise to be quiet ... now that you killed that big spider."

"Tiny spider." He kissed her forehead. "Good night, Steph."

She looked up at him and smiled. "Good night, big brother."

"Six and a half minutes older than you doesn't make me a big brother."

"No." She tapped the top of his head. "But nearly six and a half feet tall does." She nudged him out the door and closed it.

Steve grew drowsy listening to the soothing sounds of thunder rumbling softly in the distance. Maybe the squall line had fallen apart. And once Steph turned off her light, she wouldn't see any more spiders. Finally, peace in the house.

A bright flash pierced Steve's eyelids and a sharp crack jolted him awake. Lightning had hit nearby. The squall line was squalling.

Late spring could be a lively time in Nebraska with frequent thunderstorms and occasional tornado watches, but he could stay in bed unless things got really—

A wailing siren jerked him to a sitting position on the side of his bed. Somebody must have spotted a tornado in the area. He and Steph should probably grab their pillows and head downstairs.

Their father had dug a storm shelter below ground level, off the side of the basement. He had constructed it to withstand a direct hit by an F5 tornado, at least that's what the specs said.

Steve snatched his pillow and pulled the bedspread off his bed. The temperature in the cellar usually hovered around sixty degrees. If they ended up spending the night there, he and Steph would need something to keep them warm.

He walked out into the hallway.

Steph's door was closed.

He rapped on it. "Steph, we need to go down to the cellar."

The storm seemed to have subsided, and the night grew quiet except for the siren wailing in the distance.

There was no answer from Stephanie.

Steve opened her door and flipped on the light.

She wasn't in her bed.

Where is she?

The bathroom door stood open. No light on. She wasn't in there.

"Steph? Where are you? We need to go downstairs."

He checked the rooms up and down the hall, but stopped before going into the living room. Maybe she had already gone downstairs and was waiting for him. He would check downstairs. The living room was the last place he expected to find his sister in the middle of the night.

Steve hit the light at the head of the stairs and then took the steps two at a time. When he reached the bottom, a strange sound stopped him, the noise of a million bees.

The droning quickly grew into the roar of a freight train, a train that sounded like it was headed for their house.

The door to the storm cellar stood half open.

Relief washed over him. Steph must be there already.

Steve rushed to the door.

The freight train hit the house, ripping and tearing at the structure above him.

A giant vacuum cleaner tried to suck his body up into the flying debris above.

Steve dove and rolled into the storm cellar.

The storm sucked the door closed, slamming it and leaving him inside in total darkness.

"Steph, hit the push light. I can't see a thing."

He waited.

No answer.

His heart now drumming out panic, Steve's hands felt frantically for the battery powered push light on the small table.

His hand hit something and it clattered on the floor.

In his panic, he had knocked the light off the table.

"Steph, say something. Are you okay?"

Outside the cellar, a tearing noise sounded, so loud and violent it could've been the earth being ripped apart.

One of Steve's hands found the light on the floor and pushed it.

The room lit and he could see everything ... everything except the one thing needed to see, his twin sister.

Steph wasn't there. She was—no, she couldn't be. She had been raised in Nebraska. She knew what the tornado warning siren sounded like and what it signified.

He should turn on the NOAA weather radio in the cellar to hear details about the warning. But the house had already been hit. The radio wouldn't tell him what he wanted to know most, where Steph was.

Steve opened the door a crack. No more wind. No more suction.

He opened it farther and looked across the floor of the basement.

Boards and other debris littered the floor.

He looked up and gasped as a half-moon flickered between the broken layer of clouds passing overhead.

Nausea grew and bile rose into his throat.

Fearing what he would find, Steve shoved the small light into his pocket, crawled up the broken remains of the stairs, and climbed onto the ground level of what had been their home.

The devastation told him no one could have survived this kind of violence. He tried to shove that thought aside.

Toward town some lights were on. The diffuse light created a dark silhouette of the remains of his house. It had been moved thirty yards away, where it lay in a twisted, six-foot high pile of wood and furniture.

He pulled out the light, turned it on, and walked to the remains of the house. His stomach roiled, then cramped.

She must have been in the living room or he would have found her. That would mean—it would mean he had failed. His father had left Steve in charge. He was supposed to protect Steph.

He tried to picture the events of the past few minutes. He knew Steph. He thought like her. Steve could usually predict what she would do. She had seen another spider in her room and didn't want to wake him. Probably went to the couch to sleep.

Could she have survived?

Steve pulled some boards aside and saw Steph, lying beside their couch, which had been broken into two pieces. Her hands still clutched her pillow. She looked like she was sleeping, but all the blood on her head told a different story.

Had she been alive, he would have known. He could sense Steph if she was anywhere near him. He knew what she was doing, what she was thinking. He could complete her sentences, sense her fear, and feel the deep love that flowed between them every minute of every day. He should have known where she was when he looked for her.

Steve pled with God as his fingers roamed over her neck, willing there to be a pulse.

But there wasn't. And he couldn't sense her presence, because Steph wasn't there.

Half of Steve had left with her, an irreplaceable half. He would never feel whole. But, worst of all, was knowing he had failed to protect Steph. Her death was his fault.

After the memorial service, Steve made a vow. He would spend his life protecting people. He would learn to do it right. No one else would ever die in his care. Steve Bancroft could face death, but he could never look at the body of someone he had allowed to die. He would die before he allowed that to happen.

Steve unclenched his fists and sighed in a sharp blast, trying to exhale his pain and guilt. He looked at Julia.

There were tears in her eyes.

"Two years later, when I turned eighteen, I joined the Army."

"Oh, Steve." Julia took his hands. She cried softly and her teardrops splattered on his hands. "I'm so sorry."

"Me too. But I left her behind, Julia. I went into the storm cellar and—"

"But it wasn't your fault." She wiped her cheeks.

He put a finger over her lips. He had heard this before and didn't need to hear it again. "Julia, Rangers ... real men, never leave anyone behind. I left her, whether I intended to or not. That will never happen again ... as long as I live. I swear it won't!"

* * *

The intensity in Steve's voice, the tight lines on his face, and seeing him nearly out of control, frightened her. This man was a trained, powerful warrior.

Hannan's men, though they were also Special Forces, could never prevail against a man like Steve. His muscular arms circled her like bars of steel, protecting her, bringing peace and safety.

Then his arms softened, forming to the contours of her body.

Julia looked up into what had been fierce eyes.

Now, Steve's eyes focused on her, intense, but no longer threatening.

He cupped her cheeks and tilted her head upward.

Steve wanted to kiss her.

"Steve, how much do I remind you of Steph?"

"Enough. But not ... too much for—"

She placed her fingers over his lips, softly. Not ending the moment, just postponing it. "What is it you really want, Steve? Your twin sister back, or a woman who will be much more than a sister? I need to know."

133

He answered her, but not with words.

His kiss was not what she expected from a warrior. So gentle.

Was it really possible that God could create men whose jobs were to kill people when necessary, but having hearts that could leave behind the callous killing, return to a loving state, and come home as caring husbands and fathers?

If God could create such men, did that mean people like her, a person who despised killing, could have a relationship with such a man?

It was her first real kiss. Julia had never let any boy or man kiss her. Not on the lips. But how had she let her mind go on such a wild excursion in the middle of it? Somewhere in all of those thoughts, their gentle kiss had ended. She missed at least half of it and there was only one way get it back.

Steve's eyes held a puzzled expression, plain to see even in the starlight. "Julia, what are you thinking? If I shouldn't have done that, I'm—"

Julia stopped his words with a kiss that she initiated, one that she would end, but not before she savored every second of it without any distractions. As Steve would say, mission accomplished.

But, now, what must Steve think about her. "Steve ... I ... I want you to know that I've never done that before ... ever."

She had no idea if this relationship could ever work, long-term. But, for the moment, Steve Bancroft, the warrior, had stolen her mind and heart with a story and a kiss.

From somewhere in the past an old western movie came to mind—a story about a sheriff who married a Quaker. The title was something about noon. When her mind replayed the plot, Julia hit the stop button before she reached the ending.

I won't base my values on some old Hollywood movie.

She ditched the movie and focused on Steve. What if it turned out that the man with his arms around her only wanted a sister to save? After tonight, could she be that for him? It wasn't what she wanted. But maybe it was what Steve needed to heal from his wounds. If that was really the case, she would be that sister for Steve, no matter the pain.

But, if Steve wanted Julia Weiss, the woman, she was willing to see where this relationship led. But what if it led her to high noon and left her with a gun in her hands?

Could she kill someone to save her friends' lives? To save Steve's life?

She had no answer. And that meant her friends couldn't rely on her. She couldn't even rely on herself.

A verse came to mind about being immature, a child tossed to and fro by the waves, blown around by every wind of teaching. That was Julia Weiss, uncertain about important issues. And her uncertainty, at a critical moment, could get them all killed.

Chapter 15

Julia sat beside the huge glass window looking eastward, where the horizon had slowly brightened over the past fifteen minutes. High in the sky, indigo gave way to purple and purple became royal blue near the horizon. Now, a hint of yellow lined the jagged mountain tops to the east.

Seated in the rickety wooden chair they'd found in the lookout, Julia could peer out the bottom of the glass without overly exposing herself to anyone studying the lookout with night vision goggles.

She looked at Steve's G-Shock wrapped around her hand. 0355.

It had taken her until nearly three o'clock to convince Steve that he needed to sleep for a while. It had also taken an appeal to his machismo and duties as a Ranger, duties which she had said he could better fulfill if he rested.

And he had given her strict orders to wake him at 0400.

As exhausting as the climb up Bolan Peak had been, Julia couldn't sleep. Outside, somewhere in the night, highly trained soldiers sought to kill her. Inside, another battle raged between her head and her heart. This battle was the real reason why she persuaded Steve to take a nap.

Steve lay on the old wooden bed frame, breathing deep, barely audible breaths. How could he sleep so peacefully when in three or four hours their pursuers could make an assault on the peak? Maybe Rangers couldn't survive the rigors of warfare without being able to sleep when any opportunity arose.

Steve had shown her how to use the complex goggles, called a NOD. Over the past hour, she had scanned the mountainous land in the entire eastern quadrant and found no signs of the men who had chased them. But Steve had assured her that Hannan's Rangers wouldn't find her and Steve's trail before daylight.

0359. Better not be late, if she wanted Steve's continued trust.

Julia dropped from the chair to the floor, placed the night vision goggles in the chair, and crawled to the old wooden platform where Steve slept. She rose and sat beside him.

Steve lay on his left side, facing her. How would a big, strong Ranger react to being poked on the shoulder while he slept ... a Ranger who'd seen a lot of war and killing? Would he become violent like someone with PTSD? Or...

Somehow, without her noticing, his right arm had curled around her. Steve's eyes opened. "Good morning, Jules."

Jules? Where did that come from? For twenty-four years Julia had rejected that nickname, every time someone tried to tag her with it. But, with Steve, it sounded nice ... closer than friendship. Maybe too close. "Should I hum Reveille, or something? It's 4:00 a.m."

"You mean 0400. Have you seen anything?"

"Only a starry night sky, dark forests, and a beautiful sunrise in the making." She stuck a thumb out at the east window.

He slid his body toward his feet, swung his legs over the edge, and sat up beside her. "Before it gets any lighter, I should take a look while any peeping Hannanis still think they're hidden by the darkness." He glanced toward

Benjamin's goggles in the chair, then back to Julia, focusing on her face. Rather, part of her face ... her lips.

Like she had thought several times over the past few weeks, it would be nice, but probably just a nice fairy tale.

Two months ago, if anyone had told her she would spend the night with a ruggedly handsome Army Ranger in a remote Forest Service lookout, allow him to kiss her, return his kiss, and now be seriously considering a repeat, she would've considered them delusional. It was a nice delusion, but still the stuff of fairytales.

Julia couldn't. Wouldn't.

Steve's eyes flickered disappointment. He looked away and focused on the east window. "I need to start looking for any signs that they found our tracks ... or us."

He slid off the bed into a crouch and waddled to the chair, staying below window level. "Why don't you rest while I watch?"

Exhaustion hit her the moment Julia rolled onto her side on the bed frame. The cause was as much emotional as physical, and it took her mind into a fuzzy state of semi-consciousness.

Steve's story and his wounds had moved her. He had been scarred as badly as her and sharing their wounds had forged a strong emotional bond between them. Where would it lead?

Right now, she was too far gone to explore the future.

Steve sat in the chair, leaning forward, staring out the window.

The fuzziness carried her into its warm embrace, safe with Steve on sentry duty, the man who would give his life to protect her.

* * *

Steve pulled the goggles from his face and looked across the tops of the mountains.

A small arc of yellow crowning a mountain to the east leaked light onto the higher hills and mountains. Above the yellow arc, a semicircle, like a strange rainbow, ran the red side of the color spectrum from yellow-orange, to red, to deep purple.

The valleys below remained shrouded in darkness, creating such a contrast in light intensity that the goggles gathered too much light. They could damage his eyes or the goggle's sensors.

He pulled out the protective lenses Benjamin said were for daytime use. Steve locked them in place, turning the goggles into ten-power, daytime binoculars. He set them on the ledge beneath a huge glass window and glanced at Julia.

She hadn't moved since she dropped off an hour ago. This incredible woman had expended so much energy, physical and emotional, that he would let her sleep as long as possible.

She looked younger than twenty-four and her face, expressing complete peace, gave her the look of an innocent child. But, according to her experiences in Africa, that innocence had been stolen by visions of violence, the worst of mankind's inhumanity to man. Steve had fought that violence in Afghanistan, violence ideologically or demon driven by the writings of a man Steve believed to have been Satan's pawn used to delude and enslave a billion victims.

Steve turned back toward the window and picked up the goggles. He studied the ridgeline to the west, the one he had carried Julia up last night. His jaw clenched when he spotted movement on the ridge.

Five men in tac gear stood on the road, while a sixth waved to the others from a spot thirty yards below. They had found his trail.

By pushing themselves to their limits, he and Julia had reached the base of the two-hundred-foot cliff below the lookout in slightly over an hour and a half and, in another ten minutes, they had reached the lookout. Hannan's men would have to track them. It would take at least three hours for them to arrive.

Steve lowered his head, barely peeking over the window ledge. He zoomed in on the men and studied them through the goggles.

One man on the road raised his hand and seemed to be pointing directly at Steve's face. Clearly, they suspected the lookout. Would they rush toward the lookout, abandoning tracking, entirely? Probably.

Three hours had just become two. The danger sent adrenaline coursing through his veins, revving his heart.

Steve turned toward Julia to wake her.

She had already sat up on the bed and now stared wide-eyed at him. "Steve, what is it?"

He crouched, moved to her side, and sat.

Julia circled his waist with her arms and look up at him with questioning eyes, but eyes without fear. "We're going to have some company, aren't we?"

He put a hand on her shoulder and nodded. "Six visitors, in about two hours."

Julia's eyes seemed to scan the lookout cabin from one side to the other. "I'll never forget this place, or ..." She leaned against his shoulder. "But we need to go now, don't we?"

Having Julia with him might change his strategy. And there could be some real surprises as their pursuers used all of their available resources to eliminate Julia and him.

She raised her head. "Well, don't we?"

Steve weighed his answer, then found he didn't have one. "Maybe. But maybe not."

Chapter 16

0505. As Steve looked out the window to the northeast he iterated over all possible scenarios including both leaving the lookout and staying. No matter how he tried to change the ending, it concluded the same way. He and Julia would be killed by gunfire or incinerated.

He had brought Julia with him because the team believed he could protect her and fulfill his role in baiting Hannan's men. How had he overlooked the greatest danger of all?

Julia had been studying his face for the past minute, searching for an answer to her question about leaving. Steve didn't have one, not a satisfactory answer.

"Steve, we can't just stay here and let them kill us. Why can't we leave now? I can run. I won't slow you down."

He didn't reply.

The searching look in her eyes turned to a questioning frown. "Fine. If you don't want to talk to me..." She turned away from him.

He hooked her upper arm.

At his touch, Julia stopped moving.

"I'm sorry." He gently turned her back to face him. "We've got a big problem, and I don't have a solution for it, yet."

She rested her hand on his forearm. Julia had no clue how her presence affected him. Her touch, her resemblance to Steph ... it brought back all the guilt. And now this. "Jules, we can't make a run for Happy Camp."

"It's okay. I trust you."

"Maybe you shouldn't."

She shook her head. "Don't talk like that. I thought we laid the ghosts to rest last night."

"This has nothing to do with ghosts."

Frustration flooded Julia's face, just as it had back at Jeff's house when Brock questioned her pacifism. "Steve, those men could be at the base of the cliff by six o'clock. Then the shooting starts. Maybe it's time to share your plan. I can help, you know."

He turned and sat on the bed. The only answer he had come up with for this dilemma bordered on lunacy.

Julia sat beside him. "It's okay to tell me. I won't think you're crazy."

She had read him. Read him like a book. No more keeping secrets from Julia. But this plan required her to trust him even more than when they escaped Jeff's house. How could he get her to trust him when he wasn't sure he trusted himself?

Steve took her hands in his.

She scooted closer to him. "Well?"

"It's like this. As soon as the forest is light enough, that stealth chopper will take off."

Julia gasped. She scanned the horizon to the north then focused on Steve's eyes. "There is no safe place, is there?"

"I'm guessing it will take off around 0600. It could be bearing down on us by 0610. I don't know how many men will be on board. Maybe the rest of the team that went after Jeff and the others. But—"

"It has guns and rockets onboard, doesn't it?"

Steve nodded. "Guns for sure."

"I guess we can't run down the road. We'd be easy targets."

"The chopper's a Stealth Hawk, an MH-X3, a machine that supposedly never went into production. I'm thinking it did, but it was kept secret. And in a stealth configuration, I don't have a clue what kind of arsenal it carries."

"So a super-secret helicopter with six men on it will—"

"Five men. Maybe less. We took one out at Jeff's house. Don't know how many Benjamin got. A Ranger detachment has twelve men. And this team also has a pilot."

"But, Steve, if you're right, the men on the ground and the helicopter will all get here a little after 6 o'clock. What can we do?"

Steve drew a long breath and released it slowly. He met Julia's intense gaze. "We have to shoot down the chopper."

She released his hands. "Are you nuts? A silent helicopter just swoops down on us out of nowhere and you shoot it down with your M4?" She ended her rant with her eyebrows raised and a thumb pointing at his rifle leaning against the wall.

"Jules..."

She huffed a blast of air. "I'm sorry." She took his hands again. "How are we going to do this? We've only got about fifty-five minutes."

"This is how my plan works. Two of the men I saw coming our way are carrying long backpacks. Quivers filled with—"

"With thermal bears?"

"Yeah. Thermal bears and launchers slung across their backs." He paused. "So, I head down the mountain about 0530, take out one of their men, hopefully a man bringing up the rear. I steal his thermal bears and his launcher, then hurry back up to the top before the fun begins. Now, we don't have much time, so—"

"What about the helicopter?" Her eyes widened. "You're going to shoot it down like ..."

"Yeah. But not like the Apache at your house near Crooked River Ranch. This time, we give the chopper a thermal bear to warm the pilot's feet."

"While you're doing this, what about me?"

"I need two things from you. Are you any good at art?"

"You must mean the art of war?"

"Not exactly. More like sculpture. Can you rig up something that looks like the top of a person's head, peering over the window ledge?"

"I can come up with something that will look okay at a distance, but don't they have binoculars?"

"Just do your best. We only need to fool them for a short time."

"Okay. But you said two things."

"I need to be out of here and headed down the mountain in less than five minutes. So you complete the head and be ready to leave in four minutes. That leaves me one minute to find a hiding place for you among the rocks on this peak."

"Steve, you're not going to leave me here."

"Jules ... you've got to stay. You're not trained for what I have to do. I'll be moving fast, silently, and ... well, I can't take you with me."

"If we do this, Steve, you've got to promise to come back for me. I'm not afraid to die, if I have to, but I don't want to die alone. And I don't want Hannan's men getting their hands on me. Abdul, Captain Blanchard's interrogator was going to..." She looked down at the floor.

"I know, Jules. I'll do whatever I have to do to get back to you."

Julia cupped his cheek with one hand, gave him a weak smile, then searched for materials for her project.

While Julia fashioned a head using an old towel and a magazine left in the lookout, Steve searched the path up the mountain looking for the six men. Within thirty seconds he found movement a short way up the mountain. They moved straight toward the cliff.

Steve noted several landmarks to use as checkpoints while navigating down the mountain to get behind the men. He picked his likely ambush point, memorized the landmarks around it, and put away the NOD.

Julia crawled away from her creation, now peeping out the window. An incredible likeness to a human head.

He crouched and moved to the entry door in the floor of the lookout. "You ready, Jules?"

She grabbed two unopened water bottles and scooted beside him.

"Good thinking."

She handed him the water.

Before he could react, Julia wrapped her arms around him in a fierce embrace. "Promise me ..." Her voice broke. "... that you'll come back ... alive."

"I ..." He couldn't make that promise, not with certainty.

Julia looked up, reading his eyes again. "Then tell me the truth. What do you think your odds are of getting back here, taking down the chopper, and taking the men out that are coming after us? The truth, Steve." Her intense brown eyes penetrated to the depths of his heart. He couldn't lie to Julia.

"About 50-50." Either he would succeed or fail. What more could he tell her?

"But you said you'd come back. You promised me. How, Steve?"

"What will you be doing while I'm gone?"

"Praying. Praying harder than I've ever prayed in my life."

"Then there's your answer. Now, let's go."

When Steve's feet hit the ground under the lookout, he reached up, lifted Julia off the ladder, and set her on the ground.

"Steve, your phone is blinking."

He pulled it from its pocket. Steve unlocked it and displayed the text message.

"Is it from Jeff?"

"Yeah."

"Well, what does it say?"

"They had to stop and hide. I-5 is being closely monitored by the military. He has no clue when they will get to Happy Camp."

Chapter 17

Eli Vance's cane thumped on the floor of Hannan's private study. When his head appeared, the old man's face held the nearest thing to panic Hannan had ever seen.

"What's it now, Eli?"

Vance had been treading on Harrison Brown's turf for the past two weeks. Should Hannan replace Brown? No. It would be easier to let Brown think he was doing his job but let Eli do it for him.

Eli took a seat by the windows and Hannan swiveled in his office chair to face him.

"Abe, the Russians are testing your resolve."

"What are the Russians up to now?"

"Their nuclear subs are operating near our undersea data cables. You do realize what happens if they destroy one or more of those cables, don't you?" Eli's mustache twitched as it always did when the old man got nervous about something.

"Yes, we couldn't communicate with our friends in Europe, our wonderful allies who have forbid us from attending NATO meetings until further notice."

Eli coughed and shook his head. "We'd lose the ability to do electronic bank transactions and such. It would be disastrous."

"Okay, you threaten Russia with severe retaliation if they do anything."

"If they do anything?" Vance's bug-eyed stare clearly called Hannan a fool. "If they were to take down the right satellite, too, you would have no way to threaten them. Abe, you need to take care of some external national security threats, or the internal threats won't even matter."

"Now that you've warned me, you can go, Eli." Internal threats, external threats. Without the government hitting on all eight cylinders, things were spinning out of control. If he could just get the nation back under his control, he could then focus on foreign relations.

After Eli left, Hannan's thoughts turned to internal threats and to Deke, who was long overdue in reporting the results of his attack on Daniels and company.

What we have here is a failure to communicate.

And Deke would suffer the consequences. After all, he had been at the target area for at least three hours. How long did it take a thermobaric rocket or two to destroy a house and kill its inhabitants? Four or five seconds?

Hannan hit Deke's secure sat phone number on his call list and waited.

Two rings ... three rings ... four rings.

They got Blanchard, but no way could this ragtag bunch take out Deke after he ambushed Daniels and company.

A voice came through the phone. "Deke here."

It was not a confident sounding voice. At least the captain was alive, but depending on his news, that could change. "This is your Commander-in-Chief. Did you capture anyone or are they all dead?"

"Mr. President, sir ... we don't know, yet?"

"What?" Hannan squeezed the arm rest on his office chair until it broke off in his hand.

"Sir, we're still sifting through the burnt rubble looking for body parts."

"What have you found?"

"Well, nothing yet, sir. There's a lot of rubble."

And as soon as Hannan no longer needed Deke, that's what his military career would become ... a lot of rubble. "Tell me this, Captain Deke, did anyone get away?"

Silence.

"Deke?"

"A man carrying a woman entered the forest to the east. Half of my men are tracking them down, while the other half looks for bodies."

"I told you that, unless you could capture Bancroft, to take them all out. Total destruction. Now tell me, how did two of them get away?"

"But, sir, they—"

"Who shot first, Deke? You or them?"

"They did, sir. They killed one of my men, then we launched the rockets. Two at the house and one at the runners."

Not good. Somehow Daniels' band knew they were coming, despite the use of the secret stealth chopper. They were waiting for Deke and his men. "Who shot at you and where did they shoot from?"

"A man on the roof, Mr. President. We think it was the Israeli."

Great. "Mr. Levy. He's Sayeret Matkal. You won't find him in the rubble." Hannan paused. "You need to understand this, Deke. I degraded my security to send you to Oregon. This was a winner-take-all mission with risk involved. You're not going to find any bodies in the rubble. All seven got away. And you'd better find them or ..." Hannan stopped. He was running out of threats. If Deke ran or went rogue, Hannan had no one he could rely on to capture or kill Deke. "Just get them, Deke, especially Daniels. You do that and there's a big promotion waiting for you."

Chapter 18

With Julia hidden in a crevice on the south side of the huge monolith crowning Bolan peak, Steve ran down the mountain at top speed, trying to control his body. He had taken up too much time hiding Julia and then convincing her to stay hidden.

Now, he plotted his footsteps six or seven in advance, letting his trained reflexes guide his feet to the spots his vision had recorded while he scanned further ahead.

His route down the mountain took Steve around the shoulder of the peak, and nearly 400 yards from the route up the mountain used by his quarry. He might still have enough time to pull this off if he didn't stumble, start a rockslide, or anything else that would attract attention.

Julia's eyes still haunted him as they begged him not to go. Then, failing that, they begged him to promise that he would make sure Hannan's men would never touch her.

That got to him. After picturing her eyes, he struggled to concentrate on his dangerous descent. If he injured himself, his promises to Julia would all be broken.

Steve leaped a downed fir tree, landing on a patch of bare dirt. Good. He was below the rocky area near the mountain top. The dirt would provide better footing and reduce the noise from his footsteps.

Four hundred yards below him, the top of the tall snag appeared slightly to Steve's left. At this landmark, he planned to cut left and intersect the men's trail, hopefully behind them.

He slowed, taking greater care to silence his steps.

In another two minutes, the sounds of several men moving up the mountain came from below him, to his left.

He cut toward them using vegetation for cover.

They muttered, discussing something.

Steve crept closer and peered through fir bows.

One of the men pulled binoculars from his face and pointed up at the lookout. An argument ensued. Maybe about what to do regarding the head staring at them from the lookout window.

While the men continued their argument, their focus was on one another and the peak.

Steve used the time and a small stand of trees to move behind the six men, who were only a quarter-mile below the cliff. He had to strike before they reached the cliff.

He crept slowly toward them, stopping when he reached the edge of the trees.

While Steve watched, the argument between the Hannanis ended with five heads nodding in unison.

The sixth head held a pouting face.

As the other five continued up the mountainside, the loser lagged behind. He also carried an RPG launcher across his back, and a quiver with two arrows in it, arrows with fat thermobaric warheads.

Using the stealthy movements Steve had learned for stalking human prey, he moved from trees to rocks, using whatever cover the mountain afforded. He continued dogging the laggard, hoping the other five wouldn't look back. Fear that they might turn around kept Steve from going as fast as he would've liked. Nevertheless, he quickly closed ground between him and the man carrying the RPG launcher.

The group of five was no more than 300 yards below the cliff face.

Steve had only two or three minutes left. If he let the time expire and the chopper showed up, he and Julia would both die.

Though the situation was not ideal, he would have to make his move now. Timing it so his prey was near a large boulder, Steve charged.

The man tensed and stopped as Steve approached in bounding strides. The soldier swiveled toward Steve and tried to raise his rifle. He was a fraction of a second too late.

Steve took the man down rolling him behind the boulder and ended this man's participation in the battle, permanently.

Only two of the men carried launchers. The odds were 50-50 that this man had tried to kill Julia. Killing was never something one wanted to do, but Steve found it hard to feel badly about taking this man's life.

Steve quickly slipped the launcher and rockets from the soldier then pulled his shirt off. Steve slipped the man's shirt on, hoping this would slow recognition that he was the enemy.

Two hundred yards ahead, the other five approached the base of the cliff.

Steve was out of time. He sprinted straight up the mountain toward the cluster of five men in the distance.

He slowed as one man glanced his way, then accelerated when the man's attention turned to the rock face in front of them.

When approaching the base of this cliff, it appeared that the only way to reach the lookout on top was to climb up the cliff. A notch on the cliff face provided a fairly easy climb to the top. But the five men seemed reluctant to expose themselves on a cliff face where they would have no cover.

Steve closed within a hundred yards, keeping a small fir tree between him and the group of five.

They appeared to be discussing how to climb this cliff to reach the lookout. By this time, they must know that the head peering at them was not a real live human being.

Though the timing was not quite right for him to attack, Steve had to take them out now and return to Julia.

Steve loaded the launcher with a rocket and prepared to fire.

One of the five pointed his direction and barked out a command.

The other four swiveled toward him.

Steve launched the rocket.

It ignited with a whoosh and a flash and pushed Steve's shoulder backward.

One man raised his gun.

Steve ducked, covering his face before the blinding flash could sear his eyes.

He replayed the rocket launch in his mind. The rocket had headed for a spot a few yards to the left of the men. Close enough. It would either kill or injure them all, taking them out of the fight.

Steve scanned his targets.

Five men down. No one moving. Now to rescue Julia.

He loaded the last rocket into the launcher and began his sprint up the mountain, around the cliff to the place near the lookout where he had hidden Julia.

With only a hundred yards to go, Steve slowed. Looking across the flat top of Bolan peak, the lookout lay to his left. The crevice in the rock, where he'd hidden Julia, lay to his right.

With a whoosh and a muffled roar, a helicopter leaped up over the peak in front of Steve.

He had no time to hide.

The strange looking chopper rotated a side door toward him and an M240 with a man on the other end swung his way.

No gunfire. What was happening? Was the shirt he wore causing them to hesitate.

He scanned the scene in front of him.

A figure in denim shorts appeared on top of a large rock in plain view of the chopper. Julia.

Now she waved her arms at the killing machine.

She had drawn the pilot's attention and the chopper pilot rotated the side door, filled with an M240, toward her.

Steve's violent heartbeats threatened to rip open his chest as he prepared the rocket for firing.

While the people on the chopper may not have known who Steve was, they recognized Julia as their enemy.

She just stood there waving her arms.

The M240's staccato cracking kicked up a deadly line of dirt and rocks that exploded into the air.

The line of destruction from large caliber bullets that would tear a human body to shreds moved across the ground straight at her.

Steve yanked the launcher onto his shoulder and prayed as he fired the rocket.

Julia's body toppled off the rock to the ground behind it.

The rocket penetrated the Stealth Hawk. A huge ball of fire filled the sky followed by the concussion of the powerful explosion.

The helicopter dropped to the top of the cliff. It exploded again, then tumbled down the cliff face, sending a trail of fire downward to the bottom of the cliff and into the trees beyond.

Now a roaring wild fire had been ignited.

How many of Deke's men had been on the chopper? There was no way to know.

Steve turned away from the fire and sprinted toward the spot where Julia had fallen. When he reached her, she had risen to her knees.

She stretched her arms toward him.

His eyes scanned every inch of her body looking for blood or any other signs of injury.

There were none. He released the breath he'd been holding.

She met his gaze, body shaking, and a weak smile on her lips. "You came back for me."

She wasn't hurt, only frightened. But she had violated her word to stay hidden. To save his life, this woman had walked into what was almost certain death.

That thought stopped his words, strong words that his emotions wanted to assault her with, a tongue-lashing she would never forget.

Their gazes locked.

A mixture of fear, uncertainty, and something far more tender in her eyes washed away his anger, completely.

Now she was in his arms clinging to him as if she would never let go. Her body shook.

"Julia ... I told you—"

"Steve ... I broke my word, but don't be mad, please."

Arms around her, Steve looked down into her eyes. "If you ever—"

"I won't. I promise. But this time, I didn't have a choice."

Didn't have a choice? He didn't have time to dwell on her meaning. "We need to get off this mountain, now. I hit five of the men with a rocket. They went down, but I don't know if they're all out of the fight."

"What about the other man?"

"He's out of the fight, permanently."

"So what do we do now?"

Steve ditched the launcher and the empty rocket quiver, then shucked the shirt he'd slipped on.

"Where are the bottles of water you took?"

"Behind me in the crevice where I hid." She whirled, stepped down into the crack in the rock, and returned with the water.

Steve shoved the water into his small pack and locked his hand around Julia's wrist.

She locked her hand around his wrist.

He pointed down the mountain. "We've got to run as far and as fast as possible. But we've got two choices. You make the call."

"Me? Steve, you're the expert—"

"It's your body we'll be taxing to the limits. We can go sixteen miles across mountainous terrain to Happy Camp, or twenty-four miles by dirt road, a mostly downhill marathon."

"I've never run a marathon. I'm a sprinter. We run like crazy for a hundred meters and stop."

"And we haven't eaten since yesterday. So we go sixteen miles through mountains?"

"No, Steve. I want to try the marathon. At least we'll have a road to run on."

"You sure, Jules?"

She nodded.

"Okay ... we go down the mountain first, perpendicular to the Happy Camp road, leaving them bogus a trail in case anyone tries to follow. After a while, we stop leaving a trail."

Julia gave him a weak smile. "Lead the way."

Steve turned to the southwest. "Remember to drag a foot every once in a while and kick a few rocks loose, until I say stop."

"Got it."

He tugged her arm and they were off, running down the mountain.

Eight minutes later, about a mile below the lookout, a large rock outcropping appeared ahead. Steve slowed to a walk as they moved out onto the rocks, then he pulled Julia to a stop.

"Now we walk softly, leave no tracks, and we head toward Grayback Road. Ready for a walk?"

"Can I have some water first?" She looked a bit winded, but still seemed strong and game.

He pulled her water bottle from his pack. "Only two swallows."

After eight minutes of walking, they approached Grayback Road. "Before we expose ourselves on the road, I need to check for Deke and company." Steve scanned the mountainside above and checked the sky for any low-flying aircraft. Nothing. They were clear to go.

He studied Julia sitting on a tree stump, resting. She had one shoe off and was checking her heel.

"Do you have a blister?"

She looked up. "No, just a little sore spot."

"We need to take care of our feet. They keep us alive. Let me know if it gets any worse."

She nodded and put her shoe on.

"Twenty-three miles left to Happy Camp. You ready for this?"

She nodded. "Lead the way."

They were off and running, again.

As the morning sun rose higher in the cloudless sky, the day grew hot. Too hot for a marathon. Steve's shirt was wet enough to ring out the sweat.

He slowed to a stop as Julia fiddled with her blouse. She unbuttoned the lower buttons and tied it as high as possible above her waist.

They each took two swigs of water.

Despite their situation, it was impossible to ignore Julia's shapely body. Even with her sweaty hair, the perspiration making dust tracks down her cheeks, she was beautiful. But her ability to draw physical strength from a mysterious reservoir somewhere deep inside of her feminine exterior, was an even greater attraction.

Julia Weiss was a woman full of mysteries, and it seemed she had won the last bit of Steve Bancroft's heart. That was frightening, yet at the same time exhilarating. But what was she doing?

She wasn't running in a straight line and her stride was uneven, almost off-balance.

Steve pulled Julia to a stop. "Something's wrong. What is it?"

"I'm just a little tired. How far have we come?"

"About twelve miles."

"Halfway?"

"Yeah. Now tell me how you feel. You're shaking. I can see that. What else?"

"I feel a little weaker than I should, dizzy, and my headache is making me nauseous."

"It's low blood sugar. We can't have you vomiting. That would give us a real problem." He looked down the road. They had been running a series of switchbacks for the past two miles. One more lay ahead before the road approached the creek lined with bushes and trees. "Can you make it to the next switchback?"

"I think so."

"There's food ahead. Blackberries. They grow all over southern Oregon and Northern California."

"How do you know that?"

"Survival training. And ripe blackberries are packed with sugar. They'll stop your symptoms and keep you going for a while, provided you get some fluids in you."

After they rounded the switchback, Steve pulled her off the road toward the creek. The blackberry bushes were loaded with berries, ripened by the August sun.

A small flock of birds squawked their protest as he and Julia drove them away from their feast.

Steve pulled out the water bottles and studied Julia standing by the blackberry bushes.

She had already crammed her mouth full of berries. Purple juice ran down onto her chin.

"Stop gorging. It'll make you sick."

She chomped on the berries deliberately squirting out more purple juice. "I'm not gorging, just replacing blood sugar."

"You said you were nauseous. Did you know that overexertion, dehydration, and low blood sugar are all causes of vomiting?" He shoved her water bottle at her. "Here drink some water."

She finished chewing the mouthful of berries, tilted her head back and took a swig of the water, then pointed up the mountain. "Look, Steve."

Two figures ran down the road, several switchbacks above them.

Julia crouched behind the berry bushes. "How far away are they?"

Steve knelt beside her. "About two miles, unless they start taking shortcuts across the switchbacks."

They had to outrun them, or outsmart them. Julia had nearly hit the wall a few minutes ago and the blackberries weren't going to keep her going for twelve more miles. "Julia..."

She looked up at him hopeful and expectant, with trust in her eyes.

Steve's phone tickled his side. He pulled it out. "It's Jeff. Let's see what he has to say before we make any decisions. Eat some more berries, but don't gorge."

She pulled more berries off the vines as Steve put the phone to his ear.

"Steve here."

"Are you both okay?"

"Yeah. Were halfway to Happy Camp. Had some action on the mountain. I'll fill you in on the details later. We've got to go now. Two of Deke's crew are dogging us, about two miles up the mountain."

"Wanted to let you know we're moving again. We're on old Highway 99, almost to Ashland. If no problems arise, we'll reach Happy Camp in about three hours."

"Listen, Jeff, if you don't see us before you get into Happy Camp, go through the village and up Grayback Road. We'll flag you down when you get close. But keep in mind that if these two men see the van, they'll have a description. Getting to Eastern Oregon alive could get a bit iffy. Gotta run now." Steve ended the call.

If the men saw the van ...

Steve must ensure that they couldn't.

"Come on, Julia. Jeff and the others are about three hours out, so we've got some evading to do."

Julia swallowed a mouthful of berries. "Can't we just outrun them?"

"Are you up to that?"

She smiled and purple juice ran out the corners of her mouth. "Sprinters are always good for another half marathon."

"Really? I thought they just ran like crazy for about ten seconds then stopped."

"Nah. I'm juiced now. Let's go."

He looked at the purple stains around her mouth, covering her lips. "That you are."

Ten minutes later, Steve stopped behind a Madrone tree big enough to hide them and stop bullets. He waited for the two men to come into view. He pulled out his NOD, now on a daytime setting, and scanned the switchbacks on the lower part of the mountain.

In a few seconds, they appeared on the last switchback by the creek. Only a mile and a half away, now. By their dirty uniforms, they appeared to be a captain and a sergeant.

Steve looked at Julia who stared up at him from where she sat at the base of the tree. "We need to hide here and ambush them."

Julia's face morphed from wide-eyed shock to mortal pain. "You can't just murder them."

"It's not murder. They're trying to kill us, Julia. This is self-defense."

She didn't reply.

For the past five minutes, Julia had sat with her arms folded, silent. At least she would be safe behind the big tree when the shooting started.

Up the road, the sounds of footsteps crunching in the dusty gravel on the shoulder of the road grew louder.

Steve knelt in firing position and aimed his gun.

He glanced her way.

Julia covered her face and tears ran through her fingers.

He tried to ignore her words of protest, her crying. He should've been able to ignore it all and do his job. But could he?

Two men stepped into view on the road.

Steve aimed at the sergeant's chest, then slowly, almost involuntarily, the gun barrel lowered. The gun cracked in rapid-fire as he shot a short burst, swinging his aim across the man's legs.

The sergeant went down hard. He'd never fight again without a new set of knees.

Deke dove for the ditch.

Steve sprayed bullets, but they only kicked up dirt on the bank above Deke's head.

Steve studied the ditch, barely deep enough to hide a man. He watched for a couple of minutes. Still no Deke.

Fifty yards up the road a quick movement caught his eye.

Steve turned and fired, but Deke had made it into the trees.

"We've got to go, now, Julia!" He pulled her to her feet, then shot a long burst into the trees where Deke had disappeared, heading up the mountain away from their position.

If he got Julia around the next bend in the road, they could probably outrun a cautious Captain Deke. And the terrain plus the vegetation would give Deke no shots at them if they maintained their lead.

Alone, without his chopper, it was hard to guess what Deke might do. If he had some kind of support left in the Cave Junction area, he would probably return and Steve and Julia would be safe. But Steve couldn't count on that.

He pulled Julia into a run, which she seemed to welcome, and she kept his hand as they ran. What did that mean?

Five minutes later, Julia squeezed his hand. "Steve ..." Her words came chopped apart by heavy breaths. "What about the ... wounded man? I know ... you didn't kill him... because..."

"Yeah... because..."

A single sharp crack sounded in the distance behind them. "I didn't kill him, but Deke just did."

No reply from Julia. She kept his hand in hers and simply ran, staring down the road ahead of them.

What was she thinking? Did it even matter with this seemingly unbridgeable chasm between them? Steve shut off the troubling questions and ran down the dusty road.

Soon pulsations came through his hand and ran up his arm. He glanced at Julia. Her eyes were wide, glassy looking, like she was facing death. She ran with an uneven gait, limping on her right leg.

Steve scanned her bare leg down to her cross trainers. Blood painted an ankle red and the back of her right shoe wasn't a dusty white anymore. It was dark red.

He pulled her off the road toward the creek and hid behind some bushes. "Why didn't you say something, Julia? I could've—"

"No, Steve. We had to run. I could've gotten you killed if we'd stopped."

She might still get them killed by dissuading him from shooting Deke, but this wasn't the time for that discussion.

Steve pulled off her shoe and winced as he saw the slab of skin missing from her heel. He'd seen men try to run with lesser injuries to their feet. They had all failed. Somehow, Julia drew on an inner strength that still puzzled him.

He had a small medical bag in his pack, but this foot would take too long to doctor and she still wouldn't be able to run on it.

He dropped her bloody shoe in her hands, scooped up Julia and stood.

"No, Steve. Please don't carry me. I can—"

"This is the best way to beat Deke." Steve checked the road above them, then ran toward Happy Camp.

When he picked up the pace to a sprint, Julia laid her head on his shoulder and cried softly.

What was going through that head of hers? What was going through that soft head of his? If he had done his job, they wouldn't be running now and Julia's heel wouldn't look like freshly ground hamburger.

Steve's arms ached, now. His blood sugar had long since bottomed. Julia had nearly slipped from his hot sweaty arms several times, but Happy Camp finally came into view.

He picked a sheltered spot along the road, a place with a view up the road in case Deke wandered in. They would wait here for the van.

It might be a long, lonely wait, as Julia hadn't spoken a word since he scooped her up and began the final run. She seemed to be deep in thought where he'd set her down in the grass by a Maple tree.

A good sign, or a bad one? He'd wait for her to tell him. Right now, he needed hydration or his body would rebel against the abuse he'd given it over the past two hours. Steve guzzled water as fast as his stomach could tolerate it.

A silent two hours later, a white van rolled through the village toward their hiding place. Steve recognized Jeff in the driver's seat.

When the van approached, Steve flagged it down and climbed in behind Julia.

Benjamin's smiling face surprised him. He'd had no confirmation that Benjamin was still alive after Jeff's house was nuked.

He and Julia took the empty seat in front of Brock and KC in the back row.

Benjamin cocked his head. "Steve, you look like you saw a ghost? "

"I thought *you* might be one."

"That's not theologically correct." Brock's voice came from the back seat.

Steve shook his head. "But you get the drift. So, what happened when they blew Jeff's house all to blazes?"

Benjamin grinned. "I had made it to the trap door when the overpressure hit. It blew me out the door, but I landed on my feet, running full speed, and I didn't stop until I reached the church."

"We all got away, somehow," Jeff said. "But, right now, we need to park before we reach I-5. It's nearly three o'clock. We can leave about ten o'clock this evening, after dark."

"Let's drive a few miles toward I-5 and then hide his van for a while," Brock said. "It looks like a couple of us need some rest."

Steve looked at Jeff in the driver's seat. "How safe are we in the van?"

"Darkness will eliminate satellite detection," Brock said. "But this is a pink area. There are a few Hannan supporters, so we have to evade the police. If they get a description of the van ... we're toast."

Jeff nodded as he drove away. "Yeah, bro. Even taking the back roads to Eastern Oregon doesn't eliminate all the risk. We still have a few miles to go on I-5 and an hour or so along Highway 97 before we head into the back country."

Steve reached for Julia's ankle, spun her around in the seat, placing her ankle in his lap.

She didn't say anything. Wouldn't meet his searching gaze.

He started cleaning and dressing her heel. "One chopper could take us all out, giving Hannan a huge victory to crow about. He'd get some more supporters if he pulled that off."

Julia still remained quiet staring at the floorboard while he dressed her ankle.

Brock snorted his disgust. "If that happens and the red states start caving, it's curtains for the USA."

Allie sighed. "Then we need to pray that we make it back to Central Oregon tonight, safely."

Julia's tears started flowing again. She met Steve's gaze, as he finished dressing her wound, and mouthed the words, "I'm so sorry."

Steve was sorry, too. Sorry he'd let Julia influence him. Sorry he hadn't killed Deke, who now could help Hannan locate them.

Despite his sorry state, her words warmed his heart. But a lot of relational damage had been done in the last three hours. Knowing that and the danger that lay ahead of them, though he was dog tired, he'd probably miss another night of sleep.

Chapter 19

Surely Captain Deke, with his remaining men and a Stealth Hawk, could find seven people running around on the ground, trying to hide. So why hadn't Deke reported in?

In the past, it had been because of bad news. Whatever the news was, Hannan wanted it now. He hit Deke's secure phone number and waited.

"Captain Deke here, Mr. President."

Hannan listened. No background noise. Even the Stealth Hawk would make enough to hear over the phone. "Where are you, Deke?"

"Sir, I'm about thirty miles south of our original target."

"I don't hear the chopper. Don't tell me you ran over those mountains."

"As a matter of fact, I did, sir. At least most of the way."

"So you ran after Daniels?"

"Uh ... no, sir. It turned out to be the Ranger and the Weiss girl."

"Where in the blazes are Daniels and Banning?"

"They ... uh ... got away."

"Didn't you send the chopper after them?"

"We thought they went into the mountains. We attacked their position this morning, only to find we'd been lured away by that Ranger."

"And a girl who just got over Ebola. Brilliant, Deke. Did you get them? Where's the chopper? What's the status of your team?"

Silence.

The churning in Hannan's stomach was soon going to produce nausea, or something just as compelling, that would send him running for his private bathroom. "Give me your status, now, or I'll rip those bars off your uniform myself."

"I have information, sir."

"I'll take that later. Status. Now! You ..." Hannan's slurs spared no part of Deke's family tree.

After Hannan ended his tirade, a sharp blast of air came through the phone from Deke's end. "Sir, all of my men are dead. The Stealth Hawk was shot down and destro—"

"Deke! I can't believe I actually trusted you to oversee my personal security in case of an attack. You can't even protect yourself when *you're* doing the attacking." Hannan fought for control to get the last bit of useful information Deke might have. "Did you kill any of Daniels' group?"

"Maybe one. We're not sure."

Hannan lowered his voice though he wanted to scream at the man. His tone would convey the message Deke needed to hear. "You're fired."

Deke would know what he meant. It was a death sentence, unless Deke was a man of many disguises.

"Mr. President, don't you want to hear my full report?"

"Why? You accomplished nothing except to get twelve men killed and a 200-million-dollar, top-secret aircraft destroyed."

"If you refuse to hear it, you'll never know."

Impertinence. Sarcasm. Hannan had heard enough from this incompetent commander of cowards. First Blanchard and now Deke. Hannan only needed a few good men. This president's army was supposed to be full of such. Why couldn't he find them?

What about all the men you riffed and forced out for their religious beliefs?

He refused to answer that question. Trained warfighters were trained warfighters.

But are they truly warriors?

He shoved the second question from his mind.

"Well?" Deke said.

He might as well hear this. "Okay, survivor, give me the good news."

"I picked up their trail after the ambush and—"

"Ambush? You mean *they* ambushed *you*? I thought—"

"Mr. President, do you want my report or not?"

"Go ahead."

"After they killed my weapons sergeant, I followed them to the edge of Happy Camp."

"Is that all you have."

'No. They hid there for a couple of hours ..."

Deke was obviously dragging this out. Probably his way of getting a measure of revenge for being fired.

Hannan waited.

Silence.

He'd never heard this level of disrespect from Deke. But getting fired can do that to a man with a big ego. "Alright, tell me the good news."

"They got into a white Chevy van, about six or seven years old. The van turned around and headed east on Highway 96, toward I-5."

So they were headed back to Eastern Oregon. There was only one way to end this stalemate and Hannan wanted it ended now. These six people—or was it seven—had given him far too much trouble and, in the process, wiped out two Ranger detachments, a Stealth Hawk and left only the incompetent and not-so-loyal Captain Deke alive.

Maybe this was a good thing after all. He'd found what Deke was made of before Hannan had to trust the man with POTUS's life on the line.

It was time to call in an army to take out Daniels and company. No more black ops. No more detachments of special warfighters. He would bring a whole company after these rebels, with an arsenal that could wipe out an entire city.

"Sir?" Deke's voice sounded far too confident after the meager information he'd given Hannan.

"Deke, you're still fired."

"What if I get Daniels for you?"

"You tried that and failed. Got all your men killed."

"No, sir. I think some were only wounded."

"You think? What's that creed that you guys recite say about that?"

"I didn't leave them in the hands of the enemy."

"Blast it, Deke! You get my drift. You're a failure and—"

"But what if I complete the mission and get Brock Daniels?"

"I'm not giving you any more men."

"But I'll need access to intel, sir?"

"You can have that. If you manage to kill Daniels, and have proof, maybe I'll reconsider."

"Don't worry, Mr. President. When I kill Brock Daniels, you will have ample proof."

Hannan terminated the call.

Deke had to know that there was no place for him in Hannan's future plans, no place for failure. Deke was expendable. He had to earn his way back to Hannan's good graces or the man was dead. Knowing that, Deke was certainly motivated enough to do the job, but could he?

His words played again in Hannan's mind. "Don't worry, Mr. President. When I kill Brock Daniels, you will have ample proof."

He had sounded sure of himself, not cocky and not desperate.

So what did Deke know that he hadn't told Hannan? He knew something. Regardless, with a company of Rangers, 200 highly trained executioners, Hannan didn't need Deke.

Where Daniels and company would go next wasn't hard to deduce. It wasn't like they had many options left. They would be found in Central Oregon, surrounded by an overwhelming force, killed, and roasted by the media with all kinds of manufactured evidence, exposing Daniels as a ruthless, deceiving, power-hungry young man.

In the wake of Daniels' death, Hannan could already see the red states recanting and the entire resistance crumbling. Then, he could end martial law and give the people what the progressives wanted, not that he gave a rip about that. Most of the citizens would love him, certainly those with a hand stretched out to the government. The others would be silent or they'd be prosecuted as criminals. And Hannan would rule until he grew tired of the role and passed it on to a person of his choosing.

With Daniels gone, life would be good and Hannan's legacy would be a tribute to his greatness among all the world leaders in human history. He was so close to having it all and only one person stood in his way ... a twenty-four-year-old kid with delusions of grandeur.

Chapter 20

The Van couldn't have been more than fifteen minutes from Happy Camp when Julia hit the wall. Fatigue she hadn't experienced since her bout with Ebola turned her body into a blob of silly putty that seem to be conforming to the shape of Steve's shoulder.

They had only exchanged three words in the past four hours, "I'm so sorry." Julia's words. But they seemed to be enough to melt the polar ice cap that had formed after the shooting incident.

Steve leaned back in the seat and Julia's head slid into a comfortable position against his neck. She turned toward him and nestled into this place of security and ... maybe much more.

His arm curled around her shoulders and his hand slid down her side until it found her hand.

Almost instinctively Julia's free arm reached around Steve's waist. What would the others think seeing her wrapped around Steve and in his embrace? She had never allowed any man to hold her, let alone so intimately.

Exhausted, and with every muscle in her body aching from the brutal run, she didn't care what anyone thought. This felt too good to worry about trivial things.

Julia woke from her nap when the van stopped.

Jeff eased it forward, bouncing gently on its shocks and then brought it to a complete stop.

Benjamin stood and opened the side door. "I'll watch the main highway to make sure no one is curious about our hiding place."

KC's hand touched Julia's shoulder. "Get some rest you two. You need it. Brock and I want to check out the Klamath River."

"Don't expose yourself along the river," Benjamin said. "There may be fishermen and boats."

"We'll stay hidden." Brock's voice.

"Allie and I just want to walk around a bit, stretch our legs. But we'll watch the van," Jeff said as the van bounced to the rhythm of Allie's footsteps.

The van bounced again, then the driver's door closed.

Julia was alone with Steve. So very tired, but no longer sleepy. She closed her eyes to rest them.

"You okay, Jules?" Steve's voice was low and soothing as he spoke softly near her ear. His first words in nearly five hours.

"Mmmhmmm. Except for the blister on my heel."

Steve's muscles flexed, as he leaned forward.

"Don't move, please. My foot is fine."

Steve relaxed beside her again and adjusted his arms, cradling Julia even more snugly. "You probably should try to sleep. We'll be traveling most of the night tonight."

"Shouldn't you sleep, too, Steve?"

"I'm tired, but a little..." His voice trailed off as he mumbled something that sounded like "distracted."

In his arms, she was a distraction? Julia smiled, but kept her eyes closed. Now that Steve was talking to her again, she needed to keep the conversation going until they had worked through the events of five hours ago and their aftermath. "I must smell awful after all that running?"

173

"I've smelled worse."

"Steve, that's no way to—"

"You ought to smell a detachment of Rangers when it's a hundred and twenty in Afghanistan. But you're different. I've never smelled anyone so..."

"Can we talk about something besides BO?" Another subject came to mind, but Julia didn't want to destroy this moment. She rephrased her question. "How long can a guy be a Ranger?"

"Once guys reach thirty-five or so, it's pretty tough. I've heard it gets really hard to stay in top shape. But then I hadn't planned to go career when I enlisted."

Good. Steve had taken the subject where she wanted. "What about now?"

"I still plan to get out at some point."

"When's your current enlistment up?"

"In about ninety days. But—"

"But your enlistment could be in limbo in ninety days if Hannan's still around." Julia opened her eyes and looked up at Steve's face.

He clenched his jaw. "Yeah. But any way you look at it, his days are numbered."

At the moment, Julia was concerned that her days with Steve might be numbered. Craig wanted Steve in DC. Deke wanted Steve dead. And she wanted him right where he was, by her side. "Did you make any plans for after you leave the Army?"

"I ... well ... Julia, I did two rotations in Afghanistan. I saw kids orphaned by the war. I saw little girls married off to what in America we call pedophiles. I saw young boys abused by perverts in positions of authority. The US government told us it was just their culture, but it was pure evil embedded in their worldview—reduce people to nothing more than a man's property and you can do anything you want to them. I was ordered to ignore it, all of it." Steve's voice grew intense. "But I couldn't. I did some things that could have gotten me in a lot of trouble, but Craig bailed me out." Steve's sigh sounded more like a moan. "If I knew how, I'd like to help kids who have no one to care for and protect them."

Had someone told Steve to tell her this? Someone who knew her hopes and dreams. Maybe Jeff or Allie? "You're not pulling my leg are you?"

"No. Do I need to? You got a charley horse after all that running?"

She'd given herself a lot of reasons not to fall for a man like Steve. But since she first met him, she had a feeling there was more to Steve than her concept of a warrior. And she had misjudged him, badly. But even worse, she'd said things she shouldn't have.

Julia tried to blink back her tears, but they fell, followed by a steady stream that ran down her cheeks and splashed onto Steve's hand.

"What's wrong, Julia? You're crying."

"My dream..." Her voice broke, more tears came. When her voice returned it quivered as she tried to speak. "My dream was to start an orphanage somewhere in Central America. But that's almost impossible for a young, single woman to do on her own." She stopped. Had she said too much?

Steve didn't reply. He remained silent, holding her for a moment. His lips kissed her forehead, tenderly.

How could two people with such different views on important issues share the same dream? But it was true. And Steve's skills and his drive to protect others, after the guilt from his sister's death, could certainly protect Julia and a group of orphans.

Was God orchestrating something here?

The van bounced on its shocks as Benjamin bounded through the door. Steve's body tensed and he dropped Julia's hand.

"Stand down, Steve. No reason to get excited, yet. But I've seen two state patrol cars pass by on the highway in the past fifteen minutes. And we're out here in the middle of nowhere."

Brock now stood beside the open van door with KC behind him. "Which way were they headed?"

Benjamin's long sigh sounded like a punctured tire. "*Toward* Happy Camp."

The magical moment had ended. Steve sat up in the seat. "Deke. I'd bet on it. He's putting the word out about us."

Julia had caused this. The sick feeling in her stomach grew to a nauseating knot. "I'm so sorry, Steve. It was my fault. I ..." She couldn't say the words. They would paint Steve in a bad light, too.

Steve looked down, peering deeply into her eyes. His look was intense, but she saw no condemnation.

"It's not your fault, Jules." He spoke softly. "I was the one who aimed the gun and pulled the trigger."

But she had influenced him. How could something she thought was right be so wrong? Julia had endangered everyone. She shouldn't be in this group. All she did was put their lives at risk.

A thought hit her so hard it flew out her mouth before she could stop it. "If that rocket had killed me, you would all be safe."

Oh-no. Jeff and Allie were back. Julia had spoken too loudly. They had all heard her.

Benjamin's gaze swung back and forth between her and Steve. He obviously understood the issue but wasn't going to weigh in on it.

Steve cupped her chin and turned Julia's face toward his. "Jules, that's not the way to look at it. I made a mistake, but we're all okay. Rangers simply thank God they're still alive and plan their next move."

"That goes for Sayeret Matkal too," Benjamin said as he looked into her eyes. He had probably deduced what happened but, like Steve, there was no condemnation in Benjamin's eyes.

Julia didn't doubt their sincerity, but the truth didn't make her feel any better. Because the truth was she held too much sway over Steve. Yes, it meant he cared for her, but it also meant she could get them all killed if she tried to influence Steve to do anything other than follow his Ranger training and instincts.

Julia opened her mouth to voice her concern, then stopped when Steve's satellite phone lit and flashed, indicating an incoming call.

Steve pulled out the phone. "It's Craig."

Julia could guess where this phone conversation was going.

"Sir, permission to put this on the speakerphone? ... I know, Sir ... If we can't trust this group were toast ... No, I have no problem with them hearing anything as long as it doesn't put you or your mission in jeopardy." Steve switched on the speakerphone and the team crowded around Steve and Julia.

He placed the phone on the seat beside her.

"Captain Craig, here. How can I say this? I am so proud of you, all of you. You've performed on a par with a trained military force. Now, moving on to the main topic ... what is the status of Captain Deke's Ranger detachment?"

Steve leaned toward the phone. "All of Deke's men are dead or severely wounded, but Deke got away about ten miles north of Happy Camp."

"That's good news, Sergeant Bancroft. I don't think Hannan will be anxious to replace Deke's men after he lost eleven of them."

"Twelve, sir. He lost a Stealth Hawk and its pilot, too."

"Good grief, Bancroft! What have you been up to?"

"You don't want to know, sir. Suffice it to say, after Julia saved my life by flagging down the Stealth Hawk before it could fire on me, I took it out with a stolen thermobaric rocket and a grenade launcher."

"And Miss Weiss wasn't injured?"

"She's sitting right beside me, looking fine. Just a little tired after a five mile run up a mountain and a downhill marathon this morning, twenty-four miles."

"This is the Julia Weiss who had Ebola six weeks ago?"

"One and the same, sir."

Julia's cheeks grew warm. At least as warm as the looks Steve was giving her as he laid on a thick coat of praise.

"Now for the news." Craig paused. "I received news about an hour ago from a source I cannot disclose that Kingsley Air Force Base just went red."

Silence in the van.

"Well, somebody say something," Craig said.

"Sir, might there be traitors still among the people on the base?"

"Bancroft, Hannan thinks they're *all* traitors. But, no. I heard that the entire fighter wing, which is mostly Air Guards, pledged allegiance to the Constitution and is opposing Hannan. And they are not acting under the command of Oregon's true blue Governor ... for obvious reasons."

Steve frowned. "But doesn't the adjoining civilian airport cause security concerns, sir."

"Rumor has it that the base commander, fighter wing commander, and commander of the security forces had a heart-to-heart talk with the airport director and the operations manager. Other than a Hannan lone wolf attack there—"

"Lone wolf *for* Hannan? I don't think so, sir." Steve chuckled.

"Only lone wolf Deke," Julia spoke softly to Steve.

"Whose voice was that, Bancroft?"

"Julia, sir."

"And she was talking to you in that voice?"

"Yes, I believe so, sir."

"Now, how can I compete with that?"

"I don't believe you can, sir."

Julia looked at Steve and their gazes locked, warm, inviting, but Julia knew what was coming.

"Bancroft ... we need you back here. We need you, badly. Hannan's not going to replace Deke's men. He'll never trust Deke after your team nearly wiped them all out. So Hannan's not well protected, unless he runs for the DUCC."

KC moved toward the sat phone. "Craig, KC here."

"Ms. Banning ... I mean Mrs. Daniels. Good to hear from you. I'll bet you're going to tell me something about the DUCC."

"Yes. As soon as you're finished with Steve."

"Back to Sergeant Bancroft then. We've got a pilot at Kingsley who can fly you to a destination near DC. With one stop on the way, he can have you out here within five hours of departure from Kingsley, maybe faster if he pushes it. For our assault, we might need some innovative explosives work."

Julia bit her lower lip and prayed that somehow Steve wouldn't go. But that wasn't a realistic expectation.

Steve leaned over the phone. "Getting to Kingsley could be a bit dicey. We'll have to proceed cautiously, and won't you need KC's help *before* I come, sir?"

"Eastern Oregon is getting redder by the minute. My guess is that all of Oregon but the Willamette Valley will go red. Steve, after KC plants her Trojan Horse and gets the information we need, you should head for Kingsley, immediately. We don't know how long our window of opportunity will remain open."

Chapter 21

"What time is it, Steve," Julia whispered from his shoulder, her pillow since they had pulled out of their hiding place along Highway 26.

The van slowed.

"It's time to get on I-5, Jules. About 2230."

The van's turn pressed her more snugly against Steve, a place she was coming to cherish. Also, a place she could lose forever when Steve left for DC to help Craig with the dangerous assault on Hannan.

"Next stop, Weed." Jeff's voice came from the front of the van.

"If we don't get stopped along I-5," Brock said.

Allie turned from her seat beside Jeff and looked toward the back of the van. "Well, I'm not going to stop praying until we exit at Weed."

Jeff accelerated onto the freeway.

Inside the van it grew quiet.

Steve's body stiffened ever so slightly against hers. He was watching, guarding. It was who Steve was, a protector. His experiences had in part made him that way, but it seemed his willingness to fight and kill if necessary came from something even deeper.

A thought hit Julia like the ring of a wake-up call. The whole issue must be a matter of conscience. For Steve, the warrior, his conscience told him he must kill evil aggressors to save innocent people, while her conscience told her never to kill a human being. And, didn't the Bible say people shouldn't violate their consciences, because that was like knowingly disobeying God?

If that was true, then she was wrong to try stopping Steve from doing what he believed was his duty.

This conclusion could remove the mountain between them and resolve the issue that prevented her from committing to a relationship with Steve. He had practically proposed to her at one point. He said he had been looking for someone to spend his life with and found no one until she came along.

But Julia's answer, based on conscience, seemed too simplistic. Did it square with God's moral absolutes? It *was* a bit relativistic. That's what Brock would say, just before he destroyed her reasoning with apologetical arguments and theology. He would say killing was either right or wrong and she needed to come to a conclusion, the correct conclusion.

But not tonight. She would cling to her simple answer for now, and Brock didn't have to know anything about it.

A second wake-up came as a blow to the side of her head. Steve's arm had bumped her as he swiveled in his seat to look back. "Jeff, there's a vehicle in the left lane that's been closing fast for the past mile. Just now, it slowed and swung in behind us."

Seats creaked throughout the van as everyone turned to look.

Benjamin, gun in hand, moved to the side door. "Remember our plan. If we get stopped, Jeff pulls over. I disable the police car with a short burst, and keep shooting at it until we drive away. Believe me, the officer will be down in the floor board until I stop firing. We get away. His car is damaged, so he can't follow, and no one gets hurt."

"It's a good plan, but we don't need it," Jeff said. "The car took the exit."

Julia took a deep breath. She let it out slowly and nestled against Steve's neck.

His arms slid around her and held her. He could use a shower, but then so could she. Now, where was she?

Another thought startled Julia. This relatively uneventful run for the other side of the mountains was becoming mental gymnastics, a metaphysical roller-coaster ride. Taxing her mind when she was exhausted was not what Julia wanted, but the question that arose would plague her until she answered it.

When Steve got the call from Craig to go to DC, would he go? If her and the rest of the group's safety were in doubt, would Steve go anyway and make the assault on Hannan, an assault that could end this American dystopian misadventure? She wasn't sure.

One thing Julia was sure of ... if he refused to go, it would be because of her. She had witnessed the sway she had over Steve when he wouldn't shoot to kill Deke and his sergeant. And, as unlikely as it seemed, Julia Weiss, with her influence over warrior, Steve Bancroft, could alter the history of the United States ... maybe the history of the world.

Just thinking that was beyond crazy. Surely she was blowing things out of proportion, thinking irrationally, or something. But, the more she analyzed it, the more the logic seemed to hold. She might cause the assault to fail, leaving Hannan in control.

This was more than ironic. How could wimpy Julia, the weak link, the one who didn't belong in this group of awesome people—people born for greatness like Brock and KC Daniels, world-class athletes like Jeff Jacobs, world-class warriors like Steve and Benjamin, and Allie, the beautiful, Hispanic woman who glued them together like a family and mothered them all—how could Julia end up holding their destiny in her hands?

When the time came, if Steve vacillated in his decision to go to DC, she would have to make the right choice, not for Julia Weiss and not for Steve Bancroft, not for their consciences, but for the entire nation.

God, please, you've got to help me with this.

* * *

Like the other six people in the van, Steve sat silently for the next two hours while Jeff drove Highway 97 as fast as possible without drawing undue attention.

Nearly everyone was on edge, watching for that set of headlights that could signal trouble.

Jeff turned and glanced back into the darkness of the van's cabin. "Ten minutes to Chemult." He kept his voice down because one member of the group was sleeping, Julia. "A couple of miles north of Chemult, we veer off 97 onto Forest Service roads. Then we'll be safe in the backcountry all the way to Sisters."

No one replied, but it seemed that everyone relaxed a little in their seats. They were going to make it, barring a last minute encounter with police, which appeared unlikely in this remote area.

Julia must have been exhausted. She slept most of the way except for the one stop where Jeff risked getting food and water for them at a small store outside of Klamath Falls, red territory, supposedly.

Each time Julia woke, she would draw a few deep breaths, wiggle her feet, sigh, and snuggle closer to him ... if that was possible. Her arm was inside his ragged shirt. If she tried getting any closer, he was going to stop her invasion.

He chuckled softly. She would be mortified to think she had violated the bounds of propriety.

His chuckling roused her.

Here we go again.

"Jules..." He whispered. "I think you need to—"

"Oh." She sat up and pulled her arm out from the rip in his shirt, the place it had been tucked inside for the past half hour. "Steve, I ... didn't know." She folded her hands in her lap and sat shaking her head. "You should've said something. I was behaving like some hormonal teenager in my sleep."

"Asleep?" Brock's voice came from the back seat. "That's too bad, you didn't even get to enjoy it."

Steve glanced at Brock's big, shadowy silhouette behind him. "That sounds like a newlywed to me. We don't need advice from the newlyweds."

"I don't know..." Brock paused. "I'd say some bonding's been going on since you two ran off together in the woods."

"Don't tease them, sweetheart." KC's voice, soft and rather alluring.

Alluring. Just thinking in those terms told Steve he'd totally lost his focus.

The van veered sharply to the left. "Hang on, people. I almost missed the turn. Okay, we're on National Forest Service Road 200. We're safe for the next four hours, unless I get us lost out here."

Maybe it was time to get them all back on track. In a little over four hours, they would be at Julia's house and they needed to hit the ground running.

Steve cleared his throat. "You all know things are coming to a head. It's only a matter of days, or possibly hours, until Craig goes after Hannan, all the way down to the DUCC, if need be. I suggest we decide what we need to do to support that effort and make it succeed."

185

"Don't we also need a plan ... in case Craig fails?" Jeff hesitated as he spoke the words.

"Your plan would be pretty simple, Jeff," Steve said. "Run to the nearest place where you can ask for asylum. Probably Kingsley Air Force Base. Hannan would be hopping mad, looking for people to blame and people to kill. But he wouldn't attack an Air Force Base."

"Come on, guys." Brock's voice rose. "We need to be planning for success, here."

"For success..." KC said, "... I need to develop my little gift for Hannan, then I need a lot of Internet access time. I've got to detect him while he's on the White House networks in order to deliver the gift."

Steve turned toward KC sitting behind him. "Sounds like a long shot, catching him online and hacking his laptop when you don't even—"

"You worry about your own responsibilities, Mr. Bancroft. I left a back door on his laptop when all this started six weeks ago. Hannan's only partially computer capable and, after I examined his laptop in his study, he's paranoid about letting anyone touch it. I'm betting that the back door's still open. I've got the Israeli military laptop with satellite capability. But to be safe, I think we need two more laptops. One for Brock's blogging and a backup machine, just in case."

"Major Katz gave me ID and a credit card." Benjamin said. "Is there a safe place to buy the laptops we need?"

"Yeah," Jeff said. "The Super Walmart in Redmond. We can pick up food and other supplies there, too."

"You know..." KC paused. "I left my ... uh ... actually Julia's old laptop at Jeff's and Allie's the day that I—the day I'd like to forget."

"We don't want to forget all of it, Kace," Brock spoke softly.

"No. Not all of it. But the laptop might still be there."

"We can stop by and see since we'll be in the vicinity," Allie said.

"Steve?" Jeff's voice rose half an octave, begging for help.

The source of his angst had to be the four bodies of Hannan's black ops team they had left in the living room of the Jacob's house nearly a month ago ... a month of hot summer weather.

"If we swing by, I'll run in and get the computer equipment. I know how to disconnect it and which cables we need." KC was sharp. She had been there and realized the horror Allie would have at seeing the state of her living room ... and perhaps smelling it.

Brock shuffled in his seat. Evidently, he wanted to distract Allie from focusing on her house, too. "You know, I haven't blogged since the day before our wedding, four days ago. The people need to hear something. No telling how Hannan will spin my lack of blogging, especially after his attempt on our lives. He might be claiming we're dead."

Julia took Steve's hand and gave him a warm glance. "It sounds like you'll need my house for a while for Internet access and a place to stay. It's got six bedrooms."

"But, now, we only need five of them." KC's voice was low and soft. Maybe meant only for Brock's ears.

Steve looked down at the shadowy image of his and Julia's clasped hands. Maybe someday they could have a rebels' reunion and they would only need four bedrooms.

As he learned more of Julia's secrets, her strengths, which she seemed oblivious to, and about her hopes and dreams, Steve wanted her in his future. And maybe she—

"Seriously..." Julia sat up in her seat, "... how long do you think we can stay at my place before Hannan comes looking for us there?"

Steve had been pondering the question for much of the van ride. "Eventually, he'll send someone to check out the place. But keep in mind, this area is getting redder by the minute, and the Air Force Base will make him think twice before starting anything over here."

"I don't think Hannan has the stomach for a real civil war," Brock said.

But that didn't eliminate the danger to them. "Brock's right, but think about this ... twice Hannan has sent a small team of his elite Special Forces in a black operation and he's failed both times. He'll come, but I believe it will be with a much bigger force and an operation that's been carefully planned."

"And so how long, Bancroft?" Brock asked.

"I think we'll have two or three days, then all bets are off."

"Then we need another evacuation plan," Benjamin said. "But you all know the area much better than I do. If we have to hide again, it must be in a place where we cannot be observed by air or satellite."

"I know a place," Jeff said.

"Jeff..." Allie looked his way. "Please don't tell me you're thinking of the Skylight Cave?"

"You know what they say about great minds, Allie."

"But mine is thinking about that cave in a negative sense."

"Tell us about the cave." Benjamin squeezed Jeff's shoulder. "Then we can decide."

"Well, it's a lava tube, running parallel to the ground, about eight miles southwest of Sisters. It has cracks in the ceiling along the length of the cave, providing some light during the day. The cave is about a quarter-mile long, so it has places inside to hide. It will be cool during the day, while the temperature outside is in the high nineties. But we might need blankets at night. If I remember correctly, the cave temperature hovers in the sixties this time of year."

"But we won't have water or ... you know, facilities," Julia said.

Steve looked down into the dark eyes peering back at him. "Neither did the pioneers."

"I guess we'll manage." Julia sighed in resignation.

"Come on, Jules. We did just fine on Bolan Mountain."

"But we had nothing to eat, little water, and we ran a marathon so ... you know ... we didn't need to ..."

"Point taken." Jeff chuckled. "Hey, you have two special forces dudes here, survival experts, who can probably turn that cave into something with all the conveniences of home."

Jeff yanked the wheel to the right. "Sorry, guys. Big pothole in the road. You know, we'll need transportation. They might have a description of this van."

Brock tapped Steve on the shoulder. "Ask your girlfriend about that SUV parked in her garage."

KC slapped Brock's leg. "That's enough, Brock."

The van went silent, except for the sound of the purring engine.

Julia looked up at Steve. "Well, are you going to just leave it like that, Steve?"

Darkness hid her lips. Was she smiling? It looked like it. And she *was* waiting.

Steve cleared his throat. "Julia's not the girlfriend type."

Her head snapped up, eyes focused on his face.

"I mean she's the all in or all out type. Courtship headed toward the altar, or nothing at all."

Even the darkness couldn't hide her smile. "That's pretty good for a guy who's only spent one night with me."

"Come on, guys." Allie had turned sideways in her shotgun seat. "This conversation is going downhill in a hurry. It needs to be a little more productive."

Julia leaned close to Steve and whispered. "I thought it was very productive." She squeezed his hand and sat up. "About the SUV ... it belonged to my grandparents. It came with the house. I've never driven it, but I have the keys and it's practically new. If you pull up the rear seat, it seats seven."

"Great," Jeff said. We can hide the white van in the garage and drive the SUV."

"What about weapons?" Brock asked. "We only have two M4s and the handgun Benjamin gave me at Jeff's place."

Brock leaned forward toward Benjamin. "What happened to the bodies of Blanchard's Rangers and their equipment after Major Katz killed them all in that firefight?"

"We buried the bodies, Brock. They are hidden along the Deschutes River below Steelhead Falls," Benjamin said. "We wrapped their weapons and ammo in plastic and buried them south of the trailhead."

"We'll have our own arsenal," Steve said. "Are the weapons and ammo usable?"

"Some are. But some were damaged by explosions during the fight. We didn't have time to check them out and couldn't take extra weapons with us, so we buried everything, together."

"Let's see ..." Brock tapped the seat behind Steve with his finger. "There were about fifteen men when the second detachment surprised you. We should be able to get at least one M4 for each of us." When Julia turned her head toward Brock, he looked directly at her.

"Yes." Benjamin said "That's about right."

"I don't want one," Julia said and looked away from Brock.

Brock blew out a sharp blast of air. "Julia, Hannan's men are like animals. We've seen that. If they got you—"

"Stop it, Brock." KC said. You can't do that to her—force her to do something she doesn't—"

"It's all right, KC," Julia said. "Brock's right. Just having a gun might deter them, even if I don't shoot anyone."

"Changing the subject," KC said. "I just remembered that we took the router from your house, Julia. We have no way to connect to the Internet except one hardwired connection on your modem. Brock and I both need to be online."

"Kace, doesn't your Israeli laptop have satellite communications built in?"

"Yes. But what if I have trouble connecting to a usable satellite over here?"

"KC, aren't we picking up your laptop from our house," Allie asked.

"If it's still there."

"Then you can borrow our wireless router."

"That works," KC said.

Steve sat up in his seat and scanned the group in the van. "That about does it. Can anyone think of anything else?"

"Yeah," Jeff said. "How do we get you to Kingsley when Craig calls?"

Julia laid her head on Steve's shoulder. They had been together nearly 24-7 for the last month. And over the past two days, things had grown—he didn't know what else to call it but—rather intimate.

"Yeah ... uh ... let's cross that bridge when we come to it. Craig might make some arrangements with Kingsley when he talks to the pilot again. Where are we, Jeff?"

"Still quite a way south of Bend."

"Can we get any news out here?"

Jeff nodded. "There's a twenty-four-hour news and talk show radio station in Bend. Shall I try to find it?"

Allie reached for the audio system controls. "You just drive, Jeff. I'll dial the station." She turned on the radio.

The speakers in the van squawked and spit static for a few seconds until she hit the Bend station's frequency.

"... resistance grows in strength and numbers as dissatisfaction with the protracted martial law spreads across the fractured nation. The consensus from interviewing people on the streets is ... they just want it to be over. Citizens in the

blue states seem willing to agree to President Hannan's demands that they compromise rights and freedoms to bring an end to martial law. Such compromises raise two questions. First, are citizens relinquishing rights that Americans should never give up and, second ... will they ever get them back? And that's the way it is folks on this hot August night in the Dystopian States of America."

"I've heard enough. Turn it off, Allie." Brock's voice came from the back seat, angry and loud.

KC's voice came much more softly. "That's why the American people need to hear from Brock Daniels, now."

Chapter 22

At four thirty in the morning, they emerged from the back roads. Jeff pulled the van into a dirt lot at the intersection with Highway 126 on the edge of Sisters.

Julia listened as Jeff, Steve, and Brock discussed their options.

"It's going to be light enough to see us in another hour," Jeff said. "I suggest we fly down 126, hit our house as we go by, then head straight to the 24-hour super store at the north end of Redmond."

KC leaned forward from the back seat, her head beside Julia's. "To save time, why don't we divide up what we need to buy, split up in the store, grab everything and meet Benjamin at the checkout?"

"The—how do you Americans say it—tab is on me?" Benjamin grinned as he pulled out his wallet and flashed what looked like his fake ID and a credit card Katz had given him.

"Sounds like a plan but we're really cutting it close with the light." Jeff put the van in gear, veered onto the highway, and accelerated to what seemed well above the speed limit.

"Slow down, *mi amor*." Allie poked his shoulder.

"Don't worry," Jeff said. "The police have a lot higher priorities to worry about these days than someone driving ten miles over the speed limit."

"Yeah." Brock snorted a mirthless laugh. "Like which red area Hannan will attack first?"

Ten minutes later, Jeff turned onto a circle drive in front of a dark building. When the headlights swung across the front of the house, yellow barricade tape cordoned off the area. The tape had been broken in places, and loose ends waved in the gentle breeze.

"Do not cross? They made my house a crime scene," Jeff said in a whiny voice.

"Yeah," Brock said. "Finding four bodies on the living room floor, full of bullet holes and bound with tape, can cause that. Hope they found them right after we left, or ..." his voice trailed off.

Allie stared at Jeff frowning her disapproval. "You didn't tell me about that, Jeff."

No more *mi amor*. Allie wasn't happy about her living room being used for a funeral home.

This was the first time Julia had heard this part of the story, too.

Jeff laid his hand on Allie's shoulder. "That's how we got Blanchard's SUV and rescued you. Now if you don't think you're worth—"

"Enough, Jeff." Allie pointed toward the highway.

Jeff nodded and slipped the van into gear.

"I'll just grab a wireless router for us at the store," KC said. "Let's get out of here."

As the white van turned in at Julia's house above Crooked River Ranch the digital clock, on the van dash read 6:15 a.m. The sun had popped up above the distant mountains to the east a few minutes ago. It was, for all practical purposes, daylight. Had they been detected by anyone? Satellite surveillance? Traffic video?

Brock could probably post to his blog today. But would they have enough time, before being discovered, for KC to do her work?

Julia shifted her immediate concerns to her house. It was dark, except for the front porch light. A large white square had been affixed to the door. "What's that sign doing on my door?"

Benjamin slid the side door open and pulled a box from the floorboard.

"Wait before you carry everything in," Julia said. "I think we should see what that sign says." She scurried to the door, but stopped several yards away and focused on the bold print. "Quarantined for Ebola?"

Allie stopped beside Julia. "That's what you had when you met us here that night."

"That sign's a good thing," Brock chuckled. "Means nobody bothered your house while we were touring the Holy Land. Maybe the hospital tried to follow up on you and you were gone. They might have put it there."

Julia stepped closer and studied the sign. "The sign looks official, but anyone with a printer could have created it. But, you're right. Nobody would vandalize a house with this on the door. But ... I don't have my key."

Brock pointed around the side of the house. "Try the back door. KC and I left it unlocked when we ran out, trying to get away from the Black Hawk."

She looked back at Jeff. "I'll open the garage door and you hide the van."

In less than five minutes the van was hidden and everyone inside the house was busy with their tasks. Allie put away the food supplies in the kitchen with Jeff's help.

Benjamin walked the perimeter outside, probably addressing his own security concerns.

Julia followed Brock and KC into the study where they were setting up the computer equipment. "KC, I just thought of something."

KC, with a handful of cables, looked up at Julia. "What's that?"

"We're dead in the water here if I don't get online and pay my utility bill, immediately."

Concern wrinkled KC's forehead. "How do you usually pay your bills? Directly on the utility company's web site?"

"You're worried about who might see what I do and where I am, right?"

KC gave Julia her wide grin that could light up an entire room. "Hey, I thought you were computer phobic. But, yes, it might be a good idea to—"

"I'll pay through my bank, having them send a bank draft. It takes a couple of days longer, but it hides me and my location."

"Good thinking. Want to stick around and learn how to hack?" KC laughed.

"No, but call me when we can get on line. I'll have to pay the other utilities or we could lose our phone and data lines."

"Hang out here for a couple of minutes. My Israeli laptop is trying to connect to the router. When it does, we're online." She paused and glanced at Brock. "I was writing the code in my head while we were riding in the van."

Brock glanced up from the pile of packing material he was stuffing in a trash bag. "And I was working on my post, too."

Julia shook her head. "Don't geniuses' minds ever, you know, just rest?"

"Genius? He's the wrong man to ask about that." Steve's voice came from behind her. "He's just a monkey on a keyboard. Give him enough time and he can type out anything, even the whole dictionary."

Brock pointed a tiny screwdriver at Steve. "That's what they say about evolution. Give chemistry enough time and from the slimy goo it will create you."

Steve grinned. "After a detour through the zoo."

It was good to hear their banter. But this light heartedness would be confined to a few moments. Then reality would set in. What would it be like if they could all simply be friends in normal times? Well, the times weren't normal and Brock's post would have something to say about that. "So what are you going to write, Brock?"

He dropped the screwdriver and set the laptop on the office desk beside him. "I need to come up with something that clearly shows Hannan's attempts on our lives and mocks him for his failure to get us. Then end with something inspirational for our people."

"So you're going to make him mad again?" KC tapped on her laptop's touchpad.

"That's how we want him," Brock said. "Angry and careless. Come back in about an hour, Julia, and you can critique it for me."

"I'm online and good to go, Brock." KC turned and moved beside his laptop on the desk. "Give me a couple of minutes and your machine will be on, too. But remember. Whenever we access anything, we're exposing ourselves to scrutiny by people like NSA. I can hide from them, most of the time. So you'd better let me transfer your file when you're ready to post."

Julia stood and hooked Steve's arm. "Hide from NSA? I'm not even going to ask how you do that. Come on, Steve. Let's help Allie and Jeff make breakfast, then we can hear what Brock comes up with."

When they walked out of the room, KC mumbled. "Wish I could be done in an hour. I'm worried that we might run out of time here."

As Steve walked beside her in the hallway, Julia looked up at him, intending to ask about KC's concern.

The fierce look in his eyes softened. "It's okay, Julia. I'll take care of you, even if it seems like we're running out of time."

He would try to take care of her, no matter what.

That's what I'm afraid of.

After Benjamin returned from making his rounds, the seven sat around the breakfast table at one end of the kitchen while the aroma of fried eggs and bacon filled the breakfast nook. As they ate, Brock seemed to attack his food. Evidently, the post to make Hannan angry had the same effect on Brock. Maybe that was something all writers experienced, feeling the emotions expressed in their writing.

Julia scanned the people around the table. Everyone seemed to be attacking their food. Maybe it was only hunger, but Julia didn't think so. More like frustration from running half way around the globe, staying in three different homes in three days while trying to stay alive.

After they had eaten and cleared off the table, KC headed toward the hallway to the study. "If anyone who wants to hear Brock's post before I send it, follow me."

All six followed KC into the study and formed a semicircle around her computer chair. KC popped up a window on the laptop screen. "The file is ready to go to the Israeli server. Here's what Hannan and the rest of America will be reading."

KC scrolled to the top of an open document and read.

Mr. President,

The first time you attacked us with a SWAT team. They all defected because they were good police officers who had sworn to protect and serve the people of Central Oregon, not to serve you and your treasonous plan.

Then you attacked us with an Apache helicopter and tried to take us all out with a hellfire missile. Your $70 million Apache helicopter was shot down, destroyed.

Next, you sent a black ops team, special forces under the command of Captain Blanchard. He and all his men were killed. You spent four weeks contracting with Iran to sic Hamas terrorists on us. They shot an RPG into my wedding ... which I did not appreciate. The only thing that surprises me is you didn't choose a Hezbollah operative. Nevertheless, the IDF killed the little coward.

And now you send Captain Deke's Ranger detachment after us. All of his men were killed or seriously injured, except for Captain Deke who is still on the loose. And, finally, you attacked us with a Stealth Hawk. Getting sophisticated are we, Mr. President? Or, is it desperate? Regardless, I thought this $200-million-dollar bird was never contracted by the military. Evidently, you got a few of them for your own special operations. But a member of our group shot it down using one of Deke's own thermobaric rockets, a weapon intended for us.

I see a pattern of failure here, Mr. President. And keep in mind, we are just a ragtag group of seven. Three women and two men with no military training or weapons ... and two soldiers.

How can you, Abid Hannan, act as Commander-in-Chief, defending this nation, when you can't even take out a tiny band of resisters?

Your own policies have brought this situation on you, but our entire nation suffers. In a nutshell, Mr. President, this is what you have done. You have systematically removed from our military all the warriors who will fight to the death to protect our cherished freedoms and to protect their loved ones. You see, the old adage is true, there are no atheists in foxholes, for good reason. A true warrior is willing to fight and die for his country because such people believe that they are on the right side of moral issues and that God will take care of them whether they live or die.

But these are the beliefs of Christians, and a few other people of faith, who are the very men and women you have targeted to eliminate from the military. First you replaced the high-ranking officers. For months the daily list of Flag Officer assignments contained hundreds of entries. Then you initiated policies within the DOD that forced other warriors of faith to leave or violate their consciences if they remained.

So who is left to fight your battles? Men like Captain Blanchard, mercenaries with a scurvy crew of people who are not willing to risk death without a high likelihood of success and a big reward. These are greedy cowards, undisciplined men who only fight when they have an overwhelmingly superior force, which both Blanchard and Deke believed they had.

But when the resistance proved much stronger than they anticipated, they couldn't handle the situation. We defeated them and killed their men. We— three women, two men with no military training or weapons, and two soldiers.

You, Mr. President, have emasculated the military, but that was insufficient so, now, you are obsessed with gun control so we cannot fight you, birth control to please your supporters, thought control so you can make hate crimes to punish the politically incorrect, and finally, speech control. In fact, you would like to control my speech, right now, would you not?

You ask for everything but self-control. The people you've retained in the military sure don't have it. They cannot protect the USA and they won't protect you. I take no pleasure in saying this to a sitting U.S. president, but you, Abid Hannan, are as good as dead. I pray that it comes through justice— impeachment by the house, then a Senate trial with a guilty verdict for treason and murder.

To the remnant of faithful men and women in the military, standing alongside America's finest special operations forces to serve their country, the American people, and protect their way of life—warriors who will never fail their comrades, who will always keep themselves mentally alert, physically strong and morally straight—members of our nation's chosen soldiery ... may God grant that you not be found wanting, that you will not fail your sacred trust. "De Oppresso Liber."

To the American people—over the past six weeks, you have had a small, bitter taste of the loss of your God-given rights and American liberties. It has brought us pain, it has brought us fear, and it has brought death. Your own president perpetrated acts of terrorism against you, killing thousands. Continue to resist him and do not lose hope, because this dark chapter in American history will soon end. We will restore our constitutionally based, democratic republic and there will be an election to replace Hannan.

But keep in mind, he is a man that the majority of you voted for. So, in the future, before you cast your vote, remember what this man said and what he did. Remember, this time, what neo-Marxism looks like when it's forced on you in the real world. Remember what it feels like, how it tastes, and what it does to your stomach after you swallow it. After you remember, then and only then, cast your ballot.

Your Voice of Freedom,

Brock Daniels

As Julia listened, many of the events Brock described played through her memory, vivid and raw. Julia's anger that smoldered as KC read the post, burst into an inferno. "Post it, Brock!"

KC tapped her touch pad. "I just did."

Chapter 23

Julia understood Brock's work. He communicated ideas and drew out emotion through the use of words. But trying to comprehend KC's job made Julia dizzy. She stood to leave the study so KC could continue her work.

Brock sat in the big easy chair in the middle of the room. "Kace, would you explain, one more time, how your little gift for Hannan works?"

Brock's question piqued Julia's curiosity. She stopped by the study doorway to listen.

"Sweetheart, it's done and sitting on Hannan's laptop waiting for him to connect to the defense networks."

"Yeah, but how do you get the info Craig needs?"

"Are you sure you want to hear this?"

"Kace, I asked, didn't I?"

"Okay. First some history. The Executive Command and Control System used to be hosted on a computer in the President's personal study outside the Oval Office. He had access to the Nuclear Launch Codes and other critical systems from that location. But we moved all that to the DUCC when the underground command center was completed. And that's where the info we need currently resides."

"We don't need nuclear launch codes."

KC rose from her seat, walked to the easy chair, and sat in Brock's lap.

Maybe it was time for Julia to leave before the newlyweds—

Brock glanced her way. "If you want to hear this cyber-babble, feel free to stick around, Julia."

Sometimes Brock's intelligence and strong opinions could be intimidating. But Brock was being considerate, today. "Yes, I'd like to hear how cyberespionage works. I mean, that is what we're doing, isn't it?"

"Since I'm no longer employed by DISA, yes, it's cyberespionage. Something that could get me locked up in Leavenworth for life if Hannan was our legitimate leader. Where were we ... the information we need consists of cypher codes to get through doors leading to the DUCC. Most of the doors use biometrics, but they always have a backup in case of machine or software failure. Craig can use that backup to gain access."

"So how do you get the cypher codes? From Hannan's laptop?"

"No, silly." She ruffled Brock's hair. "But the DBA—the database administrator—for the defense systems in the DUCC keeps the cypher codes in a database on the classified networks. When I worked there, I sort of borrowed the ID and password for the administrator's account. I also know the DBA never changes the password ... or, if he's told to, he changes it then resets it back to his favorite password."

"Isn't that really insecure to—"

"Brock, remember that the defense networks were never supposed to be exposed to the Internet. It was Hannan's little network drop, with fiber all the way down to the DUCC, that indirectly exposed them. Since Hannan's secret connection is only used intermittently, hopefully, I'm the only person outside the White House who knows about it."

"So how does this little virus on Hannan's laptop access the codes?"

"It's called a Trojan Horse, sweetheart, not a virus. If Hannan connects to the DUCC's network, my code simply logs into the DBA's account and reads the table containing the cypher codes for the doors. It encrypts and stores them on Hannan's laptop and, the next time the laptop connects to the White House networks, the Trojan sends them, using a secure protocol, to a server out on the Internet, a server that I have access to."

KC's explanation was clear enough, but the code she wrote had to be terribly complex. "KC," Julia said, "did you have to write all that code yourself? It sounds pretty sophisticated."

"Connecting to the database, logging in and grabbing the data uses a simple scripting language. It's almost like you're sitting at the keyboard and typing in commands. But, to create a Trojan that can hide on a windows machine, that's sophisticated. I got a kit from the Mossad while we were in Israel. Major Katz put me in touch with someone."

Brock chuckled. "Hannan would literally have a cow if he knew he'd been hacked by the Mossad."

"Yes, he hates Israel with a passion. Hopefully, he will never know ... at least not until it's too late. Well, that's pretty much it. Now we wait until the encrypted codes appear on the dark side server."

"Dark side?" Julia asked.

"Don't ask, Julia. Some pretty bad people hang out there. But I don't think anyone can discover what I'm doing or find us if I hide among them."

KC was bright, brave, and it sounded like she could be a little bit crazy, but Julia admired this brave young woman who, at twenty-two years of age, held a nation's destiny in her hands. At least that's how it seemed today. "I think it's time for me to go."

Julia stood, but Brock drew her gaze. "It's good to see Steve and you together. You know, he told me six weeks ago, he had been looking for someone like you. He's a good man, Julia."

Brock's eyes had the look of a lion stalking its prey ... Julia Weiss. She needed to leave, now.

Brock's powerful arms lifted KC off his lap and set her on the floor. He stood, facing Julia. "I wish you two could iron out your—"

"Iron out our differences about violence?" Brock had started this, and Julia would finish it. He shouldn't have inserted himself where he didn't belong.

"He's a good man who loves people and hates oppression. He defends good people against evil. That's his job"

"He's trained to kill people, Brock. And my experience has shown me—"

"Experience? Julia, God gave us general revelation, you know, creation, and He gave us special revelation, the Scriptures. Then He gave us the life of Jesus to show us what God is like. But you're not accepting that. Sure, God is love, but He's also just. He is truth and He is light, but He says over and over He hates oppression and injustice. He tells us to defend the weak. You've got some points of tension in your pacifistic thinking, things that don't jive with the God of the Bible. And they will give you problems until the day you die, if you don't let God show you who He really is instead of you trying to—"

"But He's shown me a lot through what I saw in Africa." This was beginning to sound like a repeat of their heated discussion at Jeff's house. "Haven't we already had this conversation?"

"The universe, the Bible, Jesus, you can rely on those. But never place your experience before them, especially when your experience leads you to a contradiction of the only sources of truth you can count on."

"Brock, what I saw was wrong and—"

"Sure it was wrong. Bad people did evil things. But don't let evil teach you about God's ways, Julia. Steve has seen a lot of evil. He saw treacherous killings and Islamic men systematically abusing young boys and girls in Afghanistan. Steve knows that's from Satan, not God." Brock paused.

He stopped, probably because he saw what she felt, her face growing red hot.

KC shook her head at Brock. "By the way, is Steve going to DC to help Craig, Julia?"

"I don't know." She needed to end this before the harsh words she was forcibly stifling leaped out of her mouth and assaulted Brock.

Brock's eyes focused on her again. "If he is, you need to—"

"What I don't need is you intruding into my relationships ... with God or with Steve." She turned and walked out.

Before Julia turned to go down the hallway, KC stepped into Brock's arms, looking up into his eyes. "This is important to her and she's hurting, sweetheart..."

Julia walked out of hearing range, curious as to how KC's conversation with Brock would go, but too angry to stay and find out.

Chapter 24

On the other side of Hannan's desk in his private study, Eli Vance sat stroking the ends of the mustache that spanned the width of his gaunt, narrow face. "About time for the meeting, Abe. Why don't we use the Oval Office anymore? I miss that presidential seal in the carpet."

"The study has fewer holes in the wall than the Oval Office. More privacy."

A knock sounded on the door.

"Come in, Harry."

Secretary of Defense, Harrison Brown entered, followed by Greg Bell, Attorney General.

Harry took the seat on Hannan's right. "White House security is really sparse. Have more people bailed?" He met Hannan's gaze.

"You mean deserted, don't you?"

Harry broke eye contact. "I'm sure *they* don't see it that way."

"They will when I have them executed for desertion in a time of war. To address the issue, I've called in more troops to secure the entire area."

Greg Bell, shuffled some papers in his lap. "There's someone else you'd probably like to execute, after his latest blog post."

"What blog post?"

Greg's eyebrows raised. "You mean you haven't seen it?"

"I've been a little preoccupied with Russia's constant probing, threatening our underwater cables with their subs, sending military aircraft close to our air space. Now the Chinese have hinted that they could take down any nation's satellites any time they choose—a subtle warning to—has Daniels posted again? I thought we'd kept him on the run so—"

"Mr. President, he's painting you as an incompetent failure. He even lists your failures in great detail."

"You sound like you agree with him, Greg."

"Only with the fact that you have failed to eliminate Mr. Daniels. He is emboldening the resistance and it's growing. We just lost Eastern Oregon, maybe Southern Oregon, too. The most populated areas in Oregon will remain blue, but ... you really ought to read this." Greg tossed the papers he'd been holding onto Hannan's desk.

He picked up the first page and started reading. One failure after another. The itemized list of Hannan's failed military operations burned in his mind like a red-hot poker jammed into his head, searing every nerve until—Hannan took a calming breath. He would not let Daniels drive him into a rage, which was probably the blogger's intent.

Hannan finished reading the post. It was a damaging commentary coming at a time when Hannan didn't need further damage. And it galled him to admit it, but Daniels was largely correct about the military. They were proving to be gutless wonders, men who failed or ran when the going got tough.

So, Hannan would take Brock Daniels' advice and make sure Hannan's forces had "overwhelming superiority." Then they would crush this band of troublemakers. "We will soon be rid of Brock Daniels and his cohorts. I've done what I should have done in the beginning, ordered a full company of Rangers to locate them, surround them, and then tighten the noose until they are all hanged. We cannot let one nit survive."

"If this fails, Mr. President, Brock Daniels' ridicule will know no bounds, and his reputation as a modern-day prophet will only increase his influence. And as for nits, you will most certainly have a nasty lice infestation."

Eli cleared his throat. "Abe, keep in mind that you no longer have support from Kingsley Air Force Base. In fact, they might interfere."

As intelligent as the old man was, maybe Eli was finally getting senile. "Kingsley is primarily a training base. What can they do to stop us?"

"Uh ... their pilots conduct live-fire training with guns and missiles," Harry said. "They have enough weapons, sir, to wipe out a sizeable ground force."

"Then we'll take out Daniels quickly, monitoring the Air Force Base communications during the assault."

Harry Brown had been shuffling his feet for the last minute of this discussion. "Sir, last night the Air Force Base cut all communications with the DOD network—phone system ... everything. It was a sophisticated, surgical snip of all communication lines. They must have planned this well in advance."

"Then the boys at Fort Meade will have to monitor them for us."

The way Harry stared across the room, avoiding eye contact, said he still wasn't satisfied. "Suppose NSA detects preparations for air support for the insurgents?"

The troops had to move quickly, and possibly on foot, for several miles. He couldn't send in anti-aircraft equipment. The Rangers would have to fend for themselves. If they got Daniels, that was all that mattered. If aircraft got them, it was worth the loss of a hundred Rangers or so.

"Well, sir?"

"Look, Harrison ... you're my Defense Secretary, you handle that contingency."

"But, Mr. President, you've been handling these operations, personally. How can I—"

Hannan walked around his desk and opened the study door. "This meeting is over. I have some phone calls to make."

Greg Bell left the room first, walking at a fast clip.

Harrison Brown left shaking his head.

Eli Vance waited until Greg and Harry were far down the hallway. "Abe, you're willing to just sacrifice a company of Rangers to get Daniels, aren't you?"

"Why not? My cabinet doesn't think they're worth much more than what Brock Daniels described."

"Mercenaries, undisciplined men ... isn't that what he called them? You send those kind of men on a suicide mission without telling them, and they'll turn on you if any of them survive. Like I said ... someday someone's going to shoot you, Abe."

Chapter 25

Captain David Craig's patience had worn thin. Not a good thing for a commander of a Ranger detachment on a covert mission to apprehend the President of the United States. He and his men had been hiding in this safe house in an older Arlington, Virginia neighborhood for the past week, planning the assault.

Craig had been forced to trust people before spending enough time with them to develop trust. That bothered him. But he had good instincts. One look into a man's eyes, after blindsiding him with a carefully crafted question, revealed a lot. But one mistake and his mission would be over ... as would the lives of his men, leaving the US as a failed state.

Craig's problems had compounded when, two nights ago, his Weapons Sergeant, Gano—the man who had replaced Steve Bancroft—had stepped in an eighteen-inch-deep hole as they ran in the darkness to evade police. The compound fracture of the lower leg would take him out of the fray for at least two months.

What Craig needed now was first, the info from KC to make the final assault, which he believed would lead them down into the DUCC, and second, his old weapons sergeant, Steve Bancroft. Steve was a magician with explosives and this assault might require a complete magic show.

Daddy-O, his Operations Sergeant—AKA team daddy—snatched his M4 and moved to the door. "Sir, someone's coming up the walk."

"Do you recognize him?"

"Yes, sir. It's that Secret Service Agent, Belino. He's out of uniform—running shorts, tank top, and a baseball cap."

"We're in too deep with him to back out now. Let him in, Daddy-O."

At the first knock on the door, Daddy-O pulled it open and Belino quickly stepped inside.

His gray tank top was dark with sweat around his neck, down the sides and on the back.

Belino pulled off his cap and wiped his brow with the back of his hand.

"You're a sweaty mess, Belino," Daddy-O said. "I hope you're running by choice, not necessity."

"It's by choice, all but the timing. In DC, I don't normally run in the middle of a hot August day. But I've got some news you'll be interested in."

"Good news, I hope." Craig motioned toward a chair.

"No, I'll stand. Like you said, I'm a sweaty mess. This won't take long."

"Let's hear it." Craig flipped his internal switch that placed his mind in observation mode, preparing to take in and digest everything.

"I don't think I told you the last time we talked, but I have a friend who stayed behind to ... well, basically to spy on Hannan."

"And you trust this guy?"

"With my life, sir."

"What does your friend have to say?"

"The White House is like a big computer data system, Captain Craig. It's a system that's complex, full of subsystems that have evolved over the years and over many administrations. It includes security, communications systems, office help, kitchen staff, but everything is coming unglued as people choose who they're going to support, Hannan or the resistance."

"Chaos is good. Well, for us, not Hannan. But, Belino, how do you communicate with your friend without someone detecting you?"

"Like I said, the system is badly broken. That's how I've managed to keep my duty phone. I only use it to talk to my contact. But no one has even checked on it or tried to shut off service. So I can talk to my friend, until he leaves or ..."

"Yeah, or ..." Craig waited for Belino to continue.

"Well, sir, my contact says Hannan's worried about his personal security, especially while he's in the White House or working in the West Wing. He's safer in the DUCC, but he hates going down there. And he's as paranoid as ... well, for example, he seldom uses the Oval Office because of the holes in the wall."

"Holes in the wall? In the Oval Office?"

"Yes, sir. There are eighteen holes for observation by security. No mics. The holes are just used to make sure POTUS is alive and well."

"Where is this going, Belino?"

"Hannan's going to bring in more military to secure the White House and the West Wing. He would have done it already, but he doesn't know who to trust and, like I said—"

"He's paranoid."

"Yes, sir. You see, his transformation of the military wasn't as complete as he thought when this all started."

"Tell me about it, Belino. Hannan's Gestapo went down through the ranks finding all the *unsuitable* officers— Christians, practicing Jews, even some of the Muslims. The Gestapo trumped up charges to force us out by resignation or court martial. Back to your subject ... any idea at all as to when this might happen?"

"It's probably only days, a very few days. I don't know the size of the force he'll bring in, but I would guess something like a whole company of troops." Belino ran his fingers through his hair and adjusted the cap on his head. "That's all I have, so I'd better get back to my run."

"Thanks, Belino. Feel free to stop by anytime you're out for a run."

Belino nodded and headed toward the door. "Next time I'm out this way, I'll bet you're gone."

"Could be."

Daddy-O opened the door.

Belino jogged outside and broke into a run when he hit the sidewalk.

The clock was ticking now. Craig could lose his only chance to stop Hannan if they didn't make their assault before Hannan brought in an army to protect him.

If Craig's team missed their chance, things would get ugly in the US. A fractured country with more states seceding—it could lead to civil war and a lot more deaths.

Craig had to go after Hannan in the next twenty-four hours, or less. But, if Hannan retreated to the DUCC before Craig's Rangers cornered him, they would need KC's access codes or the whole mission might fail.

Should he risk the lives of his men and the future of the nation by attacking without those access codes? As his gut knotted from something Craig seldom experienced, indecision, he pulled out his secure phone and keyed in Steve Bancroft's number.

Chapter 26

Craig placed the call to Steve's secure sat phone and waited, hoping he could get enough information to make a decision on the assault. Steve could be here in approximately six hours from the time he reached the Redmond airport.

Steve answered on the third ring. "Hugo Boom, here." Sharp, clear, and confident, Steve's voice.

"Bancroft, that's no way to answer your phone."

"Sorry, sir. Just wanted to make sure it was you on the other end before revealing anything."

"It's me, but we've got a problem."

"Yeah. It started seven and a half years ago. So, what's Hannan up to now, sir?"

"He's bringing a company or more of troops to do Deke's old job, secure the White House complex. We've got to nail Hannan in the next twenty-four hours or it could be too late. I need to talk to KC, then to you, again."

"KC and Brock just walked in. Here she is, sir."

"Craig, this is KC. Before you even ask, I'm still waiting on the cypher keys to arrive via the ... well, you know."

"Listen, KC. I've got to go after our target in the next few hours or it's too late. Without the codes, is there any way I can get into the DUCC?"

"Do you have Internet access?"

"At the moment I do."

"Good. I'm sketching out your path to the DUCC as we speak. I'll put it in the secure drop box on the Israeli server. You can pick it up in about five minutes. What it will show you is the stairwell, locations of video monitors to avoid on the way down, and three doors. The first two you can probably blast through. But the final door—you'll never get through it unless you can open it, or get someone to open it for you."

Craig sighed into the phone. "So we have to catch him before he enters the DUCC or we could end up trapped, deep under the West Wing."

"We're talking about the most secure location in North America," KC said. "You can't just waltz in, you know. Without inside help and an incompetent president whose administration is coming apart at the seams, you'd never even get to the West Wing, let alone inside it."

"I'm just a little frustrated, KC. You didn't happen to memorize the key to that door, did you?"

"Craig, this isn't your run-of-the-mill four- or six-digit numeric key. It's a sixty-four-character, alphanumeric string."

"Then how the heck is anyone supposed to use the blasted key?" Craig was losing it. Something he'd done only once in the past and he still regretted it. People had died that day.

"We had a secure method of accessing the key so we didn't have to memorize it. I don't have access to that anymore, and the key changes weekly."

"Will you please check once more, KC, to see if you've received anything?"

"Sure. Be back in a couple of minutes. I have to run to the study."

"Let me talk to Steve while you check."

"Here's Steve."

"Sergeant Bancroft reporting for duty, sir."

"That's what I need. Sergeant Bancroft on duty here, ASAP. I'm going to make two plans for the assault, one plan with the access keys, the other ... a high-risk, rapid assault with an explosives expert by my side. But I pray to God we don't have to use the second plan."

"Me too. If the DUCC is nuclear hardened, I'm not sure how much help I'll be."

"Pack up whatever you need, Bancroft, and be ready to leave when I call back. I'll call the pilot first, then you. Your pilot will pick you up at the Redmond Municipal Airport, Roberts Field."

"The Redmond Airport? Is that safe, sir?"

"Safe." Craig laughed. "Bancroft... nothing we've done for the past six weeks has been safe. But nobody is going to shoot you or detain you at Roberts field unless you do something really stupid." His phone flashed and vibrated for an incoming call. He looked at the display. Belino's number. "I've got another call. Got to go."

"KC just came back in the room shaking her head. No keys yet, sir."

"That's the way this day's been going. I'll call you back with rendezvous instructions when it's time to head for the airport. Be ready, Bancroft."

Craig ended the call and picked up the incoming call. "Hello, Belino."

"Sir, I'm afraid I have some bad news."

Great. Hannan must've deployed the troops. "So, Hannan found some loyal, trustworthy troops to protect him?"

"It's not about events in DC. This is about KC, Brock, and the rest of the group on the West Coast. They may be in serious danger, sir."

Chapter 27

The group of seven congregated in Julia's dining room shortly before noon. As Julia took a seat beside Steve, the reality that he would soon leave brought an icy chill to her heart. She had faced almost certain death beside this brave, strong warrior. That had drawn them close, and it had shown her how deeply she could trust this man ... how deeply she had come to love him.

She opened her hand underneath the table, palms up.

Steve took it just as he had, for the first time, five weeks ago after boarding the Israeli Gulfstream.

So much had happened since then. Julia had learned that she was stronger than she thought and that her fears weren't as horrifying when someone she trusted and loved was by her side. That was the problem. Soon, Steve wouldn't be with her.

Steve dropped her hand and reached for his side.

Julia looked down.

Steve's phone flashed an incoming call.

He pulled the sat phone from his pocket. "It's Craig again."

Julia's stomach tightened into a cramping knot. She knew what was coming, Steve's orders to fly to the East Coast, a mission from which he might never return, but one he must attempt.

"Sergeant Bancroft here ... News for all of us... The speakerphone... Yes, Sir."

Steve placed his sat phone on the dining table. "Craig says we all need to hear this."

Julia shot him a frown. "All of us? Why?"

He shrugged and pushed the speakerphone toggle.

"Craig here. Listen everyone, I just had another chat with Belino."

"This can't be good," KC muttered.

Craig sighed into the phone. "If that was you, KC, no ... it's not good. Belino's White House contact told him Hannan is preparing to order troops from JBLM, near Tacoma, to deploy to Central Oregon. They will deploy as soon as Hannan gives the word. And Hannan has people poring over satellite data and traffic video obtained by his NSA hackers. He's looking for you and will probably deploy a whole company of Rangers to ensure you don't get away this time. Belino says Hannan is furious after reading Brock's post."

"Sir, sounds like he plans to wipe us out. Did Belino know how soon this deployment might happen?"

"Whenever he thinks he's found you. It could be a few hours or a couple of days."

Steve shook his head. "They could load a company of Rangers on their Chinooks and be on our doorstep in three hours, maybe less."

"That's why you need to invoke your evacuation plan now," Craig said.

"Here we go again." KC looked up at Brock. "Some honeymoon, huh?"

"Kace, how many people get to go from Israel to Whistler to Oregon on their honeymoon?"

"Craig ..." KC stood. "The alarm on my laptop just went off. Be back in a couple of minutes, maybe with good news."

KC trotted out of the dining room toward the hall leading to the study.

Brock folded his hands on the table. "Probably the cypher codes. Doesn't that create an interesting situation?"

"Interesting?" Steve said. "I don't like it."

"Me neither," Benjamin said. "It's an overwhelming force. We must not let them find us."

Julia met Steve's gaze. The look in his eyes stirred her heart. She knew what it meant and wanted to accept his sacrifice of love, but couldn't.

Steve was going to back out, disobeying his commander. Still trying to atone for his sister's death, he would do anything to protect Julia. Once again, she was an obstacle, a person in the way, causing trouble.

Craig's mission required Steve. That meant America needed Steve or Hannan might actually win.

Julia could not allow that. No matter the personal cost, she would make sure Steve went. The force driving him to stay must be strong if he was willing to sacrifice his career, his honor, and violate his oath. That force and Steve's will must be broken.

Julia was the problem and only Julia could eliminate the problem. No halfway measures would do. Though it would break her heart, crush her, she must drive Steve away or he wouldn't go.

The pain wouldn't last long, because Julia Weiss probably didn't have long to live, not if Hannan was sending a large body of troops to kill them. But Steve must keep his honor, his oath, and he must help Craig capture Abe Hannan.

KC ran back into the dining room, carrying a sheet of paper. "Craig, KC here. Hannan's in his study. Would you like the keys to the DUCC?"

"That I would. I had a back-up plan, but really didn't want to rely on it."

"A back-up plan for getting into the DUCC?" KC said.

"How, exactly, did you plan to do that?"

Craig chuckled "Find somebody in the underground complex to shoot and then shove their face in front of a retinal scanner."

"I think my plan is more reliable." It took KC three or four minutes to read the keys and ensure that Craig had correctly repeated them.

"Got them, KC. What's next?"

"Did you get my map of your route through the building down to the DUCC?"

"Yes. But I have a question about the map. How likely is it that you missed video cameras in the stairwell?"

"It's possible I missed some. But I only remember seeing them at the exits to floors connecting to the stairwell. There are only four such floors. The cameras are mounted above the exit doors. And the Security Center is one floor above the DUCC. Maybe you should—"

"KC, we'll take out security, if we can, on our way down."

"That's all I remember, Craig. I always used the elevator when I went down to pull my shift. The only time I used the stairwell was for a mandatory evacuation drill. It was a brutal climb out of the DUCC. I got really tired, so I may have missed some cameras."

"Thanks, KC. You may have just saved this detachment and the USA. I need to talk to Bancroft now."

"Sergeant Bancroft here, sir."

"Steve... I..." A commotion sounded in the background.

"Something's happening here. I've got to check it out. I'll call back soon as I can." The connection ended.

They needed to pack up everything from Julia's house that they would need for staying in the Skylight Cave. But Julia's mind seemed to go numb each time she tried to make a list. So she started a new list, the list of things she had to tell Steve.

"I guess our mission here is complete," Benjamin said.

"Let's make a quick list of what we'll need at the Skylight Cave."

"There's a spring for water outside the cave," Jeff said.

"Benjamin and I have filters for the water," Steve said. "We don't want anybody getting sick from parasites when we don't even have an outhouse?"

"I'll bring my Israeli laptop, maybe I can get it to connect via satellite. The batteries are good for six to eight hours," KC said.

"Kace, we're hiding in the cave for good reason," Brock said. "You're not going outside it to try connecting to some satellite."

"We don't know what might happen, Brock. I'm still bringing the laptop."

Allie pointed toward the kitchen as she stood. "I'll box up some kitchen supplies and food."

Julia hooked Steve's arm. "Steve and I will get my grandparents' camping gear from the garage."

"I can help with that," Jeff said.

Allie shook her head and gave him a look that only a fool would ignore. "No, Jeff. You're coming with me to the kitchen."

After Julia and Steve stepped through the door into the garage, Julia pulled the door shut until the latch clicked. She may not have much time until Craig called back. Craig would order Steve to go, but he would back out. She had read that loud and clear in Steve's reaction to Craig's message about the army Hannan had sent to wipe them out.

Steve's strong drive to protect had to be broken, but that meant breaking his heart. She knew no other way.

"Are there any sleeping bags out here?" Steve walked toward the shelves lining the back side of the garage.

Julia took his arm and turned him toward her. In the semidarkness of the garage, she couldn't read his eyes well, but his body language looked uncharacteristically nervous and antsy, like a man contemplating a violation of his conscience.

Before Julia realized what Steve was doing, he had her in his arms, holding her, tightly. His words came in a hoarse whisper. "If Hannan sends a large contingent of special forces, it won't be like before. Julia, they *will* find you this time and when they do, no one will survive."

She pulled her head back to see his face. "If Craig doesn't catch Hannan, America won't survive."

His eyes grew intense, blazing with a fierce emotion Julia could never remember seeing before. "Do you remember what almost happened the last time Hannan's men captured you? Remember what that creep, Abdul, wanted to do to you?"

How could she forget. The man was like Satan incarnate. Julia shuddered, then took a calming breath and put on the best bravado she could manage. "You're just trying to scare me. It won't work. God ... will ... protect me." She said the words but knew she didn't sound convincing. "You have to go and stop Hannan. Craig needs you, Steve."

"I ... I thought you needed me."

This was the dreaded moment.

God forgive me for what I'm about to do.

"I did, Steve."

Steve pulled his head back, exposing a deep frown. "Did?"

She nodded. "I thought so. But, Steve, no matter how hard I try, there are things between us that can never be reconciled, not in this life. The bottom line is ... I need God more than I need you."

Steve exhaled like he'd been punched in the stomach. "Julia, God comes first. I know that, but—"

She turned away so he wouldn't see her tears. Maybe the semidarkness would hide them. "It's more than that. When God says no, this is not something I want you to do, you have to listen to Him. And that's what He's telling me about us."

She had never lied so blatantly to anyone. She had even brought God in on her lie. Julia wanted to moan, scream, start sobbing, anything but continue this conversation. But Steve had to go, not for her, or for him, but for all Americans. And Julia Weiss was the person who had to make the sacrifice. She had done it before, but never when the stakes were this high and never had her heart been at stake.

She could do this. It would be the last sacrifice she would be called to make, because she wouldn't be alive when Steve returned ... if he returned.

"You can't mean that. I love you, Julia. I want to protect you, to—"

She pressed her fingers over his lips.

The sun beamed through the small window in the side door of the garage, lighting Steve's face. Recognition of what she had said and what she had meant showed in his eyes, a look that he'd never displayed to her, the look of a little boy, lost, alone, and helpless. Then the look vanished. His shoulders slumped ... resignation.

Steve would go. A man like Steve Bancroft would leave as graciously as possible. He would never try to force himself on a woman he thought did not want a relationship with him.

The victory of her will over his brought nothing but emptiness. If death was coming for her, she would welcome it.

"Julia, will you please do one thing for me before I go?"

"If I can, you know I will." She looked away to hide her welling eyes.

"Just ... kiss me goodbye."

She was going to lose it. No, she *had* lost it. The first sob shook her body, then came the tears.

Steve held her or she would have fallen.

Sometime later the garage door to the house opened. Brock stood in the doorway. "Sorry, but Craig needs to talk to Steve."

Julia took a deep breath, wiped her cheeks, and walked to the garage door. "Tell him Steve's coming." She closed the garage door and turned around.

Steve was there. His arms held her.

She kissed him, but not like in the lookout. This was a kiss of desperation, driven by a passion she could not mask. Julia would let Steve end this final kiss of a relationship she had killed with carefully crafted lies. And she would take this kiss with her, cherishing it to the end of what would probably be a very short life.

Finally, Steve broke it off. "Goodbye, Julia." He turned and walked inside, out of her life, leaving her leaning against the white van, her body convulsing with each violent sob.

Inside that van, she and Steve had shared their dreams ... the same dream—helping the helpless, the orphans—a dream that would never be realized.

And now guilt burned in her heart, wedging its way between her and the God she professed to love and obey, the one she had tried to make an accomplice to her lie. Julia needed to pray but, after what she had done, would God even listen?

Please, God, forgive me for deceiving him. You know I love him, but I had to do this, didn't I?

Chapter 28

Steve rode shotgun in the SUV beside Jeff as they drove to Richards Field in Redmond to catch Steve's flight.

It was over. Julia was choosing to die while refusing to let him protect her and refusing to have a relationship with him. His reason for living had been drained from him. Could he even do the job Craig needed him to do? Would he only get good men killed?

Jeff had evidently detected Steve's bad vibes and knew he didn't want to talk.

Didn't want to talk? What an understatement. He didn't want to live, because he'd failed again.

Steve had walked away from the woman he loved, leaving her to die. It was within his power to stay and use his Ranger training to save her life, no matter what Hannan threw at them. But he couldn't save all seven against such overwhelming odds. Leaving five people behind to die, while he saved Julia, violated the Ranger's Creed. And staying to save only Julia also required Steve to violate his oath of enlistment and the trust his commander had placed in him.

Life's circumstances seemed to defeat him every time it really mattered. But Julia had given him no choice. No, that wasn't true. No one had bound him and drug him away. He had made the choice to leave and it was the wrong choice.

Steve was losing Steph again, but this was worse because he had chosen to do this. No matter how hard Julia had pushed him, leaving or staying were still his choices to make, and he'd made a conscious decision to fail, to abandon her to a violent death.

Could Steve Bancroft live with what he'd done? Where he would soon be, did it even matter? He might not live beyond the next few hours.

To help him survive Julia's rejection and to preserve part of his sanity, Steve's mind went into male survival mode, numbness. If a man could shut off his thoughts and feelings, no loss could kill him ... in theory.

But something wasn't right. In one unanesthetized corner of his brain, a niggling question burned, demanding attention.

Julia had completely broken down when she told him their relationship would never work. He had seen her cry before, but never like that. When she kissed him, something happened in the middle of that kiss, something he didn't understand. It didn't end like a goodbye kiss. In fact, if he hadn't ended it, they might still be there, lips pressed together, holding each other. What did that mean?

Stop it, Bancroft. It's over. You're just grasping at straws.

"Bro, there's the pilot." Jeff's voice startled Steve, rescuing him, but leaving his question unanswered.

A man in a flight suit walked their way.

Steve looked at the gun in his lap. The M4 created another problem. Obviously, he wasn't up for this. When a Ranger can't figure out what to do with a gun, he isn't fit to be a Ranger.

He hit the down button on his window and tried to surrender to his battlefield instincts. Hopefully, they would take over and get him through the next few minutes ... and hours.

Steve snorted. "How am I going to walk through an airport carrying an M4?"

Jeff gave him a palms-up shrug.

The pilot stopped beside the door and studied Steve for a moment. "You must be Steve Bancroft."

The man in the flight suit with two silver bars on his shoulder stood about six feet tall, with a medium build, athletic looking and maybe a bit cocky. "Yes, sir. And you are ..."

"Captain John Towery." He smiled and stuck out a hand. "I'm your ride to Adventureland." Towery's infectious smile and his wit pulled Steve out of the quicksand that had been sucking him under.

Steve reached out the window and shook the man's hand. He had a firm grip, the look of a straight shooter, but his air of confidence seemed a bit over the top. Steve had heard that tended to be a characteristic of these cowboys of the wild blue yonder.

The captain pointed down at Steve's lap. "You know, Sergeant Bancroft, we don't have to go through security to get to my plane, but you can't just walk through the terminal building carrying an M4." Steve's words to Jeff, almost verbatim. "Brought a jacket for you. Might be cold up where we're going. Wrap up the gun in it. I'll bluff our way out onto the tarmac. Then we hop in, kick in the afterburner, and we're outta here. But if anybody gets testy on our way out there, whatever you do, don't pull out that gun."

"Understand, sir. I'll let you do the talking."

Steve got out and turned back toward Jeff, realizing this could be the last time he saw Jeff. It's not the kind of thing one man stays to another, not out loud. But the look in Jeff's eyes spoke it.

Steve stuck out a hand. "It was the best of times and the worst of times, but I'm glad I got to know you, Jeff. If I can,

I'll be back soon and ..." He'd better wrap this up quickly or Steve was going to choke up. "I ... I'll pray for you all and ... please take care of Julia. She'll try to sacrifice herself at every opportunity. And don't believe her when she says she can't do something. She may not look it, but she's as strong as KC. And, Jeff—"

Captain Towery tapped Steve on the shoulder. "He gets the point, sergeant. He's to take care of your girl. Now, we need to go."

The niggling, burning question returned. His girl? He doubted that. But that kiss ....

He followed Towery to the terminal building with a deformed jacket in Steve's arms, one that looked like he'd put too much starch in the wash.

Steve drew some strange looks inside the terminal. There just aren't many ways to conceal an M4 inside a jacket without looking like one is hiding something. But they made it onto the tarmac with no resistance.

Captain Towery pointed ahead at a sleek, silver jet with twin stabilizers.

The cockpit hardly looked big enough for Steve's six-foot-four frame, let alone two men. "Can two people actually fit in that thing?"

"It's an F-15E, a two-seater. Works great for training ... and for getting the right people to the right place at the right time." Towery gave Steve a sly smile, then they continued walking to the plane two hundred yards ahead.

This might have been the adventure of Steve's life—flying at Mach two across the continent in a mere two and a half hours, then making an assault on one of the most secure places in the world to capture a runaway POTUS and save the republic. The stuff of dreams.

But seeing Julia heartbroken, sobbing, telling him they were through and that he needed to go do his job—this seemed more like the great misadventure, or the great misery.

He had never failed as a Ranger. He'd only failed when women he loved were in danger. First Steph and now Julia.

Towery tapped Steve's shoulder as they walked. "Sergeant Bancroft, still worried about that girl?"

"Maybe so, sir." He wasn't going to go there, no matter how hard the captain pushed the subject.

"There are stories going around about that Daniels' group that would curl a man's hair. Even a fighter pilot. Are you a praying man?"

"Sometimes."

"I thought so. But it's hard to pray when you're really down. Makes it seem like your faith is gone. So I take it you're a Bible reading man, too?"

Steve nodded but kept his eyes on the F-15 fifty yards ahead.

"From what I heard, this is a David and Goliath story. Daniels' seven against the most powerful man in the world. Yes, David and Goliath. But we know how that story ends, don't we?"

He met Towery's gaze and saw the blazing fierceness of another kind of warrior, the one Steve had dubbed the cowboy of the wild blue yonder. Steve was in good company and he served a good God. Maybe Towery was right, but it didn't stop the ache in his heart.

"Uh-oh." The captain motioned toward two armed security guards walking briskly their way.

"Keep in mind, Bancroft, they aren't really against us, they just—"

In unison the two guard's fingers on their left hands swiped the sides of their rifles.

"Sir, those two guys who really aren't against us just flipped off their safeties."

"Well, at least they didn't flip us off."

"They're going to do a whole lot more than that."

One of the men raised his rifle.

"We have two choices, Bancroft. We go talk to them, or we make a run for it."

"No, captain. There's a third choice. You run like heck for your plane and get ready to take off."

"But they'll start—"

"No they won't." Steve jerked the coat from his weapon and fired a burst beside the two men.

The bullets sprayed chunks of concrete into an open area while the cracking of the M4 echoed off the buildings.

The two guards turned and ran for cover.

When Steve turned back toward the F-15, Captain Towery slipped into the pilot's seat and waved Steve toward him.

Steve sprinted toward the plane, looking for a way to climb in. A ladder hung down from near the cockpit. Five seconds later, the engine whined as Steve slid into the rear seat. He glanced back toward the terminal as the cockpit closed.

The two armed men ran out of the building followed by two others. "Captain Towery ... four of them, now."

The engine screamed and the F-15 whirled in place pointing a menacing arsenal at the men.

The four men bolted, sprinting toward the terminal.

When Steve pulled his helmet on, he heard the captain laughing. "That's called bandit busting." He swung the plane around in a one eighty and shot out onto the runway. "The tower's gonna go crazy but, near as I can tell, there's nobody taking off or on final. Hang on, Bancroft. I'll tell you how to gear up once we're outta here. Oh, yeah ... you might pass out right after takeoff, but not to worry."

Pass out? An invisible hand shoved Steve back into his seat and held him there as the whole world roared around him. Was he dizzy or was the world really passing by at the incredible rate it appeared—

Steve gasped as the F-15 leaped into the air, nosed upward, and pushed the breath out of him.

A loud boom still seemed to echoing somewhere. Probably inside his head. But the cockpit was relatively quiet except for a high-pitched whine.

"Lost you there for a few seconds," Towery said. Then proceeded to tell Steve to go through various impossible contortions to get "zipper suited."

After nearly pulling several muscles, Steve had wriggled into the flight suit and had his M4 and sat phone in his lap. Something about his gun drew his attention.

Good grief! He'd left the gun in automatic mode. Steve reached down and pushed the safety lever.

"Bancroft, what are you doing with that gun?"

"Just checking it out."

"Please don't tell me you were still in machine-gun mode when you climbed into my bird."

"Alright, I won't tell you that, if you won't tell me how many airport violations you committed during that take off."

"Touché. Now ... if you're comfortable enough, I suggest you take a nap. Rumor has it you've got a long night ahead of you."

"Yeah. I've heard that rumor, too."

At some point between the images of Julia playing through his mind, Steve actually did doze off. But a ticklish vibration in his lap yanked him back to consciousness. Was his sat phone actually working? It looked like it. "Captain, I've got a call coming in on my sat phone. Is that possible up here at this speed?"

"Evidently for a short while." The whine dropped in pitch like someone had pulled on the end of a slide whistle. "I'm slowing down. Maybe you can keep a connection long enough for a short phone conversation."

"It's a text message. That's probably how it got through." Steve scrolled through Craig's message, hardly able to believe what he was reading. Was he being given a second chance?

Steve stopped and returned to the beginning, reading slowly to let the significance sink in.

Hannan suspects. Must move now. Will rely on KC's info for access. Believe Daniels' location compromised. Turn back & help them. Godspeed. Craig

"What's it say? I mean ... if I have a need to know."

"Captain Towery, my commander said he can't wait for me and we must turn back so I can help Daniels' team. They're in danger. Maybe a whole company of Rangers descending on them."

Steve sucked a breath and nearly choked on it when the F-15 banked ninety degrees. The centrifugal force pushed him into the seat until his vision went fuzzy.

When the wings leveled out, the engine roared and the plane surged ahead.

"Sir, what did you just do to me?"

"We pulled a few Gs when I turned around. You're not going to pass out on me again, are you?"

"Not to worry, not going to pass out on you, captain."

They were headed westward, toward his six friends who should now be in the Skylight Cave. Headed home to Julia."

"You know something, Bancroft? I don't think we'll get a warm reception back at Redmond Muni, do you?"

"Not after I shot the place up and you threatened them with even bigger weapons."

"Where do you need to go? I mean your final destination."

"It's a remote spot about seven or eight miles west of Sisters? I need to get there the fastest way possible."

"Well I can't jettison my canopy to let you bail out of my plane. No, sir. You're getting no nylon letdown from this bird. We'll need another aircraft to get you there. One you can bail out of."

"What kind and where do we get it?"

"Madras Municipal Airport has a skydiving club. A good one."

"Can this thing land there?"

"It ain't a thing, Mr. Ranger. I call it my Silver Eagle."

"This is an Eagle and it's all silver. Not very original, if you ask me."

"Oh, it's original. Came from an old Ray Stevens song my dad used to play for me about the Doorights." Towery chuckled. "Nobody knows it, except for my DCC, but this bird's got the name I gave her hidden on it."

Chatting with Towery about his plane was the last thing Steve wanted to do. "Back to our plan. So we're landing at Madras. What then?"

"Here's what we're going to do. We'll land and you use that M4 you're carrying to make them take you to Sisters."

"Hijack a plane? Come on, captain, I don't want to have to shoot anybody."

"Then tell them you're a Red Ryder and need a quick ride to save Brock Daniels. They'll help."

"Don't you mean a red Ranger?"

"Yeah. You're a red Ranger. Beats a BB gun, anyway. Pretty conservative bunch at Madras. They'll help you if they know you hate Hannan."

"I don't hate anybody. But I despise Hannan."

"That's good enough. Bancroft, this is how we'll do it. I'll taxi you right up to the terminal ... providing you let me come in and watch you hijack that plane."

"I've always heard you fighter pilots were crazy. Now I believe it. You can come in, because I might need your word on what's going down. I don't want to end up shooting somebody."

"That works. I know a couple of the pilots there. Friends, more or less. But please tell me none of them will end up in a smoking hole because they flew you to Sisters on this sortie."

Steve replayed the captain's pilot jargon until he caught the meaning. "I don't think so. If the bad guys show, we'll need to sneak in without letting anybody on the ground know what's up."

"About the smoking hole ...you don't think so? Those Rangers on the ground—they're not going to have triple A are they?

"Come again, captain?"

"AAA, Anti-aircraft artillery."

"Sir, if we're flying in a small plane, like a Cessna, I think an M4 qualifies as triple A. But I'll do my best to keep your friends safe."

"Bancroft, you do realize that you just traded twelve Special Forces types versus West Wing security for a situation where three women, two men and two soldiers take on 200 Special Forces?"

"Yeah. I guess you fighter jocks don't have a lock on crazy."

Chapter 29

Partially covered with blankets and other supplies, Julia rode in the small back seat of her grandparent's SUV as Jeff drove down a dirt road through a sparse pine forest.

Allie rode shotgun beside him.

Brock and KC were crammed into the second seat with Benjamin.

Even Benjamin had someone, a fiancé in Israel. But Julia rode alone, odd person out. A woman who had sacrificed her own heart and Steve's for her country.

Had it been worth it? What if Craig failed and Steve was killed?

No. Deep inside her heart Julia Weiss knew the truth. A skilled warrior commander like Craig would prevail, no matter the odds. America should have one more chance at freedom, but Julia would never live to see it. Odds were, she would die in the cave that lay less than a mile ahead.

Jeff turned off the road and drove slowly toward a thick stand of Ponderosa pine. "We'll hide the SUV here, about a half-mile from the cave, and carry everything."

Julia needed to pull herself out of the depression she had slipped into after Steve left. She couldn't help this group of six with a mind mired in the muck of self-pity.

The SUV stopped.

Brock opened his door and climbed out, displaying the large US flag on the back of his white t-shirt. "Carry everything you can. Let's try to make this in one trip. We need to minimize our exposure to satellite surveillance."

Jeff climbed out of the driver's seat. "Load up, then follow me. I'll take us under the trees as much as possible. But, when I give you the word, follow my footsteps and be careful. We'll be walking along the ceiling of the cave. It has large cracks and gaping holes in it that let in light. If you slide into one, you'll end up thirty feet below, smashed on the rocky cave floor."

After five minutes of trekking through the pine forest and avoiding jagged lava rocks, Jeff stopped the group. "See the rock outcropping to our left? That's where the spring flows out from underground. This time of year it will be running low, so we'll need to filter all our water."

Allie knelt and set her heavy load on the ground. "Will somebody please remind me why we're stumbling across lava rocks carrying fifty pounds of who knows what to crawl into a big hole in the ground?"

She looked from face to face, but no one looked like they wanted to reply.

Finally, Benjamin cleared his throat. "Remaining well-hidden for the next several hours is the only way we can stay alive."

"Yeah," Brock said. "If Craig's men capture Hannan this evening, we still need to stay hidden until word gets out that his reign is over. Remember his plans for us?"

KC stepped to Brock's side. "Getting killed by an army that hasn't heard the war's over ... well, it isn't how I want to die."

"I wish Steve was here," Julia whispered to herself.

A hand came to rest on her shoulder. Allie's hand. "Me too, Julia." Allie raised her voice. "Hannan is nothing but a rattlesnake. He's the one who should be crawling into a hole in the ground."

Ahead, to their right, a rattling sound crescendoed, turning to a loud buzz.

KC dropped the load she'd carried and nearly leaped into Brock's arms.

He pushed KC behind him. "Everybody back!" Brock motioned backward with both hands, but held his ground, eyes fixed on a small bush in front of him.

Julia followed Brock's gaze to a stick, standing upright, moving back and forth. She refocused on it—a coiled rattlesnake, head erect, mouth open, fangs extended.

Brock nudged KC farther away from the snake and scooped a baseball-size rock from the ground. "This is what Craig will do to Hannan this evening." Brock's body moved like a major-league pitcher using a full windup. His arm cracked like a whip when he let the rock fly.

Brock had thrown so hard that Julia lost sight of the rock.

Thwack. The rattlesnake flew several feet away from them, its head smashed, its fangs useless, and its body writhing in death agony on the ground.

"And Steve will help Craig do that," Julia whispered.

Allie's hand squeezed Julia's shoulder.

She met Allie's gaze, saw the concern in her eyes, and Julia's tears came like a flash flood, carrying away everything—her resolve to be strong, her self-respect—everything but the agonizing pain in her heart from betraying the man she loved.

Somehow, Allie knew. Had Steve told Jeff what happened in the garage and then Jeff told Allie? No. It wasn't like Steve to reveal matters of his heart until a relationship grew deep, like it had that night on Bolan Peak when he told her his story about Steph. Allie, the mother of this band of rebels, had instinctively known.

Fighting for control, Julia blew out a breath, wiped her cheeks, and picked up the load she'd carried. "Which way to the cave, Jeff?"

Julia was third in line when they approached a twenty-foot wide hole in the lava rocks surrounded on two sides by pine trees. The trees formed two rows running parallel to the lava that had hardened forming the long cave.

Jeff dropped his load on the ground, stepped onto a ladder, and backed down into the hole.

Julia peered over the edge. A metal ladder descended ten or fifteen feet to the floor of the cave. The lava tube ran nearly parallel to the surface into a dark area about fifty yards ahead. Beyond the darkness, a blue column of light stood like a pillar, creating an explosion of white and yellow where it hit the floor of the cave. A skylight. Erie, but beautiful.

Allie dropped Jeff's load down to him, then her things. She climbed down the ladder and waited beside him.

Jeff motioned for Julia to toss her things down.

Julia tossed the blankets, but lowered her heavy pack as far as she could before dropping it to Jeff. She backed halfway down the ladder then stopped when she saw KC's face peering down at her from above. "KC, do you see the skylight?"

What had happened to Julia's voice? She spoke in normal tones but her words came out much deeper, richer, and louder.

"That's pretty cool," KC said. "We have our own sound studio without any electronics. Echo chamber, too."

Brock's head appeared beside KC. "The cave opening's like the hole in the box of a guitar. It amplifies the sound."

Benjamin's head appeared beside Brock's. "I could hear Julia's voice like she was standing beside me, and I was almost fifty yards away. It's a good thing we discovered the cave's acoustics, now. We need to speak softly."

"And carry a big stick." Brock raised his M4.

Benjamin pointed at Brock's rifle. "And pray we don't have to use it. This is a good hiding place, but if we were attacked here, I don't see how we could defend it."

A thought hit Julia like a blow to her head. A video played showing fire from an invisible flame thrower blasting through the cave, from one end to the other.

One thermal bear and everyone in the cave is dead.

Chapter 30

Captain David Craig and his ten men, dressed in tac gear and fully armed, rolled down K Street and turned onto 17th Street NW, which would take them to their destination, the Eisenhower Executive Office Building, where their assault on the West Wing and President Abe Hannan would begin.

This route had been carefully planned to avoid as many security checkpoints as possible. However, the checkpoints guarding the entrances to Washington Center Northwest could not be avoided on the way to K Street. Craig and his men had left the van near 26th Street and evaded the military and police by circling south of Washington Center and rendezvousing with the van at the corner of K Street and 19th.

Only three blocks to go. Craig turned from his shotgun seat in the van and faced his men. "Any questions before we do this?"

Blaine cleared his throat and shifted his feet. "Sir, remind me again how we're justifying killing armed security guards."

It was understandable that killing a man for doing his duty would raise moral issues. Craig expected every Ranger to consider the morality of his actions before performing them. "Blaine, at this point in Hannan's power-play and, after Brock Daniels exposed Hannan's crimes to the entire nation, any man bearing arms for Hannan, displaying an intent to use such arms against Americans, must be considered our enemy. If an armed person looks like they might use their weapon, shoot to kill. We have no other choice. Besides, Belino said everyone on the evening shift at the West Wing tonight is a Hannan supporter."

"Any other questions?" Craig looked into ten faces painted with eagerness and exuding confidence. If they succeeded today, their efforts should return the government of the USA to the people and restore constitutional rule. If not, Craig feared the nation would split and there would be war.

"You all know your assignments." Craig raised his M4 above his head. "For America, for freedom, and for the Constitution. May God be with us." He pointed toward the door of the van. "Rangers lead the way!"

He paused and shot a silent prayer into another realm, knowing his prayer was heard. Craig had already opened his heart to the answer he would receive, whatever that answer might be.

Time to focus on his men and their mission. "Fifteen seconds, then we bail out and hit the west entry to the building on the run. I'll take the lead and make the announcements. If all goes well, there won't be any resistance. But, should you detect any armed resistance, eliminate it and move ahead."

The van jerked to a stop. The side door slid open and eleven Rangers ran to the entry door of the Eisenhower Executive Office Building.

Two armed guards whirled toward Craig, eyes wide. They raised their weapons part way, then stopped.

They had seen military personnel operating in the DC area daily over the past six weeks and Craig counted on their hesitation. "Security threat, east end first floor. We've got it, but you need to lock down the building." Craig used his best voice of authority and tried to avoid any sign of hesitation.

The guards lowered their weapons.

One of the two froze in obvious confusion.

The other guard, a sergeant, kept his weapon in a ready position. The man met Craig's gaze. "Identify yourselves!"

Craig held his sat phone in his left hand and his rifle in his right. Time to bluff. Leaving his weapon pointed toward the ground, he trotted up to the guard, "No time, Sergeant. People are going to die in there in about thirty seconds." Craig raised his phone to his mouth. "Entering the building, Mr. President. Engaging terrorist suspect in thirty seconds."

The guard drew a sharp breath.

Craig pushed the man out of his way with a forearm and glanced back at his men. "He's moving to the east entrance."

The Rangers covered and moved as they cleared the central hallway.

Craig paused for a second. He never tired of watching the mesmerizing sequence of moves as some covered those advancing while two men in the rear scanned the entire area for threats.

While eleven Rangers continued through the central hallway, Craig repeated his announcement to the building's occupants, "Locking down the building. Go into the nearest office and lock your door!"

Sixty seconds later, Craig's detachment exited the building. As expected, this entrance had no guards. But across the narrow street, West Executive Avenue NW, lay the West Wing of the White House complex. The lobby door would be guarded.

As soon as the first shots were fired, the race would be on to catch Abe Hannan before he made it to the DUCC elevators or the stairwell.

Now, with less than fifty yards to go, the success of their mission depended upon boldness and surprise. If Craig stopped Hannan before he reached the DUCC, Hannan was their prisoner. If not, Craig's men had to breach the DUCC, taking out any security forces they encountered. And, though KC had given him the access codes and all known security camera locations, it was a long walk down a stairwell to reach a bunker hardened to withstand a direct nuclear hit.

Craig's men crowded around him on the steps at the east entrance to the Executive Office Building. "We go in two rows of five with a rear guard. I'll be in the first row that rounds the corner of the West Wing. Everyone in the first row rounds it, simultaneously. Allocate targets by your position and eliminate any perceived threat. Let's go, men."

Craig, Cutter, Daddy-O, Blaine, and Meyer sprinted hard toward the West Wing lobby entrance. In unison, with their free hands, Daddy-O and Blaine yanked on Velcro flaps opening the pouches from which each pulled out a flashbang grenade.

Chapter 31

Eli Vance sat at the end of Hannan's desk in the president's private study, waiting for a reply.

Hannan wasn't going to give him one. After all, the Middle East going to blazes in a handbasket was just as much Eli's fault as it was Hannan's. Besides, he had much bigger problems than some stone age tribes with 20th century weapons trying to impose their jihadist ideology on their neighbors.

"Abe, if you don't do something, you'll have jihadists storming the West Wing to kill you, the great Satan."

A knock sounded on the study door. The door flew open. Secret Service Agent Williams stuck his head in. "Mr. President, the Joint Operation Center says security was breached in the Executive Office Building sixty seconds ago by a group of men in tac gear. The intruders might already be on the White House grounds. You are to follow me to the DUCC, sir."

"Told you so." Eli's mustache twitched in what looked like a smirk. "Like I said, someone is going to shoot you someday, Abe."

The message from Agent Williams brought to mind another message, the threat made six weeks ago by Captain Craig, the Ranger commander.

... know this, Mr. President, we are coming for you. Not just my detachment of highly trained men, but Navy SEALs and other Rangers, all trained to move into any area on the planet, without being detected, and carry out our mission.

No one can stop us. Certainly not the gutless wonders you have placed in command. Some night you will awaken to fingers around your throat. They will be mine.

Hannan swallowed hard, but the constriction in his throat wouldn't go away. Surely Special Forces wouldn't make an assault on the White House in broad daylight, would they?

Williams's voice yanked Hannan back to the present. "Mr. President, we're out of time."

Hannan unplugged his laptop, shoved it and some writing materials into the laptop case and slung the case over his shoulder. Sandwiched between two secret service agents, he scurried toward the elevators to the DUCC.

Somewhere behind Hannan, Eli Vance's cane thumped on the floor at a surprising pace for the old goat.

With the acute shortage of security personnel in the White House complex, Eli would have to fend for himself.

Williams led Hannan to elevator number two and pushed the down button. The door slid open.

A loud bang slammed Hannan's head and a bright flash stabbed his eyes. The light had come from the far end of the hallway, near the lobby.

The two agents shoved Hannan into the elevator, closed the door, and pressed the button for a high-speed descent to the DUCC.

Hannan's stomach flip-flopped as the elevator dropped like a rock. When they passed level 2, a grinding sound came from the back side of the cabin. Their descent slowed and the grinding noise grew louder.

"We've got a problem," Williams said. "We're nearly to level 4. If we make it to—"

"*If* we make it?" He had Hannan's attention now. "Agent Williams, it's your job to ensure that we do make it."

Williams pulled on a red emergency handle and the elevator ground to a stop as it announced level 4. "We made it, sir, but this elevator is out of commission."

The doors opened.

"We'll have to take the stairwell down to level 5, the DUCC."

"How far is that, Williams?"

"One hundred twenty-five steps, if I remember correctly, sir."

"Williams ... that flash and the explosion—what happened in the lobby?"

"I heard gunshots just before the explosion. Though I couldn't see anything, if I had to hazard a guess, Mr. President, I'd say the guard outside is wounded or dead. ROTUS and Agent Brown got flash banged. They will probably be okay. And, whoever the attackers are, they're in the West Wing, right now."

Hannan and the two agents scampered down the stairwell for about thirty seconds before reaching level 5.

They exited the stairwell and hurried to the DUCC's doorway. Williams pushed his face up to the retinal scanner. The bulky door opened with a loud click. Air hissed from the crack around the opening door. When it swung open, the hiss turned into a wind, blowing into Hannan's face.

The three stepped through the door and into the intermediate chamber, where they would wait for the DUCC door to close and the pressure to stabilize in the chamber.

A few seconds later, the final entry door to the DUCC opened. Hannan stepped through it to what he hoped was safety.

He moved to a worktable and pulled his laptop from its case, along with a pen and a pad, and set them on the table. "Williams, how safe am I down here?"

"Mr. President, even if the intruders get to the elevators, they have three security doors to get through, including the nuclear hardened door we just came through. Each door requires a person's biometric information to be in the system or they don't get access. You're safe here, sir."

But what if someone actually made it to the DUCC? Hannan scanned the room containing a few rows of chairs, work tables lining the left wall, a large conference table in the center of the room, and several wall-mounted monitors on the front wall. The back side of the room had five doors on it, two for private workrooms, two for restrooms, and one for the hallway to the geek work room, home of the network monitors.

Network monitors. He thought of KC Banning. If there was one traitor among the geeks, might there be more? "Agent Williams, who do we have on this level, right now?" Hannan sat at the worktable.

"For your protection, Mr. President, we have myself and Agent Logan. Two military guards are covering the communication center down the hall. It's swing shift now, so only two unarmed network security analysts are on duty there. On level 4, above, we have two security guards watching the video monitors. They're armed, too."

"Are you sure the geeks are unarmed?"

"Yes, sir. They've never been armed."

Was he being paranoid? No. There had been an attack on the West Wing and the attackers had probably gained a foothold there. Soon security forces would gather and either drive them out, or call the military to do that.

But the DUCC seemed to be safe. No weapon—nuclear, thermobaric, human, or cyber—could reach Hannan here. But he needed to reach that thorn in his side, the brash blogger with delusions of grandeur, Brock Daniels. And no one could be allowed to hear Hannan's plans to make that happen.

He looked up at Williams. "I need some privacy."

"Mr. President, that's what the workrooms are for. You need to—"

"No, Williams. You and Agent Logan need to guard the door to the DUCC ... from the outside. I'll call you when I need you."

Williams's frown brought his thick black eyebrows together. "But, we are responsible for your—"

"You are responsible for obeying my orders. Leave. Now!"

Logan opened the door and Williams shot Hannan an angry glance as the two men left Hannan alone in the room.

He started the military comm software and placed a call to John Wiley, the lead NSA analyst tracking Brock Daniels.

"Mr. President, I was about to call you, sir."

So Wiley knew who was calling. He had probably recognized Hannan through use of the computer program that Hannan was not supposed to be using. Eventually, there would be fallout from his violations of chain of command, but he wasn't going to dwell on that. It would only result in a massive headache. "Wiley, do you have any news for me?"

"Yes, Mr. President. Satellite tracking data showed us that a vehicle, we believe is the white van spotted near Happy Camp, arrived at the house of Julia Weiss about daybreak this morning. It parked in the garage. A few hours later, someone drove a black SUV from the garage to a remote location south of the small town of Sisters, Oregon."

Sisters? Six weeks ago, Blanchard had fought forces supporting Daniels near Sisters. "Do you know what's at that remote location?"

"Yes, sir. Something called the Skylight Cave. It appears that our targets are trying to hide from satellite detection by going underground, literally."

Hannan picked up his pen. "Do you have the GPS coordinates of that cave?"

"I do, Sir. But, isn't Harrison Brown handling—"

"No, Wiley. I'm handling this one."

Hannan wrote down the coordinates and ended the conversation.

He retrieved the info for the 75th Ranger Regiment, second Battalion, and located the contact information for one of the company commanders, Captain Scott. Hannan placed a call via the comm software to Scott's secure phone.

"Captain Scott, here."

"Scott, this is the Commander-in-Chief. I spoke to your commander a short time ago. Are your men ready?"

"Yes, sir. We have eight Chinooks fueled and ready. We're awaiting your orders."

Hannan read the GPS coordinates to Scott. "It's a cave called the Skylight Cave. And here are my orders. Do whatever you have to do to make absolutely certain that none of the terrorists escape, even if it means blowing them to Hades, where they belong."

"Question, sir?"

What was Scott thinking now? "Go ahead."

"If we *can* capture any of them without anyone escaping, should we—"

"*Only* if you're sure none of these treasonous little ..." Hannan finished with a graphic vilification of these friends of Brock Daniels. "Do you understand, Captain Scott?"

"I understand, Mr. President. No one will escape, even if we have to hit the cave with our SMAW and kill them all."

Chapter 32

Julia wandered through their campsite in the cave, looking for something to do—anything that would get her mind off from Steve. She stopped beside Allie, who pulled a propane burner and a small canister from her backpack. In less than two hours, three hungry men would expect dinner and Allie, filling the mother role, was determined to prepare it for them.

Allie stopped and read the back of a sealed package. "Stew for six people requires a half gallon of water."

"Allie," Julia waited for Allie to look her way. "Don't use up all our drinking water. I'll go to the spring and get a gallon of water."

Brock looked up from the air mattress he planned to inflate. "All the comforts of home, except running water."

"And no bathroom.," KC added.

Jeff stepped off the ladder at the cave's entrance. "Oh, there's running water. It's just a hundred yards away. But Benjamin dug us a latrine. It's not far from the entrance."

"It had better be far enough," Brock said.

"You got that right." Jeff chuckled. "Because, after the inversion sets up in the evening, smells become concentrated near the ground and, in this cave, they'll come right down—"

"Enough little boy humor from the little boys." As she approached, Allie shot a disapproving glance at Jeff. "And don't try to tell us it's just meteorology, Mr. Weatherman."

Brock blew into the air mattress, while KC stretched the other end out across a smooth, level part of the cave floor.

Brock blew in another breath, then pinched off the valve. "By the way, where's Benjamin?"

Julia stopped by the ladder with the plastic water jug in her hands. "He went out about ten minutes ago to scout the area and make sure we're still alone."

Jeff's footsteps sounded behind her.

She turned.

Jeff pushed an M4 at her. "Here. You'd better take this ... just in case."

Julia had conceded that point earlier. She took the gun from Jeff and, as she'd been instructed, checked the safety lever.

Jeff studied her as she examined the gun. "The magazine's full. Be careful out there. Oh, I left a rope outside. If you can't climb down the ladder with the water, you can lower it into the cave."

Julia nodded, put down the water jug, and stuck her head and an arm through the rifle sling. "Be right back. Almost as easy as turning on the tap."

As she climbed out of the cave, Allie's voice echoed from behind. "What was that noise?"

KC laughed. "It was Mr. Windbag, here." She pointed at Brock.

Allie cocked her head. "Are you sure? It sounded more like rolling rocks."

Julia walked out of hearing distance, looking for Benjamin, but realizing that hearing distance was at least 50 yards from the mouth of the cave, even if they talked softly. With the cave's acoustics, they needed to whisper, especially at night.

This was where Brock had killed the rattler. She studied the bushes and rocks around her, looking for snakes before heading down to the small stream.

The brook burbled out from a wide crack in the volcanic rock.

Julia quickly filled the gallon container with the cool, clear water. This water didn't look like it needed filtering, but parasites could wreak havoc on a person's digestive tract. In that condition, climbing a ladder and running thirty yards to the latrine—she would filter the water before anyone could use it.

Julia capped the container and stood to return. Still no sign of Benjamin, but she heard voices from the cave.

Correction—one loud, unfamiliar voice. A man's voice, harsh and angry.

She hurried back to the mouth of the cave, walking softly on the rocks as she approached it.

Whoever it was, it wasn't the army that was coming to wipe them out. But even one stranger discovering them would mean trouble.

Julia set the water down and pulled the strap of her M4 over her head. She flipped the safety lever to automatic. The mere act of preparing to fire sent her heart into a wild pounding rhythm. As she brought the menacing-looking weapon to a ready position, Julia crept toward the mouth of the cave. She peered in. No one in sight.

She pushed the lever to safety, then turned around to climb down the ladder. Having her back to the cave, though she had seen no one, made her feel like a mouse turning its back on a hungry cat.

When her feet hit the cave floor, Julia leaped behind a large lava boulder near the cave's entrance, and waited.

The angry voice returned, barking out commands.

Julia gasped when she peeked over the rock and saw two men in dirty tac gear holding KC, Brock, Jeff, and Allie at gunpoint.

One of the men she recognized. Deke.

The other must've been a survivor of Steve's RPG attack on Deke's men.

Benjamin would know what to do. But where was he? She looked up to the top of the ladder. No such luck. She was on her own.

Julia had dealt with fear many times over the past three days. But, without Benjamin, this could be—no. God wouldn't force her to—

Deke ended Julia's musings when he put the business end of his rifle against the back of KC's head.

He wouldn't just—yes, he would. This man would pull the trigger if it suited him.

Would stopping him be Julia's responsibility?

Benjamin, where are you?

"Daniels, hands on your head and push your face against the cave wall ... now!"

Brock took his time, but stepped up to the wall.

Deke barked out more commands.

Even if Julia could find the courage to shoot, there wasn't enough separation to avoid hitting her friends.

All four now stood against the cave wall.

Deke walked up behind KC and scanned her body from head to foot, slowly. He ran his fingers through her long, red, curly hair.

Julia shuddered. The man was obsessed with KC. This could go downhill in a hurry as it had when Abdul had become obsessed with Julia.

KC twisted her head around and looked at Deke's face. Her eyes widened, her cheeks turned red, and she spat in the man's face.

He yanked on her hair.

KC gasped but didn't cry out.

Julia had heard of KC's courage in the face of danger. But was this courage or KC's bad temper?

Deke wiped the spittle from his dirt-smudged face.

"Ms. Banning, you have no idea who you're up against or what I can do to you."

"I'm not Ms. Banning. I'm Mrs. Daniels and I know a wuss when I see one. You're a coward, a wimp who couldn't even—"

"Kace, stop it!" Brock shuffled his feet like he might turn around. If KC didn't stop provoking this man, she could get Brock killed.

"That's good advice coming from a man who was just about to lose his wife." Deke turned to the other soldier. "Johnson, did you send the message?"

"Yes, sir. But Hannan hasn't replied."

So Deke was Hannan's hand-picked man, a man like Abdul. An animal. Julia had to end this now. She pushed the safety lever to automatic and planted the butt of the gun against her shoulder.

Could she keep the powerful weapon under control when it sprang to life in her hands?

Another question blindsided her. Could these men have gotten past Benjamin if he was alive and well?

No. Her heart hammered out panic. She truly *was* on her own. Whatever she did or did not do, Julia Weiss would have to live with it.

Or die with it.

Chapter 33

Craig brought his men to a halt and looked down the hallway to the elevators. No one.

Blaine had already checked the study and the Oval Office.

How had Hannan gotten away so quickly? Earlier, KC had detected him online from the study. Maybe someone from the Executive Office Building warned the Secret Service agents in the White House.

Time for plan B, down the stairwell. "Cutter, Blaine, watch our six. This may take a minute or two."

Craig faced the ground-level entrance to the stairwell. He couldn't use the two scanning devices on the left side of the door, but the strange-looking keypad mounted on the right side of the door looked promising. He pulled the slip of paper with KC's cypher keys on it and carefully entered the long sequence of numbers for the first door.

The door clicked and Daddy-O, the tallest member of the team, pushed it open, checked above the door, then slapped a strip of duct tape across the video camera mounted there. Security would notice, but they couldn't see whom or how many were in the stairwell.

The team entered the stairwell leading down more than 3,000 steps to the DUCC. Their descent would be brutal.

"Sorry, men. But you're going to be sore tomorrow morning."

Daddy-O ripped off another piece of tape. "We'll take sore over the alternative."

"Me, too. We need to hurry, but tell me if your legs give out. We'll take a short break. And whenever we spot a door, Daddy-O applies the tape to the camera. Any questions?"

"Just one, sir," Blaine said. "How long is this descent?"

"You would ask that. With a few short rests ... twenty minutes."

"Lord, help us."

Craig smiled and shook his head. "I second that, Daddy-O. Now, let's go."

Twenty minutes later, Craig's knees ached and his quads quivered from muscle acidity. That no one had fallen was a minor miracle.

Twenty feet below, the door for level 5 came into view. "Daddy-O, we need your services."

The tall team daddy took the lead and, a few seconds later, slapped tape over the last video camera.

By now, security would know that someone was moving systematically down the stairwell. But how would they respond? Craig prayed that he and his men could enter the DUCC before a force could be assembled and intercept them.

Craig pulled out the paper with the cipher keys on it. "Listen up," he spoke softly between heavy breaths.

The men clustered around him on the stairwell landing.

"There will likely be guards at the door to the DUCC. They should be visible when this door opens. When it does, the loud click will probably draw their attention. I want Daddy-O and Blaine beside me. I'll shove the door open at the click. We flash bang any guards, but have your guns ready. If they make any movement to fire at us, take them out. Any questions?"

257

"Sir," Cutter said. "Can you give us about thirty seconds to pay our oxygen debt?"

"Only thirty seconds. The danger of another force arriving down here grows by the second."

Two minutes later, with Daddy-O and Blaine on either side, Craig punched in the final number.

The door clicked and he shoved it open.

Two armed men guarded a large door.

Two objects flew into the hallway.

Craig shielded his face and covered his ears.

Simultaneous explosions sent searing flashes that singed the hair on the back of Craig's hand.

When he looked up, the two men lay on the floor.

Four Rangers rushed in and drug the two unconscious men into the stairwell, and handcuffed the guards to the railing, out of reach of the door scanners, and applied duct tape, liberally.

Craig stopped in front of a mammoth door, waiting for his four men to return.

"Remember, this is a two-step process. The DUCC is pressurized to prevent air contamination. KC said no one would hear us until we go through the second door. We don't know how many people are inside until the door opens, and we don't know if they know we're coming. If you have to shoot, don't shoot the president. Any questions?"

No replies.

Craig turned to the bulky door and keyed in the cypher. When the door unlatched, air hissed around its edges. The hissing turned to a brisk breeze when the door fully opened.

All eleven Rangers fit easily in the intermediate chamber, but thoughts of being trapped inside it sent claustrophobic impulses through Craig's nervous system. He fought to quell them, then gathered his men around him. "The next door isn't locked. Hannan should be on the other side. Any final questions before we pay him a visit?"

Daddy-O and Blaine moved beside Craig with M84 flashbang grenades in hand.

"God bless us and God bless America, because Hannan sure won't." With his M4 in his right hand, Craig cranked the door handle and shoved.

Chapter 34

Hannan hadn't talked to Deke in over twenty-four hours. In their last conversation, Deke had asked for, and Hannan had granted, access to intelligence information about Brock Daniels. It was a decision that Hannan now regretted, because it made Deke a wildcard in this drama unfolding in Central Oregon.

The odds were slim, but Deke might prevail and Hannan would begrudgingly grant him hero status. But Deke could mess things up, royally.

Hannan clicked on the link to open the inbox of his comm software. At the top of the list sat a message from Deke with a date-time stamp of 6:55 p.m. Eastern, fifteen minutes ago.

Hannan opened the message and drew a sharp breath as he read it.

Entering cave where Daniels group is hiding. Will have them in custody in a few minutes. Awaiting orders for their disposal.

Deke must have contacted Wiley at NSA to get Daniels' location. But Scott could arrive soon. If Deke botched this by allowing anyone to escape, he would destroy the whole plan.

Hannan quickly opened a window to reply to Deke, hoping it wasn't already too late to stop an incompetent commander who'd lost his men and a top-secret chopper.

When Hannan started typing, a loud buzzer jolted him like a lightning bolt. "What the—"

A voice came over the PA system, the voice of a man breathing hard. "Code red! Code red! This is security on level 4. The stairwell has been breached. Repeat—the stairwell has been breached. Intruders are descending toward the DUCC. Keep all doors locked and remain inside a secure room until we notify you that the underground complex is secure. We have called for assistance and will update the status as it changes."

Hannan cursed Deke. He cursed West Wing security and he—Hannan stopped.

What if this turned into a worst-case scenario? The intruders had come through at least one door protected by biometric scanning devices. As impossible as it seemed, they could possibly breach the DUCC, itself. If so, Hannan might need Brock Daniels and company as bargaining chips.

Hannan finished his reply to Deke.

West Wing breached by insurgents heading down to DUCC. Suspect defector, Captain Craig. Capture Daniels and group. Keep everyone alive, especially Daniels and Banning. Insure none get away. We may have a hostage situation here, soon.

He pressed send, then ran several possible scenarios through his mind. What if Scott's Rangers from JBLM arrived now and decided to annihilate everyone in the cave? If Scott was still flying, contacting him may not be possible. But Hannan needed to try, anyway, or he might have no bargaining chip in what could turn into a high-stakes negotiation.

He reached for his phone, but jumped to his feet when the inner door to the DUCC flew open.

A powerful-looking man, dressed in tac gear and with his face covered, stood in the doorway holding an assault rifle.

Icy fingers squeezed Hannan's heart, because he knew the man, instinctively.

Craig.

Chapter 35

Julia hadn't moved from her hiding place behind the boulder near the cave entrance. The two grimy looking Rangers with their guns on her four friends hadn't given her a chance to creep closer to them.

"Keep your hands up and your faces against the cave wall!" Deke appeared to be studying the four people in front of him, sizing them up.

What was he going to do with them? She still couldn't shoot for fear of hitting her friends.

Couldn't shoot? Was she actually contemplating shooting another human being? The question created a nauseating ache in her stomach.

Brock towered above everyone in the cave. She had seen how powerful and deadly Brock could be to any threat.

Evidently, Deke saw Brock's capability, too. Deke kept his distance and kept his M4 trained on Brock. "I'm going to collect your guns. One move from you, Daniels, and I'll shoot that freckle-faced ..." Deke's description of KC became vulgar.

Julia didn't even know what some of the words meant.

Brock's clenched jaw and flexing muscles told her enough.

"Getting comms, sir." Johnson's voice.

"Inside the cave? Must be the skylight above us. Cover them, Johnson, and give me the radio."

"It's a text message." Johnson gave Deke the comm device.

"The DUCC might be breached by insurgents?" Deke looked up from the phone and stared at Johnson. "If Hannan is taken, do you know where that leaves us?"

Johnson snorted. "Yeah. Two soldiers without a country and with no reward for capturing these two apes ... and these two delectable beauties."

The way Johnson spoke brought more nausea. Julia tried to shake it off by focusing on the events playing out on the other side of the continent.

Craig must already be on his way down to the DUCC. But it didn't make sense. How did Steve get there so quickly? Only one answer seemed plausible ... Steve wasn't with Craig. If not, where was he?

Julia stopped her speculation when Deke spoke again.

"Find something to tie them up with, Johnson. We're going to need these four, for a while."

"Then what?" Johnson asked.

Deke's gaze roved all over KC, again. "If things go badly, we kill the apes and the two women will have to be the reward for two soldiers without a country. And I get the redhead."

Johnson barked a mirthless laugh. "I've always preferred the dark-haired ..." He continued with several ethnic slurs of the worst sort as he studied Allie.

Jeff turned his head and shot Johnson a vicious looking glance.

KC's face had turned red. She lowered her hands to her sides and turned to face Deke, glaring at him. "I will kill you unless you kill me first. That's how it will be and that's all you'll get, you scrawny, little s—"

"Kace, turn around," Brock said. "Don't let those boneheads' taunting get to—."

Brock stopped when a metallic click from one of the rifles echoed through the cave.

Even Julia realized the two men would already have loaded cartridges in their guns' chambers. The click had been for dramatic effect, and it had worked.

Maybe after Deke had tied up all four he would leave them on the floor of the cave. That could give Julia a clear shot at the two men.

The things they talked about doing to the women turned Julia's stomach and, at the same time, brought anger as hot as the lava rock she hid behind had been when it flowed into this tube called the Skylight Cave.

She tried to shove the anger and other distractions out of her mind and focus on her goal. To save her friends, Julia had only one option, shoot Deke and Johnson. But, when it came time to pull the trigger ...

Can I do it?

Chapter 36

Craig trained his gun on Abe Hannan as the would-be tyrant plopped into a chair and reached for the laptop keyboard in front of him. "Hannan ... hands off that laptop, now! Freeze! If you want to keep breathing." Craig moved the laser sight onto Hannan's forehead.

Hannan winced, then turned and tilted his head back, staring at Craig ... down the bridge of Hannan's nose. "The infamous Captain Craig, you little ..."

Craig tried to mentally deflect Hannan's vulgar character assassination, but the sewer flowing from his mouth wouldn't stop. "Close your filthy mouth! Now, Hannan!" Craig's hands squeezed on his weapon as he fought the urge to send this man into eternity.

Hannan took his hands off the laptop and met Craig's gaze. "But you need to realize that—"

"No! You need to realize that it's over, Abid."

Hannan jerked erect, rigid in his chair after hearing his birth name. Slowly, a smile spread across his face. "Brock Daniels is dead."

"What?" Had the troops arrived and killed them? He studied Hannan's face. Craig's assessment ... the man was desperate and bluffing. "Do you really expect me to believe that? At the very moment when you become the hostage, your not-so-special forces capture one of our—"

"Not one. Four of them." Hannan's eyes focused on the laptop as the lighted screen flickered, turning Hannan's face from white to red. "And Daniels will most certainly be dead, along with his friends, unless—"

"You'll be dead if you don't shut your mouth." Craig's gut balled into a huge knot. "Daddy-O, cuff our illustrious president, while I check out his laptop. And leave his hands in front. We might need them."

With a quirky grin, Hannan stared at Craig, keeping his bravado while the team daddy cuffed the president's hands.

Craig spun Hannan's laptop around on the table to study the screen. A large modal window shone brightly, glaring at him with angry red letters.

To Captain Craig or to whom it may concern,

Daniels, Banning, and another couple are facing the cave wall with M4s pointed at their heads. I would suggest you free president Hannan, now. If you do not, Ms. Banning will soon start screaming and screaming and... you get the point, I'm sure.

Captain Deke.

Chapter 37

Julia checked the safety lever on her M4 again. Automatic mode.

Brock and KC lay on the cave floor, their hands taped behind them.

The man called Johnson had finished taping Jeff's hands and now worked on Allie.

When Johnson stood, there would be separation between the soldiers and her friends.

One pass through Deke's and Johnson's position in automatic mode and this nightmare would be over.

Julia eased her upper body out from behind the boulder, pulled the gun into her shoulder and raised the barrel ...

Vivid memories came storming back into her mind.

Dense vegetation around the Yoruban village surrounded her.

Her best friend, Bisi, stood beside Julia facing Bisi's jihadist cousin, Ore.

Ore pointed his gun at Bisi's face.

The staccato popping of the automatic weapon paralyzed Julia and Bisi fell to the ground, her beautiful face reduced to a bloody mass.

Julia gasped and nearly dropped her M4.

I can't do this.

Breathing hard, she pulled her head back behind the rock. Had Deke heard her? She peered around the corner of the lava boulder.

No, he didn't hear. Deke had his phone in his ear. "Who is this? ... Captain Craig?" Deke swore. "I want to speak to Hannan, now, or the four people here are going to die!"

Craig must have captured Hannan. She prayed that Deke needed Hannan alive as much as Craig wanted to save her friends in the cave. Otherwise, this would end soon and badly.

When Deke had threatened to do horrible things to KC and Allie, rage had contorted Brock's face into a frightening caricature of his usual expression. Brock was fierce in a fight and, at six-foot-five and nearly 240 pounds, he was deadly. KC said he had killed one of Captain Blanchard's men in less than a second, though Brock was handcuffed. Even if Brock managed to kill one of the men, the other one would kill him.

Julia had to end this before Brock attempted anything.

Deke's argument on the phone with Craig continued.

Julia studied KC on the ground beside Brock. The desperation in her eyes was more than Julia could bear. She looked away.

Was Deke too evil to let him have his way? Was any person so evil that she could just mow them down with an automatic rifle? Could she kill a person God had created in His image?

She had no answers to her questions.

Once again, Julia proved herself to be too weak. The kids at school were right. Wimpy Weiss they had called her. Maybe she should get what she deserved. That would be easy. Just walk out from behind the rock and let Deke shoot her.

A voice came from somewhere deep inside. Not exactly a voice, more of a thought. But it was neither Julia's voice nor her thought.

You are not weak. I made Julia Weiss strong, like Brock and KC—made for such a time as this. Only you can stop the evil. Julia, the time is now!

Chapter 38

Questions ran through Craig's mind faster than he could answer them.

Did he have the DUCC guarded sufficiently if they were attacked?

Seven of his men were outside the DUCC, four guarding the stairwell door and three at the big entry door to the DUCC. Three were in the command center with Craig. Blaine and Meyer had their guns on Hannan while Daddy-O watched the inside door.

Deke said two women, didn't he? KC and Allie. And four people. That probably meant Brock and Jeff were captives, too.

Where was Julia? And more importantly, where was the man who could save them, Benjamin?

One thing Craig could count on, if Benjamin could have been there, he would have been there. Something must have happened to him. Whatever it was, he was probably out of the fight, at least for now.

For the time being, Craig had only one option, to maintain the standoff while he tried to devise a way to end it, successfully.

He had let Hannan speak to Deke to prove the president was unharmed. Time to end that conversation.

Craig yanked the phone from Hannan's cuffed hands.

And now it was time to try a bluff by adding a little FUD, fear, uncertainty, and doubt. "Listen, Deke, if you harm any of those four people, I'll give orders to the men approaching to make sure you don't come out of that cave alive."

"What men approaching?" Deke growled back.

"Don't you know that Hannan ordered a company of Rangers from JBLM to take out everyone in the cave?"

"You, sir, are a liar. That's not going to work with me. Maybe I should start with the Banning girl, now."

Craig handed the phone to Hannan. "Tell him who's coming, Hannan, and what they're going to do."

"Deke, I ordered a company of Rangers from JBLM, 200 men, under a Captain Scott. They have orders that no one is to leave that cave alive."

Craig took the phone from Hannan. "Satisfied, Deke?"

"Well, it looks like your side loses, regardless. They'll all be dead."

"Look, Deke. Hannan is history no matter how this plays out. And if you harm one hair of anyone's head in that cave, I place a call to the Ranger company commander and you're history."

Craig's bluff had few teeth in it. No teeth that would bite Deke. Captain Scott wouldn't take orders from Craig. In fact, Scott had no knowledge of Craig, Deke, what was happening in DC, or inside the cave. The orders would have to come from Hannan.

Craig muted the phone. "Hannan, when I say so you will issue the orders to kill Deke on sight."

"Suppose I refuse?"

Craig pulled out his Ka-Bar and placed the blade against Hannan's neck. "Then you die."

"Then they die." Hannan gave Craig a smirk, but beads of sweat covered Hannan's forehead.

Craig could probably make Hannan comply, but didn't have enough time to do that with Deke threatening Brock and the others. Craig unmuted the phone. "Deke, hold on for a minute. I've got a proposal for you."

"You've got one minute, Craig. A short minute. These two women are becoming a bit of a temptation, if you know what I mean? I'm having a hard time choosing between the red-headed supermodel and the Spanish beauty."

Craig muted the phone call. Deke could do things to the women that were worse than death. He might even attempt such things to get his way.

Craig sought a solution, but he stood in the middle of a Mexican standoff while playing Russian roulette. The bullet in the spinning chamber was the approaching Ranger company. Who knew when it would end up under the firing pin?

Though Hannan had confirmed it, Deke hadn't said he actually believed there were Rangers approaching. And who knew what the Rangers would do? They might send in a bunker-busting rocket and kill everyone in the cave.

Any reward Deke expected to get for his role would have to come through Hannan. So threatening to kill Hannan was the only way to keep Deke from killing his hostages. Craig had to maintain a precarious balance of threats, a balance that would be destroyed when the troops arrived at the cave.

And Deke's reaction when the troops arrived? Craig hadn't a clue.

He ran scenarios and contingency plans through his normally sharp mind, but found only a muddle of flawed logic and ineffective tactics. He needed to tell Deke something before he killed anyone or attacked the women.

Daddy-O turned the handle on the inside door. "Sir, I'm going to make a quick check on the chamber. We don't want any nasty surprises coming through that soundproof barrier."

273

"Go ahead, Daddy-O."

Craig's minute ended with no clear plan in mind. He unmuted the call and drew a breath to speak, not sure what words would come out. "Deke, here's the deal—"

A loud crack drowned out the soft whir of the air-conditioning equipment.

Craig dropped the phone and raised his gun.

Hannan lurched forward from the chair, fell on the floor, and rolled onto his side.

Craig's head jerked toward the sound that came from the back of the room.

In front of one of the bathroom doors, a gaunt old man with a cane stood. The Secretary of State, Eli Vance. He dropped a handgun to the floor, released his cane, and raised both hands.

As shock wore off, Craig fought the urge to bash in the old man's head. Did Vance have any idea what he had just done? Would he care that he had, in effect, killed Brock and the others? Craig pointed his finger at the assassin and growled out his command. "Blaine, cuff Eli Vance. Daddy-O, get Cutter in here, now."

When Blaine grabbed Vance, Craig dropped to the floor beside Hannan. The large exit wound below his sternum told the story even before their Medical Officer, Cutter, arrived. The shot had hit Hannan's abdominal aorta. He would bleed out in a couple of minutes, and there was nothing anyone could do to save him unless he was already in the operating room with a surgical team.

When Craig dropped the phone, the speakerphone had evidently come on. Deke's voice blasted from the speaker. "Was that a gunshot? What's going on, Craig?"

If Deke knew the truth, he would kill everyone in the cave. Craig muted the phone, his available options flying through his mind too fast to catch. After the options had all flown away, only one thought remained.

God, help us.

Chapter 39

From the floor where he knelt beside Hannan, Craig glared at the assassin. "Vance, you just killed seven people."

Eli shrugged. "I always told him someone would shoot him someday."

Hannan struggled to talk.

Blaine grabbed Eli's shoulders and shoved him closer to Hannan.

The president, glassy-eyed, looked up at Vance. "Why, Eli? I trusted you more than anyone."

"Abe, after they abandoned you, you were supposed to give up, disappear, or fail, completely. But you wouldn't stop. You were poisoning the well, ruining the future for the organization. If you continued, there could be repercussions that would make it impossible to …" Eli's voice trailed off. He looked at Hannan. Something like pity flickered across the old man's face, then he pursed his lips and stared at the wall, still and stoic.

Where was Cutter? Blood pooled around the president's body, far too much blood. Maybe Cutter could do something like … perform a miracle?

"Who ordered it? Alexis?" Hannan clenched a fist in either anger, pain, or maybe both.

Eli nodded.

"Tell her she can go to—" Hannan hissed the words then stopped as the air drained from his lungs. His eyes closed and Abe Hannan became the fifth American president to die from an assassin's bullet.

The door to the DUCC opened and Cutter burst through the doorway.

Daddy-O stepped in behind Cutter and closed the door.

"He's gone," Craig said.

Cutter knelt beside Hannan's body, felt his neck, and nodded. "The bullet exited right through his abdominal aorta. It's a shame. Now, he'll never be tried and convicted for his crimes."

Craig turned toward Eli. "What's the organization and who's Alexis?"

Eli's mustache lifted on one side as he gave Craig a crooked smile. "If I told you that, I'd have to shoot you." Eli chuckled. It ended in a coughing fit that drove the old man to his knees on the floor and left him wheezing to catch what appeared to be an elusive thing ... his breath.

Chapter 40

Steve glanced at the F-15 on the tarmac as the little Cessna lifted off the runway at Madras, thirty miles north of Sisters.

The sixty-something pilot with grizzled hair that hadn't seen a barber in at least a month, shot Steve a glance from beneath equally grizzled eyebrows. But the eyes beneath those bushy brows were a brilliant blue, filled with intelligence. Right now, they were questioning eyes. "You're not planning to shoot me with that assault rifle, are you, son?"

"Wouldn't that be unconstitutional?"

"Whatever you say. You've got the gun."

"Sir, I took an oath to defend the Constitution of the United States against all enemies, foreign and domestic. That's all I'm doing. But our illustrious president has become a domestic enemy." Steve paused and adjusted the pack on his back filled with polyester and a few hundred feet of cord. "You sure this chute is packed right?"

"If it ain't, you won't get the chance to shoot me for it."

"Don't count on that, old man. But, if this chute doesn't open, some good people are going to die."

"Good people? Like who?"

"Brock Daniels, KC—used to be Banning—and the woman I love, Julia Weiss."

"The heck you say. Daniels and Banning—good people. And Miss Weiss ... wasn't she the young woman who survived Ebola a few weeks ago? Read about that in the papers."

"That's her. But you didn't read *everything* about it in the papers. Hannan's DOD got her infected with their genetically engineered version of that little bug. You know, the one that invades your body a cell at a time until it liquefies all your organs and you just—"

"Shoot, son, can we talk about something else. Medical stuff about my innards makes me queasy. You keep talking about it and you might have to fly this plane while I do some serious upchuckin'."

The small plane dropped like a rock, lifting Steve off from his seat, then he slammed down hard as the plane rose for three or four seconds. It dropped again and leveled off.

"And flying through thermals, above the desert, on a hot summer day doesn't bother you?"

"Not a bit. Son, I'm on your side, so—"

"Why don't we just say we're both on the same side, the side of the United States of America? Can't this bird go any faster?"

"This ain't that F-15 you just climbed out of, but I can crank her up to 120 or so."

"Please do it, sir. We don't have any time to waste."

The pilot shoved on a knob above his right leg and the engine wound tight. "Now, where we going, exactly?"

"About eight miles southwest of Sisters."

"Remind me ... what's there?"

"It's called the Skylight Cave."

"Well, shoot. You should have just told me. I've been there a time or two. I'll put you right on top of that old lava tube."

"No, sir."

"Quit calling me sir. I'm no officer." He pulled a hand off the wheel and shoved it at Steve. "Name's Bob Daggett."

Steve shook it. "Sergeant Steve Bancroft, US Army Ranger."

"So where do I put you down, Ranger Bancroft?"

"I won't know for sure until I see what's happening on the ground."

"Well, you'll see what's happening in ten or twelve minutes."

The plane dropped, sending Steve's stomach into flip flops, then slammed him in his seat when the Cessna bounced back up.

"Darn!" Bob, shook his head, pulled a hand off the wheel, and poked a finger into his mouth. He pulled it back out. "Let's slide west a little. Get away from the desert floor. Those doggone thermals knock my upper plate loose when I hit'em at this speed."

For the next five minutes Bob flew the plane down the foothills of the Cascades in silence, except for the drone of the Cessna's engine.

Steve ran through his mind every scenario at the cave he could think of. But it had been three and a half hours since Craig told Steve to turn back. A lot could happen in that span of time.

Bob raised his right hand and pointed at something ahead and to their left. "There's Sisters."

Steve's eyes sighted down Bob's arm. Beyond his pointing finger, a town lay nestled in what looked like Pine trees. He scanned the edges of town, then choked when he drew a sharp breath.

Southwest of town, in a field sparsely populated with Ponderosa Pine trees, only six or seven miles from the Skylight Cave, sat eight Chinook helicopters. If they came in quietly, no one in the cave could have heard them.

Depending upon how much equipment they brought, eight Chinooks could transport anywhere from 150 to 400 troops. From that location, the troops could reach the cave in two hours, maybe less.

Based on the time of Craig's call, Steve calculated the possible arrival time of the helicopters. It could have been thirty minutes ago, or as much as three hours. Maybe he was too late and Julia was—no. He wouldn't accept that.

When Steve looked at Bob, the man's blue eyes were locked on Steve. "I fought in Nam. First Air Cavalry. So I know there's a small army down there. They on your side?"

"No."

Bob whistled as he banked the plane and headed toward a mountain to the south. "If you're bent on committing suicide, I need to get you as close to that cave with as little exposure as possible."

"I'd appreciate it."

"We can use Black Butte Mountain to hide our approach for a while and keep us to the west of that army."

Steve noted that Bob's "I" had become "we." The old pilot had bought into helping Steve, but he didn't want to get the man killed or his plane shot up. "How close can you get me without them seeing me ... assuming the troops are near the cave?"

"We can snuggle up to the trees, come in from the southwest, and climb like crazy just before I drop you."

"I need a little room to navigate before reaching the ground."

"Son, I think you should minimize your air time and only use that chute to stop you from splattering on the lava rocks down there. You know, let the chute pop open just before you do. Now, show me where you want to land and, if we do this quick like, you'll be on the ground before they can react."

"You're right. Thanks, Bob. But ..." Bob was putting himself in serious danger and Steve had forced him here at gunpoint, though Captain Towery's endorsement had eased the tension a bit.

"I'll be okay. By the time they can see me, I'll be halfway through my Immelmann turn. I go down out of sight and snuggle up to the trees as I fly away to the south. They'll never get a clear shot at me. I'll never be over them, you know, like a threat. And it sounds like they're more worried about a target on the ground than some little Cessna snooping on them. I'll be fine."

"Bob ... if we both get out of this alive, man, I owe you one ... a big one."

"Tell you what. After you survive this, you bring that little gal that beat Ebola up to Madras, and I'll introduce both of you to the boys and give you a free jump."

"You got yourself a deal."

"Steve ..." Bob shoved his large, calloused right hand at Steve.

Steve shook it. Knowing it was this former soldier's way of saying goodbye, good luck, and God bless you. "God bless you, too, Bob."

"Now, listen up. In about ninety seconds, you need to move out onto that step welded onto the landing gear. When we start the climb, you count two seconds, leap as far out from the plane as you can, and pull the ripcord. Got it?"

"Got it."

"Rangers lead the way!" Bob yelled and waved Steve toward the small platform where he would jump.

Steve climbed out onto the landing gear of the little Cessna 150. They were, as Bob put it, snuggled up to the trees. So low that Steve couldn't see the ground around the vicinity of the cave. To orient himself, he looked at the spot where he thought the cave would be.

The Cessna nosed upward and the engine's drone turned to a roar.

Steve gripped the wing strut hard to keep from falling off in the steep climb. *One thousand one, one thousand two.* Steve leaped far beyond the distance needed to avoid the tail section and, at the height of his jump, tried to catch a glimpse of the cave.

In a large circle, with the cave's entrance at its center, a whole company of soldiers, at least 200, moved slowly, guns in hand, drawing their noose tighter on the cave and its occupants.

Could he make it in time? In time to what? Get shot? Was there any way to stop these men ordered by the president to kill seven terrorists?

As Steve pulled the ripcord, Bob's last words echoed in his mind, "Rangers lead the way!" The final words of the Rangers' Creed.

Another thought popped into his head as the canopy popped open above him. The men on the ground were not just soldiers, they were Rangers. That used to mean something. But, in this man's army, it only raised a question. Would they honor their creed?

Chapter 41

Julia gripped her gun, still in automatic mode, as she watched the drama unfold thirty yards in front of her.

Her four friends lying on the cave floor with their hands duct-taped behind them were at Deke's mercy. But the man's violent gestures and crude, threatening words said he knew no such thing as mercy.

Deke tossed a rock, hitting Brock in the back where his t-shirt displayed the US flag.

Brock flinched.

"Do you think it makes you an American patriot to wear a flag on your back? After you're dead, Hannan will paint Brock Daniels as a power-hungry traitor. So much for your image." Deke's eyes seemed to refocus on KC.

His grin exuded evil. He had given in to the darkness inside him and it became clear where he was headed. "On the other hand, Ms. Banning is more tastefully dressed. But, perhaps she should not be dressed at all."

Julia stiffened at Deke's vile, threatening words. She planted the butt of the gun on her shoulder and slowly raised the barrel. The words of that still, small voice replayed in Julia's mind.

Only you can stop the evil and the time is now.

"Johnson, you can do the honors." Deke waved Johnson toward KC.

Her urge to stop Deke had become a firm resolve. Julia slipped out from behind the rock and aimed her gun, targeting a point chest high, half way between Johnson and KC.

Johnson, appeared oblivious to Julia, completely focused on his task. He took a step toward KC.

Julia pulled the gun tightly against her shoulder. In one smooth motion, she squeezed the trigger and swung the barrel in an arc away from the four people on the ground.

The gun came alive in Julia's hands. The rhythmic cracking of M4, amplified by the cave, pounded her eardrums. The barrel tried to rise, like the rifle had a will of its own. Steve had warned her about this, but the higher aim only made her shots deadlier.

Johnson and Deke fell to the ground.

Deke lay still.

But Johnson moved. His hand reached for his gun beside him on the cave floor.

Julia aimed at Johnson and shot another burst. Bullets kicked up a line of dirt that she directed across Johnson's body.

He stopped moving.

It was over.

The emotional battle had already been fought and won. She had done what was required. Relief washed over her.

Julia pushed the safety lever and ran toward her friends.

Brock had rolled onto his back. He sat up, surveying the gory scene.

Julia tried not to look at the two men as she ran toward Brock.

"Julia, get his knife." Brock nodded at Deke. "It's on his belt. Then cut us loose."

Could she take a dead man's knife, a man she had killed? An hour ago, probably not. But now, the new resolve in her heart and mind to confront and fight against evil told her she could do this.

When she'd argued with Brock at Jeff's house, Brock had been right. They lived in a fallen world. She believed that as a theological abstraction, but had refused to carry her belief through to its logical conclusion, a conclusion the one true God had illustrated many times in the scriptures. When evil threatened innocent people, sometimes deadly force was the only option. That was why governments around the globe established police forces and armies.

Now, Julia understood more fully the implications of living in a sin infected world. She also understood Steve's strong desire to protect.

And I need to tell him.

Julia slipped Deke's knife from his belt.

Brock swiveled around on his rear and pushed his hands out from his back.

Julia knelt behind him and carefully sawed through the layers of duct tape.

While Brock ripped the tape from his wrists, Julia moved to KC.

When the knife cut through KC's bonds, she pulled her hands apart and whirled around to face Julia who knelt beside her. Tears in KC's eyes overflowed onto her cheeks, "Julia, please forgive me. I ... I ..."

"No, KC. There's nothing to forgive. I need you to forgive me. I acted like I was superior to you all, too good to even—"

KC slapped a piece of duct tape over Julia's mouth. "We don't want to hear any more of you putting yourself down, Julia. Not another word." KC wrapped her arms around Julia in a fierce hug. "You've done things over the last two days that I could never do. You saved our lives and Steve's, and risked your own to do it."

"Yeah." Jeff grunted the affirmation as he struggled to a sitting position. "But, if you two are through with all the girlie stuff, Allie and I would like to have the use of our hands."

When Julia moved to Jeff and Allie, a light flashed on the floor of the cave, accompanied by a buzzing sound. Deke's phone.

Brock leaped forward and grabbed it. "Hello. Is this Craig? ... We're safe for the moment. ... Julia shot Deke and his man, Johnson. Yeah. I'm sure. I saw her do it."

Julia freed Jeff and Allie, then stopped. What was that sound outside the cave? "Someone's out there." She ran toward the ladder at the cave entrance.

Jeff lunged at her, trying to stop her.

Julia pulled away, sprinted to the ladder, and stepped onto the first rung.

Jeff reached the ladder and tried to pull her off.

She kicked at him.

He backed away. "Julia, stop."

She gave him the shush signal. This was her job and she needed to do it for her friends as well as herself.

Jeff gave her a puzzled frown.

Julia motioned up, out of the cave. "We need to be quiet," she whispered. "Tell the others to keep it down while I see who's out there."

Jeff scurried back to the group and picked up two rifles, handing one to Brock.

Julia turned, looked upward, and slowly climbed the ladder. Hoping to see Benjamin, she peered out.

Movement on the higher ground to the west caught her eye. Julia ducked, then stepped down a rung, processing images of what she'd seen.

Men in tac gear. Hundreds of them. And sitting on a large lava rock was something like the thermal bear launcher she had seen on Bolan Peak. But this one was bigger and looked even more menacing.

Steve had mentioned a deadly thermobaric weapon used to kill the Taliban hiding in caves. He'd called it a serpent or—she couldn't remember. But it sounded like the deadliest of all thermal bears.

Somehow, she had to make certain the soldiers here didn't use it, or Julia and the others would all die a fiery death. That thought sent her racing heart into a wild, driving rhythm.

She had to tell these men that Hannan was a prisoner. Needed to tell them now. That would stop their attack. But how could she communicate with them without getting shot?

Julia scampered down the ladder and whirled toward Brock.

Still on the phone with Craig, Brock's eyes were filled with excitement.

She hurried to Brock, took a close look at the buttons on the phone, then reached in and muted it.

He pulled the phone from his ear. "What the heck are you doing, Julia?"

"Quiet. We're surrounded by soldiers. Rangers. Hundreds of them. We need to tell them we have Hannan held hostage or we're all dead. Ask Craig how we should do that."

Color drained from Brock's face. "We have a problem, Julia." Brock drew a deep breath and let it out slowly. "Hannan's dead."

Silence in the cave.

Steve. Was he with Craig? Was he safe? Julia needed to know about Steve. No, not just know about him, she wanted Steve here with her. She needed to beg his forgiveness and hope that somehow he would understand why she had cruelly lied to him. If she died now, Steve would never know.

He would never understand that she loved him. That the barriers between them were gone.

If Hannan was dead, Craig must have been successful. She looked up at Brock. "Was Steve with Craig?"

"I don't know. But I've got to tell Craig about the Rangers." Brock fumbled with the phone.

"Wait a minute." Julia grabbed Brock's hand. "I have an idea. Take off your shirt, Brock."

"Hold it. You're not gonna do to me what Deke tried to do to KC."

"Julia." KC hooked Brock's free arm. "He doesn't do that for anyone but me."

"How about doing it for the USA?"

KC's hands went to her hips. "No. Brock's not one of those chips and dips or whatever they call those show guys in Las Vegas."

She huffed a blast of air. "Look, I just want to make a white flag and an American flag. His t-shirt is perfect. I'll cut it in half."

Brock sighed, pulled his shirt over his head, and shoved it at her. "Take the doggone thing. I've got some more clothes in my pack."

Julia picked up Deke's knife and sliced the sides of the t-shirt, then tied the white front half to the end of her M4. She picked up Deke's rifle and tied the American flag side of the shirt to its muzzle.

Time to get out of here while Brock looked for another shirt. He would try to stop her.

"Now what?" Jeff's voice.

With a rifle in each hand, Julia turned toward the ladder.

Brock pulled a shirt from his duffle bag and looked up. "You're not going out there to surrender, Julia." He reached for her.

Julia backed away from him. "Who's going to stop me?"

He leaped ahead to block her path. "I am."

"Brock, if a man goes out there with a gun in his hand, it's threatening. They'll shoot him. But little Julia Weiss—I'm not threatening to anybody."

Brock shook his head. "Not threatening? Try telling that to Deke and Johnson."

"Move, Brock."

He folded his arms and shook his head. "Sorry, but you're not going."

She lowered her M4, pointing it at his foot. "Don't make me shoot you, Brock Daniels. But I will if you don't move. You've seen that I've overcome my inhibitions."

Brock's body stiffened, but he didn't move.

She shoved the bolt forward creating an ominous click.

Brock backed away. "Julia, Steve will kill me if I let you go out there."

"He'll kill me, too," Jeff said.

"This is okay, Brock. I know what I'm doing."

"Which is?" Brock raised his eyebrows.

Brock had thought she was crazy since they arrived at Jeff's house. If she told him her plan, it would only confirm it. "Maybe I'll just sing," she muttered.

"What did you say? Sing?"

"Have you got any better ideas?"

"Go right ahead. You can sing Michael, Row the Boat A-Shore or Where Have All the Flowers Gone while they kill you. Or maybe you can put them to sleep with Rock-a-Bye Baby so we can all escape?"

"How about I Surrender All," Jeff said.

She ignored Jeff's comment and peered into Brock's glaring eyes. "Brock, I'm not exactly stupid."

"Not exactly, but pretty doggone close."

Chapter 42

Had any of the Rangers seen Steve bail out of the Cessna? If the Rangers had posted sentries, they might have seen the chute open. That possibility made Steve doubly cautious as he moved toward the cave.

And, once he got there, what was he going to do? He didn't know, but he sure wasn't going to whistle Hail to the Chief.

What was left of Steve's uniform, his tattered shirt, might identify him as a Ranger, a somewhat out-of-uniform Ranger. But would it cause them to hesitate before shooting him? Maybe ...

His approach from the southwest, through thicker vegetation, allowed Steve to move quickly with less chance of being spotted. But, when he topped a small rise, the scene below knocked the air out of him like a punch to the gut.

A circle of at least 200 Rangers, a whole company, surrounded a big hole in the rocks, the cave opening. The perimeter of the circle, running through pine trees and across lava outcroppings, left a hundred yards between the men and the cave.

Would the Rangers draw the noose tighter and try to enter? If they did, the outcome was certain. Rangers 6,

Brock Daniels team 0. The exact score didn't matter. The game ended when the Rangers' score reached six.

Steve scanned the scene again and an icy chill crawled down his spine. He had missed the greatest danger of all. Sitting, propped on a folding bipod on top of a lava boulder, giving it a clear shot at the cave opening, sat a SMAW II Serpent, the mother of all portable thermobaric weapons. This fiery serpent had killed many Taliban as its flames roared through buildings and caves in Afghanistan.

"Steve, I ... I'm not afraid to die, but please, not by burning." That was Julia's desperate plea, before they escaped from their fiery suite in Netanya. In a cave, that's exactly how a SMAW-launched rocket would kill her. And it wouldn't simply burn her. At 5,000 degrees, the warhead would incinerate everyone in the cave.

Steve wouldn't let that happen, even if he must die to destroy the weapon. But he had another option. If he could get the commander's attention, without being shot in the process, maybe Steve could start negotiating a peaceful surrender before anyone was killed.

Success depended on the commander's first reaction to Steve and on the commander's loyalties. Since this group comprised a whole company from JBLM, it would not be uniformly loyal to Hannan like the small hand-picked black ops teams Brock Daniels and company had previously encountered. That provided a small measure of hope.

Drawing on that hope, Steve drew a breath and stepped out from behind a big Ponderosa Pine to make the biggest gamble of his life.

No one noticed. Every man seemed focused on the cave. Why? No one was manning the SMAW, so what was happening?

Steve stopped and listened. From the cave opening, a deep, rich contralto voice, with a hint of vibrato, reached him. The first three words identified the song, God Bless America.

The song came, haunting and beautiful. So out of place in a potential battlefield. The singer's intent was obvious, but which one of the women would take such a huge risk? KC?

Hearing the song, sung with that voice, stirred feelings in Steve that had been blunted by seven years of Hannan's anti-American rhetoric and actions. Steve loved America, but he hated what had been done to it. And he was more than ready to have it out right here with a company of Rangers if they would not honor their creed.

A small white flag rose from the cave opening. An attempt to surrender. Would the Ranger commander honor it?

Another small flag flew beside the white one, the Stars and Stripes.

The voice grew in volume and confidence. It sounded vaguely familiar.

A woman's head emerged from the cave, a head adorned with waves of light brown hair, waving in the gentle breeze.

Steve drew a sharp breath and nearly choked. Julia.

Two hundred guns rattled as the troops aimed them at her.

"Hold your fire, men. It's a white flag."

Who had given that command? Steve couldn't tell. Still unnoticed, he moved closer.

The men nearest Steve talked softly among themselves.

"And this is who Hannan wants us to kill?"

"She's hardly more than a girl."

"How can I shoot someone who looks like her, singing that song, carrying a white flag?"

"And an American flag."

"But she's got two M4s in her hands."

"Only to hold the flags, idiot."

This woman, who risked her life hoping that love of America still resided in the hearts of some of its military, was beyond courageous. Steve would be proud to call her his girl, but Julia had made it clear there were barriers between them that could never be broken down.

Regardless, he had to do something. Julia was nearly to the end of a song that only had one verse—only one that he could remember. Then what?

He needed to get the Ranger commander's attention. What were Daggett's last words before Steve bailed out? *Rangers lead the way.* It was part of the creed written by Command Sergeant Major Neal R. Gentry of the First Ranger Battalion, a creed Steve had memorized seven years ago, along with the Code of the United States Fighting Force.

Maybe Julia's singing had set the stage for something incredible. If not ... how many of those 200 bullets would he feel as they ripped through his body?

He shot a short prayer into another realm, wondering if God would think he was crazy. Steve pushed his gun high above his head, holding it with both hands, and advanced toward the circle of men fifty yards ahead.

He took a deep breath and belted out the words like a battlefield commander. "Sergeant Steve Bancroft, US Ranger, reporting for duty!"

The rustling of boots and metal sounded through the pines as 200 guns pointed his way.

He drew another deep breath and projected his voice. "I am an American, fighting in the forces which guard my country and our way of life. I am prepared to give my life in their defense. I will never forget that I am an American, fighting for freedom, responsible for my actions, and dedicated to the principles which made my country free. I will trust in my God and in the United States of America."

"He's wearing a uniform ... sorta." A soldier's voice.

"Captain?" Another voice. "Do we fire?"

The commander didn't reply. That was as much disconcerting as comforting.

Steve pushed the thoughts of flying bullets aside, and switched from the Code of Conduct to the Rangers' Creed.

"Recognizing that I volunteered as a Ranger, fully knowing the hazards of my chosen profession, I will always endeavor to uphold the prestige, honor, and high esprit de corps of the Rangers."

"Hold your fire!" A voice of authority echoed through the forest.

Steve noted the man who had given the command and walked toward him.

The men nearest Steve parted and let him pass.

"Acknowledging the fact that a Ranger is a more elite Soldier who arrives at the cutting edge of battle by land, sea, or air, I accept the fact that as a Ranger my country expects me to move further, faster and fight harder than any other Soldier.

"Never shall I fail my comrades. I will always keep myself mentally alert, physically strong and morally straight and I will shoulder more than my share of the task whatever it may be, one-hundred-percent and then some.

"Gallantly will I show the world that I am a specially selected and well-trained Soldier. My courtesy to superior officers, neatness of dress and care of equipment shall set the example for others to follow.

"Energetically will I meet the enemies of my country. I shall defeat them on the field of battle for I am better trained and will fight with all my might. Surrender is not a Ranger word. I will never leave a fallen comrade to fall into the hands of the enemy and under no circumstances will I ever embarrass my country ..."

They hadn't shot him, yet. Now to make his point. "Rangers, you are about to embarrass your country if you go through with this attack."

"Steve." Julia's voice, but it seemed muted now that she had left the mouth of the cave.

Before he could react, Julia ran toward him, still holding her M4-borne flags, which were no longer pointed at the sky.

"Ma'am, watch where you're pointing those guns." The commander's voice.

She stopped and handed the guns to a Ranger, who seemed anxious to relieve her of the weapons.

Steve held his gun by the butt and the barrel and slowly lowered it to the ground, leaving it there.

When he raised up, Julia, with tear streaked cheeks, ran into his arms. "You came. I should have known you would ..." Her voice faded, drowned by sobs.

Who should he speak to first? The man with the power of life or death over Julia and him? He met the gaze of the Ranger commander. "One moment, captain, then we need to talk, sir." Steve focused on Julia.

With a circle of 400 eyes on them, Julia clung to him, blubbering between her sobs. "I'm sorry, Steve. So sorry ... I lied. I've never done anything so awful ... but you still came back."

"It's okay, Julia."

"No it's not. Not what I did to you. I was a fool. Then I killed two men." She wiped her cheeks. "Just blew them away." She flung a hand away from her body, nearly whacking Steve's nose with her Velcro cast.

What must she be feeling after betraying her convictions? "I'm sorry, Julia."

"But I'm glad."

"I thought you were sorry."

"Steve, I understand now. I really do."

She was sorry. She was glad. She killed two men. She understood. That was good, because Steve sure didn't.

"Your minute's up ... sergeant, is it?" The commander stood a few steps from them. "Hard to tell with your uniform mostly missing."

"You saved me, Steve." Julia spoke softly, but the intensity in her eyes drove the point home.

In that moment, Steve read the point, not only in her eyes, but also from her mind. Somehow, her thought came as clearly as thoughts used to come from Steph. Maybe, somehow, it had. Regardless, it brought redemption for Steve Bancroft. Not the eternal kind, but the kind that would end his guilt on this side of eternity.

It's what Julia wanted for him. It's what Steph would want for him, too.

The crushing weight of Steve's guilt floated away like a downy feather in the gentle breeze that ruffled Julia's hair. Her words, and the strength of her will had removed the weight, completely.

"Your time is up, soldier." The commander's voice rose in pitch and volume.

Steve pulled his arms from Julia and popped a salute. "Sergeant Bancroft, Weapons Sergeant, 75th Ranger Regiment." He decided to go no further in defining his detachment since he didn't know Captain Craig's official status after he'd joined the resistance.

The commander returned his salute. "Captain Scott, 75th Ranger Regiment 2nd Battalion. And like you said, we need to talk."

Julia planted her hip against Steve's, hooked an arm around his waist, and squeezed with surprising strength.

What does a guy say when a girl holds him like she never wants to let go? After the long-odds gamble Steve had just won. Maybe luck was on his side. He was free from his past failure, free to pursue—he looked down at Julia's face. Why not gamble again? He draped an arm over her shoulders. "And this is Julia Weiss, sir ... my fiancé."

Julia's head snapped up.

He looked down, fearing he would see fire in her eyes, but saw only the warm, gentle look he'd seen in those dark brown eyes on that fateful day more than six weeks ago.

She leaned against him, letting his strength support her.

Captain Scott looked at Julia, studying her face for a moment. "Fiancé? Sergeant, that sure doesn't need any explaining, but why you're out here in a ragged Ranger's uniform with a group of terrorists that we came to eliminate—that's going to take some serious explaining."

"Captain Scott," Julia straightened, stood on her own, and brushed a stray wisp of hair from her eyes. "There's something you need to know before we go any further."

Scott's hand went to his hip. "Then let's hear it, Ms. Weiss."

Julia blew out a breath, then looked up a Scott's face. "President Hannan is dead."

Chapter 43

Was Captain Scott about to shoot her? Arrest her? His hands repeatedly adjusted their grip on his gun. He stared through Julia as if she wasn't there.

Had the news about Hannan's death disturbed him, or did he not believe her?

After a few seconds, Scott hung his rifle over his shoulder. His blank stare turned to a frown and his gaze bored into her. "How would a young woman, hiding in a cave in the middle of nowhere, know that?"

This wasn't playing out as Julia had hoped. Steve was oblivious to events in the cave, so he couldn't help her. She sought words to convince Scott to believe her message. "One of the men in the cave just talked to the president. Hannan was in the DUCC under the West Wing. We heard the shot through the phone. Then a Ranger, Captain Craig, told us Hannan was shot and killed."

"Whoa, whoa, whoa. Back up and let's take this one step at a time, and you'd better not be lying to me, Ms. Weiss. Now ... where's this man who was talking to the president when he was allegedly shot? I need to talk with him."

"Uh ... I shot that man. He's dead, too."

Scott swore a mild expletive, but it looked like there were a lot more words Scott wanted to unload on her. "What kind of bull are you trying to feed me, Weiss? I've never heard such a cockamamie story as—"

"It gets worse." Julia cringed, squinting her eyes as she looked up at Scott.

Steve nudged Julia. "Did Craig shoot Hannan?"

"Sergeant Bancroft, I suggest you let me ask the questions. You, soldier, are not out of the woods yet." Scott's hands went to his hips. "So, who *did* shoot Hannan, if in fact he *was* shot?"

"Secretary of State Eli Vance shot him." Julia watched Scott's eyes. Did he believe her?

"That old geezer? Those two were as thick as thieves, which they both probably were. But you know what I think? I think you all need to be locked up in the loony bin." Scott shook his head. "Or maybe I should be locked up for listening to you."

Julia jumped at the sound of two hundred rifles being raised into firing position. She followed their aim to the cave.

"Hold your fire, men." Scott barked the command, then studied the figure emerging from the cave.

Brock came out slowly, hands raised high. One of those hands held Deke's phone. "Captain Scott, we've been listening from the cave. If you know how to work this thing, there's someone on the other end who can verify Hannan's status."

Scott gave Brock the halt signal. "You can stop right there, mister. That looks like a military sat phone, but how do I know you aren't planning to blow me up with it? Let's back up ... who are you?"

Brock stretched up to his full six-foot-five and stared into Scott's eyes. "Captain, I'm Brock Daniels."

Scott spit out a stronger expletive and his hands went back to his hips. "You're the dude who started all this."

"Sir, I'd rather think of myself as one who helped finish it. Hannan started it."

Julia had been studying Captain Scott closely since his off-the-cuff remark about Hannan and Eli Vance both being thieves. Maybe they had an ally in Scott. If not, as he said, they weren't out of the woods yet.

Scott's long arm stretched out as he pointed to the phone in Brock's hand. "Prove to me that the phone is safe and I might make that call you mentioned."

Brock grinned. "Sir, I could rub my cheek against yours while you make the call, so whatever happens to you happens to me"

"You try that with me, soldier, and you won't like what happens." The captain paused, looking at Brock as if sizing him up. "A blogger. Daniels, you look more like a professional athlete."

"Had a contract offer from Kansas City, but I turned it down."

"We're getting *way* off track here." Scott pointed at the cave. "How many people are still in there?"

"Captain..." One of the Rangers stood on a small boulder that gave the man a better view of the mouth of the cave. "There's a woman coming out, unarmed."

Since Brock was out here standing beside her and Steve, it had to be KC.

A flash of red hair showed between two rocks at the mouth of the cave.

"Don't shoot captain, it's my wife. She's harmless."

"Hold your fire, men."

As KC's body rose from the hole in the ground, muted whistles sounded from around the circle of soldiers. The breeze ruffled her long, curly red hair and the late afternoon sun set it on fire. Though she was smudged with dust from the floor of the cave, KC had the look and bearing of a Celtic princess. And she had caught everyone's eye.

"KC Banning?" Scott flung his hands into the air. Public enemies number one and two. No wonder Hannan called me, personally, before we left JBLM."

"Not Banning anymore," Brock said. "KC Daniels."

"Lucky man, Daniels."

Brock's eyes returned to their usual intense look. "Only if we survive this."

"It would reduce the danger considerably if this area were secure. How many people are there left in the cave?"

Julia cleared her throat. "Just Jeff and Allie Jacobs."

Scott gave Julia a serious frown. "What about the man you shot? Was he alone?"

"No. But I thought you meant how many live people there were left."

"Ms. Weiss, suppose you tell me how many dead people there are in the cave."

"Just two Rangers, Deke and Johnson."

"And I suppose you—"

"Yes, Captain Scott, I shot them because they had made some really bad plans for KC. Do you want me to spell it out?"

"Were the two Rangers working alone?" His questioning frown said Scott didn't know anything about Deke's mission and didn't like only holding a few pieces of the puzzle.

"Deke was the commander of a Ranger detachment sent by Hannan to eliminate us with thermal bears."

Scott's face reddened and his eyes bored into Julia. "What in blazes are thermal bears? The opposite of a polar bear?"

"Sir ..." Steve said. "It's a euphemism. They shot thermobaric warheads at us."

"And you survived?"

Heat rose on Julia's neck as Captain Scott questioned everything they had done. Was it really so unbelievable? She had never fought battles before, but Julia had been there, seen it all, and it seemed reasonable enough to her. "Captain Scott, we not only survived, but we killed ten of Deke's Rangers, some with their own thermal bears, and Steve shot down a Stealth Hawk with another—"

Scott cut her off. "With another thermal bear. Mercy, woman! It's a good thing we didn't attack you with our thermal bears, you'd have killed the whole company."

For the first time since she had come out of the cave, Scott smiled at Julia.

And for the first time since she'd come out of the cave, Julia relaxed. The adrenaline rush ended, the tension drained away, and she nearly collapsed against Steve. She looked up into his warm brown eyes. "It's over. It's really over, isn't it?"

He nodded. "But you and I still have some things to discuss."

"You mean like that lame marriage proposal of yours." She gave Steve her coy smile.

"There's something else, too." Brock had been listening to them but now turned his attention to Captain Scott. "We had a Sayeret Matkal warrior with us. He—"

"You had the Israeli Special Forces on your side? It never ends with you people."

"Just Benjamin," Julia said. "On loan to us. He disappeared before Deke arrived and we don't know what happened to him."

Brock turned toward the mouth of the cave. "Jeff, Allie, it's okay. Come out with your hands up."

"Good thinking, Brock." Steve said. "I'd feel a lot better if they were all out of there before Scott's men start securing the cave."

"And I'd feel a lot better if it felt like I was in command, here." Scott took the phone from Brock. "As soon as your other two friends come out, I'll make that call."

Jeff and Allie emerged from behind rocks near the cave opening, side-by-side, hands held high.

More low whistling and murmuring came from the men.

KC moved alongside the two and walked toward the captain.

Scott watched KC and Allie walking toward them for a few seconds then shook his head. "You men sure know how to pick'em," he muttered, then raised his voice. "Roberts, take your detachment and secure the cave."

Twelve men scurried toward the cave.

Captain Scott called out to his men. "Watch out for a missing Sayeret Matkal warrior who probably thinks you are the enemy."

The twelve men immediately changed their approach. Some covered while others moved.

"If I dial the last number called on this phone, refresh my memory," Scott said. "To whom will I be talking and where are they?"

"Captain Craig will answer, and I think they'll still be in the DUCC under the West Wing," Brock said.

"If you need verification," Steve said, "I'm a member of Craig's detachment. I can vouch for you."

"One of the terrorists I came to kill is going to vouch for me?" Scott shook his head and pushed on the phone's touchpad.

Steve's arm had remained around Julia almost the entire time since she ran to him. But he released her and moved closer to the captain.

"Bancroft, if you'll stop breathing on me, I'll turn on the speakerphone."

Steve stepped back.

Julia pulled Steve close to her side, and listened, hoping for a quick resolution to what seemed like an overwhelming mess.

"Craig, here."

"Captain Craig, this is Captain Scott, company commander 75th Ranger Regiment, 2nd Battalion."

"Scott, what is the status of the five civilians and my man Sergeant Bancroft?" Craig's voice came through loud, angry, and threatening.

"Settle down, Craig. They are all safe and standing nearby. All except a missing Sayeret Matkal soldier whom we are looking for. Now it's my turn. Julia Weiss told me that President Hannan is dead, killed by Eli Vance. Can you confirm that?"

"I wish I couldn't, but it's true. Hannan's dead and Eli is cuffed, sitting in a chair here in the DUCC, wheezing like he needs oxygen."

Scott stood silent, staring at the ground for a few seconds. "That raises a big question, Craig. Who is our Commander-in-Chief?"

"The truth is ... we don't have one."

Scott swore and shook his head. "After all the trouble we've had, being placed under martial law, states breaking away from the union, and we don't have a president? That's not good."

"We haven't had a president for nearly eight years and, for the past six weeks, we've had a dictator," Brock said.

"Was that Brock Daniels," Craig asked.

Scott looked up at Brock. "Yes, it was the big guy, himself."

"He's right," Craig said. "But we're trying to rectify the situation. We've contacted Chief Justice Wendell Warrington and, since the vice president resigned, Speaker of the House, Ben Tucker, is next in line. We just reached him. But it took a little while to persuade him that he needed to be sworn in. He's as nervous as heck, but he's coming from his home in Arlington and should be here in a few minutes. But we have another problem."

"I'll bet you do," Scott said. "It sounds like you made an assault on the West Wing. If you're sitting in the DUCC with the dead president's body, it doesn't matter who killed him, you're in the hot seat and it's probably getting hotter by the minute."

"Yeah. Tell me about it. The problem at the moment is the military patrolling the city still thinks the president is in charge. So, we have a nation under martial law with troops deployed and no commander. And now a group of Secret Service Agents loyal to Hannan has secured the ground level of the West Wing, and they're pressuring us to give ourselves up. I have no doubt that my men could go upstairs and kill all of them. But it would be a lot better if we could just get the boys upstairs to stand down. Then we could swear in Tucker and start this nation moving forward again."

"You said Secret Service Agents loyal to Hannan, right."

"That's right."

"Then I've got an idea. Are you a gambling man, Craig?"

"If the odds are right. But, right now, anything I do is a gamble."

"This could scuttle your career and mine, too."

"Scott, you just worry about your career. Mine may be down the tube, already."

"Okay, I have an in with the commander of the 2nd Ranger Battalion at JBLM."

"How's that?"

"He's my fiancé's father. He's friends with commanders of both the 1st and 3rd Battalions. I know that some detachments from all three battalions are patrolling sensitive areas in DC, just not the White House. If you'll give me the phone number you've been using to contact the agents in the West Wing, I'll call my commander and see if he'll let me use a detachment or two to put the fear of God in Hannan's good old boys."

"I'm in," Craig said.

Captain Scott took the number and walked about thirty yards away from everyone to place his calls.

Excited voices came from a group of men near the mouth of the cave. Four men emerged carrying an improvised stretcher. Were they bringing out Deke's body?

There was a man on the stretcher, but it wasn't Deke or Johnson. The man raised his head. "Steve, it's Benjamin," Julia said. "How could he have gotten into the cave? He was outside when I went for water."

The men eased the stretcher down onto the ground and all wiped sweat from their faces.

"For a skinny Israeli, you sure do weigh a lot," one of the men said.

"You six his friends?" A short, stocky Ranger pulled out supplies from his pack.

"Yeah," Brock said. "A team of seven, the number of perfection."

"I'm the Medical Sergeant on our team. Sergeant Welby. And I don't want to hear any jokes about my name."

Benjamin groaned and held his head. "Sorry, I let you down."

"Benj," Steve said. "Nothing to be sorry about. You're the one who got hurt. What happened?"

"I was a little west of the lava tube and heard voices. When I came closer, I saw a rope going down one of the skylights. It was moving. Someone was climbing in near the back of the cave. I ran to stop them and—"

"You created a new skylight in the Skylight Cave." Sergeant Welby said. "The ground gave way and Benjamin got scraped up going through his new skylight, then broke an ankle and banged his head when he hit the ground twenty-five feet below."

Benjamin raised his head to look at them. "What happened to Deke and his man?"

Brock grinned at Benjamin. "I didn't see everything that happened. But somebody said an Amish girl shot them."

Benjamin met Julia's gaze and the grimace from his pain turned to a grin. "An Amish girl, you say? Amish girl, thanks for doing my job?"

"I could never do your job, Benjamin. We wouldn't be alive if it weren't for you. And, as for the Amish ways, I think I'll leave them to the folks in Lancaster County."

Her words drew a smile from Steve.

Sergeant Welby opened a container and pulled out a syringe. "You look like you could use a little something for pain."

Benjamin nodded. "My ankle would appreciate it."

The men on this combat mission were based in Tacoma. What would they do with an injured Benjamin? Julia stepped between Benjamin and Welby. "Where are you going to take him? To a hospital, I hope."

"Ms. Weiss, is it?"

Julia nodded.

"I think the plan is to fly one of our Chinooks in close and take him to the medical center in Bend. They'll probably cast his ankle and keep him overnight for observation."

"Then tomorrow he comes to my house." Julia scanned her friends around her and Steve. "You're all coming to my house as soon as Scott says we can go. And you can all stay there until you decide what you want to do." She met KC's gaze. "And where you want to live."

KC touched Julia's arm. Tears welled in the Celtic princess's eyes. "Thank you. But Brock and I might want to have a short honeymoon. Ours was rudely interrupted."

Brock draped an arm over her shoulders. "And I know just the place, Kace."

"Where's that, sweetheart?"

"The Sunview Motel. Squirrel Room, #17."

"You mean where we climbed in bed together?"

"Kace, I don't think we should get into that?"

"Brock, my idea saved our lives that night."

"It wouldn't have if I hadn't convinced the FBI that I was your husband."

"And you were *very* convincing." KC gave them her impish grin.

"Look," Julia said. "We're getting too much information about a subject that's none of our business."

Captain Scott walked back from the spot he'd been standing with the phone planted in his ear for the past several minutes. He had a smile on his face. There was a spring in his step that hadn't been there before. "That's right, Craig. They're leaving now, and you and your men are cleared to take over security of the West Wing and the White House. Once you do, if the new president has confidence in you, he will likely want you to continue in that capacity until he can clean house and insure he has people he can trust to protect him."

Craig's voice came from the phone. Evidently Scott had turned on the speakerphone for their benefit. "We're heading for the elevators now. But we need someone to pronounce the president dead before we swear in Ben Tucker."

"Can your Medical Officer do that?"

"We can't let him have the official say on that. It's too much a conflict of interest. We need to take Hannan's body to a hospital and have things done right. I think I'll call an ambulance from George Washington University Hospital once we're in the West Wing. Then we'll have the FBI pick up Eli Vance. Thanks for all your help, Scott. I owe you."

"Dude, you took all the big risks. The whole nation owes you."

Scott ended the call.

The wop, wop of a helicopter rotor grew louder.

Captain Scott knelt beside Benjamin. "We're going to take good care of you, Mr. Levy. When you get home, tell your commander thanks for taking care of this group. They're good people."

"Captain Scott," Steve said. "This whole group wants to leave for Julia's house. It's on the bluff above Crooked River Ranch. She can give you the address."

"I have no reason to hold you. But there will be investigations into all the deaths of military personnel that you were ... uh, involved with. As long as the investigators can find you, gather up your stuff and go."

Steve took Julia's hand and started to walk toward the cave.

Scott hooked Steve's free arm. "Bancroft, that's one heckuva team you put together. I don't know how you accomplished all that you did, but I sure am glad you did it. Maybe I can be proud of this man's army again. I was almost ready to resign."

"Thanks, captain. And, sir, don't resign. This country needs Rangers like you. Men that will take the initiative to do the right thing instead of jumping like puppets on a string when the CIC violates the Constitution." Steve dropped Julia's hand, popped a salute and then they were off, running hand-in-hand to the cave.

Brock and KC were already at the cave entrance. Brock waved them on. "Hurry up. We need to get back to your house, Julia, and watch history being made on TV. And I've got a blog post to make ASAP. America needs to hear about Craig. KC, can you get me online with your satellite laptop? I know exactly what I want to say."

"I can try. But no promises, sweetheart."

Julia pulled Steve to a stop before they caught up with the others. "Steve, you and I still have things to talk about."

Chapter 44

In the Yellow Oval Room of the White House, Speaker of the House, Ben Tucker, stood wide-eyed, frozen, staring at Chief Justice Wendell Warrington.

Craig placed his hand on Tucker's shoulder. "Having second thoughts?"

"No. Just a lot of first-time thoughts." Tucker swallowed hard.

"Did you bring a Bible?"

"Uh ..."

"Never mind," Craig said as he reached inside his uniform jacket and pulled out his small Bible. "You can use this one."

Craig shoved it at Tucker, but pulled the Bible back when Tucker reached for it.

"Craig, what are you—"

"Just listen for a minute. You're not putting your hand on my Bible unless you're going to tell the truth. And once you're sworn in, you'd better not cut and run or—"

"I know, I know. Or you'll shoot me like—"

"No, Tucker. We didn't shoot anyone today, only flash banged them. And we didn't shoot Hannan. Eli Vance did that. But Hannan's inner circle will likely end up in Leavenworth. I'm sure you don't want to join them."

311

Tucker shook his head.

"Let's do this," Judge Warrington said, raising his voice. "America is waiting."

* * *

A few seconds later, President Ben Tucker pulled his hand from Craig's Bible and looked up at Craig. "Now what do I do?"

This was not the start Craig had hoped for. "Tucker, why are you asking me? You're the president, for Pete's sake."

Justice Warrington pointed out the window to the Truman Balcony. A crowd of hundreds had grown to thousands on the White House Grounds, filling the south lawn to the fountain and beyond. "I already took the liberty of instructing some White House staff to plug in a mic and turn on the PA system. Now, you need to calm the fears of the people. Assure them there will be an election, soon, where they can choose a leader that they trust."

A chant started somewhere in the throng that was moving in from East and West Executive Avenues and E Street. Now the throng, including everyone moving their way, had grown to what seemed like a million people.

Craig's ten men would provide as much security as possible, but there still would be risks. Perhaps this was the time to take risks, because the people needed to see an honest man in the White House. All of America needed to see the moment as up close and personal as possible. The time had come for healing.

A spontaneous chant began from the crowd. "We want Craig!"

Why were they using his name? Craig scanned the crowd. "They're already on the White House grounds. I think we should let them come. My men will keep them out of the building. But we need to build some trust with the people.

It's worth the risk. After what Hannan has put them through, we certainly don't want to shoot anybody."

Tucker raised his eyebrows. "Let them come? That's easy for you to say. They're cheering for you. They might view me as complicit with Hannan or negligent in doing my duty."

"Tucker, uh ... Mr. President, look at them. These people aren't here to shoot anyone. This is a celebration."

The chant grew into a pulsing roar. "We want Craig! We want Craig!"

How did they know? Craig shook his head. "Brock must have posted to his blog already."

President Tucker reached out and gripped Craig's arm. The man's hand was trembling. "Will you walk out there with me?"

It's not what Craig wanted, but Tucker needed a boost of confidence. "I'll come. But remember, you're the president. Act like it."

When the two men reached the outer edge of the balcony, the chant slowly morphed to "USA! USA!"

Tucker raised his hands and the crowd quieted.

President Tucker stepped to the mic. "My fellow Americans, as most of you have heard, President Abe Hannan was shot and killed today. The suspect, Secretary of State Eli Vance, is under arrest on suspicion of murder. After our vice president resigned, as Speaker of the House, I am next in line for succession to the presidency. Chief Justice Warrington swore me in as your president—"

The roar from the crowd stopped Tucker. Was that a hitch in his swallow? His eyes welled, too. Getting emotional was a good sign. After seven and a half years of Hannan, the people needed a president who genuinely loved them rather than himself.

It took a full minute for the crowd to finish their approval.

Ben raised a hand to quell the last of the cheering. "As your president, I will keep my oath to defend the Constitution until the person you choose in the general election takes office."

Cheering broke out again. Then it morphed spontaneously to a chant. "Craig for president! Craig for president!"

Tucker raised his hands again.

The chanting did not stop. It crescendoed into a deafening roar.

What had Brock said in his post that would have gotten this reaction? Regardless, Craig needed to deflect attention to Tucker.

President Tucker turned to Craig. "They're not going to stop until they hear from you." Tucker motioned to the spot beside him. "Please?"

Craig couldn't hear him, but he had read Tucker's lips.

"Craig for president!" The chant continued.

Craig sighed in resignation, sought the right words, and stepped to the mic beside President Tucker.

It seemed that two million eyes had focused on him.

He prayed a silent prayer and whispered, "Brock Daniels, I'm going to shoot you for this." Then Craig raised his hands.

The world went silent.

* * *

Flood lights came on in the twilight, but the silence seemed eerie, especially with such an enormous crowd.

Craig leaned toward the mic. "Fellow Americans ... I appreciate your confidence, but I'm a warrior. It's what God called me to be."

A murmur rose from the crowd.

"Furthermore, I am not qualified to be your president ... well, not for two more years. But we have a plan to right the wrongs in America and prevent someone like Hannan, or an out-of-control legislature, or a legislating-from-the-bench judiciary, from wresting control from you, the citizens and from the states in which you live."

Craig looked at Ben Tucker.

Ben gave him a nod, slow and full of presidential authority. He was catching on.

Craig continued. "As soon as we can get agreement from thirty-four state legislatures, something we hope to accomplish over the next four weeks, a convention of states will be held to draft amendments to the Constitution, returning power to the states such that the power of the states cannot be subverted again ... ever."

A roar grew to earsplitting volume.

Craig let the crowd cheer for the next few minutes until the noise subsided.

"The states will decide which amendments are prudent, but they will likely include a state's power to override any abusive, unconstitutional executive orders, federal regulations, and unconstitutional Supreme Court decisions."

Cheering started again, shorter this time.

"If our nation ever ended up in freefall, this was the safety chute provided by our founders in Article 5 of the Constitution. And, my fellow Americans, it's time to pull the ripcord. If we don't, eventually another Hannan will team up with the judiciary and invite us to Uncle Sam's funeral."

Media people with video cameras on their shoulders had worked their way through the crowd. How long had he been on national TV? Craig should not remain in the limelight. It was time for Ben to speak to the people.

"Now, here's your president with some welcome news." Craig turned to Ben Tucker and saw a new look of confidence.

Ben was ready. He stepped to the microphone. "Adding to what Captain Craig said about the Convention of States—

contact your state legislatures and tell them we need the protections Captain Craig mentioned as well as the others outlined in Brock Daniels's post two weeks ago—including term limits and requirements for balancing the budget." Ben Tucker waited until the cheering stopped.

"About the election—"

The roar cut off Tucker.

News reporters swung their cameras around, scanning the cheering crowd.

Craig gave the crowd thumbs up as hope, joy, and patriotic pride swelled in his heart.

America was becoming America, again.

Chapter 45

Julia sat in the small rear seat of the SUV as Jeff turned in at her driveway, where they had left less than six hours ago. The afternoon seemed like it had lasted for days and the events it contained were surreal. The man sitting by her side was real enough, but so was the pain she had inflicted on him, intentionally.

Six months ago, if someone would have told her she was about to fall in love with a Ranger, a weapons sergeant who specialized in guns and explosives, she would have laughed at them, or insulted their intelligence with her sharp words.

Brock draped an arm around KC's shoulders. "Thanks, Kace, for getting the Israeli laptop to connect. I can't wait to see what my blog post stirred up."

When Jeff braked to a stop, Julia leaned forward and pulled herself to her feet, carefully stepping over the three M4s and enough ammunition to conduct a small war—things Steve insisted they take from the cave, just in case. "Let me slide by you, KC, so I can unlock the door. Then everybody to the great room and we'll turn on the widescreen TV and watch history being made."

Julia unlocked the door.

Everyone rushed into the great room and took a seat.

When the big flat panel screen lit, the new president spoke from a balcony at the White House.

"This evening I will give the order to all military deployed to enforce martial law to return to their original duty posts. Local police will resume their duties to protect and serve, unhindered by the military. And as of this moment, by the authority vested in me, all martial-law curfews are ended."

Brock stuck out a thumb at the TV. "From the size of the crowd in DC, I'm guessing my post went viral within minutes."

"Be quiet, Brock. I want to hear our president." KC poked him in the ribs.

"For the past two weeks, I have heard rumors that an effort was being made to organize a third party before the next election. At the time, we didn't know if there would ever be another election. I will do everything possible to allow this party to nominate its candidate. We owe our citizens an alternative to what they've had in the past ... and we never want a repeat of what we've had for the past seven years."

Cheering grew loud and President Tucker waited for it to subside.

Brock sat beside KC in the great room holding the laptop. "I just hit two social media sites. Rumors are flying around saying two-thirds of the Republicans and a fourth of the Democrats are going to bail for the new Constitutional Party being organized by Senator Carr from Texas. Did you hear about Carr's plan to clean house in the military? From general to private, top to bottom, including the Pentagon bureaucrats."

"Shut up, Brock. The president is getting ready to talk again." KC looked at Brock, but her eyes weren't saying shut up. She scanned everyone in the room and evidently realized five people were staring at her. "It's okay, everybody. Brock knows that my shut up means I love you, sweetheart, but I really wish you'd stop talking. Right, Brock?"

"Yeah, and stop talking before I slap you silly. You forgot that part, Kace."

"Then shut up, because Tucker is talking."

"It has been brought to my attention, that Israel helped save the lives of six of our citizens when Abid Hannan attempted to murder them with a black operation conducted by his hand-picked Special Forces. I thank our good ally, and look forward to rectifying the terrible wrongs Hannan has forced on a nation that fights daily for its survival amid hostile nations and continuous terrorist attacks.

"Regarding other foreign relations, I'll personally tend to the re-establishment of diplomatic relations with our allies and other friends abroad, since our former Secretary of State is in custody in a local hospital, awaiting trial. I've already contacted leaders in the House and the Senate to prepare for an expedited formation of a cabinet for my temporary administration which will only serve until the new president is elected and sworn in."

* * *

President Tucker concluded his speech and Julia turned the volume down on the TV, knowing that lively discussion in the great room would follow.

Brock shot Steve a glance. "You know, I'm really glad I don't work at the Pentagon, right now."

Steve chuckled. "You might be going to prison if you were a Hannan appointment. Regardless, it's going to be chaos at the Pentagon, trying to redeploy the regular troops, release the federalized National Guard troops, and clean house of Hannan's traitors and wusses in the military. We need our fighting force back. When Julia can sneak up on two of Hannan's choice Rangers and take them out, well it …"

Julia crossed her arms and studied his eyes. "Yes, Sergeant Bancroft."

"It proves that she's a Ranger, a good one." Benjamin had rescued Steve.

"The best," Steve said. "She saved my life too many times to count over the last few days."

She unfolded her arms and continued studying Steve's face.

"I hope Tucker, the states, and the next elected president all keep their word," Jeff said. "If not, fifty years from now, we could be in this fix again."

"I hope they keep their word so I don't have to maintain this doggone blog. I have a novel to finish, a novel that was rudely interrupted by Hannan and a freckle-faced girl."

"Is your novel a romance?" KC took Brock's hand.

"You can count on it. A romantic thriller."

KC smiled. "I wouldn't have it any other way, Mr. Daniels."

Julia glanced at KC and Brock. "I've heard Brock's and KC's story. And I think we just got the nutshell version, again." She turned toward Allie. "But you've never told me how you and Jeff got together."

"It's a long story, Julia. I'll tell it to you when we have more time. Let's just say, it all happened while I was chasing freedom."

Julia sighed. "Chasing freedom ... aren't we all. Well, Craig strongly recommended that we all stay here under Steve's protection until the nation stabilizes." Julia shook her head. "I can't bear to think about us splitting up after all we've gone through together. And, I mean this ... you're all welcome to stay here, indefinitely."

"After the firefight at our house, Allie and I will have some remodeling to do before we move back in."

"Yes we'd love to take you up on your offer, Julia," Allie said.

Jeff pointed a thumb toward the golf course on the plateau below. "Maybe I'll have to take up golf."

"Just don't swear when you hit a bad drive, Jeff." KC grinned at him. "Golf balls belonging to foul-mouthed golfers have been known to disappear on hole number five. Sometimes they end up in the canyon, 600 feet below."

"I'll keep that in mind if there are any little redheaded girls running around."

Brock stared at KC until she returned his gaze. "Kace, the lot about a quarter mile down the road has been for sale, forever. I've got enough saved up to buy it and start building a house."

"Mr. Daniels, if Hannan didn't confiscate it, I've got enough savings to buy some building materials, too."

"Then it's settled," Julia said. "You two will be staying here until you finish building your house."

"And finish my novel."

"No, Brock," Julia said. "There's one other thing you have to do." She looked at KC, who was grinning at Julia.

KC nodded and then turned her attention to Brock.

Brock eyes darted, focusing on KC, then Julia—back and forth. "I sense a conspiracy here."

Julia laughed. "You always sense a conspiracy. That's the first thing you told me about, down in Guatemala, when I mentioned your blog. But I guess you can look at it that way. Here's the deal ... you can't stay with me unless you do something that KC, Allie, and I decided you have to do, Brock."

"A blank check for my rent? This must be the high-rent district." He gave Julia a squinty-eyed glance. "Let's hear it."

"I have a phone number right here in my hand, one that KC looked up on the Internet. You need to call it, make an appointment, and put the date on your calendar."

"Look, I'm not going to see a shrink, no matter what you three women say. No way."

"Sweetheart, you *are* a bit paranoid, but not schizophrenic. We're not asking you to see a shrink. You just have to call this number and schedule yourself for the next Mariner's baseball tryout."

"Kace, that's water under the bridge. I—"

"Don't you try telling me that dream isn't still alive deep inside of you. How come, every time you get a chance, I see you throwing rocks at things, throwing really hard. And, when you try out, you'd better really try, buster. I want to see high heat with at least one pitch clocked at 105 miles-per-hour. Do you understand?"

"Alright, alright, I'll go. But, Kace, it's still just a dream. I'll probably never even—"

"Don't say it, Brock. After they clock your pitches, after you bruise the catcher's hand, and after you strike out every batter you face, they'll shove a contract in front of you so fast your head will spin."

"I'll go, otherwise KC will—well, ever since she was a kid she's had ways of evening the score. She's good at cruel and unusual punishment."

"Brock, when I turned you in to the Golf Marshall, it was only a joke. You weren't really guilty of indecent exposure."

"But, Kace, you waited an hour before you told him the truth."

"That's because you—"

"Moving right along. If you go, Brock, your rent is paid for as long as I own this house. It's got two master bedrooms, with private baths, that you married couples will want to use, because ..." Julia stopped. Her cheeks grew warm, probably pink. If she just hadn't added that "because" part.

"Because married men think they're the masters." Allie rescued her.

Steve stood and stretched. "My enlistment is up in three months. I'm getting out as soon as the chaos ends and the army can issue discharge papers, again. I'll probably be here most of that time, if Craig has his way. He's afraid that there might be some disgruntled Hannan supporters around."

Julia stood and took Steve's hand. "Now that that's all settled, would you like to take a walk with me? The sun will be setting over the Cascades in a few minutes."

Steve stood and she led him across the room.

When they reached the outside door to the great room, KC's voice came from behind them. "Good luck, Julia."

"Yeah. Good luck, Steve." Brock's voice.

* * *

Julia led him to the edge of the bluff, overlooking Crooked River Ranch and, beyond it, the canyon. Steve turned and scanned the western horizon. Somewhere in the vicinity, a small wildfire had produced enough smoke to turn the sun a reddish yellow as it hung low over the Cascade Mountains beside the snow-capped peak of Mount Washington. To the southwest, the Three Sisters jutted up above the horizon.

When God made things, true beauty could be seen by all. And God had outdone Himself when He made the woman standing beside Steve.

He looked down at Julia—her full lips parted to speak, the waves of her light brown hair dancing in the breeze, her brown eyes full of life. It was time for their talk.

"My grandparents raised me from age fourteen, after my parents were killed in Africa. After my grandparents died and left me this house, I felt guilty taking it. So, I locked it up, hired a boy to mow the grass and pull weeds, and just let it sit here for about six months. Then came the mission trip to Guatemala and, well, you know the rest." Julia stopped and waved a hand across the panorama in front of her and Steve. "I could never get tired of this view."

"I can see what you mean. A miniature Grand Canyon with a green oasis, the golf course. Would you like to fly over it? Bob Daggett promised me a free ride if you'd come with me."

"Who's Bob Daggett?"

"The pilot who flew me from Madras to the Skylight Cave so I could bail out and get myself killed by a company of Rangers."

"Steve, you took too big of a risk."

"Yeah, like you didn't? Singing God Bless America to 200 troops with their M4s trained on you."

Her head swung around from the vista in front of them to his face. "Steve, I—"

"You don't have to do that, Julia—take risks, sacrifice yourself. You are the strongest, bravest, most selfless woman I've ever known and ..." The words Steve sought eluded him ...

"You were on a roll. You didn't have to stop." Julia's coy smile tweaked one corner of her mouth.

"Okay, the most stubborn person I've ever known, bent on self-destruction—"

"You can stop anytime." Her smile faded.

"Most beautiful, most caring person—Julia, you don't have anything to prove. You've done it all. I love you just the way you are."

"And I love you. Can we ... maybe ... let Steph just enjoy where she is while you and I spend our lives together here on earth ... until we go to be with her?"

"Yeah, but aren't I the one who's supposed to do the proposing."

"Yeah? Is that all you can say? Steve, you've been living with guilt that wasn't yours. Like you told me, we live in a fallen world where bad things happen—things like people wanting to shoot you with thermal bears, tornados killing people, people we love. It's not all your fault. It's not all my fault. We can only do what we can do. But we must do what we can, even if it means shooting an evil person to protect the innocent."

"You're beginning to sound like Brock, Jules."

"Maybe. But I sounded like a cruel liar when I thought you weren't going to go help Craig after he begged you to go to DC. I hurt you because I—no, there's no way to justify what I did." Tears welled in Julia's eyes.

"I forgive you. It's done... over. We have our nation back, a place we can live in liberty, a place where our children and grandchildren can enjoy that freedom."

She wiped her eyes and smiled. "Children? I believe that's called jumping the gun. Don't you have something you want to ask me, first?"

"Yeah, I do. Would you like to fly over the ranch in Daggett's Cessna?"

"Steve, that's not what—"

"Well, would you?"

"Of course, but—"

"There's one condition. We don't land in the Cessna ... we jump out of it."

"I can't ... I couldn't ... I—"

"Julia, I'll hold you until just before the chutes open. It's a lot safer than having thermal bears shot at you."

"But I didn't choose to have thermal—"

"But you did. You ran out from the trees and became a target to protect me."

She put her arms around Steve and buried her face into his chest. "I'll jump, if you hold me." Her words came out in a hoarse whisper.

She would jump with him, even though she was afraid. He had earned her trust, the kind of trust that ran deep. Maybe he didn't deserve her trust, but he would die to keep it.

After events at the cave, only a few words had been needed and their issues were now all dealt with. Only one thing remained to be done. "Julia ... I ... I don't know if I should be doing this right now."

She pulled her head from his chest and peered deeply, warmly into his eyes.

"Julia, I don't have a house. And, when I'm discharged, I won't even have a job. But, Julia Weiss, will—"

"Yes. I don't care if we have to live in the Skylight Cave. It's still yes." She cupped his cheek. "But, Steve, the dream we shared may not require a house in the US."

"That's right. We could be living in a shack in the Dominican Republic or a hut in Guatemala. But anywhere you are, Julia ..." Steve lifted her chin, stepped close, and—

"Can I ask you something, Steve."

"That depends." The moment had been perfect. Impossible to replicate. Her timing stank. "Can I kiss you when you're finished asking me?"

"Yes. But I really need to know something. Am ... am I a good ... I mean, am I doing it right? Because I've never kissed anyone before, except you, and I don't really know what—"

"Julia, for someone who doesn't know what they're doing, you did a pretty doggone good job the last two times, so let's just—"

Her soft, full lips did a pretty doggone good job of muting his words. This woman who had no idea how good, how strong, and how beautiful she was had just given herself to him in a kiss that was perfect. At least it was perfect for Steve Bancroft.

Should he tell her it was *almost* perfect and they should practice some more? But what if she took it as criticism?

"So, Steve, how was it?"

He fumbled for words and said the first one that popped into his head. "Addicting."

"Then maybe we should—"

"That would be a good idea. I've heard withdrawal can be painful."

Somewhere near the end of their second kiss, the sun slipped behind the Cascades in a rush of nuanced color changes. Twilight began. Now it was the sky's turn to change color. Without clouds, the color changes would be slow, subtle, but still beautiful.

Julia circled his neck with her arms and pressed her cheek into his chest. "Wow. A kiss at sunset. I feel like I should break out into a song ... or something. But I can't sing."

"You sure sang in the mouth of that cave today. I heard you."

"A fluke, or maybe the acoustics. I can't sing, Steve. I've never sung a solo in my life."

"You did today. Your voice was beautiful. It touched the hearts of 200 men surrounding that cave with their weapons ready. Your song saved our lives."

"Sounds like it touched 201 men."

"God Bless America. A song that probably should have become our national anthem. Maybe today yours was the voice of every citizen who loves the USA, Jules ... the voice of freedom."

EPILOGUE

290 clicks north of Guatemala City

Julia Bancroft sat beside Steve as the four-wheel drive vehicle they had rented at the airport creaked and groaned over the humps and bumps in the small dirt road near Chisec. A mile ahead the grassy land dotted with bushes and scrubby trees became a jungle forest, extending to the tops of mountains to the west. A mile beyond the edge of the forest lay their destination.

"Steve, how do you feel about President Tucker's decision to give us all medals, the Presidential Medal of Freedom for the civilians, and Benjamin, and the Congressional Medal of Honor for all of Craig's men?"

"Jules, here's how I look at it ... it's for the American people. They need something tangible to point to, heroes to celebrate. The Lord only knows how much they need that after being beaten down by the Hannan administration for more than seven years. And it's good for our relationship with Israel to recognize the key role they played."

"I hadn't thought about it like that."

"Like what? Like a man?"

"I'm not a man, Mr. Bancroft. Besides, I can think about it however I choose." Julia leaned her head on Steve's shoulder. "Benjamin got married last week."

"Yeah, I heard. So did we. And I just realized something."

Steve paused until she looked up into his eyes. "You aren't a man."

Julia pounded his shoulder in mock fury, then rested her head there again. "The nightmare is fading away. It hardly seems real now. Hannan is buried. They showed it on TV but nobody watched."

As they passed through a field of lush green grass, the road smoothed. The grass had nearly filled in the two tire tracks. Evidently, the road hadn't been used in a while. That's probably as it should be. This road should never have been built, at least not for the purposes it had served. "Steve, what do you suppose will happen to Eli Vance?"

"Well, he's in the hospital, dying from emphysema. He'll never be prosecuted. His cigarettes have already done that."

"I'm surprised that Ben Tucker didn't even run for the presidency."

"I'm not," Steve said. "He knew his role, glue a broken nation back together and then return to being Speaker of the House. And it's certainly no surprise that Senator Carr, from Texas, won the election as the first ever Constitutional Conservative Party candidate. It wasn't even a landslide. It was total domination. Not a single state went to another candidate. And on day one, he cancelled so many executive orders that he said he had a cramp in his hand. Now, he's going after the out-of-control judiciary and restoring the culture in our military that made it the most powerful force on the planet." Steve stopped talking. He was waiting.

"Yeah."

"Yeah? Jules, why are we talking politics on our honeymoon? Are you nervous about this?"

"Nervous?" Her stomach was full of butterflies, or was it Stealth Hawks, and if it didn't settle down, they would have to stop while she lost her lunch. "A little."

Steve pulled a hand from the wheel, taking advantage of the smooth straight section of road to snag Julia's hand. "So you're ready for this, sweetheart?"

She rubbed her queasy stomach, then pulled a legal sized envelope from the door pocket and waved it at Steve. "Legally, yes. Emotionally ... I won't know until we get there. I still don't understand why no one communicated with us after we notified them about our arrival date. It worries me."

He glanced her way and gave her one of his endearing smiles that never failed to win over anyone to whom Steve was willing to show it. "Don't worry about anything but in all things give—"

"I know, Steve. I memorized that verse, too. But it's not that simple."

He squeezed her hand. "Oh, it's simple enough, just hard to do sometimes ... especially when the stakes are so high."

"Stakes high? Are you trying to—"

"No. I'm not trying to frighten you. You're doing a good job of that yourself." He braked and the vehicle groaned to stop near a cinderblock building at the edge of the forest. "End of the road."

Julia scanned the area around them—the clearing, the trail, the deserted building surrounded by a high fence topped with barbed wire and no trespassing signs.

"This was where I saw her last." Julia pointed toward the door to the building.

Steve motioned toward the trail to the right of the building. "Is that the trail?"

"Mmmhmm." Julia heard his question, barely, because her mind had drifted back several months, replaying those heart-wrenching moments when she and Brock had simply turned and walked away.

"How far up the trail?" Steve's voice yanked Julia back to the present.

"The village is a mile upstream."

So much had happened since the mission team had left Guatemala. She battled Ebola. Hannan had nearly killed all of them ... multiple times. She married a big, strong, handsome Army Ranger who would be discharged soon. A highly decorated Army Ranger. Maybe even the Congressional Medal of Honor.

Yes, so much had changed that it all seemed surreal. The envelope now stuffed in her shorts pocket said it was real, but until they reached the village ...

Steve opened her door and she slid down to the ground and into his arms. Iron hard muscles contracted around her. "Julia Weiss, how did I ever find—"

She muted his lips with her fingers. "Julia Bancroft. Mrs. Steve Bancroft. And as to how ... you know the story well enough, Mister Bancroft. I was a fool and then—"

He silenced her lips with a kiss. Then held her by her shoulders and scanned her face with the intense look of a Ranger trained to capture the details and analyze a situation with one glance. "Not a fool. Never a fool. Just a girl who saw many things no girl should ever have to see." Steve paused and smiled. "Our girl won't have to. That's a promise."

Steve knew how to plant hope in a person, especially in Julia. Warriors who could not do that couldn't lead. And Steve was definitely a leader. Fit to lead warriors and fit to lead a family.

Twenty minutes later, Steve and Julia rounded a turn in the trail and a cluster of rusty roofed huts, some made of wood and others of cinderblocks, came into view.

Julia's pulse revved as she scanned the huts.

A few Mayan women clustered near one hut, talking while a group of children, backs to Julia, appeared to be drawing in the dirt with sticks.

When Julia and Steve approached, one of the women gasped and gestured toward them.

A young girl dropped her stick and whirled to face them. "Ms. Julia!" Her shrill cry echoed up and down the narrow valley.

Looking healthy, full of life, energy and love, Itzy ran toward Julia, arms outstretched.

It was the response Julia had hoped for. But what would happen when she introduced Steve?

"Itzy ..." Julia reached toward the girl, who leaped into her arms. She held Itzy's tiny body against her chest, slipped an arm under her, serving as the chair, and held her.

"I missed you, Ms. Julia. This much." Itzy spread her arms wide, hitting Julia's nose in the process.

"I missed you, too, Itzy."

Itzy's arms circled her neck and squeezed.

With her free hand, Julia pulled the envelope from her pocket and waved it in front of the small girl's face. "Do you know what this is?"

Itzy's almond-shaped brown eyes narrowed as she stared at the envelope. Then her lips stretched the width of her light brown face. "Papers. Papers mean I not call you Ms. Julia. I call you mama."

Tears welled in Julia's eyes. But again concern tempered her growing joy. She swiveled Itzy in her arms until the slender girl faced Steve. "This is my husband, Steve."

Julia drew a breath and held it while she watched Itzy's face.

Itzy's body tensed and she studied Steve's face, finally locking gazes with him.

Steve's smile widened into its warmest expression.

Slowly, Itzy's arms reached toward Steve. "Papa."

Steve pulled her into his arms, along with Julia, where he held them in a strong yet tender embrace.

As if someone pulled the plug in a sink full of water, Julia's reservoir of horror that she'd held for so long swirled then drained, completely. And, as Steve said, their girl would never have to store such memories.

With a good person in the White House, and Brock Daniels's voice of freedom continuing to remind all Americans what it takes to maintain liberty and a morally upright nation, Itzy would have a good life with Steve and Julia in America or wherever they ran their orphanage.

America was a good nation once again. And after a thorough housecleaning, it would have a good military, led by men like Captain Craig, to ensure their protection against all enemies.

AUTHOR'S NOTES

Voice of Freedom is set in six different locations in three countries, Israel, Canada, and the USA. I've not been to Israel, yet, but the tiny nation holds a special place in my heart. Several of the other setting locations also have special places in my heart.

The lookout tower on Bolan Peak, where Steve and Julia hid overnight, used to be on adjacent Sanger Peak. That's where I remember seeing it many times as a child. As a teenager, I raced motorcycles down that mountain road and—let's not go there right now. Suffice it to say we all survived—the people, not all of the motorcycles. And there was a point at which we didn't know if we were being cast in a remake of the movie *Deliverance* or an episode of *The Beverly Hillbillies*. If you wish to pursue this subject further, email me. I may or may not answer your questions.

After the Forest Service moved the Sanger Peak Lookout to Bolan Peak, they began renting it to hardy souls who wanted a top-of-the-world experience in the Oregon-California coastal mountains. Several photos have been posted online by those who rented the lookout. The sunsets, sunrises, and night skies are spectacular. Google "Bolan Peak Lookout" if you want to see them, or look at my *Voice of Freedom* Pinterest board at pinterest.com/harryw51.

As teenagers, my buddies and I rode our motorcycles to Bolan Lake and hiked into its sister, Tannen Lake, on a three-day fishing trip. We heard from a ranger that Tannen Lake had been accidentally stocked with fish twice from the air that spring and so we caught our limit of trout each day.

This fishing adventure occurred during the heyday of Bigfoot sightings, and we were in the very center of the heart of Bigfoot country. The first evening, around the campfire, we each shared Bigfoot stories we'd heard from loggers and hunters while we listened to the haunting howling of coyotes from the ridge above the lake.

We scared ourselves spitless, with horror stories about the foul-smelling giant's escapades. But wanting to appear macho, none of us would admit our fears ... until a porcupine ran across all five of our sleeping bags at 5:00 a.m. No one was spared the chills of that experience, but only one of us ended up with any quills.

The Skylight Cave used in the story is a lava tube near Sisters, Oregon, situated on the lava-covered, eastern slopes of the Cascade Mountains in Central Oregon. I've never explored this particular cave, but I've seen spectacular photos of the eerie columns of light produced by sunshine funneling into the darkness through a skylight. You can see these on my Pinterest page, too.

Further south, some of the lava tubes are called ice caves because—you guessed it—at the bottom of the cave you can skate on ice while the temperature tops a hundred degrees at the mouth of the cave.

The skydiving club that flew Steve Bancroft from Madras to the Skylight Cave really does exist. But everything related to them in the book is purely fictitious. I really enjoyed creating their pilot, Bob Daggett.

My characters were only able to spend one night near beautiful Whistler, BC. My wife and I are not skiers so we visit Whistler in the summer to hike the trails, ride the gondolas to the snowcapped peaks. The gondola rides include the longest stretch of unsupported cable in the world, the Peak-to-Peak Gondola. One of my earlier novels, *Triple Threat*, used the Peak-to-Peak Gondola for some action scenes. This gondola seems perfect for a thriller, book or movie, but it seems that I was the first to use it.

While in Whistler, we consume gallons of coffee and I write while my wife, Babe, reads, sitting by a stream in the warm summer sun around Whistler Village.

Strolling through the village you will see tourists from all over the globe. We often spend Canada Day in Whistler to see the parade through the village, watch the fireworks, and attend the outdoor concerts.

The political setting of *Voice of Freedom* is not as pleasant as the physical setting. The story deals with the rending of America by a would be tyrant. In 2012, Charles Murray wrote, *Coming Apart: The State of White America, 1960–2010*. He focused on white Americans only to emphasize that they were not excluded from the coming apart of this nation. He thought all groups, minorities, as well as the majority, were impacted. In Murray's estimation, the rending of America is happening at the level of our core of common beliefs—religion, marriage and family, labor, ethics, and morality. His prescription for a solution is a "Civic Great Awakening," a returning to our foundations on family, vocation, community and faith—something like the Great Awakening of the 19th Century.

In part, I agree with Murray. But with two predominant, diametrically opposed worldviews present in our culture and in our politics, I am pessimistic about the nation I love coming back together. Nevertheless, I can write a story illustrating the restorative power of a taste of tyranny, a story that shows what political steps might be required to restore a fractured, failed state to a Democratic Republic.

We should heed our founders' warning that our Constitution only works for a good and moral people. So when one faction's morality becomes another's immorality, as we find in America today, the nation is fractured almost beyond repair. The USA as we have known it cannot exist under those conditions. If Americans cannot come together on core values, we will come apart on those same lines.

There are several other philosophical and theological asides to the story that readers may find interesting. One of these is Julia Weiss's pacifism, her reaction to a horrific childhood exposure to warfare, specifically to a jihadist group like Boko Haram. She learns that pacifism is unlivable in a fallen world and that self-defense, as well as defense of the helpless, using lethal force, is sometimes required.

The only thread intentionally left dangling at the end of *Voice of Freedom* is the story of the married couple, Jeff and Allie Jacobs. Their back story is contained in *Against All Enemies* book 3, *The Prequel, Chasing Freedom*, another action-packed romantic thriller set four years prior to books one and two. Look for it to release in July 2016. Turn the page and you can read *Chasing Freedom*, chapter 1.

H L Wegley

Coming Soon

Against All Enemies 3, The Prequel: Chasing Freedom, Chapter 1

By H. L. Wegley

Chapter 1

The moment the forest went silent, Jeff Jacobs sensed it. It came as an unsettling feeling more than anything audible. The sensation crept up his spine to the back of his neck.

Jeff shivered then shook off the feeling as he slowed to a stop near a stand of tall Ponderosa pines on the dusty, Southern-Oregon mountain road. He adjusted his headband to catch the drops of perspiration from a hot, July evening run before they became stinging instruments of torture to his eyes. And he listened.

Barely audible, a noise came, one that didn't belong to the forest.

It sounded again. Was it a wheezing cough?

He waited, trying to identify the sound.

The hoarse wheezing grew in volume, now accompanied by a syncopated rhythm of running feet. Thankfully, it wasn't either of his two worst fears, timber rattlers or cougars.

A slender figure emerged from the overgrown logging road ahead and ran down the main road toward him. The person sounded like someone desperately trying to finish a marathon. Someone who wouldn't.

A young woman. She half ran, and half stumbled, toward him with her long, dark hair waving behind. Her face held wide eyes that contrasted with the dust and perspiration coating her cheeks and forehead.

She stumbled and reached for him, her large brown eyes filled with terror. "Help me! Please!"

Her terror stabbed his heart in its most vulnerable

spot. In that moment, Jeff committed to helping her. For the first time in months, he had a purpose.

Off balance now, her eyes closed and she pitched forward.

He leaped toward her, trying to scoop her upper body and stop her face plant.

Jeff's hands slid under her arms.

Her falling body took him to his knees.

He rolled backward, pulling the young woman.

She landed on top of him.

The back of Jeff's head slammed against the dirt road.

He had cushioned her fall, but at what price? His left knee screamed a sharp, stabbing complaint after it folded under him. The back of his head throbbed from striking the road.

Jeff rolled onto his side, easing the woman's body onto the ground. When he straightened his knee, it stopped complaining. And he could deal with the headache, but how should he deal with the woman?

Her gasps for air had turned to deep, steady breathing, and those brown eyes that displayed terror moments before, remained closed.

He scanned her perfectly sculpted face. What did it look like without the dirt mask?

Angry voices and the sounds of running feet came from where the woman had emerged.

Warning sirens sounded in Jeff's mind. The young woman's danger would soon become his.

The pounding of running feet and the voices grew louder.

He gathered the woman in his arms, scanning the area around him for a hiding place.

On the creek-side of the road, a bushy Madrone tree had grown up from the stump of its amputated predecessor. He carried her behind its dense foliage, trying to avoid stepping on the crispy scrolls of Madrone bark that lay ready to betray him.

As he peered through a small opening between branches, two dark-complected men ran out onto the main road.

At the sight of their weapons, Jeff stopped breathing.

Both men carried assault rifles.

What started as an act of kindness had become a matter of survival.

The two men stopped.

The forest remained silent, except for the occasional buzzing of grasshoppers' wings ... and the young woman's heavy breathing.

He pulled her face against his neck, trying to muffle her respiration while he studied the men for any indication they had heard her.

The gunmen scanned the road both directions as if unsure which way she had gone.

They would soon conclude she'd been running toward the small town where he lived. From this location, she had no other good option.

One of the men gestured toward town with his gun, and the two hurried away.

Jeff also needed go toward town. The small town of O'Brien lay two miles down the road. His house, on the edge of town, was the first place of refuge he would reach.

How could he carry her home and yet remain unseen? Maybe he could follow the creek, hidden by the bushes and trees lining it. But the creek meandered all over the small valley. Following the stream would make this a three-mile trek, and if she didn't wake up soon, a three-mile trek carrying a 120-pound woman. He'd already run two miles in the ninety-degree heat.

Could he do this? Yes. He was Jeffrey Jacobs, Olympic decathlon, gold-medal contender. The words mocked him. Maybe he wasn't a contender anymore, but he *would* carry this young woman to safety.

When the men had run two hundred yards down the road, Jeff turned toward the creek. He sidestepped a patch of blackberry vines, backed through the willows lining the creek, and stepped out onto its rocky bed.

The stream was running low, channeling only a small flow of water that wouldn't impede him. The smooth, flat rocks would provide a hidden path where he would leave few tracks.

It was a good plan, but he needed to hurry, to get as far down the creek as he could in case the men returned to look for tracks. No telling what kind of trail he had left in the dust where he fell down with the girl.

But what if the gunmen waited at the edge of town, trying to prevent her from entering it to reach help? They would cut him off from his house, from the police.

As he trudged along the creek bed, Jeff explored every plausible scenario he could think of and sought a safe course of action for each one. In the end, he concluded there was only one safe course for the girl and him. He took it, praying softly as he followed the winding creek bed.

He prayed for the strength and the wits to carry this young woman safely to his home and for wisdom to determine what he should do once he got there.

Leaves and twigs crunched loudly a short distance behind him.

The men were coming to check the creek.

He broke into a labored run, trying to round the next bend before the goons with the guns emerged. His heart shifted into its highest gear. Adrenaline shot through his body.

Jeff ran hard. As he ran, he prayed that he wouldn't stumble. He prayed that the men wouldn't hear his heavy running steps and the clattering of rocks as he carried the young woman down the creek bed.

Who was she? Why was she in serious danger, danger that had already engulfed him?

Jeff glanced up into the blue sky and prayed the woman's words.

Help me. Please.

* * *

Alejandra's eyes opened. She gasped and surveyed the area around her. It was a house. Neat, clean and homey. Best of all, no gunmen. She was lying on a couch ... near a man. A knot formed in her stomach.

Her face. She touched it. The dust caked on by perspiration was gone. He must have ... The knot tightened. She clenched her jaw, raised her head, and examined her denim shorts and the buttons on her sleeveless blouse. She was clothed just as she had been when—she must've passed out when she ran toward the man, the man sitting in the chair only a few feet away.

She studied him.

He sat, hands clasped in his lap, eyes closed, but his lips were moving. Was he praying? Yes, he was. A lot of good that would do. But a man of faith ... if he was genuine, she would be safe with him. And he *was* very handsome.

Girl, you've got way too many problems to even think such thoughts.

What about Mom, Dad, and her little brother, Benjamin? Would the cartel kill them because of her? Where were the gunmen? Maybe this man could answer that question.

She pushed down on the couch with her hands, trying to sit up. Pain racked every muscle in her body. Her joints ached from the abuse she had inflicted on them during her long run.

When she glanced at the man, his eyes were open, staring at her.

The man looked safe, but she would divulge as little as possible. "Where am I?" She hardly recognized her hoarse, raspy voice.

"Let me get you some water." He returned quickly with a large glass of ice water and handed it to her.

Allie took a sip, then a big guzzle. She took a breath, then another gulp.

"Whoa. Slow down. You'll make yourself sick."

Back to her original question. "Where am I?"

He sat down in his chair. "You're in my house."

She fought through the aches and pains and sat up. "Who are you, and where is your house?"

"We *are* a little overdue for introductions. My house is on the outskirts of the small town of O'Brien. My name is Jeff Jacobs."

"Mr. Jacobs, where are the two men who—"

"You know, it's polite to reciprocate after an introduction." He smiled and propped an ankle on his knee.

That was a good sign. The gunmen must not be near or there would be no smiles, no relaxed posture. "My name is Alejandra Santiago."

"That won't do." He shook his head.

She glared at him.

He smiled. "I mean...it's a beautiful name, but if I'd tried to say it when they were chasing us, we wouldn't be—it's too long. I'll call you Allie."

"Mr. Jacobs, you can't just change my—"

"I'm Jeff, you're Allie ... for survival purposes. Deal?"

She stared at him, meaning to glare again. But the gentleness and warmth in his eyes defused her anger. "Okay. It's a deal ... Jeff." She met his gaze and gave him a weak smile.

So now I'm Allie.

She sighed, resigning herself to the name change, and took another swallow of the cold water. "Allie thinks Jeff should tell her what happened after she passed out. And she wants to know where the two gunmen are."

Jeff stood and walked to the couch.

He was invading her space. She started to protest, but there was nothing threatening about him.

Her logical mind shouted a warning while her gut instinct said, "Trust him." Torn in two directions, she tried to relax by looking away from him and through the sheer, living room curtains. It was now twilight. That meant Jeff had been with her for two or three hours and who knows what dangers he had faced. Maybe his familiarity came from some bond he felt between them, a bond she didn't feel.

She stiffened when Jeff sat down beside her.

"Allie ..." He turned toward her and paused until she met his gaze. "I caught you when you fainted. You must've run a long, long way. I've never seen anyone so exhausted. Well ... then the two gunmen came after us. I carried you. I prayed a lot, and we got away."

She had led them on a wild chase for ten, maybe fifteen miles or more through the mountains, and she, a good runner, couldn't shake those two men trying to catch her. Now, however, she feared *catch* had been replaced with *kill*. But Jeff had escaped them while saddled with her unconscious body. He must be an incredible athlete ... and smart ... or lucky.

"Have you notified anyone?"

He pursed his lips and shook his head. "Frankly, I didn't know what to do until I heard your story. You look like you're, uh ..."

"I *am* Hispanic. My home is in Nogales ... Mexico."

Jeff nodded slowly, cautiously. He was obviously trying to conceal his suspicion.

"I'm here on an international scholarship to Oregon State University."

His face relaxed.

"So now you know."

* * *

As Jeff pondered her response he was puzzled. Allie's situation didn't compute. She was an incredibly beautiful young woman. He noticed that while washing the dirt from her face. She was intelligent, educated, but she had been chased through the mountains by people who were likely drug cartel thugs.

He would have called the police immediately, but he feared she was here illegally, and since he had eluded the two men, he decided to wait, but he couldn't wait any longer. He needed to know and understand more of her story. "I'm glad that you're here legally. But, Allie, we barely escaped from two men who wanted to kill us."

His voice grew louder as memories of the shooting echoed through his mind. "You need to tell me who they are and why they shot at us. You need to tell me the whole story. I can't help you if I don't understand..." His voice trailed off after he vented his frustration, and he looked down at the floor.

When he looked up at her face, the smile was gone, and tears rolled down her cheeks. She looked so hopeless that he struggled to keep from wrapping her up in his arms. Instead, he reached out a hand.

She tensed.

But when he brushed the tears from her cheeks, she collapsed against him, sobbing. "They're going to kill my family, Jeff. And I don't know what to do."

H.L. WEGLEY